CELESTIAL

ANGELS OF ELYSIUM

BOOK TWO

CELESTIAL
Book 2 of the ANGELS OF ELYSIUM series

Copyright © 2021 by WildStone Publishing

For information contact:
OLIVIA WILDENSTEIN
http://oliviawildenstein.com

COVER DESIGN BY FRANZISKA STERN @COVERDUNGEONRABBIT
CASE COVER DESIGN BY JENNA PEARSON @JEMLIN_C
CHARACTER PORTRAITS BY CARMEN DI MAURO @CARMEN.DMDESIGN
COUPLE ART BY SALOME TOTLADZE @MORGANA0ANAGROM
CALLIGRAPHY BY TELISHA MERRILL MORTENSEN

EDITING BY *BECKY BARNEY*
PROOFREADING BY *KATELYN ANDERSON*

WHAT DOESN'T DESTROY
YOU WILL RESHAPE YOU

Angel Hierarchy

SERAPHIM
Also known as archangels.
There are seven of them.
Highest ranking celestial being.
Verities (pure-blood angels).

MALAKIM
Soul collectors.
Verities.

ISHIM
Rankers. They establish sinner scores.
Verities.

ERELIM
Celestial sentinels.
Verities and hybrids.

OPHANIM
Guild workers: professors and supervisors.
Mostly hybrids but open to verities.

FLETCHINGS
Young angels who haven't yet completed their wings.
Verities and hybrids.

NEPHILIM
Fallen angels. Disgraced. Wingless. Mortal.

Angelic Glossary

ama – mom
  apa – dad
  aheeva – love
  ayim – water
  habamehot – hide yourselves
  kalkohav – starlight
  lehatsamehot – show yourselves
  levsheh – sweetheart
  lev – heart
  leh – my
  mota – doll
  mostasheh – sweet doll
  naya – dawn
  neshamateh – soulmate
  neshamim – souls
  neshaleh – my soul
  ni – I
  sheh – sweet
  ta – you
  teh – yours
  tched - demon
  neshahadza – soulhalf

yot – are
zoya - temptresses

Prologue

I'd never loathed a city before, but never had a city destroyed me like Paris.

Paris, the cradle of love and sin.

For years, I'd deemed Jarod Adler the wickedest sinner of all. Tonight, I merited the title and a score far worse than a Triple's.

I'd harvested the soul of not one but *two* nephilim and absconded with them through the rain-slickened skies of the French capital.

Underneath a cherry tree in full bloom, I held out my palms and relaxed my fingers around the golden orbs. What in Abaddon had possessed me to lift them from their bodies? This act of folly would not only have me questioned but also demoted and tossed out of Elysium, stripped of the appendages that made me who I was. *All* I was.

As raindrops dribbled through the pale pink petals and curved around the gilded spheres, spilling onto my boots like fresh blood, I shut my eyes and tipped my head back. If gods existed, I would've implored them for advice, but we, archangels, were the ones who decided between life and death, who weighed fates and judged souls.

Tonight, though, I was no more a deity than the ant crawling across my thumb.

I wrenched my lids open and closed my fingers, springing the unsuspecting creature off. Souls pulsating against my palms, I spread my wings and readied to return to the Demon Court. But the harsh, wet winds possessed a different plan for me.

They chartered a new course, shattering my moral compass, destroying the honorable angel and awakening the flawed man within.

Chapter One

TODAY - CELESTE

I walked the length of the busy bar before squeezing in between Mister Big Man on Campus and two twittering underaged girls, sporting too much makeup and too little fabric.

"Excuse you," the blonde high schooler grumbled, her short hair swishing around a pair of hoops that could've doubled as bangles.

Without sparing her a glance, I slid my forearm across the sticky wooden bar top, giving my full attention to the guy wearing a backward baseball cap and a tight muscle tee that surely chafed his nipples.

"I'm thirsty," I mewled. "Mind if I drink that?"

He spent a hot second looking me up and down. "Are you legal?"

I pretended to bristle, even though I gave zero feathers about my flat chest and narrow hips. I licked my lips, making sure to do it nice and slow. "More legal than those two."

His pale eyes sparked as he slid the beer he'd bought the still-grumbling blonde toward me. "All yours, beautiful."

My assortment of rings clicked against the chilled glass. "I like generous boys." I pretended to lift the glass to my lips, but before the rim made contact, I stretched my index finger and ran it down the scruff on his jaw, then lower, along the column of his throat. His Adam's apple bobbed, mirroring the excitement widening his pupils. Distracting him with a slow knuckle over pecs hardened by way too many hours at the college gym, I fished his wallet out of his low-slung jeans.

3

My wing bones thrummed as though readying to evict a feather. Except thieving wasn't my style. Catching criminals red-handed was.

I pushed up on my toes and leveled my lips to his ear. "If you *ever* dose someone's drink again"—I flipped open his wallet and dragged out his driver's license—"Matt Boyd from Lafayette, California, I'll call the cops on you myself." And then I dumped the beer down his chest, getting a huge kick out of hearing him swear when the cold liquid hit his crotch.

I dropped the empty glass and his wallet on the bar, then extended the guy's ID toward Jase, my bartending vigilante sidekick and best friend with numerous benefits.

"You crazy bitch," Matt Boyd sputtered. "If anyone's going to get arrested, it's you."

I shot him a saccharine smile. Although I'd been gifted with super-human blood, I hadn't been gifted with superhuman height, so I had to tilt my head up. "And for what crime will I be arrested? Saving an unsuspecting girl from getting drugged and raped?"

As Jase relieved me of the laminated card, his fingers brushed over mine. "I'm closing your tab. That'll be twenty bucks, Mr. Boyd. Cash or credit?" He snapped a picture of both sides of his ID.

The guy's reedy lips pulsed around angry breaths. "The fucking beer's on me. Not in me!" He grabbed his wallet and shot away from the bar but came pec-to-pec with a wall of brawn.

Leon, The Trap's owner and Jase's much older brother, clapped both his hands on Matt's shoulders, then steered him back toward the bar. Where Jase was slim, Leon was a mountain of a man with more tattoos than most convicts on the guild's holo-rankers.

Leon flashed me a smile lacking a tooth from a recent brawl. Although his Harlem bar was trendy with the college kids, it was also 'all the rage' with neighborhood druggies and dealers. "Nice catch, Celeste."

Matt began to growl obscenities that would've cost him a whole bunch of feathers had he been a fletching.

"Why, thank you." I'd started hanging out at The Trap after meeting Jase last semester in my Criminal Justice class. And then I kept hanging out at the basement bar and grill for Leon's extra-greasy, extra-delicious cheeseburgers and Jase's easy company. And because you could take the girl out of the guild, but not the guild out of the girl, on busy nights, I kept an eye out for licentious activity.

"Cash or credit?" Jase repeated amiably.

Matt cranked his stubbled chin up. "The fuck I'm paying."

"You dose a girl's drink in *my* bar," Leon growled, "then try to rip me off? Jase, get Tommy."

"Who's Tommy?" Matt's voice lost its defiant edge.

"A retired Marine who just so happens to be a real talented sous-chef."

Tommy was the strong, quiet type with facial tattoos that inspired fear in most people. He'd always been perfectly indifferent to me, so I had no beef with him.

When Jase started toward the kitchen, Matt extracted a twenty-dollar bill from his wallet. "No cops. I'm leavin'. And I promise, you'll never see me again."

"That's nice, but what I want you to promise is to never drug a person ever again. Think you can do that?"

"Yeah. I'll never—" Matt gulped. "Never do that shit again."

"Good. Now hand over that stash of pills you brought into my bar."

Matt slid a hand inside his boxers and pulled out a small Ziploc, which he shakily lifted.

Leon slapped his arm away. "I don't want your fucking ball sweat in my face." He snatched my empty beer glass. "Toss it in here."

Matt dropped it in, then flipped his cap around, attempting to shade his face from the growing attention coming our way. I heard him mutter a *shit* when the head waitress and Leon's on-again-off-again girlfriend Alicia said, "Got it all on film, Leon."

"Thanks, babe." And then he dropped his voice and murmured something in Matt's ear that made the gym rat squirm and turn as white as the diamonds frosting the cross dangling around Leon's neck.

For the first fifteen years of my life, I'd been taught to reform misbehaving humans gently, by offering them a hand to guide them toward the right path. During the ensuing four years, I learned that threats and brute force worked just as well, if not better. And way faster.

Someone tapped my upper arm—the blonde with the large hoops. "My friend and I wanted to thank you."

"Don't mention it but watch your drinks next time." When the girls turned toward Jase to profess their *undying* gratitude—I swear, they kept him engaged long after saying *thank you*—I fished my cell phone from the pocket of my teal silk bomber to check the time and noticed a missed text from Muriel.

I smiled as I read it. Even though every Friday I went home for the weekend, every Thursday, without fail, Mimi asked if I'd made other plans and reminded me it was fine if I had. Weekends were sacred family time, and since Mimi was my only family now, I devoted them all to the woman who'd unfailingly cared for me after I lost Leigh.

Leigh . . . Thinking of her still hurt. She'd been my best friend, my sister, my anchor. The night she took her life, I'd been devastated. And then I'd been angry. Angry at Jarod for steering her away from her duty. Angry at Leigh for allowing him to do so. Angry at Seraph Asher for burning her wings and tossing her back on Earth with blistered crescents on her back. Angry that I hadn't been enough to keep her in this world.

For weeks, I'd hated her, and then I'd hated myself for hating her.

And now . . . now, I simply missed her. The same way Mimi missed Jarod, the boy she'd raised as her son.

My thumbs flew over the screen: *I'll try to get there for lunch, but I need to meet with my advisor, so don't wait for me if you're hungry.* And then I added: *By the way, I got us some tickets to the Saturday matinee of that play I was telling you about. The remake of A Streetcar Named Desire.*

Three dots lit up as Mimi typed. Of course, she wasn't asleep. Muriel never slept, preferring sporadic naps. I watched the dots dance and dance, expecting a long-winded answer, but all she sent was: *OK, ma chérie.*

Jase called out my name over the hasty twang blaring from the speakers. He was leaning over the bar, inked forearms splayed on the sticky wood, nose an inch from mine. He beheld me with those brown eyes of his, so many shades darker and yet so many shades softer than my own. "Want something to drink, Cee?"

I shook my head. "Nah. I'm going to head back to the apartment."

"Already?"

"It's two a.m., Jase."

"I'll miss you." The mishmash of neon signs nailed to the cement walls, ranging from a *Speedy Shoe Repairs* to a purple outline of a giant eggplant, and a smaller one of a pig with wings—my personal contribution—edged his gelled hair in bright colors.

I rolled my eyes. "You'll see me in five hours." I had an early class on Fridays, so my breakfasts coincided with the end of his shift at The Trap.

"I'll still miss you for five hours."

I laughed. The boy with whom I shared a two-bedroom apartment in a building wedged between campus and Riverside Drive flashed me his pearly whites. He had such a great smile. Such a great personality, too. He'd make a girl happy the day he decided to settle, and although he joked that girl might be me, it wouldn't. If my front-row seat to Leigh and Jarod's relationship had taught me anything, it was that falling in love was messy and painful.

I wanted fun. And easy. Jase was the perfect combination of both.

"Goodnight, Cee."

"Night, Jase." I dropped a chaste kiss on the corner of his mouth. "Be good."

"Be better."

As he headed toward a thirsty customer, I cast a look toward my neon pig. I'd thought of Seraph Asher when I'd bought it and then had smirked when Leon had unboxed the winged swine and nailed it to the wall. My ill-intent had cost me a feather, but damn if it hadn't been worth it.

Leaving the archangel's effigy behind, I wove through the dense throng of students and locals, the soles of my shoes sticking to the beer-basted concrete. I made it a few steps before finding myself trapped by two girls with pursed lips.

"Excuse me." I tried to sidestep them, but both whipped out their wings.

Oh, goody.

The brunette with the glossy curls and gold-tipped blue feathers stuck balled fists on her hips. "I just got told by my split-lipped sinner, and none too kindly, to scurry off. Wouldn't know anything about that, would you, Celeste?"

I assumed there were posters of me in the guilds because it seemed like *every* fletching I crossed paths with in New York, be they female or male, had heard of me. "Why do you assume I'd know anything about it?" I stared past them toward the glowing Exit sign.

"Because he was muttering something about getting even with a biker chick with black claws and no ass named Celeste."

Well, that was *rude*. I had an ass; it was just petite, like the rest of me. And my nails weren't filed to points, although how convenient would that be?

"I don't even own a bike." I doubted Mimi would be on board with me buying one.

"I think he was talking about your look." The other fletching gave my combat boots and black leather leggings a perfunctory once-over.

I raised my middle finger and pretended to scratch something on my upper lip. "You think?"

She flushed all the way down to her blonde roots.

"I had a plan for him," the verity said.

"I'm sorry, Blue, but are you expecting me to apologize for saving an innocent girl from ingesting a pill that would probably have gotten her raped, if not by this man, then by someone else?"

She scowled. "All you've done is provoke him."

"He'll strike again." The blonde tucked her red wings into her spine.

Like mine, her wings weren't gilt-tipped. Her hybrid status tempered my vitriolic tone because, however blinded by the celestial world, the blindfold would eventually fall, and she'd realize her feathers' lack of luster would condemn her to Elysium's lowest echelons. The best hybrids could hope for were positions in the guilds as ophanim—teachers—or in Elysium and Abaddon as erelim—celestial sentinels. Only verities got the fun gigs: malakim—soul harvesters—ishim—soul rankers—or seraphim —the crème de la crème of angels, or rather crème de la shit.

"Celeste!" Blue gasped.

My gaze instantly cycled around the room on the lookout for trouble. When I found no one barreling for me, I returned my attention to the girl. "What?"

"You lost a feather."

Oh.

That.

I glanced down at the fluffy purple, wondering why I'd lost it. For my terrible thoughts about archangels or because I'd stolen another fletching's sinner? Honestly, I was surprised only one had fallen tonight and that I'd missed the quick stab that accompanied its removal.

When the seesawing feather vanished beneath a pair of strappy stilettos, I looked back at the wide-eyed angels. "Not my first. And not my last."

I'd stopped counting a long time ago, but suspected I'd lost as many as I'd earned, considering my wings—or rather, *winglets*—were almost the same density as they'd been before Paris.

The verity crossed her arms in front of a white halter top that made her look utterly angelic. "Why did you give up?"

"What makes you think I gave up?"

My humor was lost on the two fletchings, who exchanged a look, before talking over each other.

The hybrid said, "You only have three-hundred and twenty-five . . . well, *four* now," while the verity said, "And three months left."

Even though it peeved me that they'd looked me up on a holo-ranker, I was pleasantly surprised by that figure. Since I shed feathers like a molting chicken and hadn't signed up to any celestial missions since Paris, I'd imagined I'd dropped below the hundred bar, but apparently, I'd inadvertently accomplished a crap-ton of good deeds. Although we didn't earn the amount of feathers on the sinner's scorecard when we weren't signed up to them, if we managed to help them change, even in the smallest way, we collected a feather for our kindness.

"Aren't you going to pick it up?" the hybrid asked.

"And relive my glory days? Nah. I'm a carpe diem sort of girl."

A profuse amount of white appeared around her green irises.

"Tell me something. Have I become a case study in the guild or a cautionary tale?"

The verity's entire face puckered, as though she'd ingested one of Jase's signature sour-gummy tequila shots. "The ophanim are worried about you, Celeste. Especially Ophan Mira."

"Ophan Mira?" That kicked my smile up a notch. I highly doubted the guild elder cared about her unspectacular pupil's fate. "I'm sure she's devastated by my absence. Give her my best, will you?" As I finally stepped past them and climbed up the stairs toward the street exit, the number they'd thrown at me whirled through my mind.

Three-hundred and twenty-four. Not that I'd had any intention of completing my wings, but the amount needed to reach a thousand was so preposterous I snickered.

On my way out, I blew Leon a kiss, which he pretended to catch and pocket even though he was busy chatting up a pretty blonde—I guess Alicia and him were currently *off*—then craned my neck toward the steel-black sky. Although it wasn't freckled with stars like in the guild, I thought it was the loveliest sky.

Imperfect and real.

Choked with smog and lights instead of quartz and honeysuckle.

And noise. So much noise. None of it harmonious. There were no rainbow-winged sparrows twittering arias, no quartz fountains weeping crystalline water onto night-blooming lilies. Just good-old honking yellow cabs, buzzed college students, and animated neighborhood drunks.

I loved this city all the more for its imperfections because it reflected the life I'd chosen, instead of the one chosen for me.

Chapter Two

The next morning, after meeting with my advisor to discuss my criminal justice assignment, I got on the subway and headed downtown to the penthouse Muriel had bought after I was accepted into Columbia University.

Although I hated how Jarod's caregiver had come into my life, I couldn't imagine her not being part of it.

After waking up alone in my hotel room in Paris, I'd rushed to the Demon Court where I'd forded through news vans and police barriers, shrieking Leigh's name at the top of my lungs, demanding to speak with her. It was Jarod's bodyguard, Amir, who'd finally heard my pleas. Although he'd warned me to go home, I insisted on seeing Leigh, so he'd allowed me inside.

Four and a half years later, and I still shuddered. How many more years until I could think back on Leigh and not feel like my heart was being stabbed by the letter opener she'd used to slit her veins?

I blinked away the dark memory and focused on peeling off my flaking black polish, my array of rings reflecting the strips of light that made everyone in the subway appear wan and sickly.

Mimi hated that I used the public transit, but during rush hour, there really was no better way to navigate the city.

I thought about getting a motorbike again. I'd need to get my license first. Pausing my nail-polish removal, I dug my cell phone out of my fabric tote and researched motorcycle licenses how-tos until I exited onto the sun-drenched Fifth Avenue sidewalk.

I inhaled a slow breath of early fall air. Indian summers in New England had always been my favorite season—the air tepid and full of tiny living things, the canopy of leaves and stretches of grass blanketing Central Park in lush greens. It was the season I'd missed most during the two years I'd lived abroad.

When I arrived at the Plaza's residential entrance, the doormen greeted me by name, and I greeted them by theirs, asking one about his teenage daughter and the other about his new grandchild. Mimi didn't leave the apartment often—I made sure she had everything she needed at her fingertips—but when she did go out, she dawdled in the lobby, inquiring after everyone's families. Although no angel-blood ran through her veins, Mimi was worthier of wings than most of Elysium's inhabitants.

Definitely worthier than my genitor, who'd dumped me in the New York guild the second I was out of her womb before moving to another fletching-residence. Being an ophanim meant she was allowed to travel between guilds, and yet, she'd *never* visited, never used the guilds' holographic phones to contact me and had failed to attend my wing bone ceremony—a key moment in an angel's life, almost more significant than our ascension because it was the day we could finally exit the guilds and start accumulating our precious little feathers. By that point, though, I no longer cared to make her acquaintance because I had Leigh, and she filled my quota of affection.

And now, I had Mimi.

As I rode the elevator to the twenty-first-floor penthouse Mimi had purchased with money Jarod had left in her name, I thought back on the day I'd suggested leaving her side. I'd had nowhere to go, having decided I would never again step foot in a guild, but hadn't wanted to burden Mimi. Her complexion had rivaled the white marble tomb we'd passed on our way out of the Montparnasse Cemetery where we'd buried Leigh and Jarod's bodies.

"Do you have family waiting for you, Celeste?"

"Leigh was my only family."

"And Jarod was mine."

So I'd stayed, and we'd become each other's family. And our bond forged by grief transformed into a connection wrought from love. I'd found in Muriel the mother I thought I no longer needed. After all, I'd already been fifteen and had spent five years navigating the human world with little help from the ophanim who deemed us self-sufficient the day our wing bones formed.

Muriel had taken over my education, filling my mind with knowledge that wasn't taught in the guilds. What enthralled me most, ironically, was the human justice system. I devoured books about it, learned loopholes, gobbled up the stories of the Adlers' unlawful way of exacting law that Mimi recounted while she cooked in our spacious kitchen. When I turned eighteen, I confessed my dreams of becoming a lawyer or a judge, but that would require a college education and I didn't have a single school transcript to my name.

A week later, I received three invitations to attend colleges. *"I didn't even know colleges invited people to attend!"*

Mimi had offered me that quiet smile of hers that hid a mountain of thoughts.

"They don't, do they? Normally, I mean. You did this. You got me in."

"What matters isn't how you get in but what you do once you're inside." She'd been cutting through the warm pound cake I'd helped her bake. *"So which one calls out to you?"*

As she plated two slices, I'd stared at all three letterheads, my gaze lingering on Columbia University's. In the end, I decided New York was too far away from her, so I'd pointed to the Sorbonne's letter.

The following day, Mimi stepped into my bedroom and handed me a passport. I'd gawked at it, never having owned one before, and traced her last name printed next to my first one—*Moreau*.

I'd belonged to a race; now I belonged to a family.

I dug my keys out of my tote and let myself inside the shrine of smoke-gray hardwood, black granite, and burgundy velvets that Muriel had bought the same day she'd purchased our plane tickets. We could've shared a walkup, though, and I would've been equally happy because luxury had never been important to me. Nevertheless, I appreciated the security that came with the fancy address. Even though few people knew of Mimi's affiliation to the Adler family, it only took one to destroy a life.

"Mimi, I'm here," I yelled as I stepped through the vestibule and straight into the kitchen, her usual haunt. I flung my jacket and bag on one of the island's high chairs, then washed my hands before filching a piece of *croque monsieur* from the platter atop the stove, moaning as the gooey cheese lit up my taste buds. "Mimi?"

"In here, Celeste."

I trailed her voice into the living room where she stood outlined by the blue afternoon, gaze sunk on the sprawling, green rectangle of park that stretched almost all the way to the apartment I shared with Jase. I tossed the rest of the warm ham and cheese sandwich inside my mouth before pressing a kiss to her cheek. Her skin was ice, but I imagined she'd spent her morning reading on the narrow balcony, her favorite pastime after cooking.

"*Ça va, ma chérie?*" We'd always spoken French together, even though her knowledge of English was impeccable.

"*Oui.*"

I often wondered if I'd lose my angelic aptitude to speak and understand any tongue when I lost my wings but dismissed the contemplation, mostly because I had no one to ask. Besides, I'd find out in three months.

As I prattled on about my new assignment and my advisor's advice, Mimi listened to me with rapt attention and punctuated my rapid-fire flow of sentences with her habitual warm smiles. Warm smiles, I noticed, not slicked in crimson lipstick.

The *croque monsieur* congealed inside my stomach. "Something's wrong."

"Wrong?" Her pitch was off, just like her appearance.

My heart held exceptionally still. "What is it? Do you need to return to Paris? Did something happen to Amir?"

Jarod's bodyguard was the only person she'd kept in touch with. He'd remained in France, retiring to Nice after the Demon Court was shut down and transformed into a refuge for underprivileged children.

"Amir is fine, Celeste."

"Then what is it?" I bit out each word so none would tremble. "Mimi, what—"

"Cancer."

"Cancer?" I repeated stupidly.

"Horrible thing, cancer."

The compacted cheese and ham sprang into my throat. "Horrible but curable." I swallowed hard, jamming it back down. "Right?"

"Celeste . . ."

"*Right?*" When she didn't answer, pressure built behind my temples. "Mimi?" Her name juddered on my lips.

"I fought. I fought as hard as I could, but the cancer fought harder." I froze. *No. No. No.* This couldn't be happening. "All those naps. Your diminished appetite. You said you were just . . ." What *had* she said? Oh, angels, I couldn't remember, but she'd always had an excuse. "How long—how long have you"—I pushed back a lock of hair stuck to my lashes—"known?" I whisked my lids down, up, down, but the contours of her face kept shimmering.

"*Six mois.*"

"Six months!" I choked out, feeling like she was beating my heart into stiff peaks with one of her whisks. "Why didn't you . . . why didn't you tell me?"

"Because I was hoping to win before burdening you with it."

"Burden me?" The words swerved past the giant lump in my throat. "Oh, Mimi."

Her papery thumb that forever smelled of butter and dish soap stroked my cheekbone.

"There must be . . . have you done chemo? Chemo works. Or surgery. Who's your doctor?" I took my phone out and tried to type "Best cancer doctors," but the phone slipped from my fingers and clattered onto the thick rug.

She cupped my cheeks between both her palms. "It has metastasized to my liver, Celeste."

"What does that mean?"

"That soon, I will have to leave you."

"Is there really nothing . . . no treatment . . . no . . . ?" Tears flowed out of me and pooled around the callused fingers clasping me as though I was made of glass.

She shook her head. "But you're grown up now and—"

"I still need you! I'll always need you!"

"*Ma chérie.*"

"Please. There must be something, Muriel . . . Please." I wasn't even sure who I was imploring—this woman or the angels above? I stared at the cloudless blue expanse outside the bay window, wondering if any angel was watching. "Please." Sobs tripped out of my throat and fluttered the silver-streaked auburn flyaways framing her face. Her hair was always done up so neatly but not today.

"It's time I go see my Jarod. He's probably causing all sorts of trouble up in Heaven, trouble that even Leigh isn't able to contend with."

Jarod wasn't in Heaven. He wasn't even in Hell. He and Leigh had been denied both. And soon she'd find out, because this woman, this incredible and selfless force of nature, was undoubtedly Elysium-bound.

For the first time since I lost Leigh, I wished my soul wasn't destined for oblivion. But it was too late. There was no way I could earn over six hundred feathers in three months.

"How long before . . .?" I whispered, even though I wanted to roar my heartache and skepticism about the medical proficiency of the specialists she'd visited. They couldn't possibly have been any good if they hadn't found her a cure.

"A week, possibly two. Doctors are sordidly pessimistic people."

Days? I had *days* left with her?

My tears fell faster.

My heart broke harder.

What had I done to be dealt such a hand? Was it because I'd been disrespectful to the seraphim? Was it because I'd raised my voice against the archaic laws of my people? Was it because I'd turned my back on them?

My lungs felt vacuum-packed, unable to expand and take air. I gasped for breaths between sobs.

"I have arranged everything, Celeste. You will never want for anything. And although I would like my ashes to find their way next to Jarod's, take them when you feel ready."

Another sob splintered me. She laced her arms around my hunched spine and pulled me into her with such force I couldn't imagine her body was ravaged by disease.

I wouldn't let her die.

I wouldn't let the malakim steal her from me.

I'd find a way.

I *had* to find a way.

I'd prostrate myself at the feet of the Seven and beg for her life, because this woman was all I had left in this miserably unfair world.

Chapter Three

I'd sworn never to step foot inside a guild after Paris, yet once Muriel settled in for a nap, I took a cab to the quartz dormitories. The nondescript green door filled me with such anger that I almost spun around, but in the end, I stowed away my vindictiveness, squared my shoulders, and twisted the knob.

Startlingly, the door clicked.

I supposed that while I still had feathers, the ophanim couldn't lawfully lock me out.

Guilds were always busy, but late afternoons were always the busiest. The atrium with its rampant honeysuckle vines, seven quartz fountains, and domed glass ceiling was crawling with winged girls and warbling sparrows. The sweet-floral air seeped into my lungs like glue as the crowd of fletchings split around me, their mouths parting. As I trekked toward the channel, my plan to yell until I either lost my voice or a high-placed angel flitted down the dazzlingly-bright flue firmed up.

"Fletching, you've come home."

I came to a dead-stop in front of Ophan Mira, who extended her crimson wings as though to bar me from reaching my destination. *Home?* The fact that she assumed I considered this guild my home made me wonder if she thought dementia was upon me.

"No, Ophan. I've come to call on the seraphim."

Ophan Mira tipped her head to the side, her short, peppery black hair grazing her narrow shoulders. "The seraphim are busy people. What can I help you with?"

"Can you cure cancer, Ophan?"

"I cannot."

"Then you can't help me." I tried to walk past her, but a woman with a sheet of blonde hair that reached the bottom of her wing bones stepped next to Ophan Mira, barring my path.

Since I'd never met her before, and her wings were as bushy as my old professor's, I assumed she was a new recruit of Guild 24.

"Are you trying to keep me away from the channel?" I asked pleasantly even though I was not feeling pleasant at all.

"Cancer is a natural phenomenon, Celeste. A necessary phenomenon. When souls are tired of living—"

"Natural? It's a disease! A cell mutation! There is nothing natural—"

"Calm down, Fletching."

I gritted my teeth and balled my hands. How dare she tell me to calm down! She wasn't the one with the banged-up heart.

My nostrils flared as though I'd run all three miles from the Plaza to this place, which was as much my home as the dumpster behind the greasy burger joint on the corner. "I request an audience with the seraphim."

"To discuss this cancer? Fletching, have you learned nothing during your years under my tutelage? We don't interfere in human timelines. We are not guardians of lives; we are guardians of souls. If this human has cancer, then her envelope's time has come, and her soul—if worthy—will be collected and recompensed."

"She's only sixty!" My voice snapped like fully-feathered wings.

"Six decades is a respectable lifespan."

Irritation threatened to make me gnash my teeth. Sixty was too young. "Muriel should be allowed at least two more decades!"

"Calm down, Celeste." Ophan Mira's use of my name made me blink. She so rarely used our first names.

My gaze raked over the fire-veined quartz for those posters with my face on them, but the hallway walls were smooth and unadorned. No WANTED flyer or rebellious honeysuckle vine in sight.

Her hand came up to my twitchy shoulders. I took a step back, hating when people touched me without my consent.

"I will relay your displeasure to the Seven—"

"Displeasure?" I snorted.

"—but I will not allow you to make a further spectacle of yourself in my hallways. If you'd like to wait for the seraphim's response on site, please go sit in the cafeteria, and either I or Ophan Lia"—she gestured to the new recruit—"will come get you when we hear back from them."

"I'm just supposed to trust you'll convey my message?"

Mira's thin eyebrows writhed. "Trust? Oh, Fletching, how deeply out of touch with your race you've become if you begin to question the one value we hold dearest above all—honesty."

My forever-smarting wings could attest to that being their top priority. "How unfortunate that compassion isn't what you value most." A spark of pain traveled through my wing bones. I didn't have to glance down to know a feather had just detached itself from my stupid appendages.

"Our kind isn't to blame for someone's personal choice."

"Someone? Leigh wasn't just someone. And what *choice* did she have?"

"Celeste, the cafeteria *now*, or I will not convey your message." Ophan Mira's eyes seemed to glow like the quartz around us. "Do you remember where it is or would you like Ophan Lia to escort you?"

Shriek*lessly*—I was way beyond words at this point—I spun, and the fence of feathers from the rubbernecking fletchings retracted. My pulse hammered my skull as I barged down the hallway and into the vast quartz courtyard with its raised botanical beds. I'd always thought the Elysian sky shone down on the guild, but the unwavering blue was an illusion, just like the celestial rain that sprinkled the crops through strategically-placed openings in the glass dome. Angels were such experts at deception.

I took a seat at a teardrop-shaped quartz table partially hidden by a fig tree that produced fruit year-round. Fletchings favored the tables closer to the slab of quartz with its perpetual offering of warm grains and steamed fish, chilled juices in glass jugs, and toppling pyramids of jewel-toned produce. The fragrance of my childhood turned my already upset stomach.

As I waited, I folded my legs, refolded them, jiggled them, staring down the few fletchings who had the audacity to stare back. Eventually, they all averted their curious gazes. Bored of eye-battling, I fished my phone out and messaged Muriel to tell her I was running an errand and to call me when she woke up. And then I opened my browser. The only word I'd managed to type in earlier sat tauntingly in the search bar: *best*. To add insult to injury, my search engine was suggesting a drop-down list of *best*s—best movie, best Chinese restaurant, best hotel in Manhattan, best gyms.

Freaking gyms? I never exercised. Hated it. With a passion.

"Hi." A light voice startled me out of choking my cell phone.

I peered up at the owner of the voice, a golden-haired child with a thick side-braid and charred-brown eyes. When she climbed onto the chair next to mine, keeping her little legs bent underneath her for leverage, I snapped, "What are you doing?"

Instead of growing large and watery, her eyes stayed soft, and she smiled. "You look sad."

I scanned the courtyard, imagining this was some sort of set-up, the ophanim trying to cajole me by sending a cherubic emissary, but no teachers roamed the cafeteria, and most of the fletchings had left.

"I'm Naya."

I set my phone down. "Shouldn't you be with Ophan Pippa, Naya?"

She wrinkled her button nose. "She's telling a story about monsters. I don't like monsters."

"The world's full of them, so better get used to them."

"Have you ever met a monster?"

I thought about Tristan. And then I thought about Asher. Different kinds of monsters but both monstrous. And then, as per usual, my wings got gypped of a feather. "Yes."

She blinked her wide eyes at me. "Are they really scary-looking?"

"No. Most look like you and me."

"You don't look like a monster."

"I'm sure the ophanim would disagree."

"Why would they disagree?"

"Because . . ." Where to start? "Because, for one, I've decided to make my life among humans."

She slid her bottom lip into her mouth, as though contemplating why that would make me a fiend. "My favorite color is my apa's wings."

Or not. "What's your favorite color?"

I settled back into my chair. Children were inquisitive and created links between disjointed topics at the speed of light. I'd apparently driven Leigh nuts with my non-linear way of thinking. "Black. Black's my favorite color."

"Black isn't a color."

I gestured to my leather leggings and black T-shirt that read *5'4 but my attitude is 6'2* in bold white—a gift from Jase for my twentieth birthday last month. "I beg to differ. Black is a color."

"Black is the absence of light."

I frowned, not because of what she'd said . . . technically I knew black wasn't a color, but because I was surprised someone so young was aware of this.

"I also like purple." She looked up at the deepening sky. "Violet. Not lavender."

"You'd like my wings, then."

"Can I see them?"

I kept my sparse plumage magicked away, despising what it looked like and what it represented. Only once a year, on December 19th—the anniversary of my wing bone ceremony—did I allow my electric purple feathers to spill out of my back.

"No." At my clipped answer, the child pursed her lips but didn't hop off her chair. "How old are you, Naya?"

"Four and a half. And you?"

"Twenty."

"My apa is one hundred and forty-three."

Naya was a serious daddy's girl . . . I almost inquired about her mommy but decided it wasn't my place to pry. Nor did I care. It wasn't like I would ever see the child again.

"Why are you sad?"

I blinked. Here I thought I looked angry. I twirled my phone a few times before answering. "Because someone I love is dying."

Her brow puckered. "Death isn't the end."

I'd forgotten how early the brainwashing started. "For some people it is."

"This person you love, they're bad?"

"No. They're extraordinary." The lump, which had sat in my throat like a phantom limb, began to expand again.

"Then why are you sad?"

21

"Because I don't want her to die."

"But you'll see her again." She pointed a stubby finger toward the sky. "In Elysium."

"I won't."

Her frown became so pronounced that she looked like she'd stolen a few wrinkles off Ophan Mira's forehead. "But you have wings."

"I do, but I won't complete them in time. Do you know what happens when you don't complete them?"

Without hesitation, she said, "You become nephilim."

"Bingo. The worst sort of monster."

"Nephilim aren't monsters."

My head jerked back in surprise. "I . . . agree." I leaned forward. "But don't voice that too loudly around here. I think we're the only two people who share this belief."

"I like sharing something with you, Celeste."

My heart gave a slow, painful squeeze, but then the squeezing was replaced by total stillness. "I didn't tell you my name. How do you know my name?"

She bit the inside of her cheek as though in deep concentration before a huge grin split her face. "My head told it to me."

Her head? I stared at her until it hit me what she meant. She must've heard it screeched by Ophan Mira earlier. Stone carried sound like a tunnel carried wind.

Speak of the angel . . . Ophan Mira circled the fig tree. "Fletching, the sera—" Her lips stilled at the sight of my table companion. "Fletching Naya, what do you think you're doing here?"

"I was spending time with my friend." Her hands were linked together on the quartz tabletop as though she was in the middle of a business negotiation.

I found myself smiling at how she didn't quiver or balk.

"Your . . . *friend*?"

Rude much, Ophan? Was I not worthy of friends?

Naya shifted on her seat. "Celeste and I are friends."

"How . . . *wonderful*." Since Mira's feathers were now soldered to her wing bones, none fell. Had she been a fletching that lie would've cost her. "However, it's bedtime. Please proceed to the dormitories. Ophan Pippa is awaiting you."

22

A great sigh escaped Naya's small chest. "Fine." She lurched off her chair and then, completely unexpectedly, wrapped me in a hug, crushing the teal silk of my bomber. "Bye, Celeste."

"Bye, Naya." I was so stunned by her show of affection that I didn't embrace her.

As she rounded the table toward Ophan Mira, she asked, "Will you come back and play with me?"

No. I needed to say no. "I . . . I . . ." One glance at Mira's tight face had my good sense flooding back. "Probably not."

I'd come for one reason and one alone: to help Mimi. If the angels proved incapable or unwilling to aid me, I'd have no purpose to visit guilds, much less form relationships with younger fletchings who I wouldn't see for years to come since, pre-wing bones, children of Elysium weren't allowed out of guilds, their bodies as brittle and mortal as humans.

Her bottom lip quivered. "But we're friends."

"Fletching Naya," Mira pinched out the little girl's name, "off you go now."

She blinked up at the ophanim before returning her stricken gaze to me. Tears dribbled down her cheeks, glistening like crushed diamonds. She wiped them away and then she whirled and ran, making my heart feel as brittle as a dried petal.

Mira tracked Naya's swinging golden hair until she vanished into the hallway that led to the children's dormitories. "She's an exceedingly . . . *emotive* little girl."

Yet another thing wrong with our world: angels extolled empathy and yet advocated emotional detachment. Leigh had been too compassionate with her sinners. "Being emotive isn't a flaw, Ophan."

"Did I say it was?" If my feathers had been on display, her frosty tone would've iced them over.

"So, can the seraphim help me, Ophan?"

"No. But they did urge me to have you visit the Ranking Room to check on her score and to remind you to aid her in not compromising her natural death."

I snorted. "I'm not going to help her commit suicide."

"I never said you would." But she was thinking it. I could see it in the

23

myriad of shallow grooves crosshatching her centuries-old skin. "Perhaps you should check your score, too."

I stood up so abruptly the chair skidded on the quartz. "I know my score."

"You do?"

"Yes. I do."

"May I know your plans?"

"Live each day as though it were my last because one of them eventually will be." I strolled toward her, stopped to twist a fig from its branch, then chomped into it. Impeccably ripe. I was tempted to spit it out. Instead, I swallowed.

"Celeste . . ." She leveled her wary eyes on mine.

I sensed she wanted to tell me not to waste my angel-given gift. In the end, she tacked no extra words on to my name.

"Farewell, Ophan."

Before leaving, I strode through the curved, sliding glass doors of the Ranking Room and hopped onto a seat at the long bar that belted the circular room. I pressed my dry palm into the glass panel until the holo-ranker whirred to life, then sketched Muriel Moreau over the cool glass. Her face appeared in three-dimension, so incredibly realistic it felt like she was sitting across from me. Her lips flexed then straightened, and her luminous navy eyes met mine, sending waves of tenderness lapping over me.

I scrolled through her profile until I caught sight of her rank. Only then, did I release the breath I'd inhaled back in the cafeteria: 7.

From a celestial standpoint, it was an incredible score. Her soul, once harvested, would be brought to Elysium and given the choice between remaining there forever or returning to Earth inside a new body for another lifetime. In my opinion, though, her soul was faultless and deserved not even a single digit, but I'd come to learn my views of right and wrong differed greatly from the ishim's.

I craned my neck toward the sky beyond the domed glass with its fake streaks of orange and pink. Elysium didn't deserve someone like Mimi.

She probably wouldn't stay. Not once she realized Jarod and Leigh weren't there. I wished I could somehow prepare her for the disappointment, but we weren't allowed to speak of Elysium with humans. And although they believed me reckless and undeserving, I shockingly respected this law.

I returned my gaze to the single digit floating below a face I'd come to know better than my own, and my pulse shuddered in my ears, blowing away all other sounds. One day soon that face would no longer exist. This profile would vanish. The woman I'd come to love would be gone.

Ears still ringing, I checked what had cost Mimi seven points: *patricide*.

My leg stopped bouncing. My blood stopped pumping. Mimi had killed her father?

For a moment, I sat there stunned, and then every sound in the circular room crescendoed, overriding the silence. If she'd killed him, then he'd merited it. I'd never pried into her life, the same way she'd never pried into mine. Even though our pasts had shaped our personalities, neither of us had permitted it to shape our relationship. I respected her enough to keep abiding by our unspoken agreement and let the story of her sin fade into the ether along with her body.

Warily, I pressed my palm into the glass panel, signing on to Mimi so that no fletching disturbed her from here on out. Once the words **ASSIGNED TO CELESTE FROM GUILD 24** appeared in big block letters over her flickering portrait, I shut the holo-ranker off and left the guild, once and for all.

Chapter Four

"And then what happened?" I asked, hands slotted beneath my pillow.

For the past two days, Muriel had been regaling me with stories about her past. I'd heard some of them already, but not this one. As we laid on her king-size bed, the clock on her nightstand displaying the time in glowing red letters—4 a.m.—her cold fingers slid through my hair. Since yesterday, she hadn't gotten up. She blamed her lethargy on her lack of sleep, and yes, we hadn't been sleeping much, or at least I hadn't. She'd actually been dozing off a lot, sometimes in the middle of our conversations.

Selfishly, I wanted to keep her awake. I wanted to stack as many moments as I could with her so I could reach for them in the coming months. Having gone through heartbreak already, I knew that first year would be the hardest.

"So what did Pierre do?"

Her lips, so very pale without lipstick, curved wistfully. "He took me to a shooting range. Taught me how to handle everything from guns to rifles."

I rolled my eyes. "How romantic."

She turned her head and opened her eyes. "It saved me, Celeste."

"Saved you?"

Her hand stilled in my long chestnut hair. "From my father."

My molars jammed together. I'd promised not to meddle, but the question slid out. "How did he hurt you?"

"How only men who lack self-control and morals can."

I'd never picked anyone higher than a forty, but I was no stranger to sin. Just because I didn't pick the truly high rankers didn't mean I hadn't scoured their profiles and the crimes they'd committed to earn their scores. Atrocious crimes. Irredeemable. Which was the true reason I'd stayed away, not judging them deserving. They were monsters, more terrible than the ones that populated Ophan Pippa's stories.

My mind went to Naya then. I thought about how one day she'd have to deal with these sinners, decide whether they deserved a second chance and whether she'd be the one to give it to them. Usually, the dangerous ones, especially the men, were left to the male fletchings, but some girls took them on. Leigh had.

Except Jarod wasn't all that terrible, having earned his triple-digit score because of a mistake committed by the man who'd inspired my purchase of the neon pig with wings.

"Is your father still alive?"

"*Non, ma chérie.*"

"How did he . . . *pass*?"

"Painlessly. Unfortunately." Her attention drifted to the pearl-gray ceiling. "My aim was too good."

"I'm so sorry, Mimi."

"Whatever for?"

"That you suffered at the hand of someone supposed to love you."

"Hmm." She slid her hand over the soft duvet. "I'm not. If he'd been kind, I wouldn't have met Pierre. If I hadn't met Pierre, I wouldn't have learned how to shoot. And if I hadn't learned how to handle a gun, Isaac Adler would never have hired me, and I wouldn't have gotten to raise Jarod and then you." She ran a knuckle across my cheek. "I believe everything happens for a reason. Even the terrible things." Mimi mistook my silence for lack of understanding, because she added, "What doesn't destroy you will reshape you. Remember this, Celeste. Remember that the same fire that transforms sand into glass can turn logs into ash."

Unless it was angel-fire. Angel-fire transformed something into nothing. It cremated wings and destroyed souls.

I rolled onto my back. "I don't like fire."

"A life without fire would be cold and dreary, *ma chérie.*" She traced one of the purple arcs rimming my eyes. "Now, get some sleep, and in the morning, we can make crêpes so that I can demonstrate the wonders of fire. Unless you'd rather eat raw batter."

I side-eyed her, matching her wan smile with one of my own. "Can you tell me more about Pierre? What happened to him?"

"He was part of the foreign legions."

"And?"

"Close your eyes and I'll tell you the story of how Pierre and I started, and then of how we ended."

Ended. How I loathed that word.

I forced my lids to lower as she started her story. As though my mind had made a secret pact with my heart about not wanting to hear the ending, it shut off while Muriel and Pierre were still blissful and together.

I STARTLED AWAKE WHEN DAWN CREPT AROUND THE EDGES OF the thick burgundy damask, damning myself for having missed out on precious time with Mimi. Rubbing the shards of sleep out of my eyes, I rolled over.

When my gaze met a set of eyes I hadn't seen in years, one I'd hoped never to look upon again, I sat up.

If the seraphim had come, then that meant only one thing: Mimi was gone.

Chapter Five

"No!" I crawled toward Muriel, not paying Seraph Asher any mind.

Her face was smooth, free of the pain and melancholy she'd carried for decades. I pressed my cheek against hers.

"You left me without saying goodbye," I croaked into her ear.

"Celeste . . ." Asher's voice tossed me back to the darkest time in my life.

I pulled away from Mimi, palming my cheeks that dampened so fast the tears felt like they were bleeding from my very pores. "*You*, shut up." My brow puckered as my wing bones tensed and expelled a feather. "*Mother feather.*" I shut my eyes until the ache subsided and then I reeled my lids up and fastened my gaze to the man who'd forced my friend to ascend before incinerating her wings.

Leigh was dead because of him.

"I didn't know soul-collecting was among a seraphim's tasks. Don't the leaders of Elysium have better things to do than ferry around souls?" My spine jammed tight as another feather tumbled from my wing bones.

"I understand you're in pain—"

"In pain? I'm not *in pain*. I. Am. Enraged, Seraph." My voice was barely above a whisper, but it must've packed a punch, because Asher squared his broad shoulders and folded his arms, straining the brown suede ensconcing his torso. "First Leigh, now Muriel." I gathered her hand between mine and pressed it to my cheek, begging her fingers to caress my skin one last time. "Can't you bring her back? I know she can't live forever but—" My voice caught. Wavered. I snapped my lips shut before the sob swelling inside me could rend the miserable air.

You promised me weeks.

And crêpes. You promised me crêpes!

My tears dripped around her knuckles, wetting the calluses left behind by her beloved whisks and wooden spoons.

Who am I supposed to go home to on weekends?

Who am I supposed to complain to on bad days? Or on good ones?

Oh . . . Mimi.

"You know, Seraph, she's going to hate you once her soul takes its Elysium form and realizes what you did. Or rather what you *didn't* do, which is save the boy she loved. A boy whose soul didn't deserve to be erased."

"Are you done?" Although the contours of Asher's body were blurry, his cyan irises cinched by a stroke of bronze were in perfect focus.

"The day I'm done decrying the injustices committed by our kind is the day I'm dead, so no, I am *not* done. But one day, I will be. Could be in three months. Could be in seventy years. Who in Abaddon knows when this body of mine will fail? When death will finally silence me? What a celebration that'll be throughout the guilds, huh?"

Asher's jaw hardened while tendons and bones writhed in his tanned forearms, still folded and jammed against his chest. "Are you done *now*?"

"Wasn't I speaking English? Oh wait . . . that wouldn't matter since you're fluent in all languages." My shoulder blades struck each other. Another feather gone.

"Celeste, stop it."

"Why? Am I hurting your feelings, Seraph? I didn't think you had any." The ishim plucked me again, and I gritted my teeth, until I realized that the hot slices of pain were muffling the one lancing in my chest. Then my jaw relaxed, and I welcomed the discomfort.

Asher growled low and long.

"Bet you're regretting having volunteered to collect Muriel's soul, huh?"

His lips thinned, amplifying the small lines bracketing them as well as the ones edging his eyes. Angels didn't age when in Elysium or Abaddon and aged extremely slowly within guilds, and yet Asher seemed to have aged ten years since I'd last seen him in Paris.

I sat back on my heels and directed a vitriolic glare his way. "Why is it that you made the trip anyway?"

"To uphold a promise I made Leigh. One I failed to keep."

"What promise was that, Seraph?"

"To help you."

"Help me?" I almost laughed. *No.* I did laugh. And then I stopped laughing. "I hope it wasn't to help me ascend because I have zero interest in channeling upward."

We stared off. If he thought I'd avert my eyes first, he really didn't know me at all. Then again, why would he know me? It wasn't as though we'd spent hours together in the past. The most time we'd been in each other's company was the rainy afternoon he'd collected me from the Demon Court to give Jarod time and space to explain what he'd done with Asher's help.

Deep down, I knew Jarod was more to blame in Leigh's forced ascension, but Asher should've refused to interfere. By accepting to sign Leigh off from Jarod, he'd doomed her. Had he done it hoping that once away from her lover, she'd change her mind and marry the archangel?

To think I'd encouraged her to seek out the seraphim's favor. I should've kept my mouth shut the day he'd visited the guild. I should never have gone to Paris and encouraged her to complete her mission. If I'd just stayed out of her life, then maybe she'd be up in Elysium instead of buried under cold earth.

It struck me that the fault was mine, too.

My eagerness for change had doomed Leigh.

The realization made Mimi's hand skid out of my grip and dent the thick duvet.

My stomach cramped with guilt, filling my throat with bile. I spun and scrambled off the bed, but I must've knocked into one of my fallen feathers because the bedroom vanished, replaced by a patch of sunburnt lawn fenced in by wooden spikes and wire.

"You can't starve your dog because you're mad at him." I stroked the pudgy Rottweiler pup between his floppy ears and got a sloppy kiss in return. *"He's still a baby. He doesn't understand what he's done wrong."*

Monica yanked on his leash. "He's my dog, not yours."

"I'm not trying to steal him from you."

"Then why the hell are you here?"

"I'm here to remind you that you need to go easy on him."

"He's a guard dog. At least, he's supposed to be. I might have to ask for my money back if he keeps lickin' snotty kids. How old are you anyway? Eight?"

I balled my hands. "Eleven."

"Whatever. You're a kid. A kid who's gettin' on my nerves, and I'm runnin' all out of nerves between you and him." She nodded toward her dog.

"What's his name?"

"Rambo."

"That's a good name for a guard dog."

She stared at the ball of black fur a moment, and I sensed affection there. "Let's hope he ends up deserving it. Yo, Rambo, sit. Now."

Rambo did not lower his haunches to the ground. Instead, he stared at me as Monica dragged his little body across the patchy grass. I understood her need for a guard dog. Especially since she lived alone with her kid sister and mother, but the only way she'd get Rambo to obey was by mixing some warmth into her authority.

"Do you have treats?"

"Treats? Little girl, I barely got food enough for myself and my family. I don't got no treats. Besides he's done nothin' to deserve one."

I dug through my backpack and took out a granola bar. It was probably not the healthiest dog food, but it didn't have chocolate inside, so I assumed it wasn't too awful for the canine. "Can I try something?"

She eyed me and then the crinkling wrapper. And then because she wasn't evil, just tired and eager for a quick fix, she sighed and relented. "If he shits all over the place, you're pickin' it up."

"Deal. Can you unclip him?"

Monica lifted a pierced black eyebrow, but again, she conceded. The second Rambo was loose, he leaped toward me, tongue wagging.

I broke off a corner of the granola bar. "Rambo, sit."

The dog jumped at me, trying to get the food, but I kept it high.

"Sit, Rambo, and this is yours."

He fell back on all fours and then started licking my calves and ankles.

I started to laugh because it tickled. "Rambo, sit."

Monica was staring at me, arms crossed in front of her navy tank top which matched a bruise she sported along her left bicep. I wasn't sure how she'd gotten it but suspected someone had given it to her.

I crouched and pressed my index finger right above Rambo's tail. "Sit."

The dog sat.

"Stay."

His tail started wagging, and he sprang up.

"Sit." I pressed the spot again and he sat. This time, when I said, "Stay," he stayed. I fed him the chunk of granola, which he gulped without tasting.

I made him go through these two commands several more times, and then I handed Monica the granola bar and got her to do the same thing. After an hour, with the sun beating down on our heads, Rambo was sitting and staying like a pro.

But the best part was that when he licked Monica's bare toes, instead of scolding him, she crouched and scratched her puppy between the ears.

She'd earned one of her three sinner points for mistreating Rambo. My mission had been to remind her that kindness paid off more than cruelty. Once I'd earned my three feathers, I spent my allowance on a two-months' supply of dog food before stepping out of her life.

I emerged from the memory like a deep-sea diver gone too long without air. Asher loomed over me, fingers cinched around my biceps.

Even though he'd saved me from faceplanting, I snarled, "Take your hands off me!"

His fingers sprang open, but he didn't step back, just like he didn't look away. Was he hoping the memory contained in my feather's shaft would make me calmer, more pliant?

I pressed a trembling hand against my spasming abdomen. "Take her soul and get out."

The bronze tips of his turquoise feathers swayed as he pivoted and rounded the bed.

I wouldn't turn around.

Wouldn't watch him seize Mimi's soul and carry her away.

But as I sat back on my heels and squeezed my kneecaps, my gaze collided with the framed mirror propped against the wall.

I didn't want to see.

But I did.

33

I saw everything.

I saw Asher lay his palm on Mimi's rib cage.

I saw the golden threads of her soul rise from her lifeless husk and adhere to his hands. The delicate pull he exerted on the silken strands. The glinting orb resting calmly in his palm, whole and shimmering.

I wanted to scoop Mimi's soul out of his hands and cocoon it between mine. Stow it away in the jewelry box she'd given me for my sixteenth birthday. The one she'd filled with sixteen rings, one for each year she'd missed. She'd laughed when I'd laid down my spoon full of *crème brulée* to slide each and every ring on. They were apparently meant to be worn separately. I never did. I kept them together.

If only I could've kept her soul and mine together, too.

Asher's eyes met mine in the mirror.

"Go away," I murmured.

A violent storm was battering my insides, threatening to destroy my weakening dignity.

Instead of using the door, he opened the window, snapped his wings, and sprang off the balustrade into the dawn-smudged sky.

Chapter Six

Long hours later, I phoned the lawyer Mimi had instructed me to call, a Mr. Alderman. He arrived and took charge while I sat on the couch like a zombie, clutching a throw pillow to my smarting chest and staring listlessly at the slow dance of the clouds outside the bay windows.

Since she'd died at home, Mr. Alderman called the police, so they could attest she'd died of natural causes, and then the coroner came to pick up her body. When a cleaning crew disembarked, I snapped out of my trance and yelled at them to go away.

Mr. Alderman tried to calm me. "Miss Moreau, Muriel asked that her clothes be removed, so you wouldn't have to—"

"I want *nothing* touched," I gritted out. "Not the sheets, not her clothes, not her toothbrush. *Nothing.*"

The man was reasonable enough not to fight me. "Okay then. Once you're ready, you just call me, and I'll arrange everything." He patted his thighs ensconced in fine gray wool. "One last thing. Your caregiver informed me of her desire to have her ashes interred in the Adler crypt."

I pressed my lips together, not ready to discuss burying her because burying her would take her away from me for good. Not to mention it meant a trip to Paris, to Leigh, and I wasn't ready for that yet.

Before leaving, Mr. Alderman made me sign sheet after sheet of paper. He said it was so I could take possession of the accounts and the deed on the apartment, but for all I knew, I was signing everything away to random people. My eyes ached too much to comb through the legalese, and deep down, I didn't even care for material possessions. Especially the mob's.

Sure, Mimi had explained that the money Jarod had left her was untainted, that it was earned by his uncle's horseracing stables, that all the blood money had been distributed to charities and associations, but could I trust Jarod's word? Even though he hadn't been intrinsically evil, he'd still run an empire of violence and coercion. Once my thoughts and emotions untangled, I'd call Mr. Alderman to discuss the creation of new charities, because I didn't want or need Jarod Adler's money, clean or not.

I finished inking his papers, and he tucked them all away in his fancy leather briefcase.

"Can I get you anything before I leave, Miss Moreau? Food? A lift to your campus apartment?"

The sky beyond the penthouse windows was a periwinkle smeared in peach and gold. I was about to call out Mimi's name—she so loved sunsets—when I remembered she was no longer here, and my heart broke into my throat.

"Miss Moreau?" Mr. Alderman shifted on loafers so shiny they reflected his pearly round face. "Anything before I leave?"

I shook my head and stood from the couch. He proffered his hand, probably imagining I was coming to shake it, but I floated past him and unbolted the terrace door. Wrapping my hands around the glass railing, I looked upon the city I adored even though it was now empty of the people who'd made it special. The duck ponds in Central Park glittered like foil, and the clusters of leafy elms and maples shivered over the snaking cement paths along which humans meandered like ants. The world stopped spinning for no soul.

When all the colors bled together, I curled up on the firm sofa cushions of the outdoor couch and closed my eyes, goosebumps skittering up my bare arms and the slice of stomach on display between the hem of my faded *Ringmaster of the Shitshow* T-shirt and the elastic waistband of my cotton leggings.

Distantly, I thought of eating and showering but lacked the will to do either. If Mimi had been here, she would've force-fed me something delicious, but she was no longer here. Had she reached Elysium yet? Had she found out that her boy hadn't made it into the land of angels? Had she learned what I was?

I thought of the man she'd told me about last night—Pierre. Was he in Elysium? I'd forgotten to ask Asher.

Asher, who'd promised Leigh he'd take care of me.

How egregious.

When had she asked this of him? After he'd wrenched her away from the man she loved or while he'd scorched her wings? And then I thought of the feathers I'd lost this morning. Did they still litter the rumpled duvet or had one of my many visitors inadvertently absorbed them?

Eventually, the litany of deliberations lulled me to sleep, and I dreamed of Rambo and Monica. I dreamed they were inseparable and had rescued each other more than once over the years. I woke up with a smile that quickly faded at the sight of the dark, quiet apartment.

A new dawn had broken over the city, burnishing the towers of glass, bricks, and metal, vanquishing the monochrome hues of twilight. I tried falling back asleep, disinclined to face this new day.

Mimi's fragrance drifted from the soft fibers of the cashmere throw pulled up to my neck and crept around my bruised heart like one of the guild's honeysuckle vines, torturous and comforting. I cocooned myself in the warm blanket, grateful for the heat it afforded my chilled skin.

But then I jerked into a sitting position, and the cover collapsed around my waist. Had Mr. Alderman tucked me in before leaving? He'd been the last to depart, and no one else had the key to my apartment. Draping it around my shoulders like a cape, I plodded back inside. I expected silence but was met with the distinct sound of something sizzling. My heart pounded as I crossed the living room and rushed down the short hallway toward the kitchen. Had someone resuscitated Mimi? Was that even possible?

My socked feet skidded as I came to a brutal stop. And then my heart sank like a tossed penny. "How the *feather* did you get in? And what exactly do you think you're doing?"

Asher glanced over his shoulder at me. "I landed on the balcony where you were sleeping, and I'm making you breakfast." He'd gathered his hair into a topknot and traded his suedes for a white T-shirt and a pair of denim jeans, which made him look different. Slightly more . . . *human*. Still entirely unwelcomed.

"Not hungry."

"Muriel told me you'd say that."

My heart performed a slow pirouette. "Y-you spoke with her?"

"For a considerable amount of time."

How *unfair*. Although I longed to ask about their conversation, I wanted Asher gone.

He plated scrambled eggs, then pushed the plate toward me. "You need to eat."

As he rummaged through every drawer in the kitchen, probably on the hunt for cutlery, I stared at the curdled yellow mound, stomach seesawing like a fallen feather.

The throw . . . *he* must've put it on me.

I shed it where I stood and backed up. "Since you found your way in, you'll undoubtedly be capable of finding your way out."

I spun around and retraced my steps to the living room, heading toward my wing of the apartment. I slammed the door, finding great satisfaction in how hard the wood thwacked the frame and how shrilly the latch clicked into the lock plate.

A scorching shower later, I sprawled onto my silken sheets and grabbed my cell phone, powering it on for the first time since Friday. I had several missed calls, all from Jase. I didn't bother listening to voicemails since he'd blown up my screen with text messages.

JASE: *Pizzas are on their way. Where are you?*

JASE: *Movie or series?*

JASE: *Celeste?*

JASE: *Pizzas are here.*

JASE: *I'm down to my boxers. Those horrible ones with your beautiful face on them.*

JASE: *If you don't get home soon, I'm eating all the extra eggplant topping from your pizza.*

JASE: *Celeste, it's okay if you forgot about me and made other plans but text me to tell me you're safe.*

JASE: *Okay, now I'm fucking worried.*

JASE: *Please call me.*

JASE: *I'm about to file a missing person's report. No joke.*

JASE: *Celeste, goddamn it. Call me!*

I finally did. He yelled at me for three solid minutes after I said "hello." Once he'd gotten his stress out, I told him about Mimi, then asked him for a redo of pizza night before remembering it was Tuesday. He worked on Tuesdays. His only nights off were Sundays and Mondays.

He told me to shut up, that he'd get someone to cover his shift, and then he asked if I wanted him to come over to the penthouse, and although I was tempted to invite him over, I said no. Jase was my friend, my best and only one, but he'd never met Mimi, never come to this apartment. Out of habit, I'd kept this part of my life private, because my past wasn't easily explained.

After I ended the call, I shot an email to my advisor to explain my absence, then watched TV, dozed, woke up to commercials about hair loss. I tried to sleep again but to no avail, so I donned a gauzy black sweater, my leather leggings, zipped up my combat boots, ran a brush through my snarled hair, then gripped my phone and ventured out of my bedroom.

I froze on the threshold of the kitchen.

Asher was still *feathering* there. He sat in one of the high chairs, drinking water from a crystal glass. Or maybe straight-up vodka. I used to think alcohol cost feathers but learned it was a heap of poop. We could drink, do drugs, and have wild sex as long as we did the first two in moderation and the last in private.

"I put your eggs in the oven, so they wouldn't get cold."

Pursing my lips, I made my way to the fridge, yanked it open, and grabbed a bottle of water.

"Celeste, please eat something. If you don't want eggs, I know how to cook a few other things."

"Which part of 'leave' didn't you understand, Seraph?"

His palms flattened against the black stone island. "Great Elysium, you're stubborn."

"Did you think two deaths and four years would make me easygoing?"

His eyes hardened, looking more and more like the jeweled marbles we used to roll around the guild's floor when we were kids. "If you eat, I'll leave."

"*Hmm.* Tempting." I twisted the cap off my water and took a long swallow. "I have a better idea. *I'll* leave, and *you* can stay and eat your eggs." I grabbed my bag from where it still sat on the chair beside him, pulled on my teal bomber, and pocketed my cell phone.

"Celeste!" The seraphim's voice was sharp enough to give me pause.

"*What*?"

"You have less than three months to finish your wings, and six-hundred-and seventy-five feathers to go. We need—"

"*We*?" I cocked an eyebrow. "*We* are not a team, Seraph. I am *me* and you are"—*a nuisance*—"*you*."

I felt very generous about not tacking on a bunch of other descriptors: a detestable angel with a God-complex, a puppet of Elysium, worse than a Triple.

One of those thoughts cost me a feather. I squeezed my jaw as it popped out of my wing bones and flicked the doorknob, exiting onto the small landing that gave way to our private elevator.

"Besides, I don't want to ascend, and unlike Leigh, *no one* forces me to do anything I don't want to do." A smile knocked into my lips as the elevator dinged open and I traipsed inside. "Even though I'd love to see someone try." I added as Asher appeared in the doorway.

"Where are you going?"

"Home." When his eyebrows dipped, I realized my mistake—he didn't know about my shared apartment uptown. I pressed the lobby button and tapped my boot as the doors crawled to a close. Could they go *any* slower?

A hand shoved them back open, and then Asher was standing there, his hulking frame grazing either side of my normal-sized elevator. "Home?"

I puffed out my chest, attempting to make myself look bigger, tougher. "The guild. Ouch." The ishim plucked another feather from my invisible winglets.

He surveyed its decline. "I'm guessing your destination isn't the guild."

I screwed my lips tight, picking silence over additional torture. The elevator began to emit a low-pitched, extremely disagreeable squeal. "Can you let the door go, please?"

"I can."

And he did.

After he got in.

I scowled the entire way down.

And then I told him to get lost, which won me a look that made my fist itch for action. The ishim mustn't have understood my intent because they didn't steal a feather from my wings.

After we'd exited the Plaza and crossed into the park, I said, "Stalking costs humans points on their scorecards."

One of his blue-green-bronze eyes squeezed tight. "Good thing I'm not human, then."

I stopped walking and spun on him. "Seraph, I'm a lost cause. Voluntarily and enthusiastically so. I'm sure your conscience is weighing heavily on you right now, but I'm not interested in being *saved*, so please—"

"I heard you enrolled at Columbia. I assume you live on campus."

I growled. "Was I being too subtle when I—"

"Muriel's very proud of you for being ambitious and feels terrible that you won't be graduating."

I sputtered. "Why wouldn't I get to graduate?"

He tilted his head to the side, and a dark gold lock fell out of his leather hair tie. "Because Mimi—"

"You do *not* get to call her that!"

Already every passerby, be they male or female, was gawking at Asher, but my raised voice just funneled more attention our way. Even the leashed dogs cocked their heads toward the seraphim and his big *angel* energy.

BDE was a thing; BAE was Asher's thing.

"Muriel asked me to guide you back on the right track."

I shot him a tart smile that displayed all of my pretty white teeth. "Elysium's no longer the right track for me."

Every feather on the wings he hadn't bothered magicking away twitched. "Celeste . . ."

"Tell me, Seraph, did she slap you for what you did to Jarod and Leigh?"

The bronze tips of his feathers devoured the noon sun and spit it back into my eyes.

"Jarod picked Leigh's fate, Celeste."

Had I possessed superpowers, the anger beating in my chest would have leveled every skyscraper in a ten-mile radius. "Blaming others for your mistakes is childish and unbecoming of one of the Seven."

The beginnings of a rumble seeped through the unyielding line of his lips.

"I miss Mimi. She was everything to me after I lost Leigh. *Everything*. I have no clue where I'd be today if she hadn't taken me in. What I do know is that I cannot and *will* not sacrifice my new dreams for my old ones. Leigh's death changed me. Changed what I wanted out of life. Changed how I saw the world." I moistened my raw throat with a swallow. "Mimi probably deigned talking to you because she's mature and forgiving. Two things I'm not."

"Clearly."

I didn't react to the taunt since I'd brought it upon myself. "If you have any respect for me, you'll leave me alone. You did it once, so I have no doubt you're capable of doing it again."

I kept my chin tipped up, defying him to challenge me. When he didn't, probably too busy grinding his molars down to stumps, I whirled on my heels and strode down the elm-shaded path. Only when I reached Bethesda Terrace did I hook a glance over my shoulder.

The golden boy of Elysium was *finally* gone.

Chapter Seven

When I reached my fourth-floor walkup, I was light-headed, and my skin was filmed in sweat. Every bone in my body hurt, every muscle trembled. Even batting my eyelashes was painful. I was such a mess.

I dumped my bag on the beaten-up couch Jase had salvaged from the previous owners of The Trap. I'd wanted to replace the black leather monstrosity with something new, but my suggestion was met with a categorical no. Jase was easygoing about almost everything except his couch. So after I'd signed my name on the lease next to his, I'd scrubbed the worn thing down with water and white vinegar until it smelled less like dead cow, human ass, and old beer.

I didn't bother calling out my roommate's name since he was in class. I knew his schedule because it was almost identical to my own. Across the small hallway, his bedroom door was ajar, revealing a bed made with military precision, blinds pulled all the way up, and neither a dropped sock nor a discarded pair of boxers in sight. Although he hadn't followed in his Army father's footsteps like his brother Leon, he'd been raised by a stickler for neatness, and it had fashioned his personality.

I wasn't a slob, but I was most definitely not OCD about tidiness. I often left a T-shirt draped over the back of my desk chair and open, annotated textbooks everywhere. Since I'd moved in, though, I made a conscious effort to pull my comforter over my pillows in the morning, fold my towels in our shared bathroom, and hand wash my dirty dishes. And when I forgot, I usually came home to all three done for me.

I went inside my bedroom with its bare cream walls, white oak furniture, and hexagonal-shaped wall of windows that led out onto the building's fire escape. Two pigeons were presently perched there, skinny talons wrapped tightly around the railing, purple-gray feathers ruffling. I remembered being jealous that they were born with all their feathers, that they didn't have to earn them. I'd never admitted this to anyone. Not even to Leigh. I mean, who admitted they were jealous of rats with wings, which was the way most New Yorkers viewed their city mascots?

As I drew the curtains closed, something glinted on the flat rooftop across the courtyard. I squinted, heart ramping up at the idea that Asher or another verity had followed me, but it was only bulky ventilation units and TV antennas.

My pulse settled back, and I shut out the glaring sunlight. After kicking off my boots, I curled up on my bed and studied the plain wall over my desk. I loved art, yet had never decorated a bedroom. Not in the guilds, not in Mimi's Parisian apartment, not at the Plaza, not here. Did I never feel the need to stake my presence or did I simply never feel at home anywhere?

Probably the latter. From a young age, we were taught that our true home was Elysium, that the human world was simply a stop on our way to our final destination.

I fished my phone out of my jacket, which I hadn't bothered removing, and looked up artsy pictures. I scoured three websites before finding what I was looking for. I ordered two giant prints mounted on aluminum and covered in plexiglass. I was done with the brainwashing. Done with being a vagabond. This world was it. My terminus.

After laying my phone on my nightstand, I closed my eyes. I didn't think I could sleep again, but soon the cooing of the gray street birds faded, replaced by the sound of waves crashing upon bone-white sand. Leigh was there, peach hair blowing around her oval face, green eyes lambent with happiness, platinum wings shimmering as though encrusted with diamonds.

How can you smile after what our people did to you?

What they did? What did they do, Celeste?

They let you die. They burned your wings.

44

My wings are right here, honey.

And they were, but that wasn't right.

Leigh had lost her wings. Seraph Asher had reduced them to ash.

Hadn't he? Suddenly, her wings burst into flames, melting like wax around her bare feet. She didn't scream. Didn't cry. Didn't move. Just stayed still and stoically accepted her fate.

Leigh! Leigh! I reached out for her, but she stepped back.

And back.

And back.

"It's okay, Celeste." Her voice was strange, a little husky.

"It's not okay! Your wings. They're gone. It's not fair."

"Celeste . . ." The timbre was so deep. So masculine. "Babe, wake up. You're having a nightmare."

My eyes flipped open and landed on a set of brown ones, a scruffy jaw, and dark hair slicked back with gel—Jase.

Not Leigh.

"No one's burning anyone's wings off." A smile toyed on his lips. Of course, Jase thought this was funny since people didn't have wings in his version of the world. He slid a lock of hair off my forehead and ran it through his fingers before tucking it behind my ear. "I brought back some pizzas. Extra eggplant."

My stomach rumbled even though I was pretty sure that anything I swallowed wouldn't stay down. Rubbing my eyes, I sat up and peered around my somber bedroom.

"And extra wine. Not on the pizza."

I tried to smile but my lips were too limp. Had today really happened? Was Mimi really gone? Had Asher really cooked me eggs? It all felt so surreal. "Shouldn't you be at work?"

"I told you, I'm all yours tonight."

Emotion sparked in my chest, filling the cavernous, cold hull with a little heat.

"Want to talk about it?"

I wasn't sure if by *it* he meant my nightmare or Mimi's passing. Since I wanted to talk about neither, I said, "No."

"Want a hug?"

"Yes."

He wrapped me in his tattooed arms, and I rested my head at the base of his neck, inhaling his woodsy-ginger scent. We didn't talk, even though his throat bobbed. Probably with unasked questions.

I appreciated his silence.

His friendship.

His hug.

Him.

"I ordered some art for my room."

He stayed silent for a couple of heartbeats. Was he worried about me drilling holes in the immaculate plaster? I wasn't sure why that was my first thought. Perhaps because *I* was worried about disfiguring his apartment.

"Finally."

I pulled away. "You don't mind if I decorate?"

"I mind that you're asking."

"This is your home."

"This is your room."

"I'm just renting it." I crimped the comforter.

"Still your room." He rested his palm atop my tensed hand, forcing my knuckles to relax. "Especially now."

Now that I had nowhere to flock to on weekends.

My eyes felt like they'd been burned by a lighter. I shut them, trying to repress my rising sorrow.

Lips—warm, soft—touched mine. Hesitantly. And then with less caution. The familiar pressure of Jase's mouth thrust my sadness aside, tucking it behind a surge of raw need. The need to feel both something else and nothing at all. My fingers rose to his head and danced through his stiff locks, pressing him closer, closer, closer, until we were only air and heat and beating blood.

I let his fingers and mouth strip me bare, soothe me in ways words couldn't. It was a superficial sort of comfort but comfort nonetheless. Too soon his weight and heat were gone, and I was left alone in the dark, naked and cold, sated but empty . . .

So very empty.

Like my walls.

As the toilet flushed and a bin snapped shut, he asked, "Pizza and wine?"

"I'm not hungry." I curled onto my side and breathed. Just breathed. Keeping the tears at bay but failing to stave off the overwhelming sadness.

"Okay." Hinges groaned. "Try to get some sleep then, Cee."

As the door closed, I choked on the floating shards of my heart and muffled my sobs in my rumpled pillow.

Jase didn't come back because, although we slept together, we didn't do sleepovers.

Tonight, I wished he'd forget about my rules, come back inside, and hold me.

He never did, so I ended up holding myself.

Chapter Eight

As Jase and I walked across Columbia's quad the next day, he said, "Cee, go home."

I blinked. "Huh?"

"Home. Go home."

Home was Mimi, and Mimi was gone.

"You're in no state to attend classes."

I hugged my heavy textbook tighter. "I'm fine."

"You're not fine."

"I think I know myself better than you do."

His lips thinned, and he took a step back. "You're right. I know nothing about you." Like the dream version of Leigh, he backed up and up and up. "Not for lack of trying," he bit out, leaving me standing alone in the middle of the grassy quad.

I locked my knees as the elegant brick and stone buildings bloated and shrank around me, dizzying, suffocating. I tipped my face up to the sky and stared at the sun until it charred my pupils, made them ache like the rest of me, blurred the world, burned away its colors and scents and sounds and movements.

My phone chirped. A glance at the screen revealed a message from Mr. Alderman: *When and where would you like us to deliver Muriel Moreau's ashes?*

My knees softened, and I fell.

And fell.

And fell.

The world grayed and fragmented before becoming as dark as obsidian.

CUPBOARDS BANGED. WATER GUSHED.

I rolled over, expecting open sky but a pale-gray ceiling loomed overhead and crushed-velvet sapphire drapes framed a black, starless rectangle. I sat up so quickly, my bedroom blurred and my giant flat screen TV and mirrored closets swam. Hadn't I left the Plaza yesterday? Wasn't I on campus? How did—

Another bang had my heart swinging into my throat. The sound was close. In my en suite.

"Jase?" I called out tentatively.

Unless it was my doorman, but what would he be doing in my bathroom? Not only would it be odd but also highly inappropriate. I called out Jase's name again.

The man who stepped out of my bathroom didn't have tattoos or dark hair.

I wrapped the bedsheet around my torso even though I was still fully clothed—black T-shirt with the word *Spitfire* drawn in fake flames and leather leggings. Slowly I let the sheet drift down. "You're back, Seraph."

"Being back implies I left."

My mouth went dry. "Didn't you?"

Asher crossed his arms over a white T-shirt that seemed so at odds with his status. Tendons flinched under his Elysium-sun burnished skin. "Your boyfriend seems . . . *nice.*"

Yeah, right. "I didn't know you'd met."

"After you fainted. He ran back to help you."

That sounded like a Jase-thing to do. "You should've let him."

"So, he could do what? Take you back to your uptown rathole and screw you awake?"

I gasped. "His apartment isn't a rathole. And he isn't my boyfriend. Just my roommate." Why did I feel the need to clarify my relationship?

49

Asher leaned against the doorframe, tucking his monstrous turquoise wings into his spine. "Maybe you should tell him that."

"Maybe you should mind your own business."

"You are my business."

"I am *not* your business."

"Celeste, trust me, if it was up to me, I'd let you *carpe diem* the shit out of this world."

Had he just sworn again?

"I thought you were the big guy on campus, Seraph. I thought you didn't take orders. Thought *you* made the rules."

His feathers twinkled in the faint light trickling out of my adjacent bathroom. "I am. I don't. And I do."

"Then why in Abaddon are you so intent on making me ascend? Did you not fill your yearly quota of ascensions?"

His lips twitched. I must've imagined it, though, because the archangel possessed zero wit and even less humor. "I've already told you, Celeste. Muriel demanded that you complete your wings."

"Mimi would never demand that of me."

"And yet, she did."

"Why? And why would she ask *you* of all people to help me? Her son's murderer."

Darkness swept over the seraphim, trapping shadows beneath his dramatic cheekbones. "I ran you a bath and ordered food."

"I'm not your kid."

He dipped his chin into his neck. "I'm fully aware that you're not my child, but somehow you became Muriel's, and since she's no longer here to take care of you, you're stuck with me. Now get up, clean the stink of your boyfriend off your skin, and meet me in the kitchen."

I didn't blush. Ever. Yet my face filled with heat. *The stink of my boyfriend?* Who the feather did he think he was?

"Stop thinking up ways to make me fly off into the night and leave you behind."

"Oh, Seraph." My lips curled into a cruel smile. "I wasn't thinking up ways to make you flit away. I was thinking up ways to murder you."

A feather didn't loosen from my wing bones. Perhaps because it wasn't a lie, or perhaps because the ishim didn't care about my threat. After all, it wasn't like I could kill the archangel. Only another archangel had that power because the sole way to kill an ascended was by burning away their wings with seraphim fire.

Asher snorted, and although he was still steeped in shadows, his eyes gleamed, a slash of blue against the monochrome. "Well, entertain yourself with these visions in the bath."

Before I could respond, my bedroom door clapped shut.

Chapter Nine

After a long soak in my bath where I visualized all sorts of ways to piss the archangel off enough so he gave up his little help-a-fletching-earn-her-wings crusade, I settled on the simplest method of grating him—provocation. I selected a tight black tank that displayed my perky nipples and paired it with black panties, neither skimpy nor sheer. If I'd owned a bra, I would've worn that instead, but I didn't own bras since I had so little to boost and wasn't interested in false advertisement.

The only thing that set me apart from a child or a boy was my defined waist and curved ass, and both were on perfect display. Armed with a lot of naked flesh, which was sure to make the prim archangel squirm, I padded into the kitchen where he was arranging take-out cartons. He wasn't kidding when he said he'd ordered a lot of food. The island, which was huge, was invisible underneath the multitude of ecological cardboard containers.

"Did a restaurant have to shut down for the night?" I gestured to the ridiculous buffet.

He stared up, and the container filled with fried calamari he'd been trying to squeeze between a heap of pinkish noodles and a block of parmesan cheese slid from his fingers and flopped onto the floor.

He glared at me and then down at the poor calamari as though they, too, were dressed inappropriately. "I think you forgot your pants."

"What would I need pants for? I'm at home."

He crouched and scooped the fried rings up by the handful before tossing them back into the grease-stained container. He must've grown annoyed with cleaning up the normal human way because his fingers lit up with fire, and he incinerated the remaining squid loops. And then he shoved the box into the garbage underneath the sink. Even though his fire had probably chewed away any oily, fishy remnants, he washed his hands, then washed them again, the muscles in his back bunching and jerking underneath the thin cotton.

"So, how's life, Seraph?"

He flipped off the faucet but didn't turn. Just kept his broad back to me and planted his wet palms on the edge of the black stone sink top.

"Did you ever end up getting married? Oh, wait, can you? You only had one month to seal the deal with a lucky fletching. Sorry, a lucky *verity* because hybrids were banned from entering the competition for your hand, what with our plumage being so very bland."

His knuckles whitened, and his fingers flexed. *Crack.* The black stone broke off from the metal basin.

He stared at his fingers.

I stared at his fingers. "Did you just break my kitchen?"

He let out a low growl that sounded excessively unangelic. "I'll have it fixed in the morning."

"I'm no stonemason, but I don't think it can be stuck back together."

"I said, I'll take care of it," he barked, still not looking at me.

Someone has a temper.

Operation aggravating-the-seraphim was working marvelously well.

He slid the hunk of black stone onto the countertop, knocking over the dish soap bottle. He righted it, then spent an inordinate amount of time finding the exact angle at which to set it. When he finally turned around, turquoise eyes as lambent as nebulas, he kept his gaze affixed to my forehead.

"So?" I leaned over the island and sniffed the dishes, making sure to keep my butt propped in the air even though lazy me longed to drop into one of the bar chairs. "Did you find your perfect little consort?"

"I did not."

I tried to stifle my genuine curiosity under copious nonchalance. "Because you ran out of time?"

"Because I decided I didn't want any more complications in my life."

53

"Complications? That's offensive to my gender." I plucked a cherry tomato off a plate and popped it inside my mouth, sinking my teeth into the thin skin until the juice sprayed out.

How long had it been since my last meal? I'd skipped breakfast two days in a row and lunch and dinner and then lunch again for obvious reasons. The tomato went down like a sour cherry. The last time I'd eaten was with Mimi, in this kitchen.

To escape my lurking grief, I asked, "So, celibacy, huh? Sounds dreadful."

Asher's dark brows slanted. "I'm not here to discuss my life choices."

"What shall we discuss then? *Ooh.* I know. Elysium politics." I cocked my hip against the island. "I have *so* much to say about that."

"I'm certain you do."

"Where should we start? How about the law on nephilim souls? Because guess what I found out after you dumped Leigh back into the human world? Nephilim have souls. Oh, wait. You knew that. *Duh.*" I added a dramatic eye-roll. "I didn't, though; Leigh didn't either."

His jaw sharpened.

"Know what I think?"

"I'd rather you don't tell me."

I pushed off the island and walked over to the big male, getting right up in his face, which was a feat when he had an entire head on me. "I think I should return to the guild and enlighten our people. I think angels-in-training deserve to know the truth."

We were so close I could see the vein along his temple swell and flutter with silent anger.

"All our lives, we're taught not to lie, and yet we are brought up on lies. Don't you think that's feathered up, Seraph?"

"Celeste . . ." He ground out my name, his jaw barely flexing to shape the two syllables.

"What, Seraph?" I asked sweetly.

"Once you ascend, I invite you to bring this up with the Seven."

"Except, I'm. Not. Ascending." I punctuated each word with a light tap of my index finger against his rigid chest.

The hand he'd crushed the countertop with rose and wrapped around my intrusive finger. For a heartbeat, I thought he might smash my phalanxes, but he simply dragged my hand away from him, then let go. And then he stepped to the side.

Unfortunately, he didn't fly away. Just headed to the fridge and opened the door. He grabbed a bottle of water from the door and uncapped it. "Want one?"

"I don't want water."

"A glass of milk?"

"What I want is for you not to change the subject. What I want is to hear you're going to use your position to educate the young."

Instead of a venomous riposte, I got a sigh. "I'm only one man."

"A powerful one."

"Perhaps, but there are seven of us. To amend a law, four of us need to vote in favor of it."

"Well, have you even brought it up?"

"I have. Twice."

"And?"

He shut the door of the fridge slightly harder than necessary. "And if it hasn't changed, you can imagine my request wasn't popular among the Council members."

"So, what? You give up?"

"I'm not giving up, but insisting—" He cut himself off, swigged some water, then rubbed the side of neck. "Insisting gets you attention."

"It also gets you results."

He let out a soft snort. "By that logic, I should simply keep insisting you complete your wings and you'll end up doing it without brute force."

"My wings are a personal matter. Nephilim souls are a public one. *Should* be a public one."

"You're so mutinous, and yet you're giving up on the fight. Why is that?"

"My voice will never carry like yours can."

"It'll carry in Elysium."

"I may be a hybrid, but I'm not dumb."

"What has one got to do with the other?"

"You're just trying to mollify me to change my mind about ascending."

He drained the water bottle, then flattened it into a disk. "Although it *would* make my life easier if you'd work with me instead of against me, I've never met anyone as vocal as you are."

"Leigh had a loud voice. She also had pretty verity feathers. Pure-verity feathers. And look what happened to her, so excuse me for being obtuse about working my ass off to earn feathers if I'm just going to end up losing them."

Asher's eyes darkened like spilled ink. "She didn't lose them. She gave them up."

"You think I won't follow in her footsteps if I repeatedly get shot down by the mighty powers-that-be?"

"I didn't think giving up was your style."

"It isn't. My style is enduring, even after everyone gives up on me."

"Who gave up on you? Muriel and Leigh?" Rough breaths made his chest expand. "They didn't give up on you. They died. There's a big difference. So, I'm not sure who you're talking about right now because no one gave up on you. *You* gave up on *us!*"

The power of his voice resonated inside my marrow. "I never returned to a guild after Leigh . . . after it happened." I took a breath. "I was *fifteen.*" Another breath. "No one came for me. In four and a half years, not a single angel came for me. You may disagree, but in my book, indifference is giving up."

Without another glance at the vibrant buffet, I stalked back into my bedroom and locked my door. I shut my curtains, picked up my phone with shaky hands, and sent Jase a message that I was fine, that *no, I hadn't been abducted.*

ME: *See you tomorrow?*

His answer was slow to come. *Lunch at Trap?*

ME: *Sure.*

Before shutting off my phone, I read Mr. Alderman's message again, the one that had made me faint. I typed out a quick answer: ***Please have them delivered tomorrow morning to the Plaza. Thank you.***

And then, probably because I'd spent an inordinate amount of time sleeping and was wired from my conversation with Asher, I ended up powering on Netflix and watching three entire seasons of *Modern Family*. How I wished I'd been born in a loud and crazy family instead of a hushed and submissive one. I only wallowed in self-pity for a few minutes. Then I decided that wallowing served no purpose and I would take action.

I would build a loud and crazy family of my own, adopt lots of children, since nephilim were infertile, and maybe marry a man. Or two. Some countries allowed women to have multiple husbands, right? Then again, two men sounded like a headache. I'd stick to one.

A good one.

A long-ago talk with Leigh surfaced in my mind. We'd been finishing up lunch in the Versailles gardens when she'd tried to convince me that soulmates existed. Had Jarod truly been hers? Even though I'd laughed— had I laughed? Maybe I'd just shaken my head—I did wonder if it was true.

Would Asher know?

I smirked at the idea of bringing it up. Although, come to think of it, if he hadn't left, discussing romance would surely get him to leave. No man—winged or not—enjoyed discussing love.

Although I didn't tap my fingers together and laugh like a deviant, my smirk turned into a grin that stayed on my lips. All. Night. Long.

Chapter Ten

T he next morning, as I padded out of my bedroom, fully dressed this time, I heard voices coming from the kitchen. Two. One was Seraph Asher's. I never got to confirm who the second speaker was because when I reached my destination, the archangel was clicking my front door shut.

As he turned toward me, he speared his hand through his hair, dragging it off his face. The yellow strands hit his shoulders and curled there. Had he slept over? And if he had, *where* had he slept? Maybe archangels didn't sleep. Would explain why his white T-shirt wasn't rumpled. Unless it wasn't the same one.

"This arrived for you."

My gaze drifted to the vase he slid atop the cleared island. Not a vase. An urn. My bones softened, and my saliva thickened. I swallowed back the viscous sourness, reminding myself that the woman I'd loved wasn't inside the golden canister. She was safe in Elysium.

Safe in Elysium . . .

I'd unpack that thought later.

I eased my fingers off my cell phone and laid it on the island.

"Are you finally going to eat something?" Asher asked.

"First, coffee." I headed toward a cupboard, the one above the ruined stone countertop, and grabbed a polka-dot cup, my heart pinching at the feel of the decorated porcelain Mimi had treasured so greatly she'd carted the whole set over from the Demon Court. As I carried my cup to the fancy built-in expresso machine and woke it up, I asked, "Do you want coffee?"

"I'd love one, thank you."

"Long? Short? Sugar? Milk?"

"Short. Black."

As the cup filled with charred deliciousness, I returned to the cupboard. "Did you sleep here?"

"I did."

I switched out his cup for mine under the machine's spout and brought his over amiably. "Were you worried I'd run off?"

He lifted the cup, which looked so dainty between his long fingers. "You found your pants."

I looked down at the supple leather hide that hugged my legs. "Most men would be disappointed, but you seem quite pleased."

Since his mouth was hidden by the cup, I watched his eyes for a reaction. The corners crinkled slightly, but perhaps that was because Mimi and I favored bitter beans, and the archangel found them too tart.

He drained his cup, though. "Might be because most men are after your body, and I'm after your soul."

"Except my soul's attached to my body. Always will be." Since my options were death or everlasting winged life. "They're a packaged deal."

He set his cup down, then flattened both his palms against the island. "Perhaps I should change my tactic, then."

"Your tactic?"

"To get you up to Elysium."

I sipped my coffee.

"Perhaps seduction would incite you to ascend."

The scorching liquid went down my airway, and I coughed. "Elysium, no." I wheezed as I put the cup down and coughed some more, apparently not done choking on coffee and his heinous proposition. Several inhales through my nose later, my insides settled, and I pressed my own palms on the island across from him, mirroring his stance, shoulders back, arms straight. "There is *nothing* I loathe more than a murderer, Seraph, so if I were you, I wouldn't waste my time attempting to seduce someone who despises you."

His mouth leveled off, and the vibrancy of his irises dimmed. "I wasn't volunteering for the job, Celeste."

"Well, don't even think about sending anyone else to try, because another huge turnoff for me are wings. Especially the bushy, glittery kind."

He stared at me a good, long time. "Verities aren't the source of all evil."

"Of course not. The evil ones are the nephilim. Isn't that right, Seraph?" I wasn't sure why this conversation wasn't costing me feathers. Not that I was complaining.

"Thank you for the coffee." He carried his cup to the sink and rinsed it, his vertebrae as tight as traffic on Fifth Avenue during rush hour. "Once you're ready to head to the guild, come get me. I have a phone call to make. I'll be on the terrace."

As he retreated, I called out, "I won't be going to the guild. I'm going for lunch with Jase. My *friend*. And you won't be coming, because you're not invited."

He stopped under the arched doorway, tension rippling up his spine and down his arms, making bones realign and tendons roil. And then his wings—glittery, turquoise, thick—spilled out. I hoped he'd use them to swoop off my balcony and once and for all.

He turned his head. Not fully. Just angled it in a way that I could see the harsh line of his jaw and a single flaring nostril. "You're being a brat."

"How does living *my* life the way *I* want make me a brat?"

He pivoted, this time completely, his feathers stretching a little wider around him, but not so wide that their tips grazed the satiny walls. "Because you're picking this life out of spite. For me. For your kind." He hit me with a glare so powerful I wondered if it was infused with magic—invisible bolts of angel-fire maybe, or a spray of angel-dust, although I wasn't sure how dust could hurt since it was only used to conceal. "Hate me, *fine*, but don't hate who you are."

"Who I am is Celeste Moreau."

"Who you are is a child of Elysium."

"What has Elysium *ever* done for me but fill my mind with lies and my heart with"—I carved my hand through the air, searching for the correct word—"*injustice*." After a much-needed breath, I hissed, "Do you know how awful fletchings are to one another? How judgmental? How competitive? Do you know what it feels like to have skimpy wings that don't even *feathering* shine?" My body shook like a geyser about to erupt.

"No. You don't. Because you're a verity. You might not have had things handed to you, but you had access to *everything*. Want to know what my dream was?"

A vein throbbed along the side of his neck, revealing a pulse that might not have matched my own but nonetheless struck hard and fast.

"My dream was to become a malakim. But guess what? Hybrids aren't allowed to guide souls. So don't tell me I'm picking this wingless life out of spite. I'm picking it because I like who I became outside my quartz cage. I like who Leigh and Mimi made me." I panted as though I'd just completed a marathon and beat out the fastest runners.

Asher's shadowed gaze traveled to the floor. Even though I didn't care if my outburst had cost me all of my feathers, I looked down. Found nothing purple blunting the smoke-gray hardwood.

My eyes prickled. My nose and face, too. Hot. I was hot. And furious. I balled my hands into fists to stop them from shaking and circled the island toward the row of high chairs, on the hunt for my bag. I needed to get out of here. Get away from the selfish and stubborn archangel who wouldn't take no for an answer.

"Where's my bag?"

"In the living room." His tone was dulcet, as though he sensed speaking any louder would set me off.

Fists locked at my sides, I strode toward him. He didn't shift to the side but he did tuck his wings in. Unless I plastered myself to the wall, I'd make contact with his feathers.

"Move."

The overgrown angel didn't budge. "What you said is true. It isn't fair that hybrids lack the opportunities offered to verities."

"So glad we can agree on something. Now, move."

"Ascend and become the voice of hybrids."

"Not interested. Now can you please—Whatever." I shoved away his wing.

He snapped it in but too late. I'd done the forbidden—touched another angel's wings. And not just any angel but an archangel. He could probably punish me for it. Have the ishim pluck my wing bones.

I grabbed my bag and jacket, then returned to the hallway. Asher was still standing there, but he'd done away with his wings, probably worried he'd soil his pretty feathers further on my hybrid skin.

"No one has *ever* touched my wings." His tone was harsh again. "Not without my consent."

"Shouldn't leave dangling what you don't want manhandled."

This time, when I passed by him, he had the good sense of adding space between our bodies.

"I hope it was torturous." I puffed out a slow breath as the ishim finally chastised me, schooling my features to hide my reaction to the shrill ache of another lost feather.

"I've visited your memories, Celeste. This isn't who you are."

Was he talking about the feather he'd picked up at the guild the night he'd announced his wish to find a consort? Or had he found others?

It didn't matter.

Looping my bag across my torso, I said, "I was sand, then. The angel-fire you used on Leigh's wings, it touched me, too, Seraph, and it transformed me."

Mimi's last words finally made sense. I'd been sand and now I was glass. Sharp and breakable but no longer amorphous and malleable.

Backing away, I left the winged dictator to parse out that thought in the company of my ugly purple feather.

Chapter Eleven

It took the entire subway ride uptown for my bones to stop rattling. As I emerged above-ground, I debated turning around. Jase didn't deserve to be subjected to my ugly temper. He might've been used to my mood swings, but never had my mood swung so hard. I pulled out my phone to cancel but then tucked it back into my pocket. I owed him an apology for having told him off before fainting.

I reached The Trap before he did and slid into the far booth Alicia had saved for us, the one under my winged pig. Instead of procuring me joy, the sight of it dampened my mood. I was tempted to ask for another table, but the place was packed with students enjoying Leon's signature, smoke-broiled burgers and house fries, so I flattened my back against the brushed cement wall and pretended the pig wasn't there.

As I waited for Jase, I answered an email from my advisor, then responded to Mr. Alderman's texts about having received Mimi's ashes, and that, no, he didn't have to book my flight to Paris, that I'd do it myself at some point.

Alicia bustled over with a basket of nachos, guacamole, and an iced coffee. "Courtesy of the chef."

I smiled up at her. "Tell the chef he's just made my day."

"Will do, hun. Do you want anything else while you wait?" The neon eggplant above the doorway of the unisex bathroom purpled her black skin and platinum hair, which she kept shaved on one side and braided on the other. She'd adopted the edgy style after her third break-up with Leon and had kept it throughout break-up four and five.

"I'm all good. Thanks."

After she was gone, I pulled up a travel app and began to check flights for Paris. I was about to input my credit card number when Jase strode into The Trap in his usual daywear—sweatpants, soft T-shirt, and baseball cap.

As he dropped in the booth across from me, he flipped his cap around. "Sorry. Professor Williams asked me to stay after class. Wanted to discuss breathing during public speaking. Apparently, I don't do enough of it." He shot me a crooked grin. "She asked where you were by the way. Told her you were dealing with some family things."

Family things. How to carve my heart right out . . .

A lock of his dark hair slipped through the snapback and grazed the edge of his raised eyebrow. "Who was that guy yesterday?"

Couldn't I get one Asher-free hour? Just one? Was it too much to ask? "He's someone from my past." The wall seemed harder, cooler against my stiff shoulder blades.

"Like a boyfriend?"

"No. The opposite of a boyfriend."

"Not sure what the opposite of a boyfriend would be."

"A person you have *zero* affection for."

Alicia dropped by the table, jotted down our order—the usual—and left.

Jase set his inked forearms on the table, muscles twisting under the decorative ink. "Did he hurt you?"

"Not physically."

"I knew Abercrombie was an asshole." His voice smacked of animosity. "I shouldn't have let him take you."

"Abercrombie?" I reached for a nacho and scooped up a little guac.

"Couldn't remember his name, so I gave him one."

I didn't bother telling Jase Asher's name. After my irreverence, the archangel had surely given up on me. Perhaps he was up in Elysium, sitting upright in his quartz throne, since he wasn't the type to slump, negotiating how quickly the ishim could divest me of my remaining feathers. How many did I have left anyway? Three-hundred and fifteen? Three-twenty?

The thought that he'd actually considered helping me earn six hundred plus feathers before the end of the year struck me as ludicrously amusing.

"Why are you smiling?"

I chomped on my chip, then chased it down with coffee. "I like the nickname." *Abercrombie.* Even though Asher wasn't an all-American ripped teen, it suited the all-arrogant muscled angel well.

"What did he do to you, Celeste?"

I bought myself a couple of seconds to think up a plausible answer by pulling on my straw, filling my stomach with more ice-cold liquid. "Remember that girl I told you about? The one who was like a sister to me?"

"Leighton?"

"Leigh. Before she died, she went to live with him."

His eyebrows drew low. "They were married?"

"Not exactly. More like he wanted to marry her, but she didn't want to. Anyway, he kicked her out."

His brown eyes flashed with loathing. "Who the fuck kicks women out onto the street?"

I probably should've added the part where she begged to leave, but it felt irrelevant since she'd never asked to enter Elysium in the first place.

Tendons pinched tight in his strong neck. "I'm real sorry I let him take you yesterday."

"It's okay. Like I said, he's not dangerous. He's just . . ."

"An asshole?" Jase supplied.

I nodded. And then I waited to feel a twinge, but no feather detached itself, probably because I hadn't spoken the word myself.

"What was he doing on campus?"

"He knows Mimi." Her name brought a brutal flare of pain behind my ribs. "*Knew* her."

"So, he came for her funeral."

Since it wasn't a question, I didn't answer.

"Did he leave?"

"Hopefully." I glanced toward the door as though expecting to see him standing there, in Leon's underground restaurant, trimmed in colorful neon light.

Thankfully, he wasn't there.

Our food came, and I wolfed it down even though my stomach ached and protested, having shrunk from my days of accidental fasting. When Alicia had showed up with our platters of oil-slicked burgers wedged between sesame-dusted buns, I'd steered the conversation away from Asher and had kept it away during the remainder of lunch.

Outside the restaurant, Jase slid his baseball cap around to shade his eyes from the glaring sun. "Are you coming to Goldstein's class this afternoon?"

I hadn't planned on attending but why not? The only other place I needed to go was Paris.

Eventually.

I ended up walking back to campus with my roommate. At some point, he speared his fingers through mine, and although I allowed him to hold my hand, I kept my grip slack because I didn't want him to misconstrue our relationship.

INSTEAD OF GOING BACK TO OUR CAMPUS APARTMENT AFTER class, I claimed I needed to go pack up Mimi's stuff. Although true, it wasn't the reason I was heading downtown . . . the hand-holding was.

The heat of his skin lingered like spider threads over mine, a deeply unsettling sensation.

"I'll see you later at The Trap?" Jase asked as he walked me to the subway.

"Not tonight. I need to put some stuff in order at home, then fly out to Paris. That's where Muriel wanted to be buried."

I hated using Mimi to escape this uncomfortable situation. What I needed was to sit down with Jase and go over the lines in this friendship that needed to stay uncrossed with a thick-tip permanent marker. We weren't kids. We were adults. And the adult thing to do was be honest.

I'd adult after my trip.

"Want me to come with you?"

"To Paris?"

He shrugged. "Or to your apartment. I can help you box stuff up." When I bit my lip, he added, "I'm good with cardboard."

I should've returned his smile, or at the very least, squeezed his arm and thanked him. Instead, I said, "It's Thursday. Your busiest night."

"I don't need to go to work. Not if you need me, Celeste." His eyes locked on mine, probed mine. "Do you need me?"

"Um . . ." I chewed on my lower lip.

My aloofness smudged Jase's expression and eventually killed his enthusiasm. "Guess not."

"Jase."

He started backing away.

"Jase, you *know* me. I like to keep parts of my life separate. That's what I do. That's what I've always done."

"Is that why you never introduced me to her? To keep your life tidy? Or is it because you were ashamed of me?"

"Ashamed of you? Why would I be ashamed of you?"

"Because I'm a scholarship kid with an ex-convict for a brother."

"I'm not ashamed of you, Jase, *or* of your brother. I admire you both."

He stopped retreating but kept the distance between us. "Then, why?"

"Because it was never the right time. And Mimi was a recluse. And —" I carved the air with a frustrated hand, my array of rings glinting in the afternoon sun. "Fine. Come with me! I'll show you where I went on weekends."

He let out a deep snort. "Pass."

My hand dropped back along my side. I was stunned that he'd refused, and also not. *I* wouldn't have taken myself up on my offer. "That came out—"

"I don't know what secrets you're trying to guard, but I'm sad you feel the need to guard them from me." And with that, he spun and walked down the block, sidestepping a mother as primly dressed as her toddler.

Chest heaving, I balled my hands, my nails biting into my palms. Perhaps I should've extended a real invitation instead of the flung-out annoyed version. Just so he could see I had nothing to hide. Before heading down into New York's dank and dark underbelly, I shot him a text containing only one line: my Park Avenue South address along with the apartment number. I had secrets but none in the home I'd shared with Mimi. My secrets were buried in Murray Hill, in a quartz residence hidden behind a narrow green door.

Jase would probably be too proud to come over now, but in case he changed his mind, the ball was in his court.

Chapter Twelve

Jase hadn't come over after his shift. Not that I'd truly expected him to. What I *had* expected was a text message, but the last words on our chat had come from me. The following morning, even though my body felt like it weighed as much as a semi and my mood was the consistency and color of the sky—curdled, morose gray—I pulled myself out of bed.

As I drank coffee and chewed crackers that hurt my teeth, I stared at the hallway where I'd lost a feather yesterday. It was no longer there, which could only mean one thing: Asher had touched it. Unless he'd picked it up with kitchen tongs and dumped it in the trash, a very real possibility considering how angry he'd been.

I pulled out another cracker, the plastic wrapping crinkling, and stared again at the urn, a dab of gold against the dark stone of the island. A cruel reminder of the woman I'd lost.

A tremor shot through my wrists and into my fingers. The cup slipped and shattered in polka-dotted fragments around my socked feet. The blue dots danced atop the white. Instead of crouching and picking up the pieces, I just stood there.

My chest trembled and expanded, then squeezed so tight I winced. "It's a cup, Celeste," I murmured to myself.

But it wasn't *just* a cup. Like her ashes, the porcelain tea set had been a part of the woman I'd loved.

I wasn't sure how long I stood like that, surrounded by the fragments

69

of porcelain jutting like the shipwrecked hull of a yacht, the shallow puddle of coffee stretching and soaking into my socks, but the warm liquid turned cool, then cold.

I needed to go to Paris. Lay the remains of her earthly body next to the boy she'd cherished even though it wouldn't reunite them. I backed up, tracking wet footprints across the apartment. When I reached my bedroom, I peeled off the socks and dumped them in my hamper, then the rest of my clothes came off, and I stepped into the shower. Soon, I was wrapped in thick, white steam, the only clouds I'd ever touch. As I toweled my heat-pinked skin, I booked myself a first-class flight to Paris for that evening, then checked my messages again to see if Jase had written back.

Nothing.

Once dressed in a long-sleeved black shirt and my usual leather leggings, I rooted around my drawers for my passport. The only thing I found was a strip of pictures that made my breathing trip and stumble. Leigh had taken me to the movies the day I'd earned my first feather. I didn't remember which movie we'd watched, but I did remember pulling her into a photobooth and immortalizing us on glossy paper. I was ten, a child, while she was fifteen, already a woman with the pink-orange hair and soft curves she'd so hated, but which in my eyes, in Jarod's eyes, in Asher's eyes since he'd winged her, had made her gorgeous.

The past decade had chiseled my cheeks and anger had sharpened my expression, nevertheless I still resembled the girl in the picture—freckled, dimpled, with hair and eyes the exact same shade of ruddy-brown. Lack-luster. I didn't need to have my wings on display to show off my hybrid heritage. Nothing about me sparkled.

As I swept my thumb over the side of Leigh's face, I wondered what Jase saw in my androgynous body. It couldn't possibly appeal to him. And neither could my gristly personality.

Every time Mimi had insisted I was beautiful, I'd laughed it off, laughed each compliment she'd ever given me off, but they'd still sank deep, penetrating into my toughened heart and tenderizing it.

I cast one last look at the glossy strip and dropped it back into the drawer, refocusing on my task: locating my damned passport.

Mimi had probably stashed it in the safe. I crossed the living room and barged into her bedroom but froze on the threshold. The rumpled bedsheets and a lone purple feather tucked between the nightstand and the bedframe grew closer then receded, close then far, again and again. I slapped my palm against the doorframe to keep myself from getting swept up in the current of my overwhelming emotions. My rings clinked when they met wood, the bands digging into my skin.

In that moment, I regretted having thrown out the cleaning crew. I hadn't wanted them to erase Mimi, but the proof that she'd lived, that she'd just recently *stopped* living, felt like tongues of fire gliding up and down my chest, scorching me from the inside out.

My knuckles ached from my tight grip. I let go and retreated into the living room. It took me several breaths to remember what I'd gone seeking in Mimi's sanctum.

My passport.

Right.

I stared toward the open doorway. I couldn't board a flight without it. And if I didn't board a flight, I couldn't get to—

My thoughts shrilled to a stop. There was one other way I could travel. The idea took root and bloomed, feeling more and more like the best one I'd had yet. Sure, I'd sworn off guilds, but guilds had channels. The only thing I needed was an escort. I didn't see how or why an ascended would refuse to fly me through. Buoyed by the cleverness and expediency of my plan, I collected my jacket and bag. I was about to pluck the urn off the island when I thought better of traveling with a breakable jug. I grabbed one of the vibrant Hermès silk scarves Mimi always tied around her neck and spread it on the island.

Her fragrance—Guerlain's citrusy *Acqua Allegoria*—gusted off the colored threads, seizing and squeezing my heart anew. I removed the lid off the urn and upturned the ashes. The gray powder flecked by slivers of white bones made my skin grow cold and clammy.

It's not Mimi.

Swallowing around the lump in my throat, I folded the scarf until the grains of her body were as tightly bundled as a newborn infant. I tied several knots, then slid it into my fabric tote, before heading downstairs and into a cab.

Cheek pillowed against a headrest that felt plasticky and smelled like dandruff shampoo, I watched the city smear past, so drab it looked devoid of color. Raindrops pelted the windshield, softly at first, and then the drumming turned raucous, muffling the chilly whoosh of air coming through the vents and the loop of frivolous news and movie trailers playing on the monitor.

Traffic was horrendous, so the ride took longer than its usual fifteen minutes. When we finally pulled up, I tapped my credit card against the payment terminal, stooped over my tote to protect it from the downpour, and dashed toward the angelic temple.

Hair streaked with rain, I strode into the atrium with its counterfeit blue sky and gushing fountains. A rainbow-winged sparrow swooped low, twirled around a quartz angel statue before perching on a honeysuckle vine and darting its beak into a white bloom to sip its nectar. Once sated, it leaped off and resumed its chanting, joining its voice to its peers presently haloing a small group of delighted children sitting cross-legged with their heads tipped up.

Ophan Mira stood at the helm of her rapt audience, regaling the children with the history of our kind. However uptight she was, she was a wonderful teacher and storyteller. I wondered which chapter of history she was recounting and whether it was a human or celestial one. I drifted closer and caught the name Arion.

The first malakim, one of the fathers of angels, a man forged of sky and flame who rose from the Nirvana Sea along with six other angels, four females and two males, several millennia ago and colonized Elysium before venturing down the channels.

Where Arion descended to Earth, his consort Olba traveled to Abaddon. Apparently the channels leading to either world sat opposite each other in the Canyon of Reckoning—one wreathed in dark glittery smoke, the other in pale lavender.

Arion returned from his first trip to Earth with a soul, the first harvested. When he learned Olba hadn't yet come back, he released the soul in the care of one of his sisters and traveled down the dark flue. There, he found a deserted world made of polished obsidian.

This was usually the part in the story where Ophan Mira breezed over his journey through the somber, barren land, fast-forwarding to his findings: an immense, snapping fire pit. There, edged by firelight, he found Olba's limp, wingless body, dripping blood from hundreds of gashes. At first, he blamed an assailant for his consort's wounds and the fire for the absence of her wings, but then, he uncovered dried blood and ribbons of skin beneath her fingernails and realized the gashes were self-inflicted. But what of her wings?

He scooped her up, unfortunately inhaling some smoke. Its magic seized and tortured him, making Olba appear like a monster. He dropped her and flew toward the channel, but before returning to Elysium, he realized his mistake and went back for his consort. This time, he held his breath as he picked her up and didn't breathe until the smoke cleared in the channel and he stepped out in Elysium.

As though she'd been holding her own breath, Mira expelled a deep exhale. "Unfortunately, without wings, she could no longer stay in Elysium."

"How did they know she couldn't stay?" one of the children asked.

Mira looked down at her pupil. "They just knew."

Classic. Shut down a perfectly reasonable question with a perfectly inadequate answer.

"Thus was born the first nephilim," Mira continued. "What happened to her? Does anyone know?"

A redheaded child stuck her hand in the air.

"Yes, Juniper."

"Olba went crazy in the head, aged, and died."

"Correct," Mira concluded gravely. "So, Fletchings, what is the lesson to retain from the Legend of Arion and Olba?"

The same redhead said, a tad too excitedly considering the depressing subject matter, "That an angel cannot survive without wings."

"Exactly, Fletching Juniper. Exactly."

I didn't miss the way Mira's eyes narrowed as though warning me that this would be my fate if I forfeited my wings, that I would eventually lose my mind and die. Granted, it wasn't an ideal ending, but it beat living forever with a bunch of feathered, sanctimonious louses.

My spine tensed, and a feather dropped from my invisible wings.

Mira's mouth pursed as she followed its waltzing plummet.

"Ophan Mira?"

The familiar voice jolted my attention off my downy deserter.

"Yes, Fletching Naya?"

"What happened after she died?"

"What do you mean?"

"What happened to her soul? Did Ryan—"

"Ah-ry-on," Mira corrected her.

"Did Ah-ry-on bring it back up to Elysium?"

"Nephilim don't have souls, Naya," the redhead know-it-all said.

A gasp escaped Naya. She stared at Juniper, then swung her gaze back to Mira. "Is that true, Ophan?"

I expected Mira to confirm it. After all, this was what she'd spent years hammering into our gullible minds.

But instead, she said, "No. They have souls, but they're often too damaged to retrieve."

"The sparrow's wing was damaged the other day," Naya said, "and you healed it, Ophan."

Mira's already narrow body seemed to grow reedier. "You cannot compare a bird's wing to an angel's soul."

Naya's voice rose again. "Did Ah-ry-on at least try—"

"Enough!" Mira's shout silenced Naya and most of the sparrows. At least her sternness had been preceded by some kernel of truth.

I was about to walk away when Naya's shoulders began to shake. Remembering all the times I was silenced for demanding answers that were never given, I said, "Naya raises a valid point, Ophan."

The little blonde's neck spun. "Celeste!" Before my next breath, she'd sprang to her feet and skipped to my side.

As her arms encircled my thighs, I added, "Since nephilim *have* souls, perhaps we should try healing them instead of abandoning them." I laid a hand over her head and stroked down one pigtail, then the other. "Humans are worthy of second chances. Why not angels?"

Mira's lips thinned. "When the damage is too deep, it cannot be repaired."

Naya peered up at me. "I *knew* you'd be back."

Guilt stilled my hand.

Naya released my leg and pressed her palms together. "Can I go play with Celeste? Please, Ophan Mira, pretty please."

My heart cramped at Naya's enthusiasm.

Although Mira's lips were still AWOL, her expression gentled. "I could be wrong but I doubt Fletching Celeste came to play."

Naya wrenched her head back to look at me. Was I grimacing? I must've been because her smile fell and she took a step back.

I didn't want to lie, and not because I cared about preserving my feathers for once. "Ophan Mira's right, Naya. I came to access the channel." When her eyes began to shimmer, I dropped into a crouch and touched her shoulder. She didn't shrug me off, but her little bones bunched up. "Naya, soon, I won't have access to the guilds, and you won't have access to the outside world, so becoming your friend wouldn't be fair." I left out the bit that by the time she might have access to the outside world, my mind will have gone the way of Olba's.

Unless that was part of the legend. Something to scare us into preserving our wings.

Naya wiped her cheeks. If the situation had been reversed, I would've tossed away her hand a long time ago, but she wasn't like me.

She was all gold ringlets and cherubic innocence. "You shouldn't give up, Celeste."

"I only have two and a half months left, sweetie, and a whole bunch of feathers to earn. Trying isn't even an option anymore."

The other children hissed as though realizing they were in the presence of a future nephilim.

Naya's skin tone competed with the acres of stone surrounding us. "Pick a Triple."

I cocked my head to the side. "You know about Triples?"

"I know they're not all monsters."

I couldn't remember how old I'd been when I was told about the ranking system, but certainly not this young.

Sure enough, one of the children asked, "What's a Triple?"

They were so sheltered and unprepared for what lay beyond their quartz crib, but it wasn't my place to knock down the walls that gave them a false sense of security—it was the ophanim's place. I challenged the guild professor to explain it to them, and surprisingly, she did. In broad and vague lines, she told them about sinner points.

As Mira spoke, I said, "I'd need to reform more than one Triple, Naya."

Hope glowed in her eyes.

"It sounds easy but it's not."

"Sometimes, it is."

I frowned. Had her father told her stories about Triples? Had he reformed one? Maybe he'd told her about Leigh and Jarod, although I really doubted an angel would tell his kid about the verity-turned-nephilim and her beloved Triple.

"Most of the time, it isn't." I touched the tip of her nose before rising back to my feet. "If you still want to play—"

"Yes." The word came out rushed and breathy.

"Okay." I smiled for the first time today. The first time in a few days. "Ophan, can I borrow Naya for an hour?"

Mira stared unflinchingly at me, as though trying to gauge my intentions. She probably thought I'd use that hour to fill Naya's head with insidious ideas and her heart with false hope. I expected her to say no.

"One hour, Naya. And then it's bath time."

"Okay, Ophan." Naya's grin devoured her face as she reached out and took my hand. "Can we start with—" She squealed in delight, ridding me of several decibels of hearing. "Apa!" Instead of letting me go and running to him, she tugged on my hand, whirling me around toward a group of three angels standing on the threshold of the atrium.

I waited for the male ishim to open his arms so that his daughter could jump into them, but it wasn't the ishim's arms that opened.

It was the archangel's.

A nerve twitched beside Asher's left eye as he sank onto one knee. Like a windblown ribbon, Naya's hand glided out of mine, and she dashed toward those open arms.

Chapter Thirteen

Asher was a father?

He said he hadn't found a consort, yet he had a child?

Had he fathered Naya while he was searching for a wife or after giving up on finding one?

A piece of our conversation drifted into my mind. He'd spoken about not wanting any more complications. Did he consider Naya a complication, or her mother? Who was her mother? I gazed at the female ishim standing beside him, a woman with a narrow face and a pale mane that bounced against gold-lilac wings. Her eyes were as dark as Naya's and her hair as blonde, albeit curlier. Was she the mother? Wouldn't surprise me the seraphim had picked an ishim. After all, ishim were verities. Not quite as highly ranked as malakim, though, but still at the top of the celestial totem pole.

When Naya peeled herself away from Asher and greeted the ishim by their titles—Ish Eliza and Ish Damon—I deduced the female ishim wasn't her mother. Which was reassuring because there was something so hard about her features. I instantly disliked her, and since I liked Naya, I didn't want her to have a mother like that.

Naya skipped away from Asher and returned to me. "Apa, this is Celeste."

Oh, he knew who I was. "You have a daughter, Seraph."

A pulse throbbed at the base of his throat at my *not-quite* question.

Naya wrapped her hand around mine again. "We're going to play hide-and-seek."

His gaze zeroed in on our locked hands. I could tell he wanted me to release Naya's hand, probably rip it away from hers before I sullied his little girl the same way I'd sullied his wings yesterday.

"Hide and seek?" His voice was as rough as the stubble coating his jaw.

"I promised her one game."

"How . . . kind."

I snorted, knowing he didn't think me kind. "Won't you join us, Seraph?"

"I can't. I have"—he skewered me with his ocean-colored glare—"things to take care of."

Naya pouted. "You always have things to take care of, Apa."

His expression softened instantly.

"He's an archangel, Fletching Naya." Ish Eliza's superior tone made my dislike of her grow so immensely fast that I worried all of my feathers would pop off my wing bones. Astoundingly, none even loosened.

Naya gave a resigned sigh. "I know he has more important things to do than play with me."

Carve my heart out, why don't you?

I squeezed Naya's hand to remind her I was there, ready to play with her. "Want to count or hide?"

"*I'll* count." Asher's deep timbre resonated against the domed glass ceiling. "You two go hide."

Again, Naya almost took out my eardrums with her happiness.

"Can we play too?" asked the redhead.

"Yes. Everyone can play," Naya announced magnanimously.

For some reason, I imagined Ophan Mira hiding, and that filled me with amusement. And then I imagined Ish Eliza joining in, and I outright laughed.

Asher's searing gaze impaled me anew. "Would you like to share the reason for your pleasant mood, Celeste?"

"I would, but I might . . . *molt*."

He shook his head, which made a tendril of hair escape his manbun. "If it was so terrible, you would've already *molted*."

"True." Still, I didn't share my musings. "Tell me, Seraph, what with cavorting with Triples and burning off wings, how on Earth, or rather on

Elysium, did you find the time and energy to have a child?" I delivered my taunt sweetly and quietly, so it wouldn't reach Naya. Only its intended target.

Asher's expression didn't only darken; it went pitch-black.

Naya tugged on my fingers. "Come on, Celeste."

I let her pull me toward the hallway that led to the youngest angels' dormitories, as Asher, through gritted teeth, began to count.

AN HOUR LATER, OPHAN PIPPA CAME TO RETRIEVE NAYA FOR her bath. Although she didn't want to leave her father, she ended up accompanying the ophanim.

I hadn't spoken once to him during the game; he hadn't either. Before leaving, though, I felt the need to say, "Your daughter's very sweet."

His eyes didn't shift away from the corridor down which she'd been whisked. "She is."

The silence between us was wrought with so much animosity that a mere spark would surely make the air combust.

Still not looking my way, he said, "I thought you were done with guilds."

"I need to use the channel."

He side-eyed me. "To go where?"

I dipped my chin. "Somewhere."

He turned, pinning me with a formidable glower. "No Ophan will escort you through a channel without my consent."

Wow. "Way to sling that mighty power of yours around, Seraph."

He ground me some more with his eyes.

I backed up, one palm pressed protectively against my purse and Mimi's bundled ashes. "I guess I'll use the human way to travel to Paris then."

"Paris?"

Well, *feather.* I hadn't meant for my destination to slip out. Whatever.

I began to trek toward the atrium when he asked, "What are you going to do in Paris?"

I glanced at him over my shoulder. "I had a sudden craving for macarons." *Pop* went my wing bone.

He tracked my feather's demise. "I'll take you."

I must've lost my hearing along with that feather because I thought I heard Asher offer to take me. "Um. What?"

"I said I'll take you." He stalked brusquely toward me, then overtook me.

I didn't particularly want to travel with the archangel since holding onto one's escort was a prerequisite, but I wanted to travel at the speed of light more than I *didn't* want to touch him, so I trotted along behind him.

As we rounded the last hallway and entered the smoky shaft of pure Elysian light, I asked, "You're not planning on dropping me off in Abaddon along the way, are you?"

A corner of his lips hiked up. "Unfortunately, Abaddon's only accessible through Elysium."

Since he lacked a sense of humor, I deduced the crooked smile was the beginnings of a cruel sneer. "How unfortunate indeed."

He offered me one of his hands. To think the same hand that cradled Naya had burned off Leigh's wings.

Holding my bag close to my body, I slid my palm over his, and we shot up into the ether.

Chapter Fourteen

T he second we landed in the Parisian guild's channel, an exact replica of the one back in New York, I snatched my hand from his.

As I walked out, I tossed a, "Thanks for the lift," over my shoulder.

He followed me. And not just through the hallways, but through the rose-covered atrium. Okay . . . so maybe he'd brought me here because he had business in Paris. At least, his unsolicited company distracted me from the stabbing pain of being back in Guild 7 without Leigh.

I didn't let my gaze roam over the pink blooms crawling over the white walls or the seven fountains that were different from the ones back home, not in size but in representation. The flora, the sculpted angels, and the layout were the only things that differed from guild to guild. Everything else—the fake Elysian skies, the fire-veined quartz, the chanting sparrows—were entirely the same.

We ran into no one, probably because it was the middle of the night here. Fletchings and ophanim were all tucked into bed or enjoying what the city had to offer on weekends. When Asher opened the door and then proceeded to hold it for me, I finally stopped walking.

"You're not trailing me, are you, Seraph?"

"Last I checked, walking ahead of someone isn't trailing."

Seriously? I crossed my arms. "You know what I meant."

"You're either here to get something from the apartment you shared

81

with Muriel or to bury her ashes . . ." He stared at my bag as though trying to detect the shape of an urn through the fabric.

"What does my reason for coming here have to do with your ongoing presence?"

"I was simply making sure you reached your destination painlessly. Consider it a thank you for playing with Naya."

"Thanking me for playing with your daughter offends me."

His eyebrows drew together.

"Check the ground, Seraph."

"Why?"

"You obviously think I'm lying."

His gaze didn't even flick to the sidewalk. "I don't always think the worst of you, Celeste."

"That's hard to believe."

"So, where is it you're going?"

"Will you leave if I tell you?"

"No."

"Then enjoy not knowing." I walked ahead of him, arms loosening from their knot and returning to my sides.

The door banged shut, hopefully behind the archangel.

"It's the middle of the night, Celeste."

No such luck.

"You shouldn't be walking around by yourself."

I tried to remain silent. Failed spectacularly fast. I wasn't the strong, quiet type; I was the spindly, chatty type. "I'm an adult. I'm pretty sure I'll be fine. Besides, I was planning on taking a cab."

"Taxis are on strike."

"I'll take the subway then."

"Also on strike."

I squinted toward the boulevard, but it wasn't yet visible at the end of the sinuous, pedestrian street.

"You know the French as well as I do, Celeste. They're always striking."

He was right. In the two years I'd lived here, there'd been a protest a month about something or other. Usually, it had to do with working less and earning more.

His wings materialized at his back, their bronze tips shimmering in the glow of the cast-iron lanterns protruding from the limestone façades. "I could fly you to where you need to go."

"You're kidding right?"

"Do I look like I'm kidding?"

"No, you look very serious, which is worrisome."

"Why is it worrisome?"

"Because. You're offering to *carry* me."

"Are you worried I can't?"

If my heart wasn't presently clocking each one of my ribs, I might've snorted, but I was too busy trying to space out my breaths so I didn't sound as shocked as I probably looked. "I wasn't questioning your strength, Seraph." I took in the thick biceps jutting from his brown suedes—not body-builder huge but ridged with hard muscle.

"This isn't some devious ploy to dangle you over the Eiffel Tower until you accept to complete your wings."

My mouth went dry. "That was *not* where my mind had gone."

"Then why do you look like you're about to be sick?"

"Because your offer to cart me around the sky without a seatbelt is unsettling."

"Have you never been airlifted by an angel?"

"Nope. I'm a land girl. And this land girl really enjoys walking. Besides my destination is one arrondissement over, so I'll just see myself there. On foot."

As I started to turn, he asked, "Are you frightened?"

I paused. "Of what? You?"

"Of flying."

I blew air out the corner of my mouth. "Course not." My wing bones niggled. *And* niggled.

Those big arms of his crossed over his broad chest. If I hadn't met Eve's mother, Asher's fellow archangel, I would've assumed seraphim were cast from different molds than the rest of us.

"But you, on the other hand, should be frightened."

"Of what should I be frightened, Celeste?"

"Of me accidentally—or not—grazing your precious feathers again, Seraph."

"I survived the first time. I'm sure I'd survive another attempt on my wings."

"Attempt?" I smirked but then wiped that smirk away because he was a hateful person who deserved only cold-shoulders and glowers. "Look, if your angle is to show me what I'll be missing out on—"

"I have no angle."

"Your compassion knows no bounds, Seraph, yet I'd still rather walk." And so I did, my feet eating up the silvery cobblestones.

A moment later, the air shifted, and the scent of Asher—wind, suede, sunshine—swirled around me again. Elysium, the archangel was stubborn, and this was coming from a particularly headstrong girl. If I pretended he wasn't there, would he leave?

I tried that approach for a whole minute after which I said, "Can you please find another fletching to"—I licked my lips right before the word *annoy* could pop out of my mouth—"*assist?*"

Instead of taking the hint, he said, "I met your mother the other day."

My stride faltered. Was he trying to press more of my buttons? Why in this world and in his would he bring up my genitor? "I don't have a mother, Seraph."

"You do."

I pursed my lips.

"She lives in Guild—"

"That woman was a womb, not a mother." Because I couldn't leave well enough alone, I asked, "Why did you meet her? To discuss my *predicament?*"

"Since you want nothing to do with me, I thought she might be able to get through to you."

I gave a dark chuckle. "Did she even remember she had a daughter?"

"She did but didn't want to get involved."

"Surprise. Surprise." Why couldn't I simply be indifferent to her? "Speaking of mothers, Seraph, who's Naya's?"

He studied the glass façade of the restaurant on the corner where a lone waitress scrubbed down tabletops. As we passed, her gaze drifted to Asher, and the dishtowel slid out of her hand, hit the edge of the table before flopping onto the floor. Since she couldn't see his wings, I assumed she'd been awestruck by his physique. Unless she had a thing for cosplay. In his brown tunic and matching pants, the archangel looked like he'd just taken a break from arm-wrestling a lion. She tracked him all the way to the boulevard, tongue lolling out of her mouth. Asher, though, was totally oblivious to his big angel energy.

When we reached the boulevard, I reiterated my question, "So? What lucky verity did you impregnate, Seraph?"

"Naya's mother was human."

Surprise was a weak word for my reaction to his answer. "Was?"

He set his pained gaze on a zooming taxi. "She's dead."

"Oh. I'm sorry."

A cab careened down the lane reserved for public transport vehicles, sending a gust of cool wind through Asher's feathers.

I gasped. "You lied about the strike!"

"So I did." He sounded positively unapologetic.

"I didn't know the golden boy of Elysium had it in him to mislead poor, unsuspecting fletchings."

Asher rolled his eyes. Actually rolled them, like one minute his pupils were directed on me, and then they were on the inky sky. "I'd hardly call you poor or unsuspecting, Celeste."

I smiled.

Once his eyeballs leveled back on my face, the archangel's expression transformed into a softer one that made him seem amicable. But that look was all smoke and mirrors.

Asher *wasn't* kind. He was the powerful brute who'd stolen my best friend.

He must've sensed the direction of my thoughts because his smile vanished, and he sighed. "What did I do now?"

"It's not what you did now; it's what you did then. I can't forget and I can't forgive."

When I walked away this time, he didn't follow.

Chapter Fifteen

The cemetery was deserted, and its gates sealed. It hadn't even occurred to me that it could be closed.

I peered through the cast-iron bars for a flashlight-toting guard. Finding none, I walked the length of the stone wall in search of a watchman's post when a body landed in front of me.

A very lively one.

As Asher retracted his wings, I jerked backward. "What is wrong with you? You don't sneak up on people like that."

"I'd hardly call it sneaking."

"Pounce! You don't pounce in front of people."

"So you did bring the urn . . ."

Anger with a hefty side of annoyance evened out the beats of my heart. "Why are you here?"

His face dipped. "I came to pay my respects to Leigh and Jarod."

I narrowed my eyes. "You never respected either of them when they were alive. Why start now? Is it your conscience? Does it finally bother you?"

Shadows pooled in the hardening planes of his face. "You have no idea what you're speaking of."

"I was *there*. The afternoon you stopped by to inform Jarod that your little plan worked. That Leigh's wings were complete. I was *there* when you escorted a red-eyed Leigh through the channel to Elysium. I was *there* when you threw her back on Earth in the hotel room you so kindly paid for. I was *there* when Mimi found her body. Their bodies. So don't you feathering dare tell me I have no idea what I'm talking about!"

Asher shifted his jaw from side to side.

"Now, get· out of my way." I sidestepped him, purposefully not giving him a wide berth so I could ruffle his feathers.

I expected him to whisk them away, but he neither magicked them out of existence or tucked them in, and their tips grazed the shell of my ear and the side of my arm. Even through the thick silk of my bomber, I felt their gossamer pressure, and it made me shudder. Either Asher had the worst reflexes, or he'd done it on purpose, sensing it'd grate me just as much as it grated him.

"Ah ... life without wings ..."

Abaddon, lend me strength.

"Care for a lift *now*, Fletching?"

I froze, not because of his offer, but because of the loathed title. "I may have wing bones, but I'm no fletching." I took off again, my pace so brisk the cool evening air snaked around my neck and up my spine, causing goosebumps to scatter. I pulled my jacket closed and hugged my arms around myself.

The air churned, lifting the ends of my long hair. I took it my message had finally permeated the archangel's hermetic skull and prompted him to take flight.

"Don't bite," he rasped.

Don't—

I started to turn to give Asher another piece of my mind, since one had clearly not been enough, when he locked his arms around me, pinning my own beneath his, and yanked me off the pavement.

As the sidewalk grew smaller, I held my breath. And then we were plummeting. Right into the graveyard. The landing wasn't as brutal as I'd anticipated, but it still knocked the air out of my lungs. The second his arms slipped away from me, I whirled around and smacked both my palms into his pecs, shoving him so hard he would've keeled over had he been human. Instead, *I* stumbled back. He caught one of my elbows to steady me. As soon as I'd gotten my balance under control, I snatched my arm away.

"You don't just grab people and fly off with them!"

"Technically, I hopped. High."

"You know what I mean!"

"Better be quiet. Screaming will attract attention."

The vein in my neck throbbed and throbbed. I was going to kill this bird-man! My wing bones tightened and pushed a feather out.

Asher trailed its descent. "Thinking of me?"

"Oh, you have no idea," I whispered darkly.

He had the audacity to smirk. The unicorn noodle had the audacity to smirk! But then his gaze climbed back up my face, and his amused expression vanished. "Well, perhaps stop or it'll make my mission harder."

"Your mission? Did your palm slip on top of a celestial holo-ranker and sign you up to me?" I injected my question with sarcasm to hide my curiosity.

"Angels cannot sign on to other angelic beings."

I studied the dark cemetery, trying to get my bearings and remember how to get to the Adler crypt. "Look, thank you for the lifts. Even the one I didn't ask for. But *please* . . . flit the feather away, Seraph." I started up the wide road, then went right.

"It's the other way."

I gritted my teeth. If I'd been pettier, I would've kept walking in the direction I'd picked, but because I wanted to get this over with quickly, I listened to Asher. His gaze prickled the side of my face as I strode past him and then the nape of my neck as I strode away. Wind combed through the branches of the lindens, making them click like old bones. The sound effect combined with the darkness made me shiver. I tried to remind myself that the soil beneath me enclosed only bodies, not souls. Unfortunately, that didn't ease the eeriness.

I stopped at the next main road, trying to spot a familiar marker.

"Keep going straight."

Ugh. Without acknowledging him, I followed his instructions.

A few minutes later, I reached a pillar of gleaming black marble inscribed with names: Isaac, Jane, Neil, Mikaela, Tristan, Leigh, Jarod. Soon, Mimi's name would be added to the list of departed.

Breaths hitching, I traced the letters in Leigh's name. "She wouldn't want you here. And neither would Jarod."

Asher didn't answer. Had he finally gone? I looked over my shoulder. Nope. Still there.

He stood with his arms crossed and his wings tucked in tight. "They're no longer here to protest." His gaze didn't waver off the crypt's door.

"You made sure of that."

The wind slipped through the downy web of his feathers, made them flutter even though everything else about him stayed motionless. "I did make sure of that."

Instead of going off on him—it hadn't served any purpose the first few times—I pretended like he wasn't standing there. I turned and crouched, and then I pulled on the handle of the squat metal door that led down into the crypt.

A bead of sweat slithered down my spine by the time I managed to heave it open. I extricated the bundled scarf from my bag. Mimi's scent invaded me again, made my chest constrict and my eyes slicken.

She's not really gone, I reminded myself as I released her swathed remains into the dark pit.

It didn't ease my wretched pain because, even if *she* wasn't gone, one day, *I'd* be.

Chapter Sixteen

After I buried Mimi, I shoved the metal door of the crypt closed, then rubbed my hands against my thighs. Asher was still there, standing beside the marble pillar of names.

His eyebrows tipped as I prowled toward him and then tipped some more when I stopped right in front of him. I balled my hands, inhaling and exhaling slowly, replacing Mimi's warm, citrusy scent with Asher's crisp, cool one, and then I hit his chest, right where his black heart thumped.

His lips parted around a gasp at my first punch and then they thinned as I kept pummeling him. He neither backed up nor intervened. He let me punch him until my wing bones smarted as acutely as my knuckles. At some point, he caught my fists, one in each hand, closed his fingers around them, and towed them down.

"I'm not done, Seraph!"

"You're done."

"Don't you dare tell me what I am!" I tried to rip my fists away, but he held on tight.

"If feathers weren't piling up, I'd gladly let you go on, Celeste, but hating me is only damaging your wings, so calm down."

"You burned Leigh's wings! Her body's disintegrating beneath our feet because of you! Her soul . . . her soul's light was snuffed out because of you!" I managed to free one fist but not the other. Before I could swing it into his face, he caught my wrist and pushed it behind my back, then did the same with my other hand, shackling both.

"I am not your enemy."

"The whole system is my enemy, and since you're at the very top, you are *the* enemy."

His wings snapped out and curved around our bodies, incarcerating us in a cage of feathers.

"Scared the ishim will see you manhandling a fellow angel?" I spat, fighting his vise-like grip.

"No." He lowered his mouth to my ear and released a heated whisper. "I'm scared they'll hear me confess something that could destroy *her* . . . and me."

"Her?" I tried to pull away but had zero leverage what with my hands tied behind my back and a huge body bent over me.

He breathed, just breathed, each pulse of air harsher and hotter than the last. "I saved her soul."

This time, when I wrenched my head back, I managed to get a modicum of space between our bodies. "Where . . . where is it?" Her unspoken name clung to the darkness between us.

His eyes shut so tightly thin lines bracketed them. His mouth, too. I willed it to open and answer, but it stayed cinched.

"How do I know you're telling the truth?"

The canopy of feathers cast him in shadow, yet I made out the thrum of the vein running across his temple, fluttering a piece of hair which had escaped his hair tie.

"I just damned myself, Celeste"—his eyes opened slowly but not fully—"and you're asking whether I lied?" His fingers eased off my wrists, but his wings stayed put, and although no feather touched my body, I felt them everywhere.

I rubbed my wrists as though he'd hurt me; he hadn't.

I shivered as though I was cold; I wasn't.

What I was, was stunned. And upset.

Oh . . . so . . . upset.

I slapped Asher. "How. Dare. You." My wing bones tensed as the ishim pilfered yet another feather, adding to the purple mound building around my boots.

The archangel blinked. "How dare I what?"

"How dare you tell me this only now! How dare you let me believe that . . . that . . ." I didn't want to cry, but a whimper slid out. "Four and a half years, Seraph," I croaked. "Four and a half years. A piece of my heart's been dead for four and a half years."

In a deadly quiet whisper, he said, "If you're not quiet, that piece will get buried for good."

My eyes went so wide that my eyelashes grazed my browbone. I hadn't even considered that her soul could be hunted and destroyed.

"Here I was expecting a hug," he muttered, rubbing his jaw. "Or at the very least, a thank you."

"I'm sorry. For yelling and for hitting you." I stared at the purple mound that could easily have filled a small pillowcase, but then the first part of his sentence struck me. "Did you just say you wanted a hug?"

His hand fell away from his face. "I didn't say I wanted one."

Even though his daughter was effusive, I didn't think she'd gotten it from her father. Probably from her mother.

"I have questions."

"I can imagine, but not here."

"Where then?"

"I know a place."

"Take me."

His eyebrows dipped as though surprised by my quick agreement. "Are you sure?"

I nodded.

He straightened and rolled his shoulders back, reeling in his wings, exposing us again to the night and the creatures that lurked. Was the lavender-winged ishim swaying somewhere above us, attempting to eavesdrop?

"Is this place—" The word *far* turned into a squeal as my feet were whisked out from beneath me, and I was scooped up. My arms flailed, snared the archangel's neck as he rocketed upward. "A warning would've been nice," I grumbled.

I wasn't sure if he'd heard me, but when he stopped pumping his powerful wings, he said, "I didn't feel like debating the best means of transportation."

"So you took my choice away?" I tightened my grip, not caring if I was bruising him with all my rings. "I almost forgot it was one of your many talents." Taunts when dangling miles away from land were surely unwise, but wisdom had never been my strong suit. Honesty, on the other hand, I was good at.

My comment earned me a hard glare, but I quickly forgot about the glare when his body—and by extension, mine—tipped forward. My stomach rolled over. I turned my face away from the snail-shaped city below and burrowed it against the archangel's firm chest. Although not as frenzied as my own, his pulse was hurried, pounding against my forehead, nose, chin.

I inhaled the scent of black wind and warm suede until my stomach's revolutions slowed. "Are you evaluating the best place to drop me?"

We glided in silence for a few beats, before he said, "Perhaps."

I opened my eyes to check if he was serious. "I still have wing bones."

He frowned down at me.

"If you dropped me, I wouldn't die."

"I'm aware of that."

"But it would hurt." Which would probably be the point . . . I reasoned it was probably a good thing I wasn't planning on completing my wings since I had such severe vertigo and motion sickness.

"I have no intention of causing you pain, Celeste."

And yet he had . . .

"Celeste?"

"Just trying not to puke all over your pretty uniform, Seraph." I swallowed. Once. Twice. Finally, I peeled my face off Asher's torso.

He was gazing downward at the sprawling city I wasn't brave enough to look upon. The only thing I was brave enough to peek at were the rivers of stars above.

"Ask your questions, Celeste."

I blinked away from the sky. "Here?" Cool sweat iced my skin in spite of being nestled against a colossus-shaped brazier.

"There's nowhere to hide in the sky. Especially on clear nights."

Dumbly, I looked around. When I caught sight of the Eiffel Tower— the *miniature* Eiffel Tower—jeweling the night, my stomach spasmed, and I pressed my forehead against Asher's chest again. Had he brought me up here because it really was the safest place to talk, or because he was in complete control?

Didn't matter.

I sipped in a few calming breaths. *Don't think about where you are. You're safe.*

Sort of.

"Did you also save him?"

"Yes."

Surprise pared my face from the suede. "They're together in Elysium?"

"No."

"They're not together? Or they're not in Elysium?"

"Both. Neither."

"Is one of them in Abaddon?"

"No." The gleam of faraway stars edged the stubble coating his rigid jaw.

"Where are they, then?"

He nodded to the world below.

"In Paris?"

"On Earth. Not in Paris."

"Are they together?"

"No."

"You separated them?" I didn't believe in soulmates, but Leigh had, and she'd believed Jarod was hers.

Asher's attention inched away from the shimmering city and set on me. "I had no choice."

No choice? Or was he still trying to get Leigh for himself? I set that question aside for later. "Since, to my knowledge, souls don't float around Earth, I take it you implanted them into human wombs?"

"No."

My eyebrows jolted up. "Then—where?"

"If I'd placed them inside wombs, they would've been someone's child. I wanted them to be raised inside guilds so their wing bones could develop. So they would get a second chance." He squinted past my ribboning hair. "How much do you know about reincarnation?"

"Just what they teach in the guilds. That malakim must embed the soul in the womb sometime in the first trimester of life. And that if it's not done, a new soul will form, providing the world with a necessary balance of new and old."

An icy draft thrust our bodies sideways. My fingers crimped his neck, imprinting the shape of all sixteen of my rings into his flesh.

A corner of his mouth kicked up. "Relax, Celeste. I won't drop you."

"That's easy for you to say. You're the one with the wings." A strand of hair flogged my forehead. The urge to tuck it back lost to the compulsion to cling to Asher.

He readjusted his hold on me, and I let out a breathy squawk. His thumb hooked my flyaway and held it back. "Just remember that I can fly faster than you can drop."

"How . . . comforting."

His smile grew a little wider, sloughing off dozens of worry lines.

"Actually, how would you know that if you've never dropped anyone?"

His eyes sparked with what I might've called mischief had he been a child, but Asher wasn't a child. Hadn't been one in a century—more than a century. "I've never dropped anyone who didn't ask to be dropped."

"Who in their right mind would ask to be dropped? You know what, never mind. Back to Leigh. Where did you put her?"

A sigh snubbed the residual light from his features. "You're aware that some new souls don't always . . . make it?"

"You mean, stillborns? You . . . you resuscitated a stillborn?"

"Two."

"By giving them souls?"

"Yes."

"You can do that?"

"Archangels can perform *some* miracles."

"Why didn't you resuscitate Leigh and Jarod, then?"

His lids slid closed. "Their hearts had stopped beating for far too long by the time I reached them."

I didn't think death distressed archangels, but I also didn't deem seraphim capable of playing hide-and-seek.

Goosebumps suddenly pimpled my skin. Goosebumps that had nothing to do with the ambient temperature. Leigh had died four and a half years ago, and Naya was . . .

"Naya . . ." I half-gasped, half-whispered.

His lids rose, and his eyes, which didn't resemble Naya's, searched mine.

"She's—" Heat streaked across my face, through my chest. "That's why—" My throat tightened, and the pinpricks of stars bled together until Asher was haloed in light. "That's why she knew my name."

A slow beat passed. "I was afraid of that."

"Afraid that she'd know my name?"

"That her soul would recognize yours."

My heart stumbled midbeat. "Didn't you cleanse it before placing it inside her new body?"

"I did, but your souls had a deep connection, and that isn't something that can be removed. At least not without causing irreparable damage." He said this so matter-of-factly that my gape turned into a wide-mouth stare. "You two were soulmates."

"What? I thought—Jarod . . ."

"He wasn't her soulmate."

"But—"

"Mate means friend, Celeste. Jarod . . . I believe he was more. I believe he was her *neshahadza*—her soulhalf."

I was still wrapping my mind around the fact that soulmates existed. And now, soulhalves?

"*Neshahadza* possess the deepest and rarest connection." His features contorted in disgust or was it in pain? Probably disgust, considering how poorly the archangel regarded love. "Once souls lock together, it becomes impossible for them to live without the other."

As we bobbed in the black ocean, I almost forgot I was suspended over absolutely nothing. I almost forgot I was propped against a man I'd loathed for so long. A man I no longer loathed. How could I, when he'd defied celestial law and saved a worthy soul?

Two worthy souls.

"*Neshahadza*," I rolled the Angelic word around my tongue. "Does everyone have one?"

"Yes, but most people never meet theirs, and they settle for one of their soulmates."

"Do we have more than one soulhalf?"

"No."

"Did you meet yours?"

He slanted me a look that might've made me snicker had I not been at his mercy.

"You're not still pining for Leigh, right?"

His mouth curled in disgust. "Of course not! Why in the worlds would you think such a horrid thing?"

"You wanted to marry her—"

"Because her soul was beautiful. It was never a matter of physical attraction."

"She's not your biological daughter, Seraph, so technically—"

"She's a child."

"Children grow up."

He shuddered. Like, actually shuddered. "She may not have my blood, but she is my daughter in all the ways that count, and I would *never* desecrate that by pursuing her. *Never.*" He shuddered again, and it was so powerful, it made my own body shake. "Please never insinuate such a thing. It's repulsive."

"I'm sorry, but I had to ask."

"And you did. And now, the subject is closed."

I nodded.

He pumped his wings slowly, and then we glided again, skating through the glistening immensity.

"Are you raising Jarod as your son?" Since souls were genderless, I amended, "Or daughter?"

"He's a boy in this life, too. And no. I have no relationship with him whatsoever. One child's origin was complicated enough to explain."

"I bet." The strangest urge to hug the archangel came over me, but I didn't want to startle him and risk being dropped even if he swore his wing-speed exceeded my terminal velocity.

Perhaps I'd hug him later on firm ground. Before we parted ways. Could we part ways, though? I had three more months before I was locked out of guilds. Could I go back to living my life and pretend Leigh's soul wasn't part of this world?

Chapter Seventeen

"So, what happened to Jarod?"

"I entrusted him with an ophanim from the Viennese guild," Asher explained. "Tobias."

"And this Tobias . . . he knows?"

"Yes."

"And you trust him?"

"With my wings."

Little was as precious to an angel as wings. "Will you introduce the children someday?"

"Not until I've had the law about nephilim souls amended."

"You're trying to have it changed?"

"Not actively yet. Once the children prove their worth, once they both ascend, I'll begin my crusade. As for introductions, although I hope they don't meet for a long time still, you found your way to her. I imagine he'll find his way to her, or she to him, once they roam the world freely." His chest rose with a ragged sigh. "And I imagine their souls will recognize each other in some way."

"I think you've just sprouted some white hair, Seraph."

He let out a soft snort. "I'm surprised I have any hair left."

I eased my grip on his neck, not because the terror of being so far up without any walls was gone, but because I didn't want to hurt him. Not anymore. Even though he hadn't done it for me, saving Leigh felt like a gift.

"What's Jarod's name this time? Lucifer?"

Amusement smoothed his tensed face.

"Would've suited him."

"It would also have painted a target on his back." He stared at the dark city below. "Tobias named him Adam."

"Adam and Naya. I like the sound of that."

His mouth thinned. I took it he didn't like the sound of it. Was it because Naya was his little girl now, or because he still wasn't a fan of . . . Adam?

Something occurred to me then. Something that suddenly made a ton of sense. "Mimi knows. That's why she didn't call you a rump-hole and send you on your merry way."

One eyebrow quirked up. "Rump-hole?"

"Do you really need me to draw you a picture?"

"I think I can figure it out." Was that a smile? "And yes. She knows."

"Does Ish Eliza know?"

His head jerked back. "Ish Eliza? Why would she know?"

I shrugged. "Naya mentioned you two were close when we were crouched in the toy chest, waiting for you to find us."

"Ish Eliza works alongside me. She and I aren't involved, and even if we were, I would never tell her. You do realize that what I did could not only get me demoted but killed."

"You have wings."

"Which will go up in smoke if it got out that I saved a nephilim soul —*two* nephilim souls. And I suspect the Seven wouldn't stop at my wings."

"They'd burn your skin?"

"My skin? No . . . they'd go straight for my soul."

"You can burn souls?"

"Archangel fire can burn a lot of things." A vertical groove appeared between his brows. "I know you hate me, Celeste, but if you try to hurt me with this information, you'll also be hurting Naya. They won't hesitate to"—he shuddered—"burn her soul."

Although I kept one hand welded to his neck, I let the other drift to his cheek. "I don't hate you. Not anymore. And I promise to take everything you just told me to my earthly grave."

"Grave?"

"Unless you take pity on my nephilim soul."

"You're not a nephilim."

"Yet." My hand slid back to the nape of his neck.

"I thought confiding in you would change your mind."

Is that why he'd done it? "Even if I changed my mind, Seraph, there's unfortunately no way for me to complete my wings in time. I'd need to earn seven hundred feathers before mid-December."

The bronze tips of his wings fluttered as we drifted. "And?"

"And that's impossible."

"So was bringing Leigh and Jarod back." Strands of hair blew across his forehead.

"If only you'd told me earlier . . ." For the first time in four years, I regretted ruining my wings. "Sorry. It's not your fault."

"It is my fault. *Entirely* my fault. *All* of it is my fault." The pressure of his thumb, the one with which he'd whisked away a lock of my hair earlier, increased. Not painfully. More of a reminder that he was cradling my head. And body for that matter. "Allow me to help you, Celeste. Let me try to amend the damage I caused."

I bit my lower lip, slid it between my teeth, considering his proposition and its ramifications—wouldn't the help of an archangel raise eyebrows? And then I weighed our odds of succeeding—slim to slimmer.

"I know you don't think me capable of giving people choices, Celeste, but I am. And I won't force you if you really don't want to ascend. Not now that you know."

"Really?"

"Really. But I'd be disappointed if you didn't try." His mouth hooked to one side. "Not to mention Naya and Mimi—"

"Here I thought archangels were above blackmail."

"Coercion is our specialty, along with fire and impressive wingspans."

"And a hefty dose of humility."

His eyes sparked. "Is it working?"

His reason for getting me to reconsider didn't elude me—guilt was a powerful motivator—but would attempting the impossible be enough to ease his conscience? More importantly, though, what did *I* want?

I liked the life I'd made for myself on Earth. Loved college and my non-angelic best friend. Scrambling to earn seven hundred feathers would be chaotic and tiresome. Not to mention that if, by some miracle I actually did manage to accomplish it, I'd be saying goodbye to a world I'd come to love for one I despised.

"Celeste?" Asher's voice was as gentle as the wind buffeting our nomadic bodies.

I sighed. "If I accept, how exactly will you help? How exactly *can* you help?"

The cradle of his arms tightened as though, now that I was contemplating his offer, he didn't want to risk me slipping away. "I'd preselect sinners. Sign you up to them without you having to drop by the guild. Save you as much time as possible."

"It'll be a full-time job, Seraph. Don't you have to rule Elysium?"

He didn't smile. No, he was frighteningly serious. "Until your wings are complete, I will be at your side."

"Planning on holding my hand, are you?"

His torso and arms grew rigid. "I, uh . . . I—"

I rolled my eyes at his discomfort. "Relax. I was kidding."

I stared up at the stars, wishing they could advise me. If I accepted and failed, the blow would be so violent I wasn't sure I'd heal from it. But if I didn't even try, I would always wonder. And if I succeeded . . .

"To fail or to wonder?" I murmured out loud.

"What?"

"I'm weighing the consequences of my decision on my sanity."

He stayed silent, as though to give me time to make up my mind.

If I didn't die trying, I'd get to live forever with everyone I loved. "Fine. Let's do this. Or try to, at least, but if I go crazy while I still have wing bones, it's all on you, Seraph."

His grin remolded his face until it outshone the purest verity wings.

"I'd shake your hand to seal our deal, but I don't want you removing a single finger from my body at the present moment."

He chuckled. The sound was surprisingly alluring.

"Any chance that, now that you got what you wanted, we could land?"

"Your wish is my command." He squeezed me against him, then tipped forward and retracted his wings.

I shrieked as we cut through the air, plummeting so fast I tried to climb the archangel. "Not so fast! Stop! Please! I'm going to be sick. Stop!"

His wings swooped out, and although our bodies arced upward, my stomach hit my tailbone. "Celeste, you have nothing to fear." His grip on me eased, then tightened.

"I don't like speed. I don't like heights either. And I have terrible motion sickness."

"We can drift, but it'll take a while. I assumed you wanted to get back to the ground faster."

"There's no alternative way?"

"Unfortunately not."

I glanced sideways to see how much more air we needed to cover. "Why did you have to go so far up?" I mumbled when I caught sight of the Grand Palais, its domed steel-and-glass roof presently the size of a gumdrop.

"When I was a child, I believed stars were souls that had drifted away from Elysium, tired of both the human and celestial worlds." Asher's face was turned upward. "When an ophanim explained they were balls of burning hydrogen and helium, I wept."

I snorted, because the male angel was as gruff as Naya was sensitive. "I can't imagine you weeping."

His eyes returned to me, gleaming as though they'd absconded with some starlight. "You probably can't imagine I ever lost a feather during my fletching years."

I frowned. "Did you? Lose any?"

"Many."

"Not as many as me, though, right?"

"I believe you hold the record for most feathers lost."

I raised a proud smile.

"You also hold the record for most feathers earned off duty."

"Off duty?"

"Not on a mission."

"Huh. So this means that by the time I ascend, I'll have earned almost two full sets. This should at least give me access to the rank of malakim."

His throat bobbed. "I promise that once you ascend, I'll fight to give hybrids the same rights as verities."

"You have a more important fight coming up. Once the first is won, we'll move on to the second one."

The wind picked up and whipped my hair around my face. Keeping one hand anchored to the nape of his neck, I peeled the other away to press back the windblown strands. "Mimi didn't ask to come back, did she?"

A quiet smile drifted across his face. "No. She's waiting for you."

As we coasted toward Earth, I focused on Mimi's unwavering confidence instead of on how much farther we still had to go. Or rather, *I* still had to go.

And I wasn't speaking about the ground below.

Asher had done the impossible. Could I?

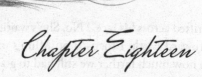

Chapter Eighteen

When we returned to the New York guild, the older fletchings were just finishing dinner or preparing to go out on the town, on missions or for fun. More than a few stopped and stared at Asher and me.

"Since I'm here, Seraph, let's stop by the Ranking Room and you can show me who I need to reform tomorrow."

"You're exhausted, Celeste. Why don't you go home, and I'll—"

A squealed "Apa" rang out, followed by a little blonde tornado headed straight for Asher. He crouched just in time to catch the incoming child.

As he rose, he smoothed the hair off her face. "What are you still doing up, you?"

My heart tripped.

Leigh...

My friend was there, in a new body, but she was right there. If I reached out, I could touch her.

I *had* touched her.

"I was trying to sleep but I had a really bad dream, Apa." She shuddered. "It was so scary. There was this man. And he was choking me."

I sucked in a breath. Could she—could she be remembering her past life? Four years ago, a man had tried to choke Leigh, a man named Tristan. He'd been Jarod's best friend, and so possessive of him that when he sensed he was losing his friend to Leigh, he tried to take her out.

Leigh had told me how scared she'd been, not so much for herself but for Jarod who, unlike her back then, hadn't been immortal. He'd stormed into the bedroom and tossed Tristan off the balcony, into the fountain in the courtyard, the one with a stone angel whose wings he'd hammered to dust as a child.

Had Asher not managed to strip Leigh's soul of this memory? Perhaps nephilim souls were different than human ones. Perhaps this was what Mira had meant about some not being salvageable.

Our eyes caught over Naya's wild mane. Worry made his pupils lance. Was he nervous about her remembering too much, about me betraying him, or about her snuffling? Was he even aware that Tristan had choked Leigh? Had she ever told him?

Asher whispered something into Naya's ear that made her bob her head a great many times, and then he murmured something else that made her pick her head off his shoulder and twist her neck.

"Celeste!"

My heart banged, its beats so loud it surely made the honeysuckle-scented air ripple. "Hey, kiddo." I tried to smile. Failed.

Ophan Pippa made her way to us. "I apologize, Seraph. I took Naya for a little stroll to calm her down so she wouldn't wake the other children. Let me take her from you." She extended her arms, which made Naya duck her head into the crook of Asher's neck and curl around him almost as fiercely as I'd clung to him when we'd dangled high above the spiraling Parisian rooftops.

"Thank you, Ophan, but I'll put her to bed." He pressed a kiss to the top of Naya's head. "After I finish up with Celeste."

The archangel was simply full of surprises tonight. *Put her to bed?* Did he tell her stories and sit at the foot of her bed until she slept? Not all parents had been like mine, but most did *not* hang around the guild, neither in the daytime nor in the nighttime.

When Asher nodded toward the Ranking Room, I backed up a step, then turned, the soles of my boots squeaking against the fire-veined quartz. Only one other fletching sat at the circular bar inside. Ironically, it was the one I'd met at The Trap with her verity friend, the night before my life was upended.

Where her gaze didn't widen at the sight of Asher and Naya, her lashes swept high at the sight of me. The infamous fletching Celeste visiting the Ranking Room was undoubtedly shocking.

I pulled out a stool, its feet scraping across the bright quartz. Asher sat next to me, Naya on his lap. As I pressed my palm onto the glass panel to switch on my holo-ranker, I stole another look at the little body that housed my best friend's soul.

Leigh and Naya were one and the same, but Naya didn't carry our shared memories. She didn't remember the endless games of *Neither Yes Nor No* we'd played. She didn't remember the feathers I'd lost when I'd been called *winglet* and had retaliated with expletives not creative enough to disguise their true meaning. She didn't remember how I'd signed up to a sinner in Paris to be at her side during her last days.

I wanted to steal her from Asher and wrap my arms around her.

I wanted to tell her all the stories about us. All we'd done together.

And then I wanted her to tell me everything would be okay.

But she was a child.

And her name was Naya.

Not Leigh.

I curled my hands into my lap and watched as Asher untangled her hair with his long fingers. There was love there.

Love and belonging.

Jealousy reared its petty head because it had been me she used to love like that . . . it had been to me she'd belonged. Well, to me and to Jarod, but not to Asher.

And now she was his.

Only his.

"Not her. She doesn't look nice." Naya wrinkled her tiny nose at the 3D image beaming out of the glass panel.

I looked at the sinner, found a woman named Barbara Hudson staring back at me, mouth so pinched wrinkles radiated like sunrays all around it. All I had time to read was her score—100—and the number of months she'd been in the system—400—before Asher leaned forward and sketched a name on the glass panel.

As the woman's face morphed into a man with bushy white eyebrows, a mass of white hair and a score of 82, I asked, "What did this Barbara Hudson do to earn a triple-digit score?"

Asher flicked his gaze to Naya before giving his head a small shake, his wind-tousled locks frolicking around his face. I assumed Barbara's crimes were too appalling to discuss in front of a four-year-old.

Asher jutted his chin toward the glass panel. "Your palm, Celeste."

Even though I trusted his judgment, I still scoured the sinner's rap sheet.

GERALD BOFINGER (20 MONTHS)
FRAUD.
82

"Is he dangerous, Apa?" Naya tucked her head under his jaw.

"No. He's harmless."

"Good. Because I don't want Celeste to get hurt."

My heart pinched at her concern.

"Don't worry, *motasheh*. I don't want that either." With those words, he scraped away my residual jealousy.

I pressed my palm against the glass panel until my name appeared over Gerald's jolly-looking face. Yes, jolly-looking. The feed playing on the loop showed the man's lips quirking into a smile, pushing up cheeks as red as the raspberry jelly Mimi used to make each spring.

I kept my palm in place until the whir of the holo-ranker was replaced by the growl of my stomach.

"Was that your tummy?" In spite of her bloated lids, Naya managed to pry her eyes wide.

"Yep." Since we were done, I stood. "Haven't had dinner yet." Or lunch for that matter. All I'd had were stale crackers and coffee. "I should get home."

Asher, who was still toying with his daughter's hair, tracked my movements, then readjusted Naya and rose in turn, unfurling his long body. I felt downright tiny standing next to him. On the upside, my face was leveled with Naya's, which lolled against his collarbone.

Suddenly, she picked her head off Asher's chest. "You can have dinner here! I'll sit with you, and we can play—"

Asher tapped the tip of her nose. "You are done playing for the day."

"Not fair." She crossed her arms and emitted a disgruntled sound that dimpled my cheeks with a smile.

"Life isn't always fair, Naya. That's why we angels exist. To make it fair." Balancing her in the crook of one arm, he turned to me. "Celeste, I'll pick you up tomorrow morning at nine."

"You don't need to pick me up. I'll meet you at—Wait, tomorrow's Saturday. Won't his office be closed?"

"His office will be but not his home."

"And you know where he lives?"

"I do."

"And by picking me up, you mean in an Uber, correct?"

He smiled, grasping the underlying meaning behind my question. He probably still had finger-shaped bruises all over the back of his neck. "We can walk. It's not far from Central Park South."

I nodded, and then, because I couldn't resist, I swept a knuckle down Naya's peach-fuzz cheek. "Sweet dreams, kiddo."

Her arms loosened from their knot, and she rubbed her eyes with her small fists. "I will now."

"You can add magical hugs to your list of superpowers, Seraph."

"I don't think she was talking about my hugs," he said, as she rested her head against his chest again.

She patted his cheek. "Your hugs are the best, Apa, but my heart is happy Celeste wants feathers again."

I met Asher's turquoise stare over her golden head. "I'll try my best to get them, but I can't guarantee my best will be enough."

Her eyebrows drew together. "Why?"

"Because I have a lot of feathers to earn." I twisted back toward the holo-ranker. "Come to think of it, I should probably check how many I have."

"Three hundred and four," the hybrid said.

When both Asher and I looked her way, her cheeks ignited, becoming as crimson as her wings, which she dragged into her spine.

Keeping tabs on me much? Instead of putting her on the spot, I thanked her for the information, and then I sidestepped Asher and Naya, skirting their gazes, not out of shame, but out of uneasiness.

How could the archangel possibly believe I had a chance of ascension? I wasn't a particularly pessimistic person, but three hundred and four . . .? Was it even worth trying?

"Celeste?" Naya's voice stopped me.

I closed my eyes, breathed in and out, then pasted on a fake smile and turned. "Yeah?"

"Will you come back to play with me?"

The only reason I'd come back was for her. And for Mimi. "If it's okay with your daddy, I'd love to."

She tilted her head up toward him, her hair cascading over the sinewy forearm wrapped around her. "Apa?"

Keeping his gaze affixed to mine, he said, "Celeste needs to concentrate on her missions, but she'll be back."

"I will," I promised, before striding out the curved glass doors and down the quartz hallway. In the atrium, a sparrow swooped low over my head, dispersing its lovely chant into my ears, then beat its rainbow wings and rose toward the star-flecked, illusory sky.

As I sat in a taxi, I researched the man I was to meet and reform tomorrow. I found a slew of articles, all of them honorific—a human rights activist, a generous benefactor, a faithful husband, a caring father, an attentive grandfather.

After learning all I could about him, I typed Barbara Hudson's name inside my browser, found out she was a lawyer who took on a lot of pro bono cases helping children emancipate themselves from their parents and women flee abusive relationships. Was she a Triple because she claimed her cases were pro bono and she made her customers pay some other way?

I was about to root around the web a little more when a message from Jase popped up on my screen: *Pizza tomorrow night. You and me?*

I hopped on that olive branch: *Yes!*

A smiley face emoji materialized, then: *Trap tonight?*

ME: *Can't. But definitely dinner tomorrow. 6 at the apartment?*

ME: *Wait. You're working.*

JASE: *I'll go in after dinner. Which apartment?*

ME: *Ours.*

The three little dots danced. I wondered what he could be typing. The dots disappeared, leaving behind an empty screen. Was he annoyed I'd called the place *ours*? Unless . . .

Biting the inside of my cheek, I sent: *Why don't we meet at my place actually?*

His answer was slow to come, even though it consisted of only two letters: *OK.*

Chapter Nineteen

S porting the pair of oversized sunglasses Mimi had bought me back in Paris, I waved goodbye to the doorman and stepped out of the lobby into the blinding sunlight. I'd slept well, and radiated energy and renewed optimism. So much so that while sipping coffee on my terrace, I'd grabbed a pad of paper and a pen and scribbled the number of days I had left and the number of feathers I needed to earn, and then came up with a dozen potential equations to reach my goal. What my calculations revealed was that I couldn't afford to dawdle and had to pick high-rankers—at least ten or twelve of them depending on their scores.

I tilted my head toward the sun and whispered, "I can do this."

"Did you doubt it?" asked a voice, which was becoming as familiar to my ears as Leigh's and Mimi's.

"Yes." I lowered my gaze from the burning star and set it on the man who'd made me crave something I'd given up on.

His eyes were on my chest. Well, on the big block letters stamped onto my black tank top that read *HEAVEN WAS BORING*. The slogan was artistically sandwiched between curly devil horns and a cute demonic tail.

"Would you like me to get you a matching muscle tee?" I asked sweetly. "I'm sure they make them in XXX-L. You could wear it on your trips to Abaddon."

He smiled, albeit tightly, as I took in *his* choice of attire—

stonewashed denim that hugged his muscular legs without looking spray-painted, and a white T-shirt that displayed toned, tanned arms that made a woman walking past us trip over the curb. Luckily, one of the Plaza's doormen managed to catch her before she got a faceful of hot pavement.

"You're far too pretty for this world, Seraph."

His eyebrows rose as though trying to glean if my statement was intended to flatter or flay. "In my hundred and forty-three years of life, this is the first time someone has referred to me as *pretty*." He brandished a Starbucks cup. "Here. This is for you."

I gaped at the drink. "You bought me coffee?"

"I did. I assumed you—"

I reached out and seized my caffeinated gift. "Thank you. That was very thoughtful." I took a sip of the dark, charred liquid, then licked my lips, trying to picture him standing in line at a coffee shop. How absurd he must've looked. "How did Naya sleep? Any more nightmares?"

"According to Ophan Pippa, she slept soundly." He speared one hand through the hair he'd chosen to wear loose. The strands glinted as though spun from molten gold and bronze. Rare were the men who could make long hair look attractive, but somehow, probably because everything else about him screamed male perfection, Asher succeeded. "Did you sleep well?"

"I passed out cold. It was delightful."

"Did you eat?"

I rolled my eyes. "Yes, Apa."

His jaw sharpened. "Don't call me that."

I frowned at him.

"I'm not your father."

I lowered the cup. "Trust me, Seraph, I know that. It was just a joke."

Asher squared his shoulders as though trying to appear more intimidating, but it was a waste of his time since no man or woman had ever succeeded in intimidating me.

I raised my Starbucks cup back to my lips. "So, where to?" My voice was dry. Gone was my good mood, squashed by his foul one.

"Sutton Square. Gerald Bofinger has a house on the river."

As we started walking east, I side-eyed him. "You know, you could've just texted me the address. I'd have found my way there. Homing pigeons have nothing on my sense of direction." I'd learned to navigate the human world after my wing bones had come in at ten. My first week out, Leigh had accompanied me everywhere, but then she'd had to concentrate on her missions again, and I was on my own.

"I promised I'd help you." He kept his gaze on the steady stream of cars flowing down Fifth.

"By assigning me sinners, not by babysitting me."

As we waited to cross, he turned toward me. "Think of me as your coach, Celeste."

I bobbed my head. "Okay. Well then, can you explain Bofinger's sin? I looked him up last night, and the man's squeaky clean."

He rubbed the underside of his jaw as though attempting to remove a smudge of dirt. There was no dirt. "He set up a Ponzi scheme, which has yet to get out."

Another Madoff. "Geez," I whispered. "How much did he steal from his investors?"

"Thirty-five billion dollars."

The WALK sign lit up, and we crossed. The archangel caused a few head-on collisions between the pedestrians. One person even stopped in the middle of the crosswalk to stare and kept staring once he'd passed her. All the while, Asher's eyes remained fixed on the transparent cube that housed the Apple Store, oblivious to the commotion.

"The SEC has received multiple reports and is looking into it, but Bofinger's covered his bases. He's transferred all his assets into offshore accounts and bought himself a property in Oman where there's no extradition treaty with the US."

"What exactly am I supposed to do, Seraph? Get him to turn himself in, or convince him to reimburse thirty-five billion dollars?"

"You need to reform him, Celeste."

"What great advice, coach. Can I call you *coach*, or will that earn me another frigid rebuke?"

Although non-verbal this time, my question earned me said-reproof in the form of side-eye. "How about just Asher?"

"It might make me forget how far above me you . . . *fly*, Seraph."

He pinched the bridge of his nose and expelled a sigh. "Call me whatever makes you happy."

"The names which would make me happy would cost me feathers, so why don't I stick to Seraph?"

His hand lowered from his face, and he shot me a slow blink, as though he couldn't believe I could think poorly of him after he'd saved Leigh. Granted, I didn't. His sense of humor could use some work, but besides that, he was actually a pretty decent guy. I kept this to myself, not feeling like buffing up his ego or debating the merits of humor. Instead, I drank my coffee and focused on coming up with a plan for the asshole that was Bofinger.

I sucked in a breath that made a little coffee dribble out of my mouth and seep into my, thankfully, black tank.

Oh, come on. I curbed my urge to rage at the ishim to avoid being burgled of yet another feather.

Asher trailed my feather's descent. "I thought last night might've lessened your distaste for me."

I didn't set him straight and admit I'd been thinking of Bofinger. Instead, I just strode on, drinking my throat-stinging coffee in loud silence.

Chapter Twenty

I scrubbed the soles of my combat boots on Bofinger's giant monogrammed doormat and rang the brass doorbell. The varnished black door opened a moment later.

"May I help you?" asked a butler dressed in an unfortunate seersucker suit.

"I have an appointment with Mr. Bofinger. Celeste Moreau." This wasn't a lie. Asher, who was presently sitting on a bench facing the East River, had phoned ahead of time and set up an appointment for me, passing me off as a potential investor. It was the only thing he'd said after I'd lost my feather, a loss he'd taken personally.

A few times, I'd sensed him wanting to impart advice, but my jarring mood kept his lips sealed and his attention fixed to the steady stream of humans milling around us, some stuffed in Lululemon on their way to workout; others trussed in last night's clubbing garb, apparently done working out.

I hated the gym and wasn't a fan of the walk-of-shame, and yet I envied them. Envied their independence. Their simple goals. Their oblivion to the celestial scales constantly weighing their souls.

The butler cleared his throat. "Please follow me." As he led me though the foyer that reeked of peach air-freshener, he glanced over his shoulder. I supposed that in my leather leggings and black tank, I didn't fit Bofinger's typical houseguest.

At the entrance of a living room with bow windows overlooking the steel-blue river, the butler extended a gloved hand. "May I take your beverage?" He was probably worried I'd spill my Starbucks drink over the fancy geometric-tiled rug.

"Sure thing." I drained what little coffee was left before relinquishing it.

"Would you like more coffee? Tea?" Guess he wasn't worried about spillage. "A mimosa, perhaps?"

Champagne cocktails at 10 a.m.? How fancy. "Water for now." If I was successful, maybe I'd take him up on his offer of a mimosa. When he left, I walked around the walnut-wainscoted room, peering at the big oil paintings, then at the silver-framed pictures of Bofinger and his family, soaking in all I could about the man.

"Miss Moreau!"

I spun around to find the white-haired financier blustering toward me, a smile stretching over his lips. He held out his hand, and I shook it, startled my eyes were level with his. Not that sinners had a proclivity to be tall, but for some reason, I'd expected a more imposing man.

In the pictures cataloguing his luxurious lifestyle, he towered over his various family members. I cast a furtive glance back over my shoulder to understand how I'd been duped. In one glossy pic, he posed from the top of a staircase with each one of his children sitting at his feet. And then in another, he stood over his wife's chair while she gazed adoringly up at him.

"What a pleasure to receive such an illustrious girl."

Illustrious? I swung my attention back to Bofinger, wishing I'd asked Asher what exactly he'd said about me.

"Your financial advisor couldn't stop singing your praises."

A smile tipped the corners of my mouth. "Did he, now? Do tell what he said exactly. Might earn him a nice raise."

"He spoke of your dedication to humanitarian causes and infallible work ethic."

I suspected my dimples were on full display. Humanitarian causes? More like celestial missions. As for my work ethic, I doubted the archangel found me all that ethical. "Did he happen to share with you how I earned all my money?"

"He said you recently inherited a large sum from a deceased relative and that you've been carefully investing it, but were interested in exploring ways to gross better returns. Where are my manners? Sit. Please." He gestured to a low, satiny couch that was as stiff as it appeared.

While I slid around the upholstered bench, trying to get comfortable against the rigid cushions, Bofinger perched on the lip of an armchair. "Ask any and all questions, my dear. You have my undivided attention."

Careful what you ask for, Bofinger. "If we worked together, how long would my money be tied up?"

"You mean when to expect distributions?"

"Yes."

His butler came back inside, toting a platter with two crystal goblets filled with water, which he placed on the glass cube, right over what looked like the head of a giant fish skeleton. Briefly, I wondered if the bones encased in the cube were real or carved from plaster.

As soon as the door closed behind him, Bofinger said, "You were asking about distributions. The most attractive opportunities require the capital stay untouched as long as possible, so I like to implement a minimum of five years, even though you'd get quarterly reporting."

I picked up my water. "What sort of risks would these *attractive opportunities* present?"

"I'm staunchly adverse to risk. Which is the reason I prefer, and encourage, long-term contracts rather than short-term ones. It's also the reason I place an extreme amount of importance on conducting a vast and thorough due diligence on any company my fund chooses to invest in."

"I read you started as an auditor for PWC before going the hedge fund way."

He smiled. "I see you've conducted your own due diligence."

You have no idea. "Like you, Mr. Bofinger, I enjoy thoroughness." After returning my glass to the platter, I folded one leg over the other and placed my palms atop my knee. "Before we talk numbers and fees"—he perked up like a dog scenting a milk-bone—"I'd like to understand a little better where my money would go. I heard your firm likes to leverage the funds it receives and borrow against them to amplify the investors' returns. Is this hearsay?"

His smile flickered. "Leveraging *is* a common practice in hedge fund management. Time is money, so larger amounts generate better investments and healthier returns."

Bofinger droned on after that, stringing big words together and spewing example after example of his fund's extraordinary successes. I had to physically clamp my lips together to avoid yawning. The only mild entertainment I got was from his thick eyebrows. They wriggled around his wrinkled forehead like those furred caterpillars I'd come across in the suburbs when I'd accompanied Leigh to visit one of her sinners. I'd crouched to stroke it when Leigh had grabbed my wrist and gasped, "Celeste, no. Their spines are toxic." Not too much harm would've befallen me, thanks to my nifty wing bones, but the experience wouldn't have been pleasant.

Bofinger was midsentence when I dropped the pretense of interested investor and said, "What do you think of the number thirty-five?"

His Adam's apple jostled under the lax skin of his throat. "I beg your pardon?"

"Followed by nine zeroes."

"Is that—" He tugged on the collar of his dress shirt, monogrammed like his doormat. "Is that what you plan on investing with us?"

"Wouldn't that be convenient?"

He blinked in rapid succession. "I'm sorry. I'm not sure I understand."

"You're a smart man, Mr. Bofinger. I'm sure you understand me perfectly."

Color rose into his cheeks, and a sheen of sweat polished his temples.

"Look, I'm not with the FBI or the SEC. I'm merely a concerned citizen."

His fingers scrabbled to open the top button on his shirt as though that could somehow help him breathe.

"You're walking on ice. Very thin ice. And yes, I know you covered your ass." Because it was also the word for donkey, it wasn't on the ishim's naughty list. As long as it wasn't attached to the word *hole*, that was. The day I'd learned ass was cost-free, it took a prominent position in my speech. "I heard you bought a place in Oman and transferred your assets into offshore accounts."

Purple. The man was purple. I hoped he didn't croak because that wouldn't earn me any feathers. I stood, grabbed his glass of water, and walked it over to him, pushing it into his hands. "Drink."

He gawped at the water for a long moment. "If you're not with a government agency, then . . . why are you here?"

"I'm here because I want to help you."

"Help me?" he squawked.

"Yes, help you." I returned to the couch but sat on its arm this time. "You have a beautiful family, and what you've done, once it gets out, will destroy them. Remember Madoff? One of his kids committed suicide. You wouldn't want that to happen to Henry, would you? Or Madeline, for that matter. You wouldn't want your wife to be thrown out of all her social clubs and insulted. Or for your grandkids to be bullied and ostracized in school. Kids can be so very cruel."

He stayed quiet, but at least he took a gulp of his water.

"I'm not asking for a confession, and I'm not wearing a wire. I just want us to find a solution before this explodes in your face. How much money do you have left?"

His eyes flicked to the door.

"Mr. Bofinger, I am not your executioner. If anything, I'm more of a guardian angel." *Ha.* I almost smiled at having slipped this nugget of truth into a human conversation. Almost, because the truth was, his Ponzi scheme was no laughing matter. "So please work with me."

"Three."

"Billion?"

"No." He shut his eyes, his skin now the sallow color of rice pudding. "Three hundred million dollars."

"And the house? I mean, houses?"

"I could get thirty, maybe forty, for this one. The one in the Hamptons is worth close to seventy, but—" He rolled the glass against his forehead. "But I've already borrowed against that one, so . . . so the bank owns it."

"What about the art?"

"Worth a few million. Twenty at the most."

I was no math wiz, but repaying investors would be like trying to take a bath in a drop of water. "Okay. And the investments? Surely not all of them are gone."

"Two investors demanded their money last month, so I had to . . ." A puff of shrill air replaced the end of his sentence, and then his sagging shoulders started to shake. "I'm going to jail. For life."

"Yeah. You probably are."

"I should just—" He peered at the white-capped East River. "Just . . . jump off that bridge."

"Then all of this will fall upon your wife and children. You don't want that."

"What do you suggest I do, then?" His shrill voice didn't startle me.

"I suggest you tell your family. You're going to need emotional support."

"Emotional support?" He balked.

"Yes. These are going to be trying times. The entire world will rise against you. To survive, you'll need people in your camp."

"I'd rather die than put them through this."

"But don't you realize they're going to go through this whether you abandon them or not? Mr. Bofinger, if you die, they will become the faces of your Ponzi scheme. If you stick around and go through the trials, then you will be protecting them. Think of yourself as a shield."

His red-rimmed eyes were focused on me and yet they were glazed in a way that told me he'd retreated into his head. Hopefully to mull over my advice.

"Also, you're going to need to call up your investors and come clean with them, give them back whatever you can, even if it isn't enough. And then call up the FBI and turn yourself in. This'll knock a couple years off your prison sentence."

He blinked out of his daze. "Why?" he croaked. "Why are you doing this, Miss Moreau? Why are you helping me?"

"Because we aren't the sum of our mistakes but the sum of how we deal with them."

I thought of the archangel, then. Of how he'd ended up saving Leigh after partaking in her death. Rectifying his wrong made him honorable in my eyes. Lovable in Naya's. But it would make him look criminal to his brethren. Perception was subjective.

Coming forward wouldn't excuse Bofinger's crime, wouldn't paint him as innocent, but it would help him take a step toward being a better man and alleviate his soul.

"Okay." Mr. Bofinger inhaled a deep, whistling breath. "Okay."

My heart thumped. Sure, it was only a word, but him uttering it . . . it was like a present. Yes, I'd met with him to earn feathers, but at that moment, I wasn't thinking about my wings. I was thinking of his soul and how I'd managed to touch it.

"Does your wife already know?"

"Not everything."

"Is she here?"

"Upstairs." He stared up at the ceiling, then shuddered and stared at his hands wrapped tightly around the water glass sitting on his lap. "She'll leave me."

I stood and walked over to his chair, placed a hand on his shoulder. "From the pictures I've seen, from the articles I've read, she adores you."

His body trembled, almost shaking my palm off. "She'll leave me," he repeated.

I extricated the glass from his fingers before he crushed it, then placed it on the platter. "Love keeps people together."

Unfortunately . . . I pressed my lips together, trying to tamp the sudden flare of anger that shot through my chest. Love had kept Jarod and Leigh together, not in life, but in death.

Mr. Bofinger slid his cell out of the holster strapped onto his belt. The phone bobbed so maniacally that I offered to help him. I located his wife's number at the top of his favorites list, and even though she was in the same house, I pressed on call.

A few minutes later, the door cracked open to reveal a perfectly coiffed and made-up blonde with an apparent plastic surgery addiction. "Gerald?" She rushed over to him, glancing at me, then back at him. "Gerald, what is it?" She pulled up an armchair and collected his hand, enclosing it between hers.

He broke down, then broke open, spilling all his dirty secrets.

At the end of his confession, the only thing she said was, "So, that's why we're moving . . ."

He swallowed, then nodded, even though it wasn't a question.

She stood. "I'll call up your secretary."

"Wait, honey, I need to talk with the children first."

"I'm not calling her to rat you out; I'm calling her so she can move up our flight. We leave tonight."

I froze, not expecting this outcome.

"But, we—honey, I have to—we can't leave the kids to deal with this." Bofinger's glassy eyes jumped between his wife and me.

"They'll come with us. Everyone comes with us." She narrowed her eyes on me. "If this brown-noser calls the Feds—"

"Please, don't threaten me. And *don't* call me a brown-noser. Do you even know the root of that word? Just, yuck." I wrinkled my nose.

"Christophe!" she screeched.

The butler trundled into the room, patting down his seersucker jacket. "Yes, Madam?"

"Show this girl out."

"Miranda, we—"

"I am not living the few years I have left without you!"

My stomach felt like I'd chucked a handful of ice cubes inside of it. I'd been right about love keeping people together.

Quietly, the butler said, "Please follow me, Miss."

Did he understand what they were discussing? Would *he* call the police or would his employers pay for his silence?

"We'll fix things from there, Gerald. Together. We will fix things *together*." Unlike her husband's frumpy expression, hers was smooth and full of resolve.

His watery eyes rose to mine.

I could feel his soul struggling to do the right thing.

I truly hoped he'd let it.

"Goodbye, Mr. Bofinger." I inclined my head toward him before I stepped out of the living room, my heart beating fast, not out of fear or disappointment but out of compassion.

Compassion for a sinner . . .

Leigh would've been proud.

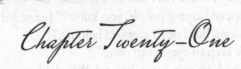

Chapter Twenty-One

When I stepped out of the mansion, my gaze went straight to the bench. Straight to the man still sitting on it, waiting for me. A part of me had been convinced he'd be gone.

"How's the birdwatching going?" I called out, as I strolled over to where he sat with his arm draped over the back of the bench and one foot propped on his opposite knee.

He turned in my direction, blue eyes traveling from the top of my head to the tips of my boots. Since I hadn't swapped outfits, I took it he was on the lookout for a sign of a scuffle.

"I'm guessing not as exciting as angel-watching in Elysium." I sat and folded my legs.

I was met with more silence.

I balled my hands into my lap, trying to keep them from shaking. "You'd be proud of me, Seraph. All my feathers are intact. I kept my cool and didn't utter a single foul word."

He still didn't talk, just kept looking me over. First at my profile, then at my hands. Was their shaking visible? I flattened my palms and squeezed them between my thighs.

"What happened in there, Celeste?" His voice was deep and raucous, lifting goosebumps on my already chilled skin.

I regretted not having taken my jacket, although would a jacket have helped? The air was unseasonably warm, the sun incredibly bright. "What happened is that I tried. But trying is sometimes not enough."

He slid the arm draped over the back of the bench a little farther, and then, tentatively, curled it around my shoulders. I drew in a shaky breath before allowing my head to loll onto his shoulder.

"I never stopped helping people, you know?" I rambled on. "I didn't sign up for missions, but I never stopped helping."

"I know. We keep an eye on our own."

Then why had no one come before? Why had no one showed an ounce of interest in my wings before Asher?

"As for being proud, I was already proud of you when you rang his doorbell, Celeste."

I tried to stretch a smile over my mouth because that was really sweet, but even my lips were shaking now. I felt like I was coming down from a high. "I never picked a sinner over forty before."

"Some of them aren't too different from their lower-ranked counterparts."

Strands of his hair brushed across my forehead. I didn't mind, but he must've minded, because he wrangled them back with his free hand. Since his arm was still around me, I assumed he didn't find the contact of my skin toxic; he probably just thought his hair was bothering me.

"I once picked a Triple." He spoke slowly, evenly. "On a dare."

I notched my head back in surprise.

His summer-sky eyes were fixed on the horizon. "I was sixteen. I'd just gotten my wing bones the year before."

"A bit of a late bloomer, huh?"

He glanced down at me, a smile playing at the corners of his mouth. "Believe it or not, back then, it was actually normal."

And now the norm was twelve, but lucky me had defied that norm. Two extra years would've been welcomed . . .

Instead of complaining about my early bloom, I said, "Sometimes, I forget how many generations separate us."

Not only had he been born in the nineteen hundreds, but he'd lived through two world wars and countless pandemics. He'd witnessed planes being built, rockets being launched into space. He'd lived before TV and the internet. According to the ophanim, holo-rankers were only installed in the guilds in the 1970s. Before then, they had tablets of sorts with black-and-white images and scrolling text, like angelically spruced-up broadsheets.

"So . . . the dare?"

His gaze rose to the crown of a tree whose leaves were mottled with amber. "I had a roommate back in the Viennese guild. Tobias."

"The one who . . . *helped* you." The one who'd taken Adam.

He nodded. "He was a year older, and bolder. So much bolder than I was." He paused. "He dared me to sign on to a man who supplied pistols to Bosnian rebels. I showed up in the man's headquarters one morning and pretended to be looking for a job as a gun runner."

I slapped my palm over my heart. "You lied?"

He tipped me another smile, which I returned. "I lost a feather—my first—but it was worth it since it won me a job. Or at least, I believed it had been worth it."

I frowned.

"On my first mission out, I tried to reason with him that firearms would only get more people killed. And most of them innocents. He asked whose side I was on, and I told him on the side of justice. He proceeded to show me what the Austrian militia was doing. The massacres I witnessed, Celeste." His Adam's apple slid up and down slowly. "He asked me if I found that fair." His jaw clenched. "On our way back from one of these bloodbaths, we were shot. Both of us. And not just once." His throat moved again. "He died; I woke up bathed in blood."

The bones in his shoulder rotated underneath my cheek as though he were lifting himself out of the gory pool all over again.

"I'd gone on horseback but had no horse when I awakened, so I went back by foot. It took me close to a week to reach the guild. A week during which I saw so many terrible things, Celeste. Things that made me question whether humanity could really be saved. If it was worth saving." He was quiet and still for a moment. "The worst part was that the man died a Triple, and even though he was far from a saint, I was outraged that his soul had been left to wilt inside his corpse."

I pressed myself away from his arm to seek the soft curves of the revolted boy he'd been behind the hard ridges of the man he'd become. "Why are you telling me this?"

"To remind you that before being an archangel, I was a fletching. A fletching who dreamed of changing the human world before he dreamed of changing the celestial one." He wouldn't meet my eyes. Just kept staring between the twitching leaves of the maple shading a piece of our bench and the snapping whitecaps atop the river. "In the end, it was the worlds that changed me."

I placed a gentle palm on his bicep, felt the tendons pinch beneath my fingers. "That's not true. Or maybe it is, but it's not the full truth. Every life you've touched, Seraph, you've changed. You've altered its course."

His eyes finally met my own, dappled in many shadows, and not all cast by the tree. "Not always in a good way. Look at what I did to Jarod. To Leigh."

"Look at what you did to me." I added a smile, but it did nothing to quiet his devastating guilt. When he made no move to get up, I rested my head back on his arm.

"I should've come for you sooner, Celeste."

"You could've not come at all."

"I made Leigh a promise."

"And you've kept it. You're here now, Seraph, so stop beating yourself up over this. If I fail to ascend, it won't be your fault."

His soundless anger was so conspicuous I could feel it beat inside his body. Several minutes later, he gritted out, "You won't fail."

This time, I was the one who kept quiet. There was no point speculating whether or not I would complete my wings. I'd try and keep trying. My thoughts returned to Gerald Bofinger. Had I tried hard enough? Most of my missions had taken me days, not hours.

If he didn't leave for Oman, I'd pay him another visit.

Then again, if he didn't leave for Oman, it would mean my words hadn't fallen on deaf ears.

Only time would tell. Hopefully not too much time, because I had seventy-seven days left, and I needed to make each one count.

Chapter Twenty-Two

Asher and I stayed on that bench in front of Bofinger's mansion a long while, both in silent contemplation of our lives. Or at least, I contemplated my life—my past, my present, and my future.

I couldn't picture myself in the land of angels, but perhaps that was because I'd never actually seen it. What I knew of Elysium was only what the ophanim had recounted: it was made of white quartz and filled with rainbow-colored creatures. The infamous Pearly Arch separated the capital from the Canyon of Reckoning, the Nirvana Sea surrounded every Elysian island, and the Nirvana mountains served as a refuge for the eldest of our kind.

I was about to ask the archangel to tell me more about the land he ruled when he stirred, mentioning his promise to meet Naya for lunch before heading back to Elysium. I stored my questions for later.

I might not have known what the far-future held, but I knew my near-future included Asher. After all, he was my coach. Or handler. More of a handler since he picked my missions and sent me on them. For a moment, I felt like a secret agent, and that reminded me of Bofinger and the Feds who would eventually storm his house.

Would he be in it when they came, or would he be sunning himself on a beach in the Middle East?

I stared at his front door, hesitating to call on him again.

"Be patient, Celeste."

My anxiety had calmed as we horizon-watched, but it was back with a vengeance.

"You should join us for lunch. It would make Naya's day."

I slid my lower lip between my teeth before declining. My body ached from the rush of adrenaline, and my nerves jangled. Besides, I didn't want to subject Asher to any more hours in my company than were absolutely necessary, or inflict my spastic mood on his little girl.

His wings appeared, unspooling slowly from the bones that held them, the tips of each feather casting tinsel across the gray pavement.

I backed up to give them room to stretch. "Thanks for sitting with me, Seraph." I took a couple more steps back. "And give Naya a big hug."

"Where are you going?"

"Home. I've been putting off going through Mimi's things. I think it's time."

"Let me fly you."

I shot his wings a grimace. "No thanks."

"Not even if I promise to fly low?"

I shook my head.

His chin dipped a little, and his eyes, which had been smudged in shadows, became as luminescent as the traffic light that had just changed to green. "I made you change your mind about your wings; I'll make you change your mind about flying."

I laughed. I mean, yes, he had changed my mind about ascending, but he'd pulled out one heck of an ace. He couldn't possibly have a second one stashed up his sleeve. "Once I have my own wings, I'll fly."

He took a step toward me. "Before you get your own wings, I'll have you enjoying it."

I raised an eyebrow. "You're not planning on snatching me again?"

"Do I look like a predator?" Six-foot-and-a-ton-of-inches moved a little closer.

"Right now, yes. You do." My pulse ratcheted up but not from fright. From something else that perhaps should've frightened me. Then again, he was an incredibly handsome man, and I was a woman with 20/20 vision.

He stopped walking and thrust a hand through his wavy mane. "I didn't mean to intimidate you, Celeste."

"Intimidate me?" I rolled my eyes. "I've been out in the world for almost a decade and have met actual scary-ass predators. Trust me, I wasn't feeling intimidated."

He searched my face a moment, as though trying to glean what I was feeling if it wasn't intimidation. My skin didn't smolder—it never had—but my appreciation must've computed because he averted his gaze. "Let me walk you home at least."

The easiness we'd shared on the bench had puffed out of existence; I wanted it back, and for this, a little physical distance was in order.

"Don't keep your daughter waiting," I tossed out before jogging across the road.

Although the archangel didn't trail me by foot, he glided high above me. I looked up once, when I crossed Park Avenue, and shook my head at his stubbornness. What did he think might happen to me between Bofinger's house and mine in the middle of the day? Was he worried the wife would try to gun me down or kidnap me, so I wouldn't tarnish her family's good name?

I chewed up the inside of my cheek after that thought coalesced because it wasn't so farfetched. Thankfully, no nondescript white van screeched to a halt in front of me and no bullet whizzed into my skull.

Yes, I would've survived the latter, but that didn't mean I wanted to experience the pain.

After arriving at the apartment safe and sound, I cleaned and I cleaned. Stripped the bed and the closet. Folded clothes and piled them into the cardboard boxes Stanley, my doorman, had kindly delivered to my front door. The makeup and perfume, I put away under the sink. I wasn't trying to eliminate Mimi's existence, just hide it so that her absence hurt less. Eventually, I'd be able to think of Mimi without my chest tightening.

As I stared around the bare room littered with boxes, I realized I wasn't there yet.

She's in Elysium, Celeste. You'll see her again.

Maybe.

I shut the door and sagged against it. And then I slid down its length, pulled my knees into my chest and cradled my throbbing forehead. Memories of her gentle voice and firm hugs spiraled and mixed with memories of her dogged attention and unwavering guidance.

I picked lint off the runner that stretched between my bedroom and hers.

Stupid cancer.

I rolled the snagged yarn until it was compact and hard, then flicked it away, wishing I could do the same with my sadness.

I was suddenly distracted by a thought: I hadn't come across the feathers I'd lost the morning Asher had retrieved her soul. Had they landed underneath the bed? I pulled myself to my feet and was about to go check when the home phone rang to announce I had a visitor.

My search would have to wait; Jase was here.

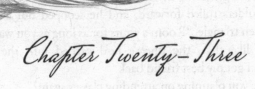

Chapter Twenty-Three

Although Jase smiled when I opened the door and divested him of two pizza boxes, it didn't reach his eyes. And then it vanished completely as I led him around the apartment, leaving Mimi's bedroom out of the tour. Back in the kitchen, I uncapped two beers and slid him one.

He wrapped his hand around the chilled glass and settled atop one of the island seats. "Why would you ever choose to live uptown with me when you got yourself a place like this?"

I took a swig of beer, the liquid foaming down my throat and sloshing into my empty stomach. "Because your apartment's on campus. Which makes it way more convenient." I reached over and snatched a slice of eggplant pizza from the box.

A small groove marred the skin between Jase's eyebrows.

I swallowed and added, "And you're in it."

Jase still hadn't touched the pepperoni pie he'd bought for himself. "So, what now?"

I grabbed a piece of paper towel from the roll and patted the grease from my lips. "I'm putting this place on the market." My gaze strayed to the broken countertop, which Asher had promised to fix. It was probably at the very bottom of his to-do list, meaning I should bump it to the top of mine. "And then, if you're still okay with me staying with you, I'd like to keep my room. At least until the end of the semester." Which would coincide with the anniversary of my wing bone ceremony. What

131

happened after that was still a big question mark. Either I'd ascend or I'd return to school. I picked up my beer and took a sip.

Jase's shoulders rolled forward, and he scooped out a cheese-and-pepperoni-laden triangle. "Room's yours for as long as you want it."

And just like that, the unease he'd carried into the apartment dispersed, and I got my best friend back.

"When are you planning on attending classes again?"

"Not until January." The prospect would make a good consolation prize if I ended up staying on Earth.

After he'd polished off his pizza, he asked, "What are you planning on doing till then?"

I chose my answer carefully. "I'm going to help people."

"People?"

"Strangers who are a little lost."

Jase stared and stared, and then he rubbed his hands on his denim-clad thighs, got up, and circled the island slowly. He set both his palms on the sides of my face and tipped my head up. The faint scent of oregano and greasy meat that clung to his skin transferred to mine. "Celeste Moreau, you are truly something different."

If only he knew *how* different . . .

"I'm sorry for having been such an asshole to you."

"You weren't."

"I was. Will you forgive me?"

"You got me my favorite pizza. Consider yourself forgiven."

"I've missed you so goddamn much." He bumped his nose against mine, but before his lips could reach mine, the doorbell rang.

Frowning, I eased away from him. "Must be my doorman." Anyone else would've been announced by telephone before being allowed up.

But no. It wasn't the doorman. There, on the small square landing, stood none other than one of the Seven.

My heart climbed into my throat because the only thing that warranted a house call from Asher was news on Bofinger, and since the archangel wasn't toting a bottle of bubbly, I suspected it wasn't the pleasant type.

"He left, didn't he?" I went for nonchalance, but my nerves made my voice crackle.

"He did."

My heart dropped right into my bare feet. I tugged my hand through my hair, but then stopped because my fingers were shaking, and I didn't want Asher to see how affected I was. *Strong.* I needed to stay strong. "Who's next?"

"Can we discuss this inside?"

"Um." I clutched the thick edge of the door. "I have company."

Like the rowboats on Central Park Lake, his eyebrows glided toward one another, tapering almost to a point. "Company?"

"Yes. Company." When his gaze climbed to a spot over my head, a spot that radiated heat and the scent of pepperoni, I sighed. Why couldn't Jase have stayed out of sight? I drew the door wider. "Jase and I were finishing dinner. Would you like to come in?"

I expected Asher to refuse, but the firm line of his mouth softened into what, on anyone else, would be categorized as a smirk, but smirking wasn't part of the archangel's arsenal of expressions. "I'd love to."

"Really?"

"I've been wanting to get to know your friend better."

"You have?"

"I have."

I really wanted to ask him *why*, but instead, I stepped to the side and gestured for him to come in. As I shut the door, I noted his apparel. Instead of human-wear, he'd come dressed in his Elysian suedes. That would be interesting to explain to Jase. Maybe, if the subject came up, I could pass it off as an eccentricity.

"I thought you hated this guy." Jase spoke quietly.

Not quietly enough, apparently.

Asher walked into the kitchen. "We made up." He didn't even glance over his shoulder as he said it. Just dropped it in coolly.

I chewed on my lip as I shut the door and returned to the island, where I propped myself on one of the high seats.

Asher opened the fridge and helped himself to a bottle of water. I could just imagine what his familiarity would look like to Jase.

Rolling the plastic between his long fingers, the archangel leaned back against the broken countertop. "So, how long have you two known each other?"

The chair legs next to mine scratched against the hardwood floor as

Jase sat down again. His knee bumped into the side of my leg as he draped his tattooed arm over my stunted backrest.

"Jase and I have been friends for a year."

"Friends? Huh . . ." Asher took a swallow of water.

I bristled. "What is *huh* supposed to mean?"

"A friend is by definition someone who knows everything, or *almost* everything, about you. Like Leigh did."

My rigid spine bumped into Jase's forearm. Why was he bringing Leigh into this? "Your point?"

"My point is that I doubt Jase knows much about you, so considering him a friend might be a stretch."

Anger shot through me. Who did he think he was? "I think you're mistaking me for Naya."

He took another slow mouthful of water. "If you'd been my daughter, Celeste, I wouldn't let you hang with a boy like Jason Marros."

Jase turned into a block of granite next to me. "Excuse me, Abercrombie, but if you don't want me to rearrange your pretty face, then I strongly suggest you keep your opinions to yourself and get the fuck out of here."

"I'd stow away those threats, Marros. Violence is *never* the answer, even though it is your favorite one, isn't it?"

Anger morphed to confusion, but I shoved it away. Jase and I were friends, and I wouldn't let Asher make me doubt this. "I invited you in out of hospitality, but since you seem unable to be cordial, I'd like you to leave."

He didn't push away from the countertop. Just kept sipping his water.

"Did you not hear me?" I asked.

"I did."

"Then why aren't you making your way to my door? Or window?" I added under my breath, not caring how Jase would construe this.

"Because I think you deserve to know what sort of man you welcomed into your home . . . and bed."

I sucked in a breath at his low blow. If he was going to aim below the belt, then so was I. "Jase is allowed his secrets, the same way I am. The same way *you* are. So stop trying to turn me against him, or whatever it is you're trying to do."

134

"Protecting you. That's what I'm trying to do."

My jaw zinged from how hard I was clenching it. "I neither want, nor need, your protection right now."

Asher finally pushed himself away from the sink, but instead of heading to the door, he stepped close to the island and leaned forward, setting his empty bottle down and bracketing it between his forearms. "Did Celeste ever tell you about the month she spent in a retirement home when she was thirteen, convincing an elderly woman not to overdose on her arthritis medication?"

My mouth went dry.

"Celeste not only gave that woman the will to live, but she was instrumental in setting her up with the older gentleman across the hall. Today, they're happily married."

Goosebumps spread over my skin. "Sylvie married Ronald?"

Asher's eyes alighted upon mine. "They did. A year after you saved her soul, Ronald asked her to tie the knot. It was quite the social affair. I heard they played bingo well into the night and all the orderlies had to wear bowties made from surgical masks."

I bet that had been Sylvie's doing. As well as pills, she'd hoarded those light blue face masks, convinced they were ruining the younger generation's immune system. I smiled at how preachy yet entertaining she'd been, but then my happiness waned as I wondered how Asher knew this. I'd never told him about this mission. Did I have a record up in Elysium?

Jase's thumb stroked my spine. "Doesn't surprise me. Celeste's an amazing woman."

Asher tipped his head to the side. "Did she ever tell you about the time she helped a wife stop verbally abusing her husband by showing her how putting him down was not only hurting their marriage but lowering the respect of their children?"

My heart ticked faster.

Cynthia hadn't been the easiest human to reform because she hadn't considered herself patronizing, merely frank. It had taken her oldest son calling his father an idiot in front of his friends—the word Greg Jr. had used was way more terrible than that, but I kept it at bay for the sake of my wings—for his mother to step up and protect the man she'd married.

"Are they still married?" I mused aloud.

"No."

I'd earned nine feathers for that mission, yet now, I felt like I'd somehow failed Cynthia and Greg if their marriage had collapsed. I didn't deserve those feathers. I'd probably lost them anyway.

I bit my lip as Asher told Jase about yet another one of my missions. He was passing me off as being such an angelic being. I mean, I was, but he was misrepresenting me.

Was he attempting to prove to Jase that my friend didn't know a thing about me, or was he trying to remind me of all the reasons a relationship with a human was bound to fail because it was built on too many secrets?

Suddenly, I sat up, bouncing away from Jase's stroking thumb. "You were the one who picked them up!"

That's how he knew about Sylvie and Cynthia and angels only knew who else! The archangel had invaded my privacy by absorbing my feathers and the memories laced within them.

Instead of gracing me with an answer—he probably felt it was obvious enough since the feathers had disintegrated—he recounted yet another morsel from my past to Jase.

Jase turned toward me. Instead of soft, his brown eyes flashed like overly varnished hardwood. "How much history do the two of you have?"

"Oh, Celeste and I, we go way back." Asher spun his empty bottle twice before adding, "Her entire life, to be exact. We know everything about one another, and when I say everything, I do mean everything."

"That's a gross exaggeration." I was trying to keep my temper under control, but the pressure building loosened my tongue. "I don't know your dick size, Seraph, yet I know Jase's, so quit trying to intimidate my friend and get out of my house!"

My stomach clenched as a feather was waxed off my invisible wings. I didn't follow its trajectory.

Jase rolled his fingers, cracking his knuckles. "You heard the girl, Seraph. Get the fuck out of her apartment."

Crap. I'd called Asher by his title, and now Jase assumed that was his name. As long as he never figured out what it stood for, I wouldn't have violated a celestial law.

Asher didn't move. Barely even twitched. "I protect my own, Marros, so no, I won't leave, but you are welcome to."

Tension made Jase's body thrum. "Your own? Celeste isn't *yours*, you narcissistic prick."

"Don't call him that." My voice sliced through the thick air.

Asher was a lot of things but not a narcissist. I'd met one. Reformed one. The archangel could be arrogant, but he wasn't looking to be perpetually admired and he didn't lack empathy. He wouldn't have brought Leigh back or raised Naya as his own if he'd been violently self-centered.

"Don't call him that?" Jase gestured spastically toward Asher. "Don't you see that that's what he is, Cee? You said it yourself. He's trying to turn you against me! Paint himself as the oh-so-righteous-and-fucking-caring guy, and me as some worthless piece of shit. And yeah, I might not be good enough for you, but I'd never try to possess you."

I leveled a pointed look on the archangel. "His bedside manner needs improving, but that doesn't make him a prick."

Asher watched me from across the island, his body so still it seemed like an extension of the black stone.

"I can't believe you're defending him." Jase's eye twitched.

"You're my friend. If he insulted you, I'd defend you."

Jase lurched to his feet. I thought he was going to give Asher a taste of his knuckles, but instead, he pulled on his vintage leather jacket.

"Where are you going?"

"Home. *Our* home. Are you coming?"

I hesitated, and that hesitation made Jase's face shutter. It was like watching every door and window clamp shut at the very same time. I caught his hand and squeezed it, trying to apologize for how badly the night was ending. "Let me work some things out here, and then I'll join you uptown."

His eyes stayed on mine a long time as though gauging if I really would. "Okay."

I gave his fingers a final squeeze before letting them go.

Letting him go.

Chapter Twenty-Four

After the front door closed, I whirled on Asher. "What in Abaddon was that?"

"What in Abaddon was what?"

I twirled my finger in the air. "Why were you so . . . so mean to him?"

"I didn't call him any names. And I don't see how pointing out your benevolence was *mean*."

"You don't see? Well, let me explain it to you, Seraph. Jase has been there for me when I've needed a friend, a shoulder to cry on, a hand to hold, a body to keep me warm. He may not be aware of my past or of what I am, but he knows me way better than you ever will."

Asher straightened, rolling his massive shoulders back, straining his sleeveless suede tunic. Jase hadn't commented on the archangel's attire, but I bet he thought Asher had come straight from the East Village. "You are aware of his score, aren't you, Celeste?"

"His—" I batted away my surprise. "Stop trying to turn me against him!"

"Forty-one. That's his score."

I flattened my palms against my ears, but it was too late. His score ricocheted around my skull. "I just told you, I didn't want to hear it."

Asher rounded the island toward me. "I'm not trying to turn you against him, Celeste." I hated that his voice penetrated through the barrier of flesh. "I just want you to be aware of the people you allow near you. You might not think I have your best interest at heart, but I do."

Doubt gnawed on my unflappable affection. I wanted to keep my ears covered and hum until Asher stopped demolishing my one and only friendship, but I chose to act maturely. I let my hands fall and cocked my chin up in the air. "Is that why you just *had* to tell me Jase's score?"

"I was informing you because I thought you might want to sign on to him next."

"What? No!" My head jerked. "Jase is my friend. I can't—I would never—No. Pick someone else. Or better yet"—I hopped to my feet, side-stepped Asher, and grabbed my bomber jacket from the coat closet—"I'll go pick someone myself."

"You're not done with Bofinger."

I froze, my hand already on the doorknob. "He left. You said he left." My breaths were coming out in pants.

"That doesn't mean he won't come back. Or that he won't do something to redeem himself. Give it a few days. I promise that if I feel like you're wasting time, I'll sign you off." He strolled up to me in that unhurried pace men accustomed to having people wait for them possessed.

I needed some air. I almost walked out barefoot and without my keys.

"Celeste, where are you going?"

"Out." Before leaving, I turned toward Asher. "And don't you dare follow me, or our agreement is off, and you can wallow in your guilt for all of eternity."

His eyes grew as gray and forbidding as the waters in the Hudson during the cold months. "Celeste . . ."

"Don't Celeste-me. You come into my house and wreck my friendship. My *only* friendship. If you're expecting gratitude, don't hold your breath." I twisted the doorknob, stepped out, and then slammed the door shut in the archangel's face.

As the elevator flew me down to the lobby, the emotions he'd stirred up expanded like depressurized air. I was livid, disenchanted, disturbed. Jase's number swam in front of my eyes as though I were staring at his profile on a holo-ranker. I didn't head into Central Park. The Park at night was not a pleasant place to be. Not even for an immortal. Instead, I headed toward Times Square.

I lost myself in the pounding of feet, the honking of cars, the squeal of brakes, the chatter of a thousand voices speaking a hundred different languages. I blinded myself with the rush of color from animated billboards, the glare of lampposts and headlights, the glow of giant screens, and the flash of theater marquees.

At some point, I wandered into a seedy bar covered in so many Broadway posters that it was impossible to tell what the walls were made of. Not that I cared. All I cared about was dulling my whirring mind. I ordered a vodka on the rocks, hoping I wouldn't be carded. I didn't want to produce my fake ID because flashing it cost a feather. The bartender delivered my order without hassling me. Then again, she had so few customers, she was probably glad I'd shown up. As I drained my glass, it hit me that I hadn't brought my bag. I dug through my pockets for some cash, but came up with a wad of gum and two dimes. I didn't even have a phone.

Being so disorganized wasn't like me. I blamed the archangel for that. Deciding I'd deal with payment later, I ordered a second drink as a woman took the stage and performed a song from the *Phantom of Opera*, which gave me actual chills. The show had been Mimi's favorite, but that wasn't the reason I was enthralled. It was the woman's voice, its languid and ethereal resonance, which clashed so completely with this hole-in-the-wall.

When I started on my third drink, abandoning any attempt at moderation, my wing bones began to thrum. However far I ran from the ishim, they were always there. Why had I wanted to ascend anyway? What was the point? Yes, I missed Mimi, but I'd gotten four years with her. Four fantastic years. Couldn't that be enough? As for Leigh—Naya—once she developed wing bones, I could see her. Guide her. Help her from down here.

I knocked back the entire glass in one swallow. When I turned toward the bartender to ask for another, the woman's brow scrunched. "You sure, hun?"

I was sure I wanted to forget the mess tonight had been. "Yes," I said at the same time as someone behind me said, "No."

I spun toward the person who'd dared take the decision away from me. "Go away, Seraph."

A new performer took the stage, a young guy with long dreads that bounced around his shoulders as his fingers danced over piano keys, filling the bar with an outrageously gorgeous melody. I took it back. This place wasn't seedy. This place was a find, a diamond in the rough. I needed to jot down the name so I would remember it come morning and return when I wasn't one-part vodka and two-parts rage. And this time, with my wallet.

I glanced up at Asher, who loomed over me like my very own body-guard. "Since you're here, Seraph"—a hiccup darted past my lips—"why don't you make yourself useful and pay this nice lady for my drinks?"

His gaze ground into mine as though trying to grind up my very soul. I was sure he thought me such an inelegant fletching but whatevs. Wasn't like I cared.

"How much have you had to drink?"

I tipped my face up and smiled. "Enough to lose a feather. Or two. Can't really feel my wing bones at the moment."

His chest got all bloated with air as he produced cash from—I didn't even know where since neither his suede pants nor his tunic had pockets —and placed it on the bar top. As he leaned across me, I got a noseful of wind and heat. "Will this cover her tab?"

I had no clue what the lady behind me answered. It was too loud. Outside and inside. And his smell. Elysium, it was distracting. I might've licked his neck had the vodka not taped my tongue to my palate.

"Are you ready to go?"

"What?" I pressed a hand to my chest, heaving a fake gasp followed by a real hiccup. "Are you asking me instead of telling me?"

His response to my taunt was a sigh. "Forget I asked. Let's go."

"Ah . . . here's the archangel I know and loathe." Hiccup.

"Celeste . . ." he growled.

"What, Seraph? You're allowed to point out everyone's flaws"—my chest tightened with a hiccup—"but we're not allowed to point out *your* flaws. 'Cause let me tell you"—I poked his rock-hard chest with my index finger—"you got *sooo*"—hiccup—"many." I hopped off my stool but miscalculated my landing and smacked into him.

"Can you walk?"

I pointed to my boots. "Don't see why not. I got two feet." I squinted. Actually, four. *No.* That couldn't be right . . .

I took a step and stumbled. Okay, so maybe I couldn't. Or at least, not well. Before I could try again, Asher picked me up as though I was a sack of rice.

My cheeks went from warm to scorching. "Put me down. You've embarrassed me enough for one night."

"You can't walk."

"I can crawl."

"You're not crawling all the way home."

"What if I want to?"

"You don't."

"Oh, so now you know what I want and what I don't want?"

"You'll thank me tomorrow."

"I will *never* thank you." I shut my eyes because the ceiling was swinging.

At least my hiccups were gone. That was nice.

And then cool air buffeted my face. That was really nice, too.

So nice that I kept my eyes closed and leaned into the cool darkness that seemed to grow brisker even though an inferno kept the length of my body toasty.

Chapter Twenty-Five

I awakened violently, acid shooting up my throat. I clamped my lips shut and sat up, darting my hand out for balance. I ended up knocking over the glass on my nightstand, and water—or was it vodka? *Please, let it not be alcohol*—spilled down my comforter and seeped into my rug. The room seesawed, and I almost toppled right out of bed but somehow managed to defy gravity and stay upright. Slowly, the room in which I'd slept appeared in dabs of muted color. I was at home. In my midtown home.

I remembered leaving it but had zero recollection of getting back. My gut clenched. I jolted out of bed and streaked toward the bathroom, slamming down onto my knees just as a jet of bile dotted with chunks of eggplant splashed into the bowl. *Ugh.* I was *never* drinking again.

I retched again, my nose stinging, my eyes watering.

What in Abaddon had gotten into me to drink so much? It was so unlike me.

Long fingers wound through my hair, dragging it away from my vile stomach contents. For a heartbeat, I thought they belonged to Mimi, but then the memory of her loss hit me along with a fresh wave of nausea. Sweat beaded along my brow as I leaned back over and emptied myself some more. When I slumped back, I caught sight of a pair of muscular calves cloaked in suede.

I rested my cheek on the toilet seat and shut my eyes. "Do you get a kick out of seeing me at my lowest, Seraph?"

His fingers tightened around the coiled rope of my hair. "What sort of question is that?"

I picked my head off the plastic seat. "I'm puking up what feels like an organ, and you're here. You're *always* here."

"Why do you keep expecting me to leave?"

"Because that's what people around me do. They leave." I laid my cheek back against the toilet seat as my skull began to bob. "When I ask them, and even when I don't."

He released my hair and stood. I expected him to walk away. Instead, water started running and steam webbed the air. And then a wet towel glided down the side of my face and neck.

Asher levered my head and wiped the other side of my face. I expected disgust to contort his features, or at the very least, disapproval, but found only concern. The words *thank you* gripped the tip of my tongue but never made their way out.

Just because he was concerned about me didn't mean he actually cared. Unlike Jase. *He* cared. Proven it so many times over. All Asher had proven was an overdeveloped sense of duty toward his people, and since I was still one of them—

"Here." He pushed a glass of water toward my mouth and handed me two white pills. "Take these and a bath. You should feel somewhat better after."

"I'm surprised you know the cure for hangovers. Can't imagine you've ever had one." I tossed the aspirin back and chased it with the water. My stomach gurgled. I breathed in and out slowly, waiting for the spasms to quiet.

"Do you want some help getting into the bath?"

I tried to imagine what he could mean by that. "Are you offering to undress me?"

Asher's cheeks didn't blaze, but his eyes did, and not in an aroused way, more in an I'm-going-to-toss-you-in-fully-clothed way, complete with nostril-flaring. "I doubt you require my assistance to undress." He turned around and strode out, slapping the door shut with so much force that the lacquered wood rattled in its frame.

I pushed myself up to standing, exulting in how easily I could torment the ancient being. Tiny aches lanced from the soles of my feet to the roots of my hair as I tottered over to the bathtub. Damn vodka. At least my stomach was no longer trying to turn itself inside out. I yanked off my clothes, then dumped a heaping dose of lavender-scented bath salts and immersed my tender body into the balmy water.

As I soaked, I shut my eyes and tried to piece my evening back together. It came back in disjointed snippets. One of them made my lids wrench open. Crap, Jase. I'd asked him to wait up for me. I needed to call him.

After my bath.

I closed my eyes and steeped a while longer. And then I climbed out and bundled myself in my thick bathrobe monogrammed with a loopy C on the breast—another one of Mimi's gifts—and brushed the fuzz off my teeth. Feeling a whole lot less queasy, I went back into my bedroom and pulled on a pair of black sleep shorts and a boxy crop top with the words *I Speak Fluent Sarcasm* scrolled across the chest. Mimi had rolled her eyes at me the first time I'd worn it.

Oh, Mimi . . . Had I really questioned my desire to see her again?

I wanted more years with her.

I thought of Bofinger as I rolled my damp hair into a bun. "Please, please do the right thing," I murmured, stepping up to the window and watching dawn paint the sky a pearlescent gray. *For the people you screwed over. But also for me. Please.*

I was sober enough to know my plea wouldn't magically carry over to his ears, but Leigh had once told me prayers never hurt anyone, so why not murmur some. Cosmic logistics aside, my whispered entreaty made me think of the day she'd told me this, and oddly enough, there was comfort in that memory.

I padded out to the living room, on a quest to find my phone and something to eat, preferably something extra-fatty and dripping in sugar. Ooh, donuts. I could get some delivered. *If* I could locate my phone . . .

A gust of chilly air streamed through the open terrace window where Asher stood with his back to me. I was tempted to walk over and lock it when lavender wings tipped in gold poked out from behind his broad body. Or rather, from in front of it.

Asher had angelic company. I imagined the visit was work-related. Unless he was entertaining angels in my house, which would be quite rude since he hadn't asked for my permission to arrange playdates for himself. Curiosity made me switch directions and head out into the brisk October morning.

I wasn't sure if he'd sensed my presence or if his company had alerted him to it, but he turned as I stepped onto the narrow balcony, revealing an ishim I didn't care for much. Not that I cared for any ishim. My spine tingled as though to remind me to stop while I was ahead unless I wanted to part with another feather. How many was I down anyway? I'd forgotten to check under my barstool last night.

"Celeste, you remember Ish Eliza?"

Like I could forget the ranker with the resting unicorn face. I slapped on a smile, which she didn't reciprocate, and leaned against the cold metal doorjamb. "What brings you to *mi casa*, Ish?"

"Business that doesn't concern you, Fletching."

"Ish Eliza . . ." Asher's voice was low and slightly admonishing.

The archangel really loved using people's names instead of forming full sentences around them. Sure, it got the message across, but it did little to show off his glibness. And the man was glib. To this day, I remembered the impassioned speech he'd made back in the guild when he was on the prowl for a consort. Had he ever entertained asking the verity next to him? Probably not since they weren't hitched, and from the way she was rubbing her feathers on his arm, it didn't seem like she would've turned him down.

"Sorry for having interrupted your cozy get-together."

I pushed off the doorframe and started to turn when Asher said, "I'll be inside in a minute."

"Oh, no need to cut your rendezvous short on my behalf. I'm plenty happy to be on my own. Plus, I need to make a phone call to salvage my broken friendship."

The blue in his eyes turned inky. "Don't make any plans. We have work to do today."

"Do we? I thought I had to give Bofinger time."

"Just don't leave."

To avoid losing a feather, I didn't answer. If Jase was awake and took my call, I wanted to suggest a greasy breakfast at The Trap to iron out the wrinkles in our friendship. As I resumed my cell phone hunt, the number 41 shimmied on the outskirts of my vision. Our relationship wasn't only wrinkled, but torn, and although holes could be mended, until I understood how he'd earned his consequent score, they'd remain gaping.

I had three options: a) cave and ask Asher, b) go to the source and confront Jase, or c) head to the guild and check on a holo-ranker.

Dread pulsated through me, reawakening the dull pounding. I squeezed my temples with my fingertips. Where in Abaddon was my damned phone? Had Asher confiscated it? Just as I had this ill-thought, I spotted it on the coffee table, next to the TV's remote control.

"Score." I grabbed it, my knuckles grazing the digital remote, managing to switch on the television.

The voice of the news anchor blasted from the speakers, drilling my temples anew. I hit the mute button instead of the OFF. Worked just as well.

My phone had three percent of battery life remaining, so I hurried to locate Jase's contact and press call. As it rang, I watched the newscaster's rouged cheeks puff as she shared what seemed like exhilarating news.

Jase's answering machine clicked on.

"Hey, Jase. I'm sorry about last night. If you don't totally hate my guts, I'd love to hang at some point today. Just call . . ." A familiar name scrolled across the ticker. "Me when . . . uh. Um. Let me call you back." I hung up and pressed the phone to my chest, the bands of my rings digging into the sparkly black silicone case. "Oh, holy Seven." I lobbed the phone onto the couch. "Asher!"

The archangel burst into the living room, the ishim hot on his wingtips. Yes, wingtips. He'd magicked his wings into existence, and the bronze-turquoise barbs fluttered from his rushed arrival. Had I sounded in such grave distress that he'd assumed I'd need to be whisked off?

His eyes scanned me from forehead to toe. "What is it, Celeste?"

Joy made me skip toward him and throw my arms around his waist. His body seized as my wrists and fingers brushed the underside of his wings. So very soft. The only soft place on his body. In the back of my mind, I knew I was committing a faux-pas, and a grave one at that. I wasn't only grazing the edge of his wings, but their most intimate spot. I tried to care about propriety. Okay, no I didn't. I didn't give a crap about propriety in that instance. All I cared about was expressing my happiness and gratitude toward my hardheaded and hard-bodied handler. Besides, if he was uncomfortable, he could just magick them away. Since he hadn't, I surmised it wasn't such a hotspot after all. It wasn't like I'd ever checked. My wings had always been a source of pain. Turning them into a source of pleasure would be confusing and disheartening if I lost them.

For the first time in years, I let myself dream that I'd get to keep them.

I bent backward to look up at him. His pupils had dilated to the point of eclipsing their brilliant backdrops, and his chest was pounding with such violent beats that I worried his heart was trying to breach his skin in order to clobber me for my insolent hug. He was positively frightening, yet I wasn't frightened.

I smiled. Didn't soften him one bit. "I did it, Seraph. Bofinger just confessed to his Ponzi scheme. He called the investors himself. He's fled the country but confessed."

His pupils shrank as his gaze sailed toward the TV. Eliza's attention flicked to it too, but then it flicked back to me, or more accurately, to my linked hands nestled in the crook of her boss's spine, right beneath the velvety vee of his wings. I expected a snarl to drop from her mouth at any moment. Almost made me want to give Asher one slow stroke just to spite her, but I took pity on his savaged feathers and released him.

"It might not count," Ish Eliza said, bowling over my exultation.

My hands plummeted to my sides, thumping against my thighbones. "What? Why?"

"Humans can only redeem themselves if their confessions are shored up by repentance." Eliza took a step closer to Asher. The second her body disturbed the air around his feathers, he made them vanish.

"I disagree, Ish Eliza." Asher's voice sounded a whole octave deeper than usual. "If this man wasn't repentant, he wouldn't have confessed."

My heart rose and rose like a fugitive helium balloon.

He looked down at me, the blue sparkling like the flames at the bottommost part of candlewicks. "Bring out your wings, Celeste. Let's see if there are new growths."

I crossed my arms. "Um. No."

His eyebrows tipped. "Why not?"

I backed up a step as though fearing he might drag my wing bones out using brute force, which, thankfully, was impossible. "Because no. Doesn't Ish Eliza have a nifty, built-in feather detector?"

"Ish Eliza does not," she answered.

Hearing her talk about herself in the third person would normally have made me crack a joke, but I was way too wired to poke fun at her. "And you can't tell either, Seraph?"

"Not without looking at your wings or at a holo-ranker. Why don't you want to bring them out?"

"Because I just don't."

A groove formed between his already tight eyebrows.

There was no way I was displaying my winglets in front of either of them. Even if they were eighty-two feathers denser.

My eyes must've shifted to the ishim, because suddenly Asher was telling Eliza to leave.

"Seraph, there is still the matter of—"

"Not now."

"But what am I to tell Seraph Claire?"

"You can tell her I'll be in Elysium before the day is done, and we can discuss the matter in person."

"She will be displeased."

"And if you don't leave now, I will be displeased!"

Whoa.

Eliza backed up one step and then another, staring daggers at me even though I wasn't the one who'd issued the thunderous command. I supposed that staring daggers at the archangel wouldn't have earned her any brownie points while glaring at someone so far beneath her cost nothing.

"Very well. I'll pass on your message, Seraph." She returned to the terrace, wings unspooling, then soared over the park before hanging a sharp turn and vanishing out of sight.

"What was that about?"

He avoided my question. "She's gone. You can bring out your wings now, Celeste."

"I'm not showing you my wings either."

The groove deepened. "Why not?"

"Because I don't show anyone my wings. Haven't in four years. The only time I bring them out is on my wing bone anniversary."

"Why?"

I blew air out the corner of my mouth. "Why are you being so obtuse about this?"

He crossed his forearms. "Because I've never met an angel who refused to display her wings."

"What can I say? I'm unique."

"Celeste . . ." He was doing it again. Growling first names as though they constituted perfectly adequate full sentences.

"My nickname in the guild was *winglet*."

"And?"

"If you had a tiny penis, would you display it?" The question whizzed out before I could choose a better metaphor. For all I knew, the archangel wasn't generously endowed. Being big everywhere could be deceptive . . . I'd found this out first-hand.

His eyes widened a notch. "Wings aren't genitalia."

"Aren't they, though? Both erogenous zones." *Someone, take the shovel out of my hands.*

"I promise not to touch them against your consent."

Whoa . . . "So, that wasn't the root of my reticence." Was I blushing? I really hoped not. I was feeling minutely hotter than before, but that was probably because Eliza had shut the terrace door. *Oh, wait . . .* it was *wide* open. I tugged at the collar of my crop top. "My wings are ridiculous. They look like dress-up props."

"Wings come in many sizes and colors, Celeste. All of them beautiful."

This time, I totally rolled my eyes. "Oh, puh-leeze."

"Besides, you touched mine . . . *again*." He dipped his chin to better look down his aquiline nose at me. "Without my consent, I might add. The least you could do is display yours."

"Not happening. And I'm sorry about having ruffled your feathers, Seraph. I'm a very unpredictable and effusive person. You really should keep them hidden when in my company."

A sigh made the sharp line of his jaw loosen. "Then at least go into a closed room and look at them."

I swallowed, knees feeling suddenly rubbery. "I don't want to do that either."

"Why not?"

"Because . . . what if there's no new growth?"

"There will be. I'm certain of it."

Another wad of saliva slunk down my throat. "Can't you just call up someone and ask them to check a holo-ranker?"

"I can, but I want you to face your wings."

"They're on my back, so pretty hard to face."

He dragged in a breath. "You know what I mean."

I gnawed on my lower lip. "Fine." Before I could second-guess myself, I went into the closest bedroom—Mimi's—shut the door, and stood in front of the propped mirror. Inhaling a lungful of courage, I let my loathed appendages materialize and stretched them as far as they went, which wasn't far. The sight of them, their sparseness, made color rise to my cheeks.

I stopped looking at what wasn't there and searched instead for what might be. I pivoted a little and then I squinted. The edges of both my wings were lined in what resembled sheared violet mink. I must've gasped, because the next thing I knew, there was pounding on the door.

"Celeste?" Asher's tone was rough and more than a little frantic. "Can I come in?"

I vanquished them out of existence because I was starting to know how impulsive the archangel could be. He'd barrel in even if I said no.

Sure enough, the door flew open. One look at my shiny cheeks made color leach from his. "Perhaps, it's too soon. Sometimes it takes a little time for feathers to appear."

I palmed my tears away, trying to stretch a smile over my lips, but they trembled too hard. "They've appeared."

"They've—Then why are you crying?"

"Because I'm . . ." What was I? Proud? Hopeful? In the end, I went with a word that summed up both. "Because I'm happy."

"Thank Elysium I'm immortal or your unpredictability would've stopped my heart a few times already."

I smiled. And then I laughed. And then I cried some more because maybe this wasn't such an impossible dream after all. I was still *far* from ascending, but in one day, I'd earned eighty-two feathers.

The archangel, he just smiled. And it was totally smug, but I didn't bait him about it because those feathers . . . I owed him for them. Even though I didn't thank him out loud, I was pretty certain my shiny eyes and curved lips conveyed my gratitude.

"Point me to my next sinner, Seraph."

Smile in place, he said, "Why don't you get dressed while I go sign you up?"

"I am dressed."

His lips fell into a very unamused line.

"Fine. I'll go put on a thong."

Reflexively, his eyes lowered to my very short shorts, and his skin tone, usually so smooth and golden, turned slightly mottled.

I patted his big arm on my way out. "And some pants." I grinned all the way back to my bedroom.

Why did I enjoy rattling the seraphim so much? Oh yeah, because I was good at it, and I loved doing things I was good at. Like accomplishing missions. I was good at that too, apparently.

Under my breath, I thanked the universe for granting my wish, even though it probably hadn't had much of a hand in it.

Unlike Asher.

After pulling on my leather leggings, I returned to the living room, ready to speak my gratitude, but the archangel was gone.

The one time I'd wished he'd been around . . .

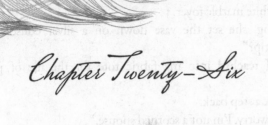

Chapter Twenty-Six

The junk food I'd scarfed down while I'd researched my newest sinner sat heavily in my stomach, not because the woman seemed particularly complicated or frightening, but because the pressure of succeeding, and quickly at that, was back.

Fernanda, a sinner worth thirty-two points, conned married men out of millions of dollars. She started by seducing them, had extended affairs, documented these trysts, then threatened to show the wives the pictures, text messages, and emails she gathered during the weeks spent working these unsuspecting chaps. She'd duped six men and was now the proud owner of a Park Avenue apartment, courtesy of one lover, a house in London, courtesy of another, a vacation home on the Amalfi Coast, courtesy of yet another, and a sizeable bank account, courtesy of all six combined.

My job: put an end to her lascivious, albeit lucrative, business.

I hugged the sumptuous orchids I'd bought as a ticket up to her apartment and stepped inside the building, arrowing straight toward the concierge's desk. After phoning my sinner, the concierge escorted me toward the bank of elevators. Inside the farthest one, she swiped a badge, pressed on 38, then backed up so the doors could shut.

When I arrived in front of Fernanda's already opened door, I was still strategizing how to go about reforming her.

"Ooh. How beautiful." She reached for the plant, her blonde locks bouncing against a silken nightie covered by a sheer robe.

She was about to close the door when I pressed it open and stepped inside her white marble foyer.

Frowning, she set the vase down on a silver console. "Are you expecting a tip?"

"No." I reached into my fabric tote for the file of pictures I'd compiled.

She took a step back.

"Don't worry. I'm not a scorned spouse."

She froze.

I extended the file.

"What's this?"

"Pictures. *Family* pictures." Since she didn't take the file, I opened it and displayed the picture of the first man she'd duped. "Remember Octavio? He's become an alcoholic and spends more time in rehab than with his wife of thirty years, not that she wants to spend time with him anymore." I flipped to the next picture, confronting her with the brutal reality of what she'd done. "This one. Gaspard. Divorced. Only sees his kids every other weekend."

Her lash line dipped low, dimming her dark irises. "Who are you, and what do you want?"

"My name's Celeste Moreau, and what I want is for you to become a better person. Shall we sit?"

"No." Her mouth barely shifted around the word.

"Fine." I tossed the picture aside, then pulled out before-and-after shots of prey number three, four, five, and six. "Hunting married men isn't a good sport. You've destroyed a lot of marriages, Fernanda."

"It takes two to destroy a marriage. Besides, we all have to make a living."

"Why married men? Why not single ones?"

"Why don't you mind your own fucking business?"

"The city's full of wealthy bachelors."

She glowered. "I'm not the sort of woman men want to marry."

"Why do you say that?"

"Because . . ." She expelled a frustrated breath. "I'm just not."

I shut the file and set it down. "Did someone tell you that?"

"My mother said there were two types of women in this world: the

154

ones who looked good on paper and those who looked good on bedsheets. Apparently, I look best on bedsheets."

"Mothers aren't always right."

A sultry smile curled her lips. "Oh, but I do look good on bedsheets."

"That doesn't have to be the only place you look good."

"Doesn't matter since I have no desire to get married. Men are all cheaters. Like you said, they think with their dicks."

"I didn't actually say that, but back to the matter at hand . . . Why *married* men?"

"Because they treat me like a prize instead of a commodity. Single men feel like they're owed my attention after they take me out on a date. Married men feel lucky I even give them the time of day."

"You shouldn't establish your worth from other people's opinion of you."

Annoyance reshaped her mouth. "I don't. I know my worth, which is why I make people pay for it."

"What about the wives? The kids? Do you ever spare a thought for them?"

"All I do is play the part the wives no longer care for. I make men feel desired and interesting again. In a way, I do the wives a favor—if I sleep with their husbands, they don't have to."

I studied her pert nose and bouncy golden locks, her busty, narrow-hipped figure. "Don't you feel guilty?"

"Why should I feel guilty? I give them their money's worth."

I twirled my finger in the air. "I'm sure you're good but this good?"

She smiled. "Believe it or not, it was Gaspard's wife who gifted me this apartment. She was worried her husband would leave her for me, and she didn't want to risk it."

"You could've turned it down."

"Turned it down? Are you crazy? Why the hell would I turn down a free apartment?" She snorted. "Have you never accepted an outrageous gift?"

I thought of the many gifts Mimi had bestowed upon me over the years. Gifts that I'd accepted but that I'd never felt owed. "You should stop while you're ahead."

"I could have a stroke and lose the use of half of my face, or worse, my brain. While I still have my health and looks, I plan on accruing as much wealth as I can."

I didn't speak for a long moment, rethinking my strategy. Even if my slideshow made her contemplate her wrongdoings, it wouldn't miraculously change her overnight, and I needed to change her overnight. Which gave me an idea. "How about I help you find an eligible bachelor?"

"I told you already, I'm not interested in single men. They're not worth my time or skill."

"Can I try to prove you wrong?"

"Why?" She crossed her arms. "What's in it for you?"

"My soul would greatly benefit from helping yours."

"That's the oddest thing someone's ever told me."

"I'm an odd girl." I opened her front door. "Meet me tonight at Dinos. Ten o'clock."

She tipped her head to the side. "What if I don't?"

I stepped out into the hallway. "Then you miss out on a free meal at the trendiest restaurant in the city."

"No strings attached?"

Right before she shut her door, I added, "The reservation will be under Moreau."

"I won't be there."

But she would. Curiosity, or maybe worry, would make her seek me out.

Chapter Twenty-Seven

I strode into Dinos at ten to ten. I didn't want Fernanda arriving before me and deciding she was no longer interested in what I was peddling. After the maître d' seated me at the limewashed bar that garlanded the restaurant, I called Jase for the tenth time, and for the tenth time, he didn't answer. I understood why he might be angry, but his silence was now angering *me*. What exactly was he trying to achieve? Did he think I'd storm back uptown to fix us?

A waiter sporting a black linen shirt and a thick Greek accent leaned over the bar and asked what I wanted to drink.

I set my phone down and ordered sparkling water. I'd think of Jase later. Right now, I needed to focus on this mission. When after fifteen minutes, Fernanda still hadn't arrived, I began to worry I'd been overly confident. I'd give it another fifteen, and if she didn't show—

"I changed my mind." My sinner glided into the seat beside mine.

"No, you didn't." I opened my leather-bound menu. "You were always planning on coming."

Smiling at my directness, she shrugged out of a fitted blazer, revealing a crimson dress that stuck to all her assets. Her gaze trawled the room. I doubted she was admiring the fishing nets that spanned the breadth of the ceiling and held thick emerald and azure glass globes fitted with lightbulbs.

"Where are all those promised bachelors?"

"You wouldn't be into the ones I know."

157

Her hand froze on its way to her water glass. "I don't understand. You said—"

"This place transforms into a club after midnight, thus our late dinner. Since la crème de la crème of New York flocks here, you're bound to find some available candidates."

The Greek waiter leaned over the bar, tendering a second menu to Fernanda. When she gripped it, he didn't automatically release it. She shot him a tight smile.

After he was called away by another customer, I angled myself toward Fernanda. "Look at that . . . you already caught someone's attention."

She spun around, eyes raking across the room. "Whose?"

"Our waiter's."

She wrinkled her nose. "No offence, Celeste, but there's no way I'm going home with someone who makes minimum wage. Not even for a night."

"Why? He could be an exceptional human being."

"Perhaps, but for me, love is transactional. If I have nothing to gain, then there's no reason for me to give." She wrapped her hands around her glass and brought it to her painted nude lips that complemented her dewy makeup and mascara-accented eyes. Asher had mentioned she was twenty-nine, but she looked younger, fresher.

"A real relationship would be good for your soul, Fernanda."

"*My* soul? I thought we were here for *your* soul." Her lips quirked with another smile. "You're funny."

I wasn't trying to be funny; I was trying to be effective.

After we placed our order, and the entranced waiter had set a glass of rosé in front of Fernanda, she said, "I haven't done a girl's dinner since I was sixteen."

"Really?"

"I don't especially like women. They're usually catty and competitive. And judgmental. God, how they can be judgmental."

I thought of Eve and her handful of densely feathered friends. How they'd always looked down their noses at me and my winglets. The only one who'd never treated me like dirt was Leigh.

Fernanda sipped her wine. "Do you have many female friends, Celeste?"

"I used to have one."

She set down her glass and wiped her hands on her napkin. "Used to? What happened?"

Like the plucked strings of the bouzouki playing in the background, the memory of Leigh strummed my pulse. "She died."

That sobered up my companion. "I'm sorry."

So am I . . .

Naya existed, but she was still a child. A child whom I'd broken my promise to hang out with. Tomorrow. I'd go see her tomorrow.

"The grilled octopus was a good choice."

I spun toward the voice, which belonged to my other bar neighbor, a handsome man sporting an open-collared pink shirt that made his deeply tanned skin pop. "Glad I ordered it then."

The man's gaze snaked over my face but didn't dip lower than my chin. He held out his hand. "Phillip."

I shook it. "Nice to meet you, Phillip. I'm Celeste." I tipped my head toward my sinner. "And this is my friend Fernanda."

"Fernanda. Italian?"

"Half." She picked up her wine and lifted it to her mouth.

I scooted my chair back, so he could see her better.

"What about you, Celeste? Where are you from?"

"I grew up in the city." I checked his left hand—no ring and no tan line to indicate one might've been there. "What about you, Phillip?"

"Originally, St. Louis, but I moved to New York for college and never left."

Fernanda planted one elbow on the bar, her blonde locks cascading over her shoulder. "And what is it you do, Phillip?"

"I'm a lawyer. Specialized in mergers and acquisitions."

I could almost hear clicking in Fernanda's brain as she evaluated what income bracket M&A would put him in. She must've decided it was satisfactory because she paid no mind to all the little plates of glistening food the waiter set down between us.

I thanked him. His dark eyes flitted to me before zeroing back on Fernanda, who was chortling at something Phillip had said. Our two-person dinner turned into a three-person one. Phillip seemed nice enough. More importantly, though, Fernanda seemed captivated.

When she excused herself to go freshen up, I became the sole recipient of his attention.

"Do you model?"

Seriously? I smirked. "I'm missing about a dozen inches to model. I'm actually studying law at Columbia."

"You're kidding? That's my alma mater." He signaled the waiter and tapped his wine glass. "Smart *and* beautiful." His attention grew heavier and heavier. If I hadn't been trying to match him with Fernanda, I might've encouraged Phillip. He was quite attractive, and I was quite single. "Can I get you something to drink, Celeste?"

I hummed. "Not tonight, but thank you."

"Sometime this week, perhaps? I'd love to hear how you're enjoying your classes." His voice had turned downright raspy. "Does Professor Goldstein still teach?"

"Ha. Yes. And still full of energy."

"Celeste."

My clipped name made me crook my neck. "Fancy running into you here." I smiled up at the scowling archangel. I imagined his dissatisfied expression was due to his presumption that I was out enjoying a date instead of working.

Phillip looked between us.

"Phillip, meet my . . . boss."

"Boss? I thought you were in college."

"I am."

"Well, hello there, big guy." Fernanda, whom I'd missed sashaying back to us, slurped up my broad-bodied handler with a thorough once-over. "I'm Fernanda." She lifted a hand, which he didn't take. Didn't even look at. Fernanda's freshly nude-slicked mouth pinched.

"Can I have a word with you, Celeste?"

I sensed he wanted to have many words with me. "Excuse me. I'll be right back." I slid off my chair and trailed the archangel through the restaurant where tables were being rolled aside to allow the growing crowd to congregate. The classic Greek tunes had been replaced by thumpier club beats.

Asher folded his arms over his white T-shirt. Seriously the man had two looks—Elysian archangel and James-Dean human. "What do you think you're doing?"

"Working."

His gaze flicked to the bar where I'd been sitting, where both Phillip and Fernanda now sat, staring at us. Their mouths moved. Good, at least they were chatting.

"I promised Fernanda to help her find an unattached man so she could change her sinful ways. Phillip's single. Before you so rudely interrupted us, I was trying to matchmake them."

A muscle convulsed in his locked jaw. *Wow*. He was really mad. "By arranging a get-together to discuss college life?"

I folded my arms, matching his closed-off stance. "Just because he's interested in getting together doesn't mean I am. Besides, how is this any of your business, and how in the worlds did you even hear it? Were you eavesdropping?"

"How you accomplish your missions is very much my concern. That man—Phillip"—he all but spit out the name of my pink-shirted admirer —"isn't interested in your sinner, Celeste. He's interested in *you*."

How long *had* he been watching us? Instead of confronting him about his stalkerish ways, I said, "So, I'll find her someone else."

"And keep Phillip for yourself?" He slanted the poor guy one heck of an embittered look.

"You know what . . . maybe I will. It's not like Jase is answering my calls." I raised my chin up a notch. "And, Seraph, if you're not pleased with the way I go about my missions, then I suggest you flock back to Elysium. I'm sure you have plenty to keep you busy up there."

He backed up, pupils flaring. Although his expression spoke volumes, his mouth didn't speak a single extra word as he carved through the crowd and out of the restaurant.

Chapter Twenty-Eight

I got home at 1 a.m., my ears buzzing from the loud music that had played in Dinos. I was beat, and my feet hurt from having danced with Fernanda until she'd found herself a man to swap me with. Then I'd sat at the bar beside Phillip and discussed law. My evening ended with an internship offer at his firm and a new contact in my phone. Even though I made no promises to call, he seemed satisfied enough that I'd taken his number.

I left at the same time as Fernanda and her suitor. Before parting ways, she put her unlocked phone in my hands. "As promised."

"I'm not sure what I'm looking at . . ."

She rolled her eyes. "My photo stream. He's gone."

I scrolled through pages and pages of selfies. There wasn't a single picture of her most recent target. "You kept your word." I returned the phone to its rightful owner.

"I did." She smiled, then turned toward her newest squeeze, who was waiting for her beside a stopped taxi. She started to walk away but spun back. "The guy who showed up earlier, all angry and uptight. What's his deal?"

She had a man waiting for her but was inquiring about another? "He has a kid, Fernanda."

"I wasn't asking for me. I was curious about the nature of *your* relationship with him."

I frowned. "He's my boss."

She hoisted the chains of her Chanel bag up. "Is he possessive of all his employees like he is of you?"

"Possessive? He's not possessive. He just takes his job *extremely* seriously."

She grinned. "And here I thought you were the astute one." She blew me a kiss. "Call me if you ever want to do dinner again. This was fun." She folded herself gracefully into the cab, and then her suitor squeezed in beside her and clapped the cab door shut.

I watched the taillights fade before setting off for home by foot. I was still trying to make sense of her parting words—about me being astute—when I walked through my dimly-lit living room and came to a dead-stop at the sight of someone standing at the railing of my terrace. A very tall, very winged someone. Whitewashed in moonlight, Asher looked like one of those angels on the covers of paranormal romances. Although most depicted us inaccurately, a few were surprisingly close to the truth, to the point where I suspected the author's awareness of our existence.

I unlocked my balcony door. "Did you come to congratulate me or tell me about my next sinner?"

Asher pivoted slowly, the tips of his taut wings catching the moonlight and tossing it into my face. "Congratulate you?"

"For a job well done. She deleted all her blackmail material and went home with a *single* man."

"Phillip?"

"No. Another man."

"What about Phillip?"

I clutched my elbows, shielding my bare midriff from the nippy air. "What about him, Seraph?"

His gaze darted past me, as though he was expecting to find I hadn't come back to the apartment alone.

"Is that why you're standing on my terrace at one o'clock in the morning? To check whether I brought a guy home?"

A gust of wind caught in his feathers and in his hair, blowing both sideways. He pushed the loose locks out of his stony eyes. "You don't need distractions."

"With all due respect, Seraph, you may be into celibacy, but I'm not. I didn't bring anyone home tonight, but I'm not going two-and-a-half months without sex." I started to turn when I decided to add, "FYI, sex does the mind and soul good."

"You have your entire life to copulate."

A corner of my mouth turned up. "Is that how they referred to it back in Austria in the nineteen hundreds?"

He scowled. "Let's stop wasting time on that subject and concentrate on what is of actual importance: your wings, Celeste."

"Great idea. Why don't you go back to the guild and look up my score?"

"Why return to the guild when the wing-bearer is right here?"

"I'm not bringing them out, if that's what you're hinting at."

He sighed. "Why must you be so stubborn? They're just wings. Wings you should be proud of."

"They're not just wings. Not to me."

"Celeste . . ." Frustration thickened the intonation of my name. "Go into your bedroom and close the door, and then fucking save me a trip and conjure them up."

"No."

He tipped his head down and shot me the archangel of all glares.

"What's with the pissy mood, Seraph?"

"We're not here to discuss my mood. We're here to discuss your wings."

"I'm not discussing my wings with a man who looks just about ready to raze an entire city block. Now, either you tell me what I did wrong—since I imagine you're mad at me—or you go cool off with a little sky stroll, and when you feel nicer, you can come back, and we can discuss my mission. Preferably after I get a full night's sleep."

For seconds that stretched into a full minute, he didn't respond, just tipped his gaze to the darkened sky as though imploring it to lend him patience.

When he squeezed his forehead, I took pity on him. Clearly, something other than mulishness was ticking him off. "Mimi used to make me chamomile tea with honey when I was troubled. Would you like a cup?"

He leveled his attention back on me, then magicked away his wings, which I took as a *yes*, and trailed me into the kitchen. After setting the kettle to boil, I dug out a tin box filled with dried yellow blossoms.

As I spooned them into the strainer, Asher took a seat at the island. "I'll have someone come fix your counter tomorrow."

I drew open a cupboard and grabbed two mugs, and then pushed up on tiptoe to reach the shelf with the condiments and honey pots. When I turned around to carry it all to the island, I caught Asher watching me.

The kettle hissed and clicked.

I filled the teapot, my throat clenching as the familiar aroma lifted and perfumed the air. How long would Mimi's absence hurt? Until I was sure I would see her again?

I swallowed. "Did she find Pierre?"

"She?"

"Muriel. Pierre was her great love." I crooked the teapot over the two mugs, then added a heaping spoonful of honey to both and mixed, driving the sweet steam upward. "She told me about him the night"—my throat tightened again—"she passed." I slid him his mug, staring at the rippling surface.

"Pierre died over two decades ago. Although he lived in Elysium for a few years, his score wasn't good enough to remain there forever, so his soul was returned to Earth. To a new form."

My heart missed a few beats. If Pierre's soul had been reincarnated, then the memories of his life with Mimi had been erased. Even if he died with a sinner score below ten this time, which would grant him access to Elysium forever, his soul wouldn't recognize Mimi's.

"I can sense your disapproval."

"Disappointment, not disapproval. She loved him very much."

"Then, one day, their souls will find a way back to each other."

"Careful, Seraph, I might label you a romantic." I smiled at him over the lip of my mug, and he smiled back. "Tell me, how would they find their way to each other? It's not like he would remember her."

"If they were soulmates, or soulhalves, his soul will remember hers in whichever form they meet."

"Really? I thought all memories were removed before the malakim returned souls to Earth."

"All are scraped away. Souls need to begin anew without being encumbered by previous lives, but fragments of beloved places and cherished people linger." His words lifted steam off the surface of his mug, which he'd raised to his mouth. "Look at Naya." His eyes slid to mine.

Like the billowing, honeyed mist, my moroseness dissipated,

flavoring the air with newborn hope. "Back to the reason for our tea party. Why'd you bite my head off earlier?"

He placed the mug down gently, then curved his long fingers around it. "I'd much rather discuss reincarnations and soulhalves."

I grinned. "Although I'd *adore* hearing your opinion on soulhalves, I'm not letting you off the hook for hopping on my terrace and shrieking at me."

"I don't shriek." Although his timbre was deep, his tone was light.

"That's right . . . you roar."

His lips shaped a smile that seemed to reach his very soul and drag it out of his fine leather boots. "And it cows everyone but you."

"Not much intimidates me, Seraph."

His bright eyes held mine over the steam. "I'm starting to understand that."

"So . . . why'd you roar?"

He shifted on his seat, and the chair legs creaked from his weight. "Remember how I told you that I'd made not one, but two mistakes four and a half years ago?"

My good humor faded. "Don't call them mistakes."

"I'm not saying that what I did was a mistake; the mistake was *how* I went about doing it. I should've planned better. Timed Adam's arrival into the male guild differently." He rubbed his jaw, his fingers scraping against his afternoon-shadow, which had grown into a midnight-one. "The fact that two new fletchings were registered within minutes of each other up in Elysium raised eyebrows, but since Adam was a baby and had angel-blood, the Seven let it slide." His hand dropped heavily from his face. "Apparently, though, Seraph Claire hasn't let it slide. She keeps pestering Tobias to come forth with the mother's identity. He's stalling, trying to figure out a solution."

No wonder the archangel had been in a crap mood.

"I should never have involved him in my mess." He took a deep breath, then let it out.

I, on the other hand, had stopped breathing. I wasn't sure how long my lungs remained empty, but when I filled them again, the oxygen burned. If the children were discovered . . . Adam would lead to Naya . . . I couldn't lose her again.

I walked over to Asher and circled my arms around his neck, then propped my chin atop his bowed head. "If you sense she might *hurt* them, bring the children to me. I'll find a way to hide them."

His shoulders rolled beneath my taut forearms. "There is no hiding from angels. There is no running from them either. Besides, do you really think I'd let you bear the burden of my crime?"

I pulled away to look down at the troubled man sitting at my kitchen island. "If you're a criminal, Seraph, then I am a saint, and since we both know I sin like I breathe, I can assure you that you are very much *not* a criminal."

He grunted. "Not in my people's eyes."

"I haven't met Tobias, but if he helped you, then he believes that what you did was just. As for the others, you don't know what they think of you. All you know is what Seraph Claire thinks, and we all know she's a—" The descriptor I was about to use was replaced by a shallow intake of air.

Asher followed my feather's tumble.

"Worth it."

He leaned back in the chair, the short backrest groaning. "I'm certain it was, but I'd much prefer if you tried to preserve your wings, because I'd like an ally *up there*, Celeste." He pointed at my ceiling.

I slid into the chair next to him, dragging my mug toward me. "Then line up my next sinner."

"You're that certain you've reformed Fernanda?"

"I'm *that* certain. And for my next mission, pick a high roller."

"Not unless I come upon another Bofinger. Sinners with high scores are dangerous."

"I have wing bones."

"Wing bones might keep you alive, but they won't keep you safe."

I tapped his bicep, which hardened under my fingertips. "I have you for that." Then I flexed my own biceps, which bulged . . . slightly. "I may look harmless, but I can cause my fair share of harm."

"Undoubtedly, but the harm you'd cause wouldn't be with your arms; it would be with your sharp tongue."

His gaze landed on the seam of my lips, which made my tired body wake right up as though my herbal tea had been laced with Red Bull. I leaned infinitesimally closer to him. A wasp seduced by fire. My body warmed and my limbs began to fizz as though my very veins had been packed with Pop Rocks. He had to be putting out some form of angelic pheromones because never had I been so attracted to a man before.

Seriously, even the turquoise depths of his eyes seemed more mesmerizing, flecked in glitter. "Celeste . . ."

My name was thick on his tongue, intensifying the thrumming in my veins.

He swallowed, and in the breadth of a single second, his stare blackened as though his pupils had been pricked. "Don't."

"Don't what?"

"Don't confuse our relationship."

I snapped out of my daze. "Excuse me?"

"Look at your skin."

And so I did, and cold horror replaced wanting heat. *No no no.* Out of all the men out there, why did I have to be smoldering a man who could actually *see* my skin glow? Why couldn't I have smoldered Jase? I lurched to my feet while the archangel glared at my broken countertop, disgust contorting his mouth.

I was by no means stunning, and sure, I wasn't a verity, but I wasn't revolting. "This happens *all* the time. You're nothing special, Seraph."

My invisible wing bones strummed, and a feather collapsed. Damn lie detectors.

His gaze lowered to the floor in time with the purple down.

I turned away before he could knead my flailing ego any more. People's opinions usually rolled off of me. Apparently, one person's didn't.

Why? Why him? Was I experiencing some sort of Stockholm Syndrome? Not that he'd kidnapped me, but we did spend an inordinate amount of time in each other's company. That was probably the crux of it. I couldn't wait for operation *save-winglets* to be over.

Successful or not.

Just to be rid of this frigid, overly-masculine being.

Chapter Twenty-Nine

I woke up to knocking. I groaned and stuck a pillow over my head.

"Go away," I muttered.

Two more loud raps. "Rise and shine, Fletching."

I sat up, fully awake now. Running a hand through my tangled locks, I strode across my room and drew the door open. The other side was empty air. Had I dreamt up the snarky feminine voice?

The knocking started up again—knuckles against glass. I turned around and yanked on my drapes.

Blonde corkscrews blowing around her knife-thin face, Ish Eliza hovered outside my window, lavender wings spread wide. "Ah. Finally. The fletching awakens. Meet me on the balcony."

The desire to close my curtains and burrow back under my rumpled comforter now that I knew no one was in my apartment was strong, yet I walked out and unlocked the glass door.

"Ish Eliza," I muttered, "to what do I owe the pleasure of your *oh-so-agreeable* wake-up call?"

"Seraph Asher was otherwise engaged and sent me over to inform you that you were unsuccessful in your mission."

Shock momentarily trumped my annoyance. "Unsuccessful?" Hadn't Fernanda deleted all the pictures? Did she have them backed up and needed to erase those so I'd get my feathers? Or had she woken up this morning and decided to return to her wicked ways?

"You failed."

"I'm well aware of the meaning of unsuccessful." I wanted to snarl but kept myself in check. "Why didn't the seraphim deliver this news himself?"

"Perhaps, he didn't feel like babysitting you today."

Could she *be* any pettier? "What's your problem with me, Ish?"

"My problem is that you're wasting our archangel's precious time. The Seven are elected to better the worlds, not help undeserving fletchings fix their mistakes."

I gritted my teeth. "First off, I never asked for our dear archangel's help—he willingly gave it to me—and secondly, my resolve to stop earning feathers was *not* a mistake—it was an informed decision."

She squared her shoulders and crossed her arms, straining her snug gray uniform. "Look, however fun this chitchat is, I have places to be. If you don't care to help Fernanda become a better person, then Seraph Asher suggested you take on your doorman, Stanley."

"My doorman?"

"Did I speak in Angelic?"

Instead of sinking to her level, I chose the quickest method to get her out of my house—congeniality. "What exactly is Stanley guilty of?"

"He's afflicted with a severe case of kleptomania. Have you ever had packages go missing?" Her gaze scanned my sprawling apartment. "You probably wouldn't have noticed . . ."

"Because I have so many useless, earthly possessions?"

Her lips arched harshly. "Did I say that?"

"No, but you were thinking it loudly."

"If I was you, I'd spend less time wondering what ishim are thinking and more time wondering how to help fluff up your little hybrid wings."

Oh . . . she did not just go there. "Get. Off. My. Terrace. And tell Asher—"

"Seraph Asher."

"—that if he *ever* sends you over to relay his messages, I'll stop trying to ascend."

"What a shame that would be."

I gripped the side of the door, picturing shoving her sparkling wings inside the space and flinging the door closed until I'd bruised every rachis. A feather drifted to the ground.

"Your mind is a vile place, Fletching. Dark as Abaddon."

I shot her a close-lipped smile and began to shut the door, squeezing the metal frame so hard the bands of my rings grooved my flesh.

"Oh, before I forget, you'll have to stop by the guild for your next sinner and use a holo-ranker yourself. You recall how they work, right?"

I shut the door in her hostile face and then I phoned up Fernanda.

Her sleepy voice crackled through the receiver after a few ringtones. "Celeste? Why are you calling so early?"

"You didn't erase the pictures," I snapped.

A beat of silence, then the rustle of sheets. "Excuse me?"

"Your blackmail pictures. You said you'd erased them, but you didn't."

"I did erase them." Her tone had become as chafing as my own.

I closed my eyes, her sinner score floating in and out of focus behind my lids.

"But now, I regret it."

My eyes popped open.

"I regret having taken advice from someone so ... *unstable*."

Remorse swamped me. I shouldn't have taken my aggression out on her. It wasn't fair that I'd expected her to change overnight. Not everyone was a Bofinger.

I thrust my hand through my pillow-mussed hair. "Fernanda, I'm sorry."

"If we'd been friends, I would've cared. I might even have asked why you're being such a bitch about this, but I don't care. My offer to grab dinner? Forget about it."

Before I could attempt damage control, she ended the phone call. I sank onto the couch, dropped my face into my hands, and rued my over-inflated confidence for allowing me to dream the road to Elysium would be without potholes.

I LEFT FOR THE GUILD A FEW HOURS LATER ON FOOT. I thought fresh air and exercise would help burn off my stress, but if anything, my walk gave me time to reflect on how I'd handled Fernanda.

Poorly. Childishly. Abrasively.

I almost turned around and went home. Almost gave up, but that would make me a quitter, and I was no quitter. Sure, my self-assurance had taken a hit, but I'd build it back up. I still had time.

When I entered the atrium, my footsteps faltered.

"What a fortunate coincidence." Eliza plucked a rolled slip of paper from her braided silver belt and extended it toward me. "I was just at the Shanghai guild with Seraph Asher, and he asked me to deliver this sinner list. He said these should last you two weeks. They're all *easy* missions. Like Bofinger."

Like Bofinger? If I remembered correctly, she'd thought he wouldn't change as swiftly as he had.

"Do not disparage my fletching's accomplishment." Ophan Mira's red wings were pulled in tight along her spine, barely poking out from behind her even tighter shoulders. "No sinner is simple and no sin inconsequential. Humans are complex, even the lowest scorers."

I blinked at Mira. I couldn't remember a single instance my ancient professor had stood up for me, and yet here she was, standing up for me.

The verity stretched out her wings. When male angels did it, it was seen as courting. When females of our kind did it, it was a show of dominance. "You forget I was once a fletching, Ophan."

"I forget nothing, Eliza."

"*Ish* Eliza."

"Pardon me, Ish. Back in my day, we didn't precede given names by titles. We were angels first, arrogant second."

Whoa. Whoa. And whoa.

Antipathy rolled off the ishim's glittery plumage, potent as the smell of honeysuckle adrift in the atrium. "I will have a word of your insolence with the Seven."

Mira said nothing.

"Once you're done, Fletching"—Eliza shoved her damned list into my chest—"inform Ophan Mira, and I'll return with a new list."

"I told you this morning that if Seraph Asher sent *you* to me again, I was done." I ripped up the sheet of vellum.

Ish Eliza's eyes held a triumphant gleam as though she'd just won some competition. I didn't think the archangel liked Eliza all that much, but since he'd decided to act like a petulant cherub, ghosting me because I'd dared smolder him, I supposed he didn't like *me* all that much either.

"What a shame." Smiling, Eliza walked away, her feathers swaying in time with her backside.

Mira's stern eyes were fixed to the strips littering the atrium floor. "Why did you destroy the archangel's list?"

Instead of answering, I asked, "Could the ishim really get you in trouble for standing up for us hybrids, Ophan?"

"I was standing up for my *fletchings*—hybrids *and* verities. The shine of wings has never meant a thing to me. Not in the past and not now. All I can hope for is that, one day, it will stop mattering altogether."

In silence, we studied each other.

I wasn't sure what she saw when she looked at me, but what I saw in her was a supporter instead of a detractor. "For that to happen, a hybrid would need to become archangel."

"I agree, Celeste, and I believe it's time."

Who was this woman and what had she done with my crabby, rule-abiding professor?

She finally let out a puffed exhale that loosened the tension cramping her body. "At least, we have a champion—Seraph Asher."

A sparrow swooped around our heads, spilling its aria into our ears.

I followed its ascent toward the fake cerulean sky. "What makes you so fond of him?"

Something flashed over Mira's face, something that made goosebumps scamper over my skin.

She *knew*.

She knew about Naya . . .

She'd recognized Leigh's soul.

Mira broke the silence with a question. "What makes you so intolerant of him?"

Even though I wished she'd let it go, I felt like I owed her for barking at the ranker. "I thought he was my friend; I thought wrong."

She gestured to the shredded list surrounding my boots. "The paper at your feet tells a different story than the one you tell yourself."

"He's not doing it for me."

She cocked an eyebrow. "Whom is he doing it for then?"

"He's doing it for the woman whose soul he collected a few weeks ago. The woman I tried to save from cancer." Saying it out loud made my ego throb like a stubbed toe.

Ugh. Why did his reason for helping me matter? Why did his reaction to my smoldering matter? I was beginning to think his absence might be a good thing. Definitely a necessary one.

"You asked why I was so fond of him." She gestured to the list. "I find his desire to succor souls commendable."

My heartbeats clanged. Was she talking about mine or Naya's? And if she was talking about Naya's, did it mean she agreed with his law-breaking?

"Some people touted that what he'd done in Abaddon was a fluke with a nice ending, but the present confirms what I've always thought . . . that it was no fluke, but an act of great heroism."

"The golden boy of Elysium," I mused out loud.

She scrutinized my expression as though trying to spot whether I'd spoken the nickname in mockery. "He is more man than boy, but he does possess a golden soul."

"What is it he did in Abaddon?"

"He saved Elysium from being contaminated by Abaddon's foul magic."

"How?"

"Why don't you ask him?"

"I would, but didn't you hear the part where he's avoiding me?" For someone so heroic, the golden boy-man was exceptionally cowardly. Not only had he broken his promise to help me, but he'd done so by way of a wing-nosing ishim . . .

"I heard, which does make me wonder what you've done."

"Oh, you know me. Something quite terrible." I rubbed the side of my index finger, the pad of my thumb bumping into my two stacked rings.

"I do know you, Celeste, and for all your defiance and snark, you don't have a terrible bone in your body."

My twitching fingers steadied at her compliment.

"He'll find his way back to you. Somehow, he always does. The same way you found your way back to . . . us."

Naya. She meant Naya.

"I have a class to teach." She turned. "Please pick up your mess before leaving."

"Could you not just incinerate it?"

"No."

Sighing, I crouched and scooped up the strips of paper, then shoved them inside my pocket. "Can I borrow Naya from her classes?"

She looked over her shoulder at me. "Would refusing stop you?"

"No."

Her cheeks softened with a smile that barely bowed her lips. "She's in art class, if I'm not mistaken, attempting to learn to paint purple feathers. Imagine that? Purple . . ."

I grinned. Not because Naya was apparently thinking of me—although that warmed me from the inside out—but because Asher had another ally. My first instinct was to message him, but I didn't have his number.

I returned to my task of confetti collection, catching Stanley's name on one of the strips. I tried to forget it, but of course, it was the name I ended up sketching on my holo-ranker after a half-hour of fruitless browsing.

I'd complained Asher was childish, but didn't destroying the list make me even more so?

Chapter Thirty

After I left the Ranking Room, I found Naya standing at an easel, dabbing purple paint onto a canvas. Her blonde mane swung and shimmered as she inspected her painting, adding more blue to her purple, swiping more curved strokes.

I watched her a short while before walking over. "Nice painting."

She twirled, and then her brown eyes grew large and she swung her arms around me. "Celeste!"

"Hey, Little Feather."

"Little Feather?"

Ice. My blood became ice. Why on Earth had I used the nickname I'd heard Jarod call Leigh?

"That name hurts my heart." Naya untangled herself from my arms.

"Sorry, I . . . I didn't mean to hurt your heart."

"Why?"

"Why what?"

"Why does it hurt?"

I longed to pretend I didn't know, but it would've been a lie, and I was trying to preserve feathers. Plus, I didn't want to lie to her. I smoothed my ponytail over the Eagles logo on my T-shirt, trying to think up something that made sense.

"What does your top say?" Her paint-smudged fingers tugged at the collar of my bomber.

I blanched, because the T-shirt had once belonged to Leigh, a gift from one of her sinners. I hadn't saved much from her closet, our body types were so different, but that shirt had traveled with me from Paris to New York. Had Naya recognized it like she'd recognized the nickname?

I cleared my throat. "The Eagles." I raised her index finger to the E, then slid it across the remaining letters, sounding each one. "They're a rock band."

"Are they your favorite?"

"No."

"Then why do you have their shirt?"

"Because . . . because it belonged to my best friend." My gaze raked across Naya's face, which looked nothing like Leigh's and yet encompassed all of its sweetness.

"And she didn't want it anymore?"

She doesn't remember it . . .

"I'm just borrowing it until it fits her again." Before she could ask why it no longer fit my friend, I pointed to the canvas. "So, tell me why you're painting a purple feather."

She whirled back toward her easel, blonde locks spinning like rotor blades. "It was a surprise. For you."

I brushed a curled tendril off her cheek. "For me? That's so—thank you, Naya," I whispered thickly.

"You can call me Little Feather if you want."

My hand stilled before falling away from her velvety skin. "I, uh . . ." If Asher heard me use that nickname, he'd smoke me with his angel-fire.

Unless he wasn't aware of how Jarod had called Leigh . . .

She shrugged a shoulder. "You can call me what you want. Except Worm."

I balked. "Why in the world would I call you Worm?"

"I don't know why I said that." She pulled her lower lip into her mouth.

A part of me suspected someone had called her that in her past life. Probably Tristan. He was evil-incarnate. If Jarod hadn't already killed him, I would've taken great pleasure in ridding the world of his soul.

"Would you mind if I painted next to you?"

Her lip popped free. "I want you to stay."

Smiling, I dragged an easel toward me, adjusted its height, then asked if I could borrow some of her paint. She'd preempted me by handing over a few squashed tubes and a brush.

As she went back to work on the purple feather, I studied her profile and traced it. I hadn't drawn anything in ages, but as I flicked my wrist and guided the brush across the canvas, I was reminded of how much I'd enjoyed creating art.

"Is that me?" she asked after a long while.

I nodded.

"You made my hair so pretty."

"I only painted what was there."

"And look at my eye. It's so big."

"You're mostly all eyes at the moment."

She gazed at her likeness. "I'm happy my hair isn't orange."

My pulse stuttered, and my gaze flicked to Ophan Pippa, who was explaining composition to another one of her young pupils.

Quietly, I said, "Orange hair is beautiful too. Every color hair is beautiful."

"But Apa has golden hair like me. And he's the handsomest man in all the worlds."

I smiled. "And you're the prettiest girl I know."

"No. You are."

My heartbeat slowed as I remembered a time when Leigh would tell me this. Back then, I was awkward, freckled and dimpled, and like Naya, all eyes. Not that I'd outgrown my eyes. I'd just grown alongside them. As for my freckles and dimples, they were all still there.

I added a stroke of peach along her likeness's neck. "Will you put this painting in your room?"

"I want you to keep it. So you don't forget me."

"Forget you? Oh, sweetie, there's no way I could ever forget you." I laid down my paintbrush and tapped two fingers to my chest. "You and I, we're soul sisters."

"Soul sisters." Her eyes sparkled. "You think our souls are sisters?"

"I know it." I crouched to her height and stamped a kiss on her cheek. "I have to go now, Naya. Your daddy left me a long list of people to help." Sometime during my meditative art session, I'd decided to grow the heck up and tape his list together when I got home.

"But you'll come back?"

"I will."

"Okay, then. You can go."

I smiled as I straightened.

"Your feather!" she cried out.

"How about you give it to me tomorrow, once it's dry?"

"Okay."

As I exited the art room, I watched Naya study her portrait. I probably should've looked at where I was going instead. Would've saved me a head-on collision into what felt like drywall but was in fact an archangel torso.

"You have paint on your cheek."

I raised a hand to my face and scrubbed.

"Allow me." Asher hovered a fiery palm over my skin.

Heat danced across the lower part of my face and then spread to places he wasn't touching.

He shifted his palm to the stained collar of my jacket. "Don't quit."

"I'm not."

"Ish Eliza informed me that you ripped my list."

"I did."

His brow furrowed. "Why?"

I canted my head to the side. "Because I was angry with you."

He curled his fingers into his palm, extinguishing the flames. "I'm sorry for reacting the way I did."

"Don't be. I think not spending time together is wise." I sidestepped him. "But please leave your next list with Ophan Mira instead of your favorite ranker."

I stalked out of the guild, a silly part of me hoping he'd follow, if only to yell that Eliza wasn't his favorite anything, but he didn't go after me because it was Naya he'd come to see.

Not me.

Chapter Thirty-One

By the end of that week, I'd gone through more than half of Asher's list, earning myself a total of one hundred and twenty-two more feathers, bringing my wing density to five-hundred-and-two. I barely slept, barely took breaks to feed myself. I strung my missions together, bouncing from sinner to sinner as soon as my holo-ranker displayed an increased amount of feathers on my profile. It wasn't a rhythm I could keep up, so I decided that the next person I'd help would be a higher scorer.

Higher than anyone on Asher's list. I thought of that Triple lady I'd seen the one time Asher and I had gone to the Ranking Room together, but then remembered his reaction to her, and although curious, I decided I didn't want to deal with a Triple. At least, not after the exhausting week I'd had.

I also decided I deserved a night off. And maybe even a full day. It was the weekend after all. Even angels were allowed to rest.

Because Jase hadn't called or messaged me since he'd left my place last Saturday, I decided I'd go find him at The Trap. I missed my friend, sinner and all. Many times I'd been tempted to sketch his name on my holo-ranker to find out his dark and dirty secret, but each time, I'd tucked my hands into my lap and resisted.

As I zipped up my artfully-ripped black jeans, his score twirled behind my kohl-lined lids—41.

And then it materialized again as I waited for my Uber next to Stanley.

"It's funny. I've been getting a lot of mail lately. You wouldn't happen to know who's been sending it, Miss Moreau?"

I kept my eyes on the steady ebb of Saturday night traffic. "Everyone deserves to receive a little care mail."

I'd ordered a few things in his name and had had them shipped to the Plaza. I wasn't sure how professional it would appear to his colleagues to receive packages at his workplace, but I hadn't truly cared. What I had cared about was that he saw his name on a shipping label for once, that the boxes he took home belonged to him.

Stanley's sin was . . . *had been* . . . kleptomania. Almost every week, he'd lift a package from the mailroom. A package he wouldn't even open, simply hoard in his basement. Eventually, he returned them to their rightful owners, which won him sighs of relief, smiles, and sometimes even tips.

The gratitude was what fueled his thievery. He'd grown up in a household where neither parent had ever expressed the faintest affection for him or for each other. As he'd described his childhood, I'd counted my blessings that I'd had Leigh and then Mimi. For all the pain love brought, the absence of it really screwed people up.

"Muriel always said you were an angel." His eyes were as slick as the midnight-blue sedan pulling up to the curb.

Hearing her name and what she'd thought of me was a poker to the heart, the pain fiery and sharp. Physically, I was an angel; but in every other way, I'd drifted so far from my race.

His throat bobbed as he got the car door for me. "Your packages. They're the kindest thing anyone's ever done for me."

I touched the sleeve of his jacket, squeezed the meaty arm underneath, and then slid into the backseat of my ride.

As the car jetted East, I said, "Actually, can you take Fifth? I need to head downtown first." I added the address of the guild as a way-point on the app, then sat back and convinced myself that what I was about to do was virtuous.

I had to give myself a long-winded pep talk before, propped on a stool in the Ranking Room, I managed to sketch Jase's name on the glass panel of my holo-ranker.

His face appeared in 3D, exactly the way I knew him to look, with a scrim of dark beard, slicked-back hair, and soft brown eyes. I rubbed my moist palms over my jeans as I read and reread his single crime: *identity theft.* Here I'd expected horrible things. Although identity theft was far from good, he hadn't assaulted anyone.

Out of curiosity, I sketched his brother's name. Unlike Jase, his score was 63. Like Jase, his crime was identity theft. But that wasn't his only one. His rap sheet was long and included larceny, illegal gambling, and arson.

I'd never thought Leon was saintly, but neither had I imagined him to be so *villainous.* Wasn't he afraid of returning to jail? Wasn't Jase afraid of *going* to jail? I traced my friend's name again, wishing I hadn't snooped, wishing Asher had never told me about his score, wishing I could go back to the way things had been. But was that even a possibility? So much had changed in my life in the past weeks.

I contemplated Jase's face a long time, debating whether to sign on to him. Ethically, it felt wrong, but sentimentally, it felt right. If I could help strangers, then I could surely help my best friend. Besides, Asher himself had suggested I reform my friend.

Before I could chicken out, I pressed my palm against the glass panel, and my name appeared over the hologram. Then I powered down the system and got up.

On my way out of the guild, I heard Naya's sweet voice drift from the cafeteria. Even though my ride was still waiting at the curb, I decided it could loiter another minute. However much time I spent with Naya, it never felt like enough.

When I reached the entrance of the cafeteria, I came to a dead-stop. She wasn't alone.

My eyes met Asher's over the top of her golden curls, which he was smoothing, his palm as large as her entire head. She had an arm curled around his neck and a smile on her lips from whichever tale he was telling her. Other children had congregated around them to listen, all of them enraptured.

My past jealousy returned.

It's not a competition. And yet I was jealous of the history they shared. Jealous of the love they had.

Before she could spot me, I spun and left.

ALTHOUGH TRAFFIC WAS HEAVY, THE FORTY-FIVE-MINUTE trip up to Harlem helped me decompress. When I reached The Trap, Leon was standing outside, taking long drags on a cigarette in the company of two college-aged girls.

"Hey," I said, as I approached him.

His eyes moved to me, devoid of their usual warmth. Instead, they were tinged with wariness.

"Is Jase working tonight?"

He blew a stream of pale smoke right into the faces of the girls, before pulling the heavy metal door open and waving them into his underground lair. "He is."

"He's been avoiding my calls."

Slowly, he nodded. "I was guessing he was in a mood because of you." He puffed on his cigarette, blew the smoke sideways since he knew my distaste for a faceful of nicotine. "What happened?"

"We got in a fight. Sort of."

Leon's eyebrows dipped toward his crooked nose. "He wanted you to commit or some shit, and you didn't?"

I frowned. "No. Why would you think that?"

"Baby bro's got it bad for you, Celeste."

My lashes lifted so high, they skimmed my browbone. "I wasn't . . . aware."

He stared at me, one thick eyebrow raised as though he didn't quite believe me.

"He's my best friend, Leon, and yeah, I love him, but I'm not on the market for a relationship. I never led him to think otherwise."

He sighed, then coughed. "Might want to tell him that."

"I will. Tonight."

He nodded, coughed some more, then flicked the glowing butt of his cigarette into the street. "It's a loud and rowdy crowd tonight." His number and list of sins flashed behind my lids, overlaying on his life-beaten face. "Good for business."

I wondered which business he was referring to, the bar's or the brothers' side business?

When his hacking cough started again, he pounded one fist against his chest.

"Want me to get you a glass of water?"

He smiled. "Nah. It'll pass. Besides, I got a beer." He raised the bottle and took a swig.

I didn't insist that water would probably be better as I slid past him and into the loud space.

He hadn't been kidding when he said it was a big crowd. I wasn't sure I'd ever seen The Trap so jampacked. Actually, I had. After midterms and finals. You could barely move around on those nights.

A Lynyrd Skynyrd song thumped atop the chatter, creating a cacophony that made my tired brain pound, but then all the sounds faded when I saw Jase and he saw me. Blood rushed around my eardrums as what I was about to attempt set in.

I almost retraced my steps, but the pain that flashed across his face egged my feet on. As I carved my way toward the bar, he turned toward a thirsty customer, then another and another, avoiding me.

"Heard you've been moody," I said when he was within hearing range.

The line of his shoulders sharpened even though he kept his back to me.

"Talk to me, Jase."

He finally turned, slapping the dishrag he'd been using to dry his hands over his shoulder. "Got nothing to say."

"Oh, I'm sure you have plenty to say."

His pupils pulsed with a cocktail of annoyance, anger, and hurt.

"I've missed you."

He stayed silent, which was crushing because Jase wasn't the strong silent type. That was more Asher's MO.

"In case you didn't realize that from the thousands of messages I sent you. And the handful of voicemails."

After a mile of silence, he asked, "Where's Abercrombie?"

I shrugged. "Probably with his daughter."

He blinked. "He's got a daughter?"

"Yep."

"And a wife?"

"No. Just a fanclub of glittery females."

"Glittery?"

I bit my lip at that slipup. It wasn't my worst one yet. "You know . . . the preened type. Lots of jewelry."

His gaze dropped to my hands and my assortment of rings.

I dragged my fingers into my palms. "Jase, he and I aren't together. Never have been and never will be. But I'm not here to talk about him. I'm here to talk about you. About us."

His brown eyes vacillated between gentle and hard. "I don't feel like talking about me, and clearly, there is no us."

"Are you sure that's clear?"

"It is now."

"Jase . . ."

He raised a hand. "Please, Cee. It's all good." His unsmiling face told me it wasn't, but at least, he'd used my nickname.

Someone tried to get his attention. He looked around, probably to see if Alicia could get the customer, but she was delivering a platter of glistening chicken wings to one of the booths, her body contorting like a gymnast's as she wended through the throng.

"Want some help? I make a mean vodka on the rocks, and I'm quite the pro at uncapping beers if I do say so myself."

He smiled. This time, for real. "Nah. I got this." He started to turn but stopped.

"Not going anywhere." I placed my elbows on the bar and got comfortable. "If you don't mind me occupying this stool until closing time, that is."

"I don't mind."

"Good."

"Good," he repeated, before heading to the thirsty dude with the raised arm.

Although he spent the next few hours taking orders, ringing up customers, pocketing tips, and scrubbing the bar-top clean, his gaze would flick to me every few minutes. At some point, he set a tall, sweaty cocktail in front of me. I hadn't touched alcohol for a week, but sensing it was an olive branch, I accepted the drink and took a tentative sip, and then another, settling in to crowd-watch while he worked. Every so often something else would show up in front of me: a small basket of fried zucchini, a glass of water, a ramequin of homemade chocolate ice-cream, a fresh drink even though I wasn't done with my first.

When the crowd finally thinned, Jase sidled up to my side of the bar. "Spotted any miscreants tonight, Cee?"

I'd spotted a few wandering hands, but nothing the receivers of those unwanted touches couldn't handle. In truth, though, I'd been too deep in my head to pay the room any real attention. My mind had been on Jase, on how I should go about reforming him, and whether it was a terrible idea or not.

I'd finally decided that even if it cost me my friendship, getting him to walk a better path, and thus, saving him from his brother's fate, would be worth the price.

Shifting on my stool, I said, "Nothing that necessitated an intervention."

He grabbed the bowl I'd scraped clean and added it to a tray chockfull of dirty dishes, which he carried into the kitchen. While he was gone, a thought struck me. Or rather a reel of memories. Me handing over driver's licenses, and Jase snapping pictures of them.

Had I unknowingly supplemented his identity theft business?

Oh, Jase . . . please tell me you didn't use me.

The door flapped open, and he strode back out, his gait easygoing like his personality. Like his smile. He was so smart, so hardworking that I couldn't imagine he'd fallen into this willingly. Leon must've dragged him over the line of right and wrong.

I twirled my straw slowly, hoping that any good I'd do, Leon wouldn't undo once I was gone.

If only new angels didn't have a century-long travel ban . . .

There were so many laws that needed amending up there. Ophan Mira had such confidence in Asher, but he was only one man. Could one man change an entire world?

And why was I thinking of the archangel again?

Oh right . . . . Because I had a ridiculous, unreciprocated crush on the man.

I downed my drink, then shoved the blond out of my mind and concentrated on the dark-haired man before me.

Chapter Thirty-Two

We got home late, and even though a part of me was tempted to delay my confrontation, I sensed I wouldn't be able to sleep until we'd talked.

I pulled off my bomber jacket and hooked it to one of the pegs by the door, the silver wings stitched into the back collapsing into shimmery creases. Chewing the life out of my lip, I mulled over how to begin. I turned, deciding to just nip it in the bud, but found myself backed up against the wall with a hot mouth covering mine, muffling the words I'd been about to articulate.

I grabbed handfuls of Jase's black T-shirt and held him back. "Jase, slow down. I need to—"

"I got it this time, Cee. I promise. Not a fucking string attached." His mouth arced back toward mine.

I swiveled my neck, and his lips collided into my cheek. "I need to talk to you before we do anything."

My body usually revved up fast at the slide of Jase's tongue, but my fizzing nerves transformed my lust into dread. He was *not* going to want to kiss me after our talk. *Or* hug me.

His eyebrows slanted over his darkening eyes, before jolting upward. "You're not pregnant, are you?"

"Pregnant? No." Out of all the conclusions to be had . . .

He scrubbed a hand across his forehead. "Thank God."

God had nothing to do with that; humans, with their contraceptives, did.

"Unlike Abercrombie, I have no desire to be a daddy."

I didn't retort that fatherhood hadn't been Asher's desire either. At least not when he'd breathed life back into Naya's infant body.

Jase fished his wallet out of the back pocket of his jeans and tossed it on the small kitchen counter. "So, what is it you want to discuss?"

"Your side business."

His eyes went flat. "My side business?"

"Identity theft."

He snorted. "Identity theft?" Another snort. "Is that what Abercrombie told you?"

I kept silent, not wanting to lie. It wasn't like I could explain holo-rankers to Jase.

"The fact that you would actually believe such shit makes me question our friendship. The guy's obviously got it in for me."

Again, I deflected speaking about my source. "The IDs I'd hand you —the ones you took pictures of—did you use them? Did you use me?"

He rammed his fingers through his gelled locks. "You can't steal someone's identity from an ID; you need social security numbers. Remember slipping me any of *those*, Celeste?" He hammered each word into the fraught air.

"Did Leon put you up to this?"

"Don't you fucking dare bring him into our shit."

"Jase, I'm not an undercover cop or a snitch. I'm your friend."

He grunted. "If you were my friend, you'd believe me instead of that pretty boyfriend of yours."

I planted my palms on my hips. "Newsflash: I know this may come as a surprise, but I *can* think for myself. Everything I know, I found out. On. My. Own. The only thing he told me was that you were involved in something you shouldn't be. Jase, you're so feathering smart. I mean, you're at Columbia. On a scholarship! Please don't throw this away on fast cash. *Please.*" I gulped in a much-needed breath. "If you need money, let me give you some, but don't—"

"I'm not a charity case. And I'm not sticking around to discuss shit that doesn't concern you." His arm shot out toward his wallet and keys, which he stuffed back into his pocket.

"I'm here because I care about you."

"Not enough."

"What?"

He walked right up to me, bumped me a step backward. If he'd been any other man, I might've felt fear, but Jase wouldn't physically hurt me. Would he?

"You don't fucking care enough about me if you're accusing me of this shit." Spittle smacked the tip of my nose.

I locked my shoulders and stood my ground. "I brought it up because I want to help you."

"I don't fucking want your help!"

His outrage wasn't uncommon—no one enjoyed facing their demons —but he was such a placid person that his heated reaction made my breathing hitch. What had I been expecting though? That he'd take it in stride? That we'd sit on his smelly couch with crumpets and tea and dissect his conscience?

"I know it's hard to look at your actions—especially the questionable ones—under a magnifying glass, but if you don't, you'll end up in jail like your brother, and I won't stand here and watch you throw away your entire future over a crime you have the power to stop committing."

"Then stand elsewhere!" He backed up. "I got an idea. Go back to your pretty little penthouse, with your pretty little things, and your pretty little blond boyfriend. 'Cuz you're not welcome here anymore."

I narrowed my eyes at him. "I'll stand where I feathering want to stand! And right now, that's here. With you. So stop trying to toss me out. I'm not going anywhere. I don't abandon people when things get tough."

"Do you even know what tough is?"

"I lost my best friend, so yeah."

"You know how many best friends I lost?"

"This isn't a competition, Jase."

"No. It's an intervention." His tight lips bowed into a frightful smile. "Well, you can save your breath. As for your fucking money, you obviously have too much of it. Less now. But still too much." That ugly smile of his grew.

My heartbeat rocketed right into my throat. "What are you talking about?"

"I'm outta here. I'll give you the day to pack up—"

"You stole my money . . ." I whispered. "When?"

He opened the door. "Be gone by Monday."

My hands trembled, all of me trembled. "I forgive you. I forgive you, Jase, but don't leave."

His brutal smile froze and then its hard edges chipped, before it thawed off his face entirely. There was great power in forgiveness.

"Just get away before . . . Just get away, Cee." And then he stepped out and flung the door shut.

"Before what?" I yelled but never got my answer.

Apparently, it would take more than forgiveness to drag Jase back to better shores.

Chapter Thirty-Three

I didn't pack up my things. What I did after Jase left was rip open the flat boxes I'd received in my absence and pull out the plexiglass pictures I'd ordered for the walls of my bedroom. And then I curled up on my bed and stared at them until oblivion swept me away.

I startled awake to pounding. The sort that could bring down a door. Pulling last night's jeans on, I hopped out of my bedroom, heart ramping up. Had Jase talked to his brother? Was one of Leon's ex-military guys trying to get to me?

"You have wing bones," I whispered under my breath. "You are not afraid."

Still, I grabbed a kitchen knife from the butcher block by the sink. Before I could look through the peephole, the door flew open. I bounced back just in time to avoid getting smacked in the face and raised my knife, knuckles white.

I expelled a violent shudder at the sight of my visitor and lowered my weapon. "What is wrong with you, Seraph?"

Asher eyed the knife and then the apartment. Without a word, he strode past me, all but punching open all the closed doors, while I went to shut the front one, not wanting an audience. The latch didn't click. I squinted down at it. Found it melted.

"Where is he?" Asher barked.

"I'm assuming you mean Jase. He's not here." I flung the knife on the countertop, then gestured to the not-quite closed door. "You broke his door."

"You weren't opening it."

"You have to stop going around and destroying things."

"I left you a list, Celeste."

"I got your list, Seraph."

"Then why did you sign on to someone who wasn't on it?"

I crossed my arms. "Jase is my friend. I'm helping all these people who aren't. I wanted to help someone who was. And by the way, *you* even suggested I help him."

My heart rate was slowly decelerating but hadn't leveled off. How could it, when, after being scared awake, I now had to deal with a truculent angel? My wing bones strummed, but the strumming didn't turn into a hot jab. Probably just the ishim's cute way of warning me to rein in my opinion.

"Well, I came to my senses. He might be your friend, but he's mixed up with lots of dangerous people. Which you're apparently aware of seeing as you greeted me with a bread knife."

I stretched my jaw from side to side, temper expanding now that my fear had shrunk. "Unlike some people, I don't dump my friends the minute I get uncomfortable."

The archangel's eyes burned with unchecked anger. "Excuse me?"

"You ran away."

"I didn't run."

"Sorry. You *flew* away."

His nostrils stopped flaring. "Celeste, I didn't run or fly away. I stepped back to give you the space you've been asking for since I came back into your life."

I rolled my eyes. "Sure. Sticking me with a list and a hostile ishim was for my own good."

His Adam's apple jostled. "You're right. It wasn't only for your own good; it was also for mine. After I failed to find a consort, I made a vow to the Seven that my entire focus and heart would go to Elysium." His voice had dropped, and dropped some more when he added, "And then I went ahead and made Naya and Adam. I didn't want another—"

"Distraction? Yeah, okay. I got that." My arms tightened. "Look, as much as I enjoyed you stopping by and yelling at me, I'm tired. Physically and emotionally. So if you wouldn't mind letting yourself out of here, I'd really appreciate it." As I padded back toward my bedroom, I added, "Oh, and if you could fire up a new latch on your way out, that'd be real great."

"You're not staying here."

I twirled around and retraced my steps, then jabbed a finger into one hard pec. "I'm not your puppet. I'm not your anything. You may rule Elysium, but you don't rule me."

He wrapped his hand around my finger and dragged it down. "You're not staying here because it's not safe. And not because the latch is broken, but because Jase's brother has killed for less."

I snatched back my finger. "I have wing bones."

"So, I should just step back and let them torture you?"

"No one's going to torture me."

"You came at me with a knife, so don't tell me the thought didn't cross your mind."

"Fine, it did, but Jase would never torture me."

Asher's jaw was granite. His entire body was granite. "He's not going to torture you because you're going to abort this mission."

I slapped my chest and expelled a theatrical breath. "What? You haven't signed me off already?" There was a shrill edge to my voice that made all the lines on Asher's body sharpen some more. "Off your game, Seraph?"

He let out a dark sound. "If I signed you off, you'd sign yourself right back on to spite me."

I flung him a tart smile. "You know me well." I retreated into my bedroom and slammed the door, or at least tried to.

Asher blocked it from closing with his palm and then shoved it back open and stalked inside. "I'll send someone to gather your things, but we're leaving now."

"I'm not leaving."

"And I'm not going to stand around and watch one of my people get hurt."

"I am not one of your people, Seraph!"

His wings materialized at his back, sharp as twin swords. "Whether you want to or not, you belong to Elysium."

"I belong to myself."

"Don't push me," he rumbled, all low and menacing.

"Or what? You'll remove me against my will?"

His nostrils flared with wild breaths. "Worse. I'll stick around until you beg me to get you away from the Marros brothers."

"You're not sticking around."

"Watch me." Smiling like someone who'd bested his enemy, he stalked back out to the living room and got comfortable on the couch. He even picked up one of the *New Yorker* magazines Jase stockpiled.

Forget seeing red . . . I'd skipped right over the color wheel to black. "He hates you, Seraph."

"I can't imagine why."

I wanted to throttle the man. "What happened to all that work you had in Elysium?"

"All done." He flipped a page, then another.

"I won't sign off until I get through to him, and I won't get through to him if he sees me in your company. In other words, you'd be dooming my wings. Are you sure you want that on your conscience?"

"I have angel-dust; he won't see me."

"But I will, and it'll destroy my focus."

"Pick another sinner then."

"No."

"Then I guess we'll be spending lots of quality time together, *levsheh*."

Levsheh? I was guessing it was Angelic, since it wasn't in any language I knew, and I knew them all. Probably meant *demon*.

"I hate you. I really *really* hate you." A hot jab to my wing bones made me hiss, but I recovered quickly. "If I never reach Elysium, it'll be on you. All. On. You." I spun, and this time, when I kicked my bedroom door, it clicked shut.

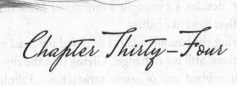

Chapter Thirty-Four

After screaming my anger into my pillow, I brushed my teeth and hair, dabbed on some much-needed concealer, and changed out of the tank top I'd slept in. My jacket was out in the living room but so was my surly guardian. I jerked the blinds up, and then shoved open the window. The air was brisk but warmed by threads of sunlight. I grabbed a sweater and knotted it around my waist, then hooked my tote to my shoulder, and sent Jase a text message asking him where he was.

Like a thief, I slipped over the sill, my boots clattering softly on the iron fire escape. I didn't move for a full minute, waiting to see if Asher would melt the lock off my bedroom door or splinter the flimsy wood with a well-placed kick. When neither of the two happened, I clanked down the rusted stairs. By the time I reached solid ground, sweat dripped down my spine.

A smile at having outmaneuvered the archangel made my dimples dig deep. I hopped down into the back alley and pressed into the shadows surrounding the building, careful not to rub up against the bricks, especially the ones discolored by piss and angels only knew what other bodily fluids. I checked my phone for a message notification, but nada.

"Where are you, Jase?" I murmured.

I surveyed the street and then the sky. A pigeon flew past, but no winged man. I darted out of the alley and speed-walked all the way to The Trap. I didn't know if Jase would be there, but it felt like a good place to start my search, what with it being a public space and lunchtime. Even if Leon was there, he wouldn't try anything on me, not with a crowd watching. Besides, I'd brought a canister of Mace that could make a bunker of soldiers bawl like babies.

Before entering the basement lair, I swiveled my head around to take in the sky and street. Still no archangel. Giving him the slip had been *way* too easy, which robbed me of some satisfaction. Palming my bag, I headed down the stairs and squinted around the neon duskiness.

Alicia was at the bar, filling a pitcher with soda. As I approached, she sent over a smile that made my swaying insides calm a fraction. If she smiled at me, then Jase hadn't told her I was persona non grata. The real test would be Leon, though.

"Mornin', hun," she said as I perched on one of the bar stools.

Before I could ask for anything, she slid me a mug of drip coffee. "Bless you, Alicia."

She winked at me as she carried over the pitcher to the waiting table, then scribbled down their brunch order. After delivering it to the kitchen, she came back. "We got two specials today: scrambled eggs with —with, um . . . blackberries."

"Blackberries?" That was an odd mix. I frowned until I saw her attention was elsewhere.

I glanced over my shoulder. When I caught sight of white T-shirt and blond manbun, my molars clicked. Should've known Asher would sniff out my trail.

He settled two stools down from me without so much as a glance in my direction. I slid my teeth against each other, debating whether to storm off or pretend he wasn't there.

I went with option two. I needed to speak with Leon ASAP and running away would be a setback. Besides, I was hungry.

Alicia blinked. "Be right over, sugar." She refocused on me. "So, where were we?"

"You were telling me about those scrambled eggs with blackberries," I muttered.

"Huh? Why would Leon put berries in eggs?"

"He was feeling experimental?"

She let out a soft snort. "That man does love to experiment. Anyway .

. . the blackberries are on the buttermilk pancakes. The scrambled eggs come with maple bacon and avo-toast. Tempted by either?"

Not feeling like making up my mind, I said, "I'll take both."

She slanted me a coy smile. "You and Jase worked up an appetite last night, huh?"

I was about to set her straight when I remembered Asher was *right there*. "You know us too well." My answer would thoroughly annoy the archangel, who deemed sex a waste of time. "Leon's in the kitchen, right?"

"Manning the grill. You need him?"

"I'll stop by to see him after I eat."

"You got it." She flipped the sheet on her pad, then stepped toward Asher. "Hiya. I'm all yours, now. What can I get you?"

Over the thick lip of my coffee mug, I muttered, "Birdfeed with a side of humility."

I didn't think Alicia heard me, but Asher's lips clenched a little, which told me he probably had.

"Some black coffee would be appreciated."

"Comin' right up." As she passed by me, Alicia widened her eyes and flapped a hand to fan herself.

Pretty on the outside; petty on the inside. Crazy how a single letter could make such a difference.

Staring at the muted baseball game over the bar, I asked, "Is your dust defective?" His gaze drilled a hole in the side of my face. "'Cause you're *very* visible."

He shifted on his stool, denim whispering against the black vinyl. "I said I wouldn't show myself if Jase was around, and from what I can see, he's not."

"Maybe he's in the kitchen."

The batter got a homerun.

Asher rolled his head from side to side. "Actually, he's at the college library."

I jerked my gaze to his face, which was angled toward the TV. The pale light defined his profile while the neon insignias filled it in with pinks, oranges, greens and yellows.

How? How did he know?

"Fire escape was a nice touch, *levsheh*."

"Stop calling me that."

"Stop trying to escape me."

"Never."

"Then get used to your new nickname."

So much for pretending he wasn't there. I side-eyed him. "What does it mean? Bane of my existence? Demon child? Foul soul?"

He smiled, flashing some of those pearlescent white teeth.

"Whatever. I don't care." I turned my attention back to the baseball game. I'd ask an ophanim later. Or not.

I let it roll off me like water on feathers. A breath snagged in my throat . . . what if it meant *winglet*?

No . . . he didn't loathe me enough to call me that. Did he?

"So, what's your plan?"

"Like I'd tell you."

The kitchen door flapped open, and Alicia reappeared with a platter of food destined for the booth beneath my glowing pink swine.

I smiled to myself. "See that winged piglet on the far wall?"

Asher glanced over his shoulder.

"I gave it to Leon last year. Wanted to add to his collection." My wing bones strummed. "Guess who I had in mind when I purchased it?" Another tremor echoed through the invisible bones. *Pluck me already . . . see if I care.*

"I'm going to go out on a limb and say me."

"You spotted the resemblance too, huh?" I hated how spiteful he made me. To think I'd hugged and then smoldered him a few days ago . . . *ugh.*

"I'm flattered."

"Flattered?" That torpedoed the smile from my face. "Why in the world would you be flattered?"

"Because I've been on your mind for over four years."

I set down my coffee mug harder than necessary. "*That's* your takeaway?"

"What can I say?" He tipped his mug to his mouth and drank, then nonchalantly angled his body toward mine, his long legs falling open. "I try to see the best in everything and everyone."

Anger slithered under my skin. Again, my wing bones thrummed, but didn't toss off a feather.

I refocused on the game. "Well, I wasn't thinking any positive thoughts when I bought it."

"I bet. My spirit animal would've surely been a dragon if you had."

Egotistical much? "So, what's *your* plan, Seraph?"

"My plan is to watch over you. If that entails watching you eat a breakfast suited for a small family, then so be it."

I wanted to growl and would have if I hadn't just thought of a great plan to shake off my guardian. I scrolled through my contact list for my favorite nail salon. I dialed them and booked myself a mani-pedi and a bikini wax.

Before hanging up, I turned to Asher. "Since you'll be with me all day, should I book you a chest wax?"

He turned dangerously chilling eyes my way.

"Right. You don't have any hair on your chest. A massage then? You look a little tense."

Ice-cold blue burnt into me.

Smirking, I said into the phone, "That'll actually be it for today." She asked me what sort of treatment I wanted down there, and I said, "A Brazilian. Three p.m.'s perfect. See you later." I hung up and laid my phone on the bar. "We're going to have *such* a fun day."

Alicia came back with two laden plates. After she checked up on Asher, who still didn't order anything to eat—rude—she bustled away.

I picked up my avocado toast and took a small bite. "If you insist on staying at my side while I get my crotch waxed, can I hold your hand? It's surprisingly painful."

His eyebrows lowered, eclipsing the sliver of residual brightness.

I nibbled on the toast again. "Should I interpret your silence as a hard pass?"

His glare turned downright scorching.

I licked a glob of avocado off my finger, sensing he was two seconds shy of storming off. But those two seconds turned into twenty minutes. And he was still there. He'd break before the salon. I mean, no respectable guy would watch a girl they barely knew get her ladybits waxed, let alone a girl they *did* know.

Once I'd polished off both plates, I hopped down from my stool. "Hey, Alicia. My neighbor's gluten-intolerant and wanted to hear all the options you have for people with sensitive bowels." I was pleasantly surprised my statement hadn't cost me a feather.

What it did cost me was another scathing glower.

I tightened the knot on the sweater tied around my waist. "I'm just going to thank the chef for all that delicious food. Be right back."

Asher had one boot on the ground, but since Alicia had rushed over to discuss gluten-free options, he politely stayed put and listened.

I slinked around the bar and pushed open the flap door. "Hi, Leon."

He stood by the grill, a sweat-soaked bandana tied around his forehead. "Celeste!" His wide grin soothed my nerves.

I leaned a hip against the stainless-steel countertop. "That avo-toast. You need to add it to the regular menu."

"Tasty, huh? It's the smoked paprika."

I glanced at the busboy washing dishes on the other side of the kitchen and at Tommy, the sous-chef with the questionable style in facial art. "Leon, can we talk a sec?"

"Sure."

I bit my lip and looked around the kitchen. Dropping my voice to a whisper, I said, "Jase and I got into a fight."

"Happens to the best of us. Alicia and I are at each other's throats at least twice a week."

"He didn't tell you what we fought about?"

"Boy doesn't talk much. Not even to me. You know that." He flipped over two glistening patties.

"Leon, we fought about what you guys . . . *do*."

His dark eyes slid over to me. "What we do?"

"Your side business."

The congenial smile melted off his pockmarked face. "Have no clue what you're gettin' at, Celeste."

"Do you really want to discuss it here?" I nodded toward his staff. The busboy had his back to us and might not have spoken English, but he was still in the vicinity. As for Tommy, he was studiously slicing a purple onion, but I had no doubt he was listening.

Leon slowly set down his kitchen tongs. So slowly. Too slowly. "I have no secrets from my employees."

Tommy looked up then. Of course, he was part of the operation.

"Pull Jase out. That's all I came in here to ask."

Leon shifted, and his diamond cross reflected the spotlights from the extractor hood. "Jase is an adult and makes up his own mind."

"Jase adores you. He'd do just about anything for you. Including handing over his roommate's banking information."

Leon dipped his chin into his neck.

"I'm not here to threaten you, or ask you to transfer the money you stole back into my account. I'm here to ask you to cut Jase loose, force him to concentrate on law school. He gets caught, and he can kiss his future goodbye."

"I made a good future for myself, and I didn't go to any fancy, over-priced school."

"The Trap's great. Truly, I admire all you've done here, but you're one mistake away from getting shipped back to jail."

He wiped his thick hands on his black waist-apron. Fresh bruises marred the skin on his knuckles. "Yeah?" It felt like he'd gotten closer, but it must've been my imagination since his army-green crocs hadn't budged off the grease-stained white tiles.

Still, I took a step back. When my shoulder blades connected with a wall of brawn, I released a gasp. I prayed it was Asher, but the hand that clamped over my mouth reeked of raw onions. A glance toward the chopping station made my throat squeeze tight. I slid my fingers into my bag and uncapped the pepper spray. Before I could raise it, a knife settled underneath my chin.

Immortal. I was immortal. I was going to be fine. *Eventually.*

"Hey, Jesus!" Leon called out to the kitchen porter. "How do you feel about a bonus?"

The boy, who couldn't have been older than sixteen, stalked toward us, wiping his elbow-length yellow rubber gloves down his thin thighs. The fact that he hadn't taken them off was more than a little alarming.

I should've listened to Asher. Should've let him get me out of this. Or at the very least, escort me into the kitchen. I'd let my trust impair my judgment. Stupid. I was so incredibly stupid.

"I knew you'd be a liability. Told Jase he should've gotten rid of you, but he was so pussy-whipped." Leon approached and slid one meaty thumb over my cheek, digging it into my dimple.

I wanted to retch.

"I'm real sorry, Celeste, 'cause you were sweet. And quite useful."

"Don't do this," I yelped, the palm digging against my lips muffling my voice.

Angry more than frightened, I bit down on Tommy's hand and swung out the Mace, depressing the trigger. A stream hit Leon square in the face. Jesus flipped around, spewing Spanish curses. Good. He must've gotten an eyeful too. I turned the can on Tommy just as the knife bit into my flesh, drawing a river of warmth down my neck. My fingertip slid off the trigger, and the metal canister crashed onto the floor.

All the sounds around me fused together into one low, rustling hiss. My vision dotted, grayed. And yet in the sea of blacks and whites, I caught sight of vivid turquoise. I opened my mouth to utter Asher's name. It came out as a whisper. *Good.* That meant Tommy hadn't sawed through my airway.

I wasn't sure how I'd ended up slumped on the floor, but that's where I was, sitting on dirty tiles with sharp drawer handles jutting into my spine. A slow blink brought the kitchen into soft focus, but the sounds . . . they were all still rushing together, overlaid by the rhythmic beat of my heart.

Wings out like an avenging angel, Asher smashed his fist right where Tommy's jaw intersected his ear. The ex-convict crumpled like a water-logged towel. Then the seraphim stretched out his arm and sent a bolt of fire into the other two's blinking, wet faces. The fire caught in Jesus's hair, spread across Leon's bandana and down their kitchen scrubs, chewing the stained fabrics.

Horrified. I was horrified. "Don't . . . don't kill them, Seraph," I murmured.

It wasn't so much because I cared about them, but because I knew angels weren't supposed to mess with human timelines. If Asher sent them into early graves, there would be consequences.

He crouched down before me, his glare sharper than his scowl, and it was a mighty severe scowl. "My fire won't kill them."

Good. That was good.

"Hope you enjoyed your last moment of freedom, Celeste, because from now on, you and I . . . we're going to be glued at the fucking wing bone."

The archangel's intent was probably not humor, but the picture it brought up was nonetheless amusing, and my lips bent. "You'll scare off my sinners, Seraph. And then I won't earn—" Pain streaked down my neck at the effort it took to move my mouth, and I winced.

He raised his palm and sent a burst of heat over my wound. I sucked in a breath and held it in until he was done searing the blood off my skin.

"Good call," I murmured. "A bloodied neck would probably freak out more than one customer."

From the corner of my eye, I saw the flap door open, and then Alicia was standing there, shrieking.

She dropped the platter she was holding. Ceramic and glass shattered and sprayed the tiles. "What the hell happened in here?" The door flapped closed, banging into her backside, sending her stumbling a couple steps forward, her sneakers crunching over the broken crockery. "Leon?" Her voice was so shrill it hurt my eardrums. "Baby, what happened?"

"The asshole used the blowtorch on us." His voice warbled over the gush of water. "I got half a mind to call the cops."

Asher's gaze zeroed in on Leon, who stood at the sink with Jesus, both of them splashing water over their blistered skin. "Oh, you should absolutely call them, Leon Marros. I'm certain they'd love nothing more than to reconnect with you."

I focused on the white cotton enclosing Asher's broad chest, on the galaxy of red dots. Was that my blood? I swallowed back the surging bile, but the jet was stronger than my throat muscles. I spun my face away just in time to avoid staining Asher's shirt some more. The eggs, the pancakes, the avocado, the blackberries . . . they splashed the tiles beside me. Although unpleasant, I was glad to rid myself of food cooked up by cruel men.

I itched to call Jase on Facetime to show him my throat. But what if he wasn't stunned by his brother's savagery?

Worse, what if he condoned it?

He wouldn't. Jase was fundamentally good.

His score shimmered in front of my eyes—41. Forty-oners weren't the best but they were better than—what was Leon's score again? Sixty-something? Would it be a hundred now that he'd attacked me? *Wait.* Tommy had attacked me, not Leon. Leon had just given the order. Tommy would be the Triple.

"Let's get you home. And not to that ratnest you call a home," Asher added with a grumble.

I was done fighting him on this. "Okay." My voice felt stronger, clearer. I palmed my throat—smooth. "Wait . . . did your—did you heal me?" Could angel-fire weld wounds?

"You'll still have a bruise. Now, can we go, or do you have some more things to discuss with your friend's brother?"

"Actually, I have lots more to say to him." I pressed my palms into the tiles. Before I could get my feet under me, I was hoisted up. An *oomph* escaped from my newly-healed throat. "Seraph, I can walk."

Maybe.

"I am *incredibly* angry with you right now." His growled words barely moved his lips.

"Nothing new there." I curled an arm around his taut neck.

He harrumphed.

Sighing, I rested my head against his clocking heart, choosing not to battle him on his method of transportation. After all, I really wanted to get out of here, and the quicker the better.

He strode right past a shell-shocked Alicia, stomping over the shimmering sea of cracked glass at her feet. When we entered the restaurant, mouths gaped so wide pieces of food fell out, and then phones rose.

"Didn't you burn away the blood?" I whispered.

"I was a little busy patching up your throat." The deep rumble of his words pulsed against my forehead.

I copped a peek at my chest, swallowing when I noticed the scarlet hue of my skin and the soaked collar of my light gray T-shirt. Out of all the days I'd foregone wearing black.

When we emerged, brisk air licked up the sides of my face, icing the mixture of sweat and blood.

"Celeste?" someone gasped.

I peered around Asher's bicep toward a set of narrowed, purple-smudged eyes. "Jase!"

My friend's wariness turned to disgust when he took in the male holding me.

I tugged on Asher's arm. "Set me down, Seraph."

"No."

"I'll stay by your side. Just put me down." When he didn't, I tacked on a *please*.

He grumbled something but relented. When I wobbled, he wound his arm around my ribs and then, muttering again, dragged my body against his, locking me against the side of his rib cage. His stronghold kept me from faceplanting, which I was grateful for. I didn't need any more bruises.

"Your neck?" Jase's voice made me refocus. "What happened to your neck?"

Before I could answer, Asher snapped, "Your brother happened to her neck."

Jase's body seized up on the patch of sunny sidewalk. "Leon wouldn't strangle Celeste."

"Strangle? I was cut, Jase. Tommy did it, but it was on Leon's orders."

Jase reached out and yanked down the collar of my T-shirt, not enough to expose my breasts but enough to piss me off. "I don't see a cut."

Before the growl forming at the back my throat could emerge, Asher grabbed Jase's fingers and flung them away.

Jase stumbled backward, color shooting into his face. "Don't fucking touch me, Abercrombie, or I'll—"

"You'll do nothing." I shut him down, afraid his score would rocket up if he so much as entertained murderous thoughts about the archangel.

Jase's lashes rose. "Whose blood is it?"

"Mine."

"If it was yours, you'd have a fucking cut!"

"Stop yelling."

"Stop lying!"

"Jase, I'm not . . ."

"Fuck you, Celeste. Fuck you for making me believe . . ."

I began to shake. "Making you believe what? That I care about you? That I care what happens to you? I. Do. Care. I care so much I went to talk to your brother about getting you out."

Police sirens wailed. I wanted to plug my ears, but my arms hung limp at my sides, my fingers drawn into my palms.

"Did you kill him, Celeste?"

"If you think I'd be capable of killing a person, then you don't know me at all."

"You've changed." His gaze flicked to Asher, who'd remained surprisingly silent and still beside me. "And not into someone I want anywhere near me, so I'm going to say this one more time. Get your shit out of my apartment or it ends up in the dumpster." Jase backed off with erratic shakes of his head and then vanished down the stairs.

Instead of cutting Jase out of his brother's web, I'd tangled him further inside. "I was just trying to help," I whispered to him, to myself, to Asher. "What a mess." I batted my lashes to clear my eyes of the foolish tears dripping out.

I'd failed Fernanda. Now, Jase.

Asher's palm splayed open on the small of my back, and although I was trembling everywhere, somehow, my tailbone seemed to quake hardest. "You tried—"

"Not hard enough!"

"You tried harder than I would have."

"Because you don't like him."

"You're right. I don't. I don't have any respect for abusive men."

I pressed away from him, which ended up with me contorting my body into a backbend, since he hadn't relaxed his grip. "Abusive? Jase isn't abusive."

"He didn't use your friendship to wheedle information from you? He didn't steal your money?"

"The money wasn't mine."

"You're much too forgiving."

"Be happy I am. Otherwise, I wouldn't have forgiven your assitude."

He quirked up an eyebrow. "Assitude?"

"The state of being a perpetual ass."

He still didn't look offended, which was crazy because it wasn't a compliment. "If refusing to let you go off on your own to face three pitiless sinners—two of which are ex-cons—makes me an ass, then I'll wear the title with great pride."

I started to roll my eyes at his obnoxiousness when a blue-and-white car careened down the block, tires screeching to a halt a couple feet from where we stood.

"Hold on tight." Asher's wings deployed at the same time as he scooped me up and tossed some dust to cloak us.

"Why? Please tell me we're not—"

The word *flying* turned into a gasp as Asher shot up into the bright

New York sky. Heart skittering into my throat, I crushed my arms around his neck and my legs around his waist, then squashed my lids shut and buried my face in the crook of his neck.

"Why couldn't we have hailed a cab like normal people?" I mumbled.

"Because we aren't normal people, *levsheh*."

My air-fright was momentarily dispelled by the foreign nickname. What in Abaddon did it mean? Since asking would bely caring and further undermine the whole unflappability I was going for, I bit back the question.

He suddenly leveled off, bringing our bodies parallel to the Earth's surface. My stomach met up with my heart inside my abdomen, beating so frighteningly fast that Asher was surely feeling the force of their alliance. I tightened my limbs' grip on the body keeping me from going splat.

"Besides, you made me discuss gluten and bowel movements with a stranger." His voice carried like a warm gust over the whipping wind. "Consider flying retribution."

A smile cracked through my anguish. "Fine, but don't try it on days I don't get my throat slashed."

His chest went frighteningly still. "Pick sinners from my list, and you won't get your throat slashed."

I peeked up, found his features as tense as the rest of his body. "Okay."

A few strands of hair were ribboning around his face.

I reached up and caught a piece waving in front of his eyes. "Don't want you running into a skyscraper."

A smile spread from his mouth to his eyes, jeweling the cyan depths.

Angels, the man was pretty. It was the eyes. The mouth and jawline, too. And the nose. *And* the hair. Yeah . . . everything about him was perfection.

As though he sensed me thinking about his flawlessness, his gaze lowered to mine. Stayed there.

"Seraph, please look at where you're going."

"I could fly with my eyes closed, Celeste."

The blood drained from my face. "If you so much as try to demonstrate this skill, I will *pet* your wings."

That diffused his pupils until his eyes were more black than blue. Murderous eyes.

I focused on a thready cloud unspooling like spun sugar beyond the archangel's bronze wingtips. "I should probably keep my threats for after we land."

A full minute of silence later, he said, "That was a threat?"

My gaze snapped back to his inky one, disconcerted by his reaction. He couldn't *actually* want me to touch his feathers, could he?

A peculiar heat crawled up my skin, made it tingle.

Aw, *mother feather.*

Not again.

And not up here.

Groaning, I shut my eyes, but my lids did little to block out my luminescence. To think I was plastered to the chest of the man my body had decided to smolder without my brain's consent.

"I changed my mind, Seraph. Please drop me."

A vibration settled over the rhythmic thuds of his pulse. It took my burning ears a millisecond to decipher the sound—laughter. He was laughing at my predicament.

"It's not nice to make fun of people when they're at their weakest." I really needed to locate the dead-man switch on my smoldering because if I continued to light up in his presence, I wanted it to be on my terms.

His laughter slowed to an elegant chuckle. "You mean, at their shiniest?"

"I'm going to let go now." I forced myself to slacken my death grip.

He pressed his mouth into the crown of my head. "Go ahead, *levsheh.*" The king of Elysium and of mixed signals tucked me in closer. "I've got you."

Chapter Thirty-Five

After depositing me on my balcony, Asher asked if I had someone in mind from his list for my next mission.

I shrugged. "Someone without a penchant for violence would be awesome."

His eyes strayed to my neck, which made my palm rise to the raw skin. The dried blood flaked off beneath my fingertips.

"Just text me where and who I'm meeting." I started to turn. "And if I have a cover story."

His gaze was still stuck to my collarbone, and from the downward shape of his lips, I deduced what had befallen me at The Trap aggrieved him.

"I'll see you"—I was about to say *later* but switched it to—"soon." Unlike the word later, soon didn't smack of desperation. Besides, I was glad to be alone. I needed a shower and space to process all that had happened.

After he leaped off my balcony, wings stretched as wide as a bird of prey, I went inside and threw my T-shirt into the trash, then peeled off my jeans but tossed those in my overflowing hamper. Once I'd rid myself of at least two layers of epidermis, I put on a load of laundry, uncorked a bottle of white wine, and settled on the couch in front of blissfully vapid reality TV. Halfway through the second episode of Desperate House-wives of somewhere or other, I remembered Jase's threat of dumping my

209

belongings. I must've phoned up eight moving companies before I found one that could fit me in the following morning.

I texted Jase that they'd be at the apartment at 8 a.m.

His message: *I said today. And what the fuck happened to my lock?*

I ground my teeth. Since I couldn't explain the lock, I texted back: *No one's free today.*

JASE: *Then tell them they can pick it up from the back alley.*

I sat up, royally pissed at his pettiness now. *Stop being a jerk.*

JASE: *Or what? You'll have the cops who cuffed Leon drop by my place?*

The news of his brother's arrest momentarily stilled my grinding molars.

ME: *I'm sorry.*

JASE: *Are you?*

ME: *Yes, Jase. I am.*

For the longest moment, no answer came up on my screen.

JASE: *Get your shit out today.*

I sent him a bunch of messages asking him to be reasonable, but no three little dots danced to show he was composing a reply. I punched a throw pillow and growled at it and then I tossed it across the room, but instead of landing on the rug, it landed in a set of big hands.

"What have I done now?"

I glared at Asher, even though, for once, it wasn't him I was mad at. "Believe it or not, you're not always the cause of my bad mood."

He dropped the cushion on one of the couches, humor fleeing his expression. "What happened?"

"Jase is being an ass."

I'd seen the archangel look angry, annoyed, frustrated. Never had I seen him look like he wanted to snap bones. "And you were conversing with him, why?"

"Because I was trying to coordinate the removal of my personal effects from his apartment, and the soonest I can get a moving company is tomorrow morning, which isn't good enough for him." My nose prickled as though I were about to cry. I would *not* cry. Not over this.

"Give me your keys, Celeste."

I frowned, but it turned into a headshake when I understood he meant the ones to the apartment I shared with Jase. "I'm not getting you involved in this."

"I'm already involved."

"But you no longer need to be."

"If you're afraid he'll hurt me . . ." His voice trailed off at the crazed smile digging into my cheeks.

"Hurt you? No . . . I'm afraid *you* might hurt *him*."

"You're still protecting him after all he said to you?"

I pursed my lips. It *was* feathered up. "You're right. He does deserve my full wrath. You know what, I think I'm going to head back uptown myself—"

"No."

"—and tell him what a sparrow-louse he is, and—"

"No."

"—punch him in the throat, so that he sports a matching bruise."

"No."

I sent him a defiant glare. "Watch me."

"Celeste," he growled.

When I stalked toward the hallway, he stepped right into my war path.

I stuck my hands on my hips and scowled up at him. "I'm not in the mood to fight you on this."

"Good, because I could do with one less battle to wage."

My bones jammed together. "Naya?"

"She's fine. A little peeved you didn't accompany me to the guild earlier, but otherwise, she's fine."

My pulse quieted as abruptly as it had spiked.

"Now, will you please give me your keys and a list of what you would like me to retrieve?"

"Boxing up thongs and sex toys is way beneath your paygrade."

A divide appeared between his taut lips and then vanished. Jaw clenched, he said, all low and grumbly, "If that's all you have at the apartment, then I'm sure an internet order could replenish your loss."

Smirking, I slid my hands off my hips. "The only thing I really want is my teal jacket. Mimi gave it to me, and—"

"The one with the angel wings?"

"Yes." I pushed my fingers through my hair, a thought occurring to me. One which had niggled at me ever since she'd special-ordered the jacket from Dior two years ago. "Did she know what I was?"

"On her deathbed, Mikaela—Jarod's mother"—a groove dented the space between his eyebrows—"she mentioned angels and Elysium. Muriel attributed it to dementia and sorrow, but over time, she started to question this. Especially when she met Leigh. And then you."

I swallowed, and it hurt, but not because of the bruise. "I miss both of them so much."

Asher's palm ghosted over my upper arm, almost settling. In the end, he brought his arm back alongside his body. "Both of them miss you, too."

But one wasn't . . . well, she wasn't exactly the girl who'd left me behind. I didn't say it out loud, afraid it would somehow pain him to hear I wished Naya were someone else. She was different, but she was enough. More than enough. And I was incredibly thankful for her existence.

"Anyway. You won't need keys. No more lock, remember?" Biting my lip, I added, "He's going to hate seeing you."

"I wasn't expecting a backslap and a beer."

I couldn't even muster a smile. "Thank you."

I didn't realize I was wringing my hands together until Asher caught them and gently pulled them apart.

"You did nothing wrong today, Celeste. Besides not listening to me, that is."

I pulled one of my hands from his and slugged his solid-as-bone bicep. "Arrogant man."

"Accountable, not arrogant."

"Whatever helps you sleep at night."

A smile slid over his mouth. "Either way, since you smoldered me —*twice*—I take it the trait enthuses you."

"Enthuses me?" I choked out. "Nope. Not even a little." I pulled my other hand free—why was it still in his anyway?—and tucked some pieces of hair behind my ear. "Arrogance is extremely off-putting."

His smile turned lopsided, which changed his entire face, making him seem suddenly more . . . approachable. "I won't be gone long. Try to abstain from drinking that entire bottle of wine by yourself in my absence."

I eyed the bottle. "Better not be gone too long then."

He sighed. "Drinking is never the solution, Celeste."

"It numbs the pain."

"It only disguises it."

"My body. My choice."

Gone were all traces of his prior amusement. "Think about your wings."

"I do. That's all I think about these days."

"Perhaps *think* isn't the right word. *Care* about them."

I bristled. "I *do* care." How dare he assume that just because I indulged occasionally, I was an unworthy wing owner.

As he moved past me, I thought I heard him mutter, "Not as much as I do." But it was probably a line from the reality TV show, because all the archangel cared about was easing his conscience by helping me reach Elysium.

If he cared about me in any other way, he wouldn't always be discussing my wings; he'd touch upon my heart and body. But no . . . it was all about my soul and the damn winglets that linked us.

Chapter Thirty-Six

The rebel I was took a sip of her wine after the seraphim left, but the sweet liquid tasted sour, so I poured it out and then I upended the bottle right into the sink. Instead of tossing it though, I brought it back into the living room and plopped it onto the coffee table. It was a teeny bit childish, but I didn't want to tarnish my impervious persona by letting him think he'd gotten to me.

Damn him and his guilt-trip.

Poor Naya was in for a no-fun adolescence.

As I settled back into the couch with my legging-clad legs bent underneath me, I seethed mutely. After a few minutes, pouting got boring. Plus my stomach growled, so I picked up my phone and ordered Indian takeout.

I'd just relieved Stanley of the bagged food when the archangel landed on my terrace, my jacket draped over his forearm.

He was simmering, and I almost took pity on him until he said, "I'm surprised you can even walk straight."

So his bad mood wasn't Jase-induced . . . it was me-induced. "And I'm surprised you still think anything about me is surprising." I side-stepped him, and since he'd pulled his wings out of the way, there was no awkward feather-bender. "Thanks for retrieving my jacket. Just toss it anywhere."

"What did you do with the wine?"

"*Why* . . . I drank it." Since I had drank some, I didn't lose a feather.

"I know the sound of inebriated-you. You don't sound inebriated."

I arranged all the containers around the empty bottle. "Fine, I didn't drink it, but not because of anything you said." My wings tingled but didn't eject a feather. *Thank you, Ishim.*

I assumed he'd ask why I'd kept the empty bottle when he nodded toward the laden table. "Are you expecting company?"

I sucked a drop of green curry off my fingertip. "I lost my last friend today, so no."

He crushed my poor jacket against his torso. "Jason Marros wasn't your friend."

"He used to be."

"A true friend would never have taken advantage of you."

It was silly, so silly, but the reminder of my poor lack of judgment made me bitter and defensive. "Fine. You win. Jase wasn't my friend."

Annoyance chiseled his features.

"Does my unpopularity and guilelessness please you?" A tremor built in my feet, rose up my shins, my thighs, my torso, spread to my clenched fists. To keep Asher from spotting the trembling, I crossed my arms. "Just tell me who I have the pleasure of reforming tomorrow and go."

"No."

"What, no? It wasn't a suggestion."

"I'm not leaving when you're on the verge of"—he waved his hand in my general direction—"of breaking down."

"I'm not on the verge of breaking down; I'm on the verge of breaking *something*. Maybe your nose, if you don't get yourself and your giant savior-complex out of my house." I gathered the loose collar of my sweater, yanked on it, but it just puddled right back down my shoulder. "So. Who?"

His lips grew thinner than the distance between the cartons of take-out, and there was zero distance between any of the pleated foil containers. "I'm sorry you cared about an asshole and I'm sorry he hurt you."

"Yeah. Whatever." I doubted he was sorry.

He flung my jacket on the arm of the couch and then stalked toward me. Before I could react, he bundled me in his arms and pressed me against his chest, pinning my folded arms between us.

I tried to wriggle away. "What in Abaddon do you think you're doing?"

"I'm hugging you, Celeste."

"Well, let go. I don't want a hug." I desperately tried to free my arms, but I was well and truly trussed up.

"If Muriel or Naya had been here, they would've hugged you. And you would've let them."

I bent my neck as far back as it would go. "Well, I don't want *your* hug."

"What's wrong with my hug?"

"Your hug feels like pity, and I don't want your pity."

"Pity?" He gently gripped the back of my neck.

Okay, fine. It didn't feel like pity. At least not the part of his anatomy digging into my abdomen. Although that was probably just a physiological reaction to the friction I'd caused by squirming.

"Why don't you tell me what I'm doing wrong, so I can improve my technique?" he asked all low and gravelly, which made my damned skin break out in goosebumps. Why couldn't he have been endowed with a cartoonish pitch, complete with a squeak? "I've only ever hugged one other person, and she fits in the crook of one arm, and although she complains about a whole lot of things, she never once complained about my hugs. So? How do I make it feel better?"

"By letting me go."

Silence resounded between us, followed by a slow swallow. "I tried that. I tried it for an entire week, and then you had to go and sign on to your ex, and I went so blind with rage that here I am making a fool of myself, attempting to hold on to someone who despises all that I am and all that I do."

I sighed. "I don't despise you *or* your hugs, even though they're a tad overpowering. As for Jase, he isn't, and was never, my boyfriend."

A vertical groove formed between his eyebrows. "You slept with him. *Lived* with him."

I pressed my head farther back, which made his fingers slide off my neck. "I slept with him because it was fun and uncomplicated, and I lived with him because it was practical."

Twelve heartbeats later—I counted them—he gritted out, "His hands were all over you."

I cocked an eyebrow. "Why do you care?"

"I care because his soul's tainted, and yours . . . yours isn't."

I snorted. "I'm the top scorer on the guild's sinning leaderboard."

"There is no guild sinning leaderboard."

"But if there was, I'd have everyone beat."

"Can you please stop putting yourself down?"

"Technically, I'm putting myself up. *Top* scorer."

He huffed a frustrated breath that scraped across my forehead.

"Look, I may have been naïve when it came to Jase, but my eyes are wide open now. Do I hope he'll change? Yes. Will I be the one to change him? No. I can't. I thought I could, but friendship and business really aren't a good mix."

Asher watched my eyes as though to make sure I was speaking the truth. I wasn't sure why he was looking at my face. The air around my legs was much more telling. "Have you slept with many men?"

Every freckle on my face—and there were many—heated. Since when did I blush? And since when did archangels concern themselves with the sex lives of fletchings? And why was his palm still on my lower back? I tried to step away from him, but he kept me tightly pinned. So tightly, it felt like my heart had become unmoored and was kicking my spine.

His eyes slid closed, and his mouth pursed as though he'd just bitten down on something sour.

"Why?"

His lids snapped up, and his eyebrows tilted toward one another as though in anger. "That many?"

"That many?"

"I assume there are many if you don't wish to answer."

"I don't wish to answer because it's a very personal question. Not to mention one that doesn't concern you."

"You're right." His hand slid off my lower back and then his gaze lowered in turn, removing the last two points of anchor between our bodies.

His reaction made my heart neglect a few beats. Was he jealous or simply curious? Lowering my arms, I relented. "I had two other partners before Jase. Both in Paris. Both not serious."

He peeked at me through his long, honeyed lashes.

"I've never had an actual relationship because I've never wanted one. Never wanted to experience Leigh's heartache. Getting attached brings joy but the pain that comes with it . . . I'm not sure it's worth the joy. Yes,

I loved Mimi and Leigh with my heart and soul, but not with my body. I can't imagine loving someone with all three. The destruction of such a love . . . It would be obliterating. So, that's my not-very-exciting story. How many people have *you* loved in all those years of life you've had?"

"Like you loved Leigh and Muriel? Two. Tobias and Naya."

"And like Leigh loved Jarod? What is it you called them again? Soulhalves?" *Don't torture yourself, Celeste. Don't ask if he has one.* "Have you met yours?" I wanted to shake myself. My heart did it for me, though. It quivered so wildly it made my rib cage tremble.

His gaze flicked to the food cooling on the coffee table, stayed there. "I have met mine."

My heart dipped and stilled, and so did my trembling. "I thought —When?"

"Years ago." His jaw ticked. Once. Twice.

Years ago . . .? Had he lost her? Was this why he was so bitter about relationships?

"Why didn't you marry her?"

"Because she wasn't eligible."

I frowned.

Before I could delve deeper and uncover the root of the archangel's moodiness, his eyes settled back on mine with the force of a punch.

"You said I wasn't the first man you smoldered, but then you lost a feather."

I blinked. "Is that a question or an assessment of my wicked, deceitful ways?"

"It's a question."

"I lied. You're the first person I've ever smoldered."

"Why did you lie?"

"I lied because I was mortified, and you looked horrified."

"I wasn't horrified." His Adam's apple glided up and down his long neck.

"Well, you looked it."

"I was panicked, not horrified."

"Not sure how that's any better," I mumbled.

"I'm not allowed to take a consort."

Which I knew was a gallant way of saying he wasn't interested. Not only was I a hybrid, but I was also not his soulhalf.

I hid my disappointment under a hefty eye-roll. "I *smoldered* you, Seraph. I'm not expecting a marriage proposal. It just happened. Trust me, I wish I could *un*smolder you, but that's not a possibility, so now, I have to live with the shame of it."

"There is no shame in smoldering."

I side-eyed him. "You've obviously never winged someone by accident."

He raised a rueful smile. "No. I have not."

"King of self-control meet the queen of awkward-sparkling." I exhaled a breath. "Can you please forget my skin lit up?"

"I neither can nor want to." A touch of sadness blotted the light in his eyes. "But it unfortunately doesn't change the fact that all I have to offer is my friendship. And my hugs. Which I promise to improve on"— he smiled—"if you'll let me."

My heart bumped against my ribs, making my chest ache and my throat squeeze. "Okay fine sure." I dropped down onto the couch and grabbed a naan. The doughy flatbread was cold. Still I tore it into chunks, which I ate without tasting. What in Abaddon was wrong with me?

I eyed the wine bottle, wishing I hadn't dumped it. Sure, alcohol wasn't the answer, but there was nothing like a good buzz to ease nerves. Remembering I had a wine fridge stocked with the stuff, I got up and sidestepped the hulking archangel.

Once I was out of his line of sight, my breathing eased a fraction and my heart stopped catapulting against all the soft tissue and hard bone surrounding it. I pressed my forehead against the cool glass door of the built-in cellar and shut my eyes.

Wine. I came for some wine.

I inhaled a painful lungful of air, let it out slowly, then repeated the process. I thought of the lawyer I'd met on my night out with Fernanda. Maybe I could give him a call. Get him to take my mind off the mess I'd made by smoldering someone only interested in my soul.

But then I realized that both the bottle I wanted to uncork and the man I wanted to call were merely Band-Aids, and that even if they bought me time to recover, they wouldn't heal the wound the archangel had inadvertently inflicted upon my heart tonight.

How I wish I hadn't wanted *him*.

My gaze drifted to the counter he said he'd fix. Maybe some broken things could never be fixed.

Stifling my uncharacteristic freak-out, I returned to the living room and injected my tone with a lightness I wasn't feeling. "Ever going to have my kitchen stone fixed, Ser—" The last syllable became air at the sight of my empty living room.

Good.

He was gone.

That was good.

Then why did it feel so bad?

Chapter Thirty-Seven

My bruised throat and heart had broken my sleep into restless increments. Nevertheless, the next morning, I got dressed only to find a handwritten note in my kitchen that I should take it easy for the next two days. Even though the clock was ticking, I didn't insist on taking on a new mission. I returned to bed and nursed my wounds.

Feeling better on day two, I bought a fancy coloring book and a set of felt-tip markers, and walked to the guild to visit Naya. We sat at a table in the cafeteria and, shaded by the fragrant fig tree, spent the afternoon chattering and filling paper after paper with bright colors.

Many times, I'd looked over at her and wondered how anyone didn't recognize her soul. I mean, I was glad for it. If anyone besides Ophan Mira found out . . .

I shuddered just thinking about it.

Just as I had that thought, two gray-uniformed ishim entered the cafeteria. Although a low branch full of ripe fruit and rubbery leaves fenced us off from the rest of the cafeteria, Ish Eliza's eyes cut right across the room toward me. I hoped she hadn't come to have a talk about sinning and sinners because I was in no mood to chat about either. After taking in my table companion, her pinched lips pursed some more.

"She wants to marry Apa," Naya said, not taking her eyes off the parrot's feathers that she was carefully coloring in.

Jealousy wormed its way through me. This wasn't news, but it didn't mean I enjoyed hearing it. "And does your apa want to marry her?"

"Apa's not allowed to marry."

That hadn't been my question, not exactly, but I decided that stressing the *want* part would just make me sound desperate.

Eliza tucked in her sparkly lavender wings as she walked toward Pippa. The ishim's voice didn't carry, but I realized I wasn't the object of her visit when she, along with her fellow verity ranker, exited the cafeteria.

"Ophan Pippa said the only woman he would've been allowed to marry is my mother." Naya bit the top of her pen and shook her head, blonde pigtails flopping about the pink romper she'd paired with a sparkly unicorn T-shirt.

"Your . . . mother?" Her body's biological mother or her soul's biological one? Hadn't Leigh's mother been married?

Naya shrugged. "Apa never speaks of her, so I don't think she's alive." She glanced away from her parrot. "Did you know her?"

"No." I'd never met her body's or her soul's mother. Leigh's parents had never once visited the guild, something that had saddened my friend immensely.

I thought of my own mother then, but sighed. What was the point in thinking of someone who didn't care about you?

"How many feathers do you still need, Celeste?"

"Too many." I picked up a turquoise pen and whisked it across my wolf's face. The color was an exact match to Asher's eyes. All it lacked was some bronze.

Naya reached out and gripped my hand, making my pen drag across the sheet. "You're going to earn them all. Apa will make sure of it."

"Your apa may have magical powers, Naya"—with my free hand, I fingered the faint scar that still marred my neck—"but he unfortunately cannot magically color in my wing bones." I squeezed her hand back. "Rest assured, though, little angel, I'm not giving up."

I'd stopped by the Ranking Room before going to find Naya to check on my score. Even though I'd earned one hundred and seventy-eight feathers in three weeks, I still had a ways to go to reach a thousand. Four-hundred and ninety-nine to be exact. And only two months.

I should probably not have been taking days off.

"Let's play *Neither Yes Nor No*."

I stilled as memory after memory of past rounds we'd played reeled through my mind. "Why that game?" I asked cautiously.

"Because it's my favorite."

"That's funny. It's my favorite, too."

"I know. I mean . . ." Her brow puckered.

"How could it not be my favorite since we like so many of the same things?"

"Yes."

I grinned. "One point Celeste. Zero Naya."

Her mouth rounded. "Hey. I didn't know we started."

"I'm unbeatable at this game, but try your best."

A small smile I might've called devious, if she'd had a devious bone in her body, bent her mouth. "You love my apa."

"No." I coughed. "Whatever gave you that idea?" I sucked in a breath as a feather popped out of my wing bones. *Ugh.*

She pumped her tiny fist and smiled so wide it pushed up her cheeks. "One one. You said no." But then her nose scrunched, and her smile fell when she caught sight of my lie. "You lost a feather."

I concentrated really hard on my coloring.

"Can I touch it?"

I set down my pen and stared between Naya and the shaft that contained one of my memories. "Sure."

She hopped off her chair and crouched, then reached out to pick it up. Her eyes closed as she squished it in her palm. Soon, the purple barbs disintegrated into spangling dust.

When she opened her eyes, they were all shiny. "I didn't know people could be so mean to their ama."

I frowned, trying to remember who she might have seen. One boy I'd signed up to six years ago came to mind. Thomas. He'd thrived on insulting his mother and telling her she was overweight and lazy, and that that was the reason his dad had left. Was that who she'd seen? I'd almost given up on him, but in the end, I'd stuck around and witnessed a tearful reconnection. The boy had finally realized his father was a scumbag and he'd asked his mother for forgiveness.

I told Naya the ending of that story because I didn't want the memory stuck in my feather to dishearten her for what she'd have to do in a couple years. And then we played a few more rounds of *Neither Yes Nor No*. We ended up being tied five to five.

"I want rainbow wings when I grow up." Naya gave her parrot green eyes.

"Rainbow wings?"

"Every color feather. Except black. I don't want bat wings." She wrinkled her nose.

My lips quirked. "Good thing no angel has ever had black wings."

As we went back to coloring, I wondered if, in this new body, she'd get sparkling verity wings or if the transfer of her soul would alter the glitter of her wings. "I cannot wait to see them. Whatever color they end up being because I sense they'll be beautiful."

She beamed, and although her lips weren't shaped like Leigh's, the girl I used to know bled right through that smile.

AFTER A FULL NIGHT'S SLEEP AND A VISIT TO MY FAVORITE nail salon, I made my way toward the steakhouse to meet my newest sinner—a maître d' who made a pretty penny selling overheard business conversations to interested parties.

When I stepped into the loud, masculine space, the archangel was already seated, wearing something so unlike his usual Elysium suedes and tee-and-denim combo that I almost walked right past him. *Okay.* That was an exaggeration. He wasn't the sort of man one could walk past without seeing.

"Should I have dressed up?" Taking in the fine cut of his navy suit and open-collared white shirt, I slid into the bulky leather chair across from him.

"No. Why?" His eyes seemed a little darker than usual as though he'd had a few rough nights. Since Elysium wasn't known for its wild parties, I assumed it was work.

I gestured between my purple T-shirt adorned with the illustration of a growling tiger and his fancy suit.

He looked down at his lap as though he'd forgotten what he'd worn. "Oh. No. I dressed this way because I'm your cover story. We're having a business lunch."

I shrugged out of my bomber. "And what is it you're peddling? Glow-in-the-dark halos?"

A smile relaxed his stiff mien. "No halos. Just a chain of clothing stores."

"Nice."

His gaze scraped across my throat, across my scar and paling bruise. "How's your neck?"

"Healing."

For a moment, neither of us spoke, just stared across the table at one another. I wasn't sure what was going through his mind, but the weariness coming off him worried me.

Above the surrounding chatter, I asked, "Is everything all right, Seraph?"

"Naya said you visited."

I guessed my question would remain unanswered. "I did. We colored. It was possibly the most fun I've had in a while." I thought of the rainbow parrot that was now propped next to my purple feather painting on my dresser. "Eliza was at the guild. Do you know what she was doing?"

"Visiting a fletching who just completed her wings."

Relief that she hadn't been there for Naya or for me warred with jealousy that one of my peers was ascending while I was still so far from it. "Will you be escorting the Ascended through the channel?"

"I don't escort Ascended through the channel."

"You escorted Leigh."

"I don't *usually* escort Ascended." He leaned back in his chair, but there was nothing relaxed about his posture. "You were inconsolable that day."

"I was losing my best friend." Little had I known it was the beginning of the end. I tugged my fingers through my hair, my glossy crimson nails sailing through the deep auburn. "It's really too bad you don't escort Ascended."

"Why is that?"

"Because I was hoping you'd take me through the channel. You know, because you're my mentor and all."

And all? Could I sound any lamer? He was my mentor and maybe my friend, but that was it.

Even though the room was dusky, a spark entered his eyes. "Oh, I was planning on making an exception for you. Like you said, I'm your mentor. Only normal I'd see you to the end of your journey."

A spot of warmth touched my chest. Did he realize the effect he had on me? Sure, I'd smoldered him, but was he aware of how big my crush had gotten?

"Good. I was worried Ish Eliza would be taxiing me through the channel."

He smiled. "Poor Eliza. You really have it in for her."

"I have it in for people who regard those beneath them with disdain." Also, I had it in for people who competed for the same men, not that there was a competition since the archangel wasn't on the market. For a consort, I realized. Maybe he was on the market for a girlfriend. And maybe he was considering Eliza. After all, she was a verity. Oh, angels, what if *she* was his soulhalf? What if she hadn't been eligible because she was still a fletching back then?

"How old is Eliza?"

He frowned. "I'm not certain. Two hundred and fifty, I think. Why?"

Like I would answer that. It was silly, but his answer filled me with relief. Yes, he still had a soulhalf somewhere, but at least it wasn't the marten-faced ranker.

"They're not on the market yet." Asher ticked his head discreetly toward the man who'd appeared beside our table with a sweaty chrome pitcher and sweatier forehead.

Ah. I assumed the perspiring waiter with sideburns worthy of a Victorian novel was my flavor-of-the-day.

"They're filing for bankruptcy," Asher said.

The Jane Eyre character took his sweet time filling our water glasses.

"In other words, your company could purchase it for a symbolic dollar."

I scooted forward in my chair, feigning rapt interest. "If they're going bankrupt, why would my company want to purchase it?"

"Because they have cash on their account. Six million, which will come with the purchase."

I had no clue if companies who were going bankrupt had cash, or why they would go bankrupt if they did, in fact, have cash, but understanding business wasn't the point.

My sinner clutched the pitcher to his chest. "Would you like to hear today's specials?"

"With pleasure, Jacques." Asher nodded toward me. "Celeste, meet Jacques. The man who made this steakhouse a New York institution."

"You flatter me, Mr. Asher."

"I'm only speaking the truth."

I looked between the two men, surprised they were on a first-name basis. After hearing the specials, Jacques retreated toward one of the cream-jacketed servers and transferred our order, then walked toward another table to repeat his little water-offering-eavesdropping charade.

"Do you often wine-and-dine fletchings in this institution?"

"I never share meals with fletchings. Apart from my daughter and you." His expression became as stiff and dark as the wainscoted walnut décor of the steakhouse. "As for why I'm familiar with Jacques . . . His score keeps going up, one point after another. He's not an evil man, but if he doesn't watch out, he'll end with an impossibly high score."

"What's his going value these days?"

"Forty-four. He's sold many delicate secrets and lacks the motivation to stop."

I scrutinized the side-burned man. "So I need to motivate him . . ."

As I turned back toward Asher, my gaze snagged on a vaguely familiar face. Trying to place the man shrugging into a fitted coat made me stare a tad too long. He smiled as he slotted his phone into his breast pocket and walked over.

His name tumbled into my mind just as he reached us. "Phillip." I smiled. "We meet again."

"What are the odds?" Phillip turned toward Asher, who seemed to have become one with the ambient duskiness. "Sorry to interrupt your lunch." Phillip's green gaze returned to me. "Just wanted to stop by and check you hadn't lost my number."

I tapped my cell phone. "Haven't lost it."

"You should use it. I'll answer."

I laughed at his candidness. He tipped his head toward Asher, then winked at me before treading toward the door. When I looked back toward my lunch companion, I was met with an icy glower.

"He's a distraction." Asher shoved his napkin onto his lap. "You don't need a distraction."

I narrowed my gaze. "I may not *need* one, but maybe I *want* one."

I wasn't trying to annoy him, but my declaration firmed up his scowl. I kept expecting him to push back his chair, fold his napkin, and declare I was doomed, but he didn't shift off his padded leather seat. Not even when I cornered Jacques next to the bathroom after my main course and pretended to be tipsy on the single glass of wine I'd ordered and drank. All part of my reformation plan. Hiccupping, I pleaded the maître d' to offer me unbiased advice about my fake dealings, slipping in numbers and an actual competitor's name. After some long-winded counsel, Jacques presented Asher with the bill, chomping at the bit to get us away and sell my ramblings to the highest bidder.

As we crossed 3rd Ave, Asher's gaze dipped to my gait.

"Relax, I'm not drunk, Seraph. It was just an act."

"Did I say anything?"

"No, but I can see the wheels spinning up there." I stopped on the corner. "I'm going to walk around for a bit." An invitation to join me clung to the tip of my tongue, stayed there; we weren't the type to take strolls together.

He had better things to do. And wings. He probably enjoyed using them more than his feet, especially considering how busy New York sidewalks were.

"I need to give Jacques a day or two to go through with what I set in motion." I rolled my hair into a long rope, then let it unravel over my shoulder.

A nerve fluttered in Asher's jaw as though he meant to say something.

"If you get bored ruling over Elysium, you have my number. Actually, do you?"

"I do."

"I don't have yours."

"I'll remedy that." He pulled out his cell phone, and a second later, mine vibrated.

"Great."

I waited for him to deliver a similar line as Phillip, but no invitation to call slipped through his taut lips. And then his wings materialized at his back, but he neither stretched nor pumped them, simply stared at me with such disarming intensity that my heart spun like a flicked top inching toward the edge of a table.

Subduing my disappointment behind a smile, I zipped up my jacket and backed away. "I'll call you when I feel like I've gotten through to him so you can check my score and set me up with my next sinner."

He still didn't say a thing. Not even *toodeloo*. Not that Asher was the sort of man to say *toodeloo*, but a *have a pleasant afternoon* would've been nice.

I wished I could blame the piercing ache growing inside of me on heartburn, but it had nothing to do with the crab cakes, T-bone, and basket of fries I'd ingested. My silly little heart simply wanted someone it couldn't have . . . someone who'd proposed friendship.

I rubbed the bottom edge of my rib cage absently, and then, after a half-hour of wallowing, I scrolled through my phone for Phillip's contact. He was cute and available, and most importantly, interested.

I texted him a simple: *Hi.*

A couple seconds later, he texted back: *Celeste?*

ME: *I found your number.*

PHILLIP: *I answered.*

ME: *I see that.*

Even though I wished I were having this conversation with another man, I made plans. Plans that led to shopping for clothes that were unlike anything I owned. I momentarily hesitated to snip off the price tags, but in the end, I did. And the following night, I donned one of my purchases —a dress so white it was almost blinding and so short it was almost indecent.

And then I added another item I never thought I'd wear: stilettos.

As I stared at my reflection in the bathroom mirror, I thought of Mimi, imagined her brushing out my hair, telling me what a beautiful woman I'd grown into. She'd tell me this often, as though hoping that if she said it enough, I'd begin to believe it.

Would she think I was beautiful tonight?

I felt a little beautiful.

I also felt a lot sad.

I pulled out her favorite lipstick, a crimson that matched my nails, and slicked it on. And then I left before I could scrub it away, pull off my dress, and kick off my heels to wait for a man who wasn't coming.

Chapter Thirty-Eight

I knew I looked different when I stepped out of the elevator but hadn't realized how different until my doorman did a double-take. If only I could feel different, too. Maybe I would after tonight. Maybe Phillip would be fun and sweet, and steal my mind away from the brooding archangel.

I spent the first ten minutes of the cab ride downtown trying to pump up my enthusiasm for the date, the next ten tugging on the hem of my dress wondering what in Abaddon had gotten into me to wear it, and the last ten debating to tell the driver to stop and head back uptown.

In the end, I got out of the cab and walked to the blazing art gallery where Phillip had suggested we meet before dinner. I waited for him outside, but between garnering an unsettling quantity of attention and the brisk evening air, I headed inside. I pulled out my phone, opened my latest chats. My gaze lingered on the name beneath Phillip's: Jase.

Even though I itched to find out how he was doing, I clicked on my chat with Phillip.

ME: *I'm here.*

I waited a couple of minutes for him to answer. When my screen didn't light up, I sent him: ***Is everything okay?***

Fifteen minutes ticked by. Even though I kept checking my phone, I strolled around the gallery because I had enough pride not to stay rooted to the middle of the very white and bright space, looking like an abandoned puppy.

I'd never gotten stood up before, and it stung. To think I hadn't especially had high expectations for this date in the first place . . . I couldn't imagine how crushing it would've felt had it been someone I actually cared about.

Once I got over the sting, I made the most of my outing and walked around the maze of galleries that grew smaller and duskier the farther I penetrated into the block-long building. Instead of oppressive, though, the dim lighting and close quarters accentuated the art. It also heightened the emptiness of the galleries, the other visitors flocking to the wider and more populated space. After all, most people had come out to be seen, not to see.

The very last gallery, which was no bigger than the room I'd rented from Jase, contained a particularly beautiful piece: the Manhattan skyline made up entirely of words. I leaned forward and squinted at the scribbles. It was a poem, an ode to New York and New Yorkers. I snapped a few pictures, wanting to show Naya. Maybe we could work on a project like this together.

"I wasn't aware you were an art amateur."

My shoulders locked up at the sound of the deep timbre. Slowly, I straightened, and then slower still, I turned.

Asher was wearing a suit again, a three-piece black one this time. "Expecting someone else?"

"I've decided to mitigate my expectations of people. It greatly lessens my disappointment." Even in my stilettos, I was still several inches shorter than the archangel and had to cant my head. "However, I am surprised to see you here and curious as to how you knew where I'd be."

His gaze drifted to my short, white strapless number. Had it been made of anything other than pleated chiffon and draped silk, it would've looked cheap. But it didn't look cheap. It looked expensive. And pretty. At least, I thought so. I wasn't so sure the archangel shared my belief considering how frowny he became.

"Lucky guess," he finally said.

"The same way I don't put much stock in people, I don't put much stock in luck. Did you follow me? Track my phone? Check my location on your fletching-GPS app?"

"We don't have one of those yet, but it would be rather convenient."

"Were you worried I was being distracted?"

"No."

A woman tried to come in through the lone narrow opening, but two was already a crowd, so she peered at the painting behind me, then spun on her heels and clip-clopped away.

I refocused on Asher. "What do you mean, *no?*"

"I wasn't worried you were being distracted because I knew you'd be here alone."

My eyebrows furrowed. Until the meaning of his words dawned on me. "You canceled my date?"

His wings materialized at his back, adding bulk to his already imposing form.

"I can't believe you did that. You had no right!" Anger laced through my surprise, overpowering it so completely that I couldn't even appreciate that I hadn't been stood up.

Asher didn't even have the nerve to look impudent.

"First rule of friendship," I said tightly, "you don't go behind your friend's back and cancel their dates."

"Phillip cheated on his LSATs and on his last two girlfriends. I was looking out for you."

"I can't believe you're justifying yourself! What exactly did you tell him that he didn't even have the decency to man up and call me?"

"I told him to lose your number."

I gripped my elbows, my knuckles whitening. "You have *no* shame."

"In two months, you'll be gone."

"Or not!" I tossed my hands in the air, exasperated. "But that's beside the point!"

"You'll be gone." The archangel had ninety-nine problems but confidence in me wasn't one of them.

"Still doesn't give you any right to decide what I do during the time I have left," I hissed.

The air around his body seemed to wobble with heat as though his annoyance was fanning the fire in his veins.

"I really don't feel like being in the same room with you right now." I tried to sidestep him, but he whipped out his wings until the bronze tips grazed both walls of the gallery.

Yes, it was on the small side, but his wings were on the ridiculously enormous side.

I stopped an inch from the fence of feathers. "Pull them back or I will plow straight through them."

He didn't remove them from my path.

I glared at him. "I'm serious, Seraph. Tuck them in. Now."

"I can't."

"You can't?" I spun on him and hissed, "Why? Are they *cramping*?"

"No."

"Then why can't you fold them up or magick them away?"

"When you smoldered me, Celeste—"

"I told you to forget it." I puffed out an annoyed breath, damning my soul and skin for having lit up for *him*.

"—when you smoldered me, did your shine turn off instantly?"

"I don't see how my smolder's duration has anything to do with you not being able to get your wings out of my face."

"Celeste," he growled.

"What, Seraph?"

"I'm winging you."

Chapter Thirty-Nine

No smoke leaked out of Asher, but the veins in his hands and along his neck were distended.

I blinked at him, then at his wings, then back at him. "*Why?* Why would you wing me?"

He shut his eyes and pinched the bridge of his nose. "Because I've lost my angels-damn mind." He spoke so quietly that I barely caught his words over the thumping in my chest. When his lids reeled back up, his irises, usually so vivid and clear, were full of thunder. "Because I'm a selfish man, who has so little to offer, yet wants *everything* in return."

My breathing slowed, and the thing in my chest, the thing that coveted the archangel, in spite of him being mercurial, controlling, and inaccessible, expanded.

"I promised the Seven I would concentrate on Elysium, on our people. I swore to eschew any and all distractions, especially ones of a physical nature. Yet here I am *winging* you." He released a bitter laugh that gave me actual chills. "I don't deserve to be an archangel, and if I weren't so worried about Naya and her fate, I would've forfeited my seat. But I am *terrified*, Celeste. Terrified that she will be taken from me. But now I'm also terrified that *you*'ll be taken from me. I can't lose her, but I also can't lose you." His voice, so steady and strong, broke on that last part. "I cannot afford a distraction, but I also cannot stomach losing you to Phillip. Or to someone like him. Like Jase."

A tickle began behind my lids. Spread to my nose and throat.

234

He slanted me the most heart-crushing look. "You don't belong with them." A deep swallow jostled his throat.

"With whom do I belong?"

He ran a trembling hand down his face, as though to scrub away his frustration. "Why couldn't we have met in twenty years?"

My heart bounced. Squeezed. Bounced. Squeezed. "Where do I belong, Seraph?"

The feathered shafts whispered through the air of the small gallery as they finally began to retract. "With me, Celeste. You belong with me. *To* me." And then he was stepping forward, filling my space. Filling *all* the space. "The same way I belong to you." He unbuttoned his vest, then took my hand and flattened it against his white shirt, right at the bottom ridge of his rib cage. It was nowhere near his heart and yet something beat beneath his skin.

"I'm assuming you're not pregnant." I ended up saying, because . . . *what in Abaddon was that?*

"You haven't figured it out . . ." Not a question. Merely an observation.

He rested his own palm over my abdomen, and my stomach tensed and pressed up against the wall of skin. Wait, was it my stomach? Where were stomachs? Maybe it was my heart . . . Maybe the archangel had finally managed to knock it loose.

He covered my hand with the one not resting on my stomach. "What you're feeling is my soul."

My lashes hit my browbone. "Your soul? We can feel souls? I thought only seraphim and malakim had that ability."

"Seraphim can control all souls." He tugged my fingers a little lower, and the nudging followed. "Malakim, though, only possess the power to guide souls out of lifeless bodies and into new ones." He curved his palm around my waist, settling it against my spine. The pounding inside me took off after him like the Rottweiler pup I'd fed granola.

"Last I checked I wasn't an archangel." I shifted my hand to the side of his rib cage, and his soul bumped right along.

He lifted his hand off mine, and with the utmost gentleness, he cupped my cheek. "You can feel mine, Celeste, because my reckless soul has decided it belongs with yours." The air darkened as his wings curled around our bodies. "*Ta yot neshahadzaleh, levsheh.*" His fingertips danced up the length of my spine, then back down, before wrapping delicately around my waist. "You are my soulhalf, sweetheart."

My blood tightened and then detonated, and my skin tossed glitter across the arched expanse of his feathers. "Here I thought *levsheh* meant demon-spawn."

A taut smile flickered over his mouth. "I'm declaring my soul's inability to exist without yours, and *this* is what you pick up on?"

I shrugged, but since I was trembling, it probably looked like I'd been hit by one of those frigid winds that rushed around skyscrapers in the dead of winter.

"And demon-spawn? Why in the worlds would you think I'd call you demon-spawn?"

"Might've been your tone."

He cocked an eyebrow. "My tone?"

"Yes. You have an unrivaled way of biting my head off."

His smile solidified. "You bring out emotions I didn't even know I possessed, Celeste. Emotions I'm still not equipped to contend with." He combed back a lock of my hair, tucked it behind my ear, his fingers sweeping across the back of my conical stud before balancing on the curve of my neck. "Be patient with me, *levsheh.*"

Levsheh . . . sweetheart. Now that I knew what it meant, I decided it was a gorgeous sounding word.

"Seraph—"

"Please, don't call me by my title."

I licked my lips. That was going to take some getting used to.

"Asher . . ." Using his angels-given name was so strange that it momentarily gave me pause.

"Yes?"

"Why did you lie about having met your soulhalf years ago?"

"I didn't lie. I did meet her years ago." He beheld my scintillating skin with such reverence that my shine intensified. "At a guild banquet in my honor. I even got to see her beautiful wings that night and glimpse her virtuous soul."

My mouth slipped open, and for a moment, I lost the ability to produce sound, but then it returned with such force that my words came out shrilly. "You were talking about *me*?"

"Who did you think I was talking about?"

"*Not* me." I bit my lip. Released it. "Did you know it then?"

"That your soul would own mine? No. For the bond to happen, there needs to be physical contact, and we didn't touch that night. Thank Elysium, for you were still so young."

"When did you know then?"

"I began to wonder the day we sat on the bench outside of Bofinger's house, but found out for certain the day you hugged me in front of Ish Eliza. My soul tried to flee my body when it sensed yours."

I blinked. "All I remember was thinking you were two seconds away from murdering me for having touched your wings."

His lips bent some more, and although his expression wasn't carefree, it was mesmerizing. "You really think the worst of me."

"Before I met you, I heard stories of how great and heroic you were. The golden boy of Elysium." With the hand not feeling up his soul, I traced the shape of his smile and raised one of my own. Like his, it wasn't bright, because loss sanded down the edges of joy, leaving behind the essence without the artifice. "I had trouble believing someone could be so objectively extraordinary. But then you walked into the guild and gave your grand speech, and I told Leigh that if she did *one* thing in her life, it was to become your consort." The memory of being at her side in the star-flecked atrium that night extinguished my glow. How was it that you could miss someone who was still essentially alive? "Although I'm glad she didn't listen to me, she, too, realized you lived up to your nickname."

His breath seemed to catch in his throat.

"So don't ever doubt my admiration, Ser—Asher."

He swallowed. "You admire me?"

"For all you've done." I rested one hand on his cheek. "For all you do." I cupped the other side of his face. "And for all you still have left to accomplish."

The fence of his feathers tightened around us, every downy barb locking together, dipping us into more darkness.

Keeping my eyes locked on his, I said, "To think you're a little mine now."

His neck bowed. "I am more than a little yours, *levsheh*."

"You're also Naya's and Elysium's."

"Not in the same way."

I rested my cheek against his chest, right at the base of his throat, and wound my arms around his waist, feeling the soft brush of his feathers against my skin.

His fingers threaded through my hair and worked their way slowly through the lengths. "I'm not allowed to marry."

I pulled back. "Why do you keep circling back to that? I don't care about marriage. I swear, I don't. The only thing I care about is being with you. Is there a way for us to be together, or will it cost you your title?"

"No. It wouldn't cost me my title." He wrapped the ends of my hair around his fingers, then let them unravel, before winding them up again.

"You're just worried that I'll be too great a distraction?"

He lowered his forehead to mine. "I'm not worried you might be; I'm certain you will be."

His eyes were filled with such torment that I sighed. "So what is it you suggest? Wait until Naya has ascended?"

"I tried that already. Waiting this out. Waiting *us* out." He hung his head, and in the quietest voice I'd ever heard him use, he whispered, "Tell me to leave, *levsheh*."

I trailed my hand up his side, the downy barbs of his wings caressing my knuckles, making both of us shiver. When I reached his neck, I spiraled my fingers around it. "No."

"You deserve someone better. Someone who didn't break the highest law in Elysium."

"I hate our laws." My wing bones strummed.

And strummed.

In the end, I didn't lose a feather. Maybe because I hadn't specified *which* laws I loathed.

"Please, Celeste. Send me away."

I steeled my soul and breathed the command he wanted to hear, not because I wanted him to heed it, but because I wanted him to realize he wasn't trapped. "Leave."

His eyes shut and squeezed until their corners crinkled.

When he didn't move, I uttered the hateful word again.

His lids flipped open, and I held my breath, silently waiting to see if he'd build his walls back up, tuck in his wings, and choose his duty over his heart. I told myself that if he did, I'd forgive him, because his choice would be forged by responsibility and not cowardice.

He wound more of my hair around his fist, tipping my head farther. "Forgive me, Celeste."

My throat tightened. My chest, too.

"Forgive me for not being a stronger man."

I swallowed as a hurricane of heartbeats built and swelled, whisking up my soul and carrying it out to the remotest reaches of my body. When his lips grazed my mouth, the hurricane raged. Was he kissing me goodbye?

His kiss set fire to my skin, illuminating our cocoon of silence and darkness where nothing outside of his pounding soul and my sparkling flesh existed.

If this was goodbye, it was the cruelest parting.

I wanted him to explain what decision he'd come to, but my mouth refused to free his. Not that his seemed desirous to release mine. Did that mean—Did that mean he was staying?

When his lips parted, my poor heart leaped and soared. Or was it my soul?

Even though I craved to run my hands over his magnificent feathers, I didn't want to spook him, so I settled on dragging his face closer. A muffled groan dropped from his mouth. I gorged on it, gorged on his heartbeats and heat too. He crushed me to him, and it awakened not only my muscles but every single one of my nerve-endings. Even my invisible wings twanged, need filling each shaft and each vane.

His words ran on a loop inside my clouding mind: *Forgive me for not being a stronger man.*

Did he believe staying made him weak? How many walls—his and our obsolete world's—would he need to tear down to grasp his strength?

My navel dipped from the bulge thickening between our bodies. In a corner of my kiss-dazed brain, it hit me that if he didn't break me with his mouth and arms, he'd surely break me with that other part of him. Was it a mark of insanity how terribly I wanted to be broken by this tormented, celestial king?

How high my soul had reached . . .

I might've smirked at its audacity to have snared an immortal ruler if my mouth wasn't so intent on soaking up every last drop of our first kiss.

I never wanted it to end and yet I did, so we could collect thousands more.

My blood careened through me at such speed that my head lightened, threatening to float away and join my heart and soul wherever it was they were suspended. Repeatedly, I gasped, and repeatedly, he swallowed my gasps and fed me some of his own.

It was only after my sparkle faded that he pried his panting mouth off mine. Although he didn't release me, the knot of his arms slackened, and he freed my strands that dropped like silken ropes down my spine.

"My soul feels like it might burst." His whispered words warmed my flushed skin.

I tapped his abdomen with two fingers. "Your soul's higher up, Seraph."

He blinked, and then, once he caught on to what I'd implied, all the edges of his beautiful face smoothed, and he laughed. "Well, it has been over two decades . . ."

"What's been over two decades?"

His gaze, which had been on mine, dropped to my bare shoulder. He studied it as though it were the single most fascinating bone in the body.

"Since you've been with someone?"

His eyes narrowed but didn't shift off my shoulder.

I reached up and pushed a golden tendril of hair out of his averted eyes. "Asher?"

"Yes." He said this so roughly that it scraped across my swollen mouth and pinned it shut. "Abaddon screwed me up, Celeste."

What had he endured in the underworld? I licked my lips, eager to ask but loath to spoil the moment with memories that still haunted him.

I rested my palm on his jaw to steer his gaze back toward mine. "Well, you haven't lost your touch."

That won me back his full attention.

"If you think I'm lying, by all means, check the floor."

His gaze didn't stray off mine. "I trust you, *levsheh*."

It was silly but his declaration was almost as heady as his kiss.

His nose bumped into mine, and then his mouth slanted over mine, gently and chastely this time. And although the gentleness lasted, the chasteness did not. "Your soul has bound itself to a weak man's."

"You are not weak, but if this is your way of telling me that you'll give me more than hugs, then by all means, reduce your worth. I have enough admiration to compensate your lack of pride."

He turned his head and kissed the inside of my palm. I still didn't know if souls could wander freely through bodies, but it felt like mine had traveled right into my hand.

"Did you know that once souls find their halves, it is *physically* impossible for them to be apart? This is why I believe Leigh and Jarod were soulhalves. Why she returned to him, and why I came back to you in spite of my conscience raging at me to stay away." He delicately stole both my hands and transferred them to his chest that pounded with strong and steady beats and then lower, to the edge of his rib cage where his soul thrummed wildly.

I stroked it.

Mine. It was mine. *He* was mine.

This sparkly-winged pillar of a man was *mine.*

Chapter Forty

After he'd retrieved my jacket from the makeshift coat-check by the front door and helped me into it, Asher excused himself to speak to the gallery's owner, probably to thank him for having kept people away from the little gallery that had seen our first kiss. And second. And third. It had all remained very PG, even though my mind had wandered to many a R-rated place.

As he walked back toward me, posture so straight, gait so steady, appearance so refined, he garnered everyone's attention. Two older ladies even fanned themselves.

To think he was returning to me. I wanted someone to pinch me.

He held out his hand, and I fit my fingers through his.

As we strolled out, impatience to head somewhere private made me blurt, "Home. Let's go home."

He stopped walking and gazed down at me. "Have you eaten?"

"I'm not hungry. At least, not for food."

His pupils distended. "We have an eternity before us, Celeste."

"What if we don't?" I bit my lip. Released it. "What if in two months—"

"Don't say things like that." Thunder. His expression became thunder.

"Hey . . ." I said soothingly. "I'm just being realistic here."

He rolled the enormous knobs of his shoulders, straining the seams of his suit jacket. "No, you're being defeatist, which isn't like you."

Silence crept over us.

"Are you done with Jacques?" he finally asked.

I sighed. "Almost."

I'd stopped by the restaurant at lunchtime and cornered the maître d'
to lament that my deal had been called off because of leaked information,
and that I risked losing my livelihood . . . my very life. Yes, it was a stretch
but not completely untrue. If I didn't earn my wings, I'd end up losing
them, and in turn, my immortality.

I'd asked Jacques point-blank whether I'd said anything incrimi-
nating during my first visit to his establishment. Although he
pretended I hadn't, his forehead had slickened with so much sweat that
I could spot my reflection in its shiny grooves. His fear of getting
unmasked was toying with his conscience, the part of him I was trying
to reach. Once he—*hopefully*—retracted the information, I'd pay him
one last visit. In case my plan backfired, I'd put my backup plan to use:
sit him down and confront him like I'd done with Bofinger. I couldn't
afford to spend weeks on Jacques, but I could give him a few more
days.

To lighten the mood, I asked, "Are you putting off heading back to
my place because you're scared, or are you really that determined to
feed me?"

"Scared?"

"Of what'll happen behind closed doors and drawn curtains after
two decades of celibacy."

The archangel tipped me a slow smile. "If anyone should be frightened, it should be you, *levsheh*. You're about to lead a famished man into
your bed."

"I can't wait." Because I hadn't smoldered him in at least thirty
minutes, my skin decided to shower light over the pavement and the brick
façade of an apartment complex.

"You're sparkling, Celeste."

"Just making sure your gaze doesn't stray."

His thumb dipped under the hem of my jacket and settled on the
indent of my waist. "You don't need to smolder me to make certain of
that."

"One can never be too careful. Our worlds are full of alluring people,
all of whom would steal you away in a heartbeat."

"You're my soulhalf. There is *no one* else for me." He angled his body toward mine. "But rest assured that if anyone so much as tries to separate us, I'll extinguish their souls." He said this so very softly and yet his threat resonated in my marrow.

"Please don't extinguish any souls on my behalf." The mere idea that he might flicked off my phosphorescence, not because I was appalled, but because I was worried extinguishing souls would lead to a reprieve from the Seven, and for Naya's sake, he needed to keep a low profile.

His features tensed as though he were having the same contemplations. Or maybe he was still thinking about someone trying to separate us. "There's an excellent sushi bar two blocks away. Do you eat raw fish?"

"I eat everything."

His palm made its way to the small of my back, and we started up again. I glanced up at him, and he glanced down at me, and the ambient world stopped existing. There were no more taxis jouncing against potholes, no more boisterous chatter from passersby, no more subdued glow from streetlamps. Just him and me.

But then the world came crashing back in full surround-sound and technicolor as a scrappy man smelling like The Trap's dumpsters at closing time yelled something about how capitalism was going to bring forth the apocalypse. He stumbled. Asher shot out his hand to steady him. The man ripped his arm from the archangel's grasp, then proceeded to rail at him and his fancy, capitalistic suit.

Asher removed his jacket, then draped it over the man's dirty wifebeater. "There's money inside the breast pocket. Get yourself a hotel room, food, a bath, clothes."

I watched the drunk—or was he drugged?—man run unsteady hands down the lapels of Asher's jacket that hit him mid-thigh. He patted down the pockets, then suddenly froze and jerked his gaze toward the archangel, eyes so wide his irises bobbed in the white expanse.

Asher gripped the man's shoulder and gave it a squeeze that crumpled the fabric floating around his skeletal frame. "Every soul on this Earth has a purpose. Find yours. Make the world a better place, even if it's only for one person." He released the homeless man's shoulder and turned, and then his hand was back on my body.

I glanced over my shoulder as we walked away, found the man trembling again, possibly harder than before. I hoped I'd just witnessed the moment that would alter the course of his life.

"When I was a fletching," Asher started, "I wanted to save every human being, and for the life of me, I couldn't understand why angels didn't devote themselves entirely to ensure the famished were fed, the injured were healed, and the desolate consoled."

"And now?"

"Now, I understand the precepts taught in guilds—that the best way to save humanity is by teaching humans to save themselves." He held the glass door of a hole-in-the-wall restaurant open for me, an understated smile softening his expression. "But the boy inside still wishes I could save them all."

On the threshold, I pressed up on tiptoe and stamped a kiss on his jaw, the dark blond stubble chafing my lips. "And you doubt you deserve the role you were entrusted with . . ."

My faith in his prowess wouldn't magically expunge the weight of the world he carried on his wings, but hopefully, it'd ease the anxiety that accompanied the load. I stole his hand from his side and pulled him inside the Japanese eatery, which resembled the cabin of an old ship with its varnished wood-paneling and electric gaslights strung up over a tiny dining room, made narrower by a U-shaped sushi bar. It was packed, and yet the hostess found us two free stools. If she hadn't been salivating over my date, I might've thanked her for her industriousness, but Asher was mine, and I was apparently territorial.

I placed my hand on his thigh and narrowed my eyes at her. She looked between the archangel and myself but mustn't have deemed me threatening, because she kept gazing at him. A little respect would've been nice.

Asher draped his arm over my backrest and flipped the laminated menu. "Anything you don't like?" He moved his mouth to my ear. "Besides our hostess?"

I let out a soft snort and turned, about to reiterate that I ate everything, but got sidetracked by how close his mouth was to mine.

Before I could kiss him, our waiter showed up. Asher placed our order in such perfect Japanese it took the waiter a full minute before he worked his pen against his notepad.

"Would you like sake, Celeste?"

The glazed eyes and cracked teeth of the man we'd bumped into swam in front of my eyes, and I shook my head. It wasn't that I thought a glass of rice wine would doom my soul, but I wanted a clear mind and body tonight.

Once the man was gone, I unfolded my napkin and laid it on my lap. "I've been meaning to ask . . . how did you become Elysium's favorite hero?"

He leaned back in his chair. "I'm not sure it'll make for a pleasant dinner conversation." He slid off the little ring of paper around his chopsticks, then fidgeted with the two long, whittled pieces of wood. "Besides, what I did wasn't heroic. Any man with my power and in my situation would've done the same."

"You were an Abaddon erelim back then, correct?"

He nodded.

"Although I've never been to Abaddon, I imagine there is more than one erelim patrolling that dimension."

He didn't answer, but his thinning mouth told me he hadn't been alone in Hell.

"So, what is it you did?"

He stroked up the length of smooth wood engraved with the Japanese word for LUCK. "A soul managed to break free from his vessel, recover his human form, and break others out. By the time we caught on to the breech, he'd singlehandedly freed over fifty souls, which leaked the fumes of repentance throughout the fortress." He shuddered. "It was the wails of two of our fellow guards, who'd succumbed to the fumes, that alerted the rest of us. I flew inside the fortress and shut the airlock, the only point of entry. There are no windows. No doors either. Just glass case upon glass case of souls."

"I thought there was a bonfire . . ."

"There used to be, but our ancestors found a way to contain it and syphon the fumes," Asher explained, although he seemed a world away, back in that fortress. "I forced myself to breathe as little as possible as I raced around, not because of the fumes, but because once the airlock shuts, the air supply dwindles. I wouldn't have died, but if I'd passed out, I wouldn't have been of much use.

"Not having sinned much, my darkest memories weren't debilitating. Unlike my fellow sentinels'. One of them had shredded his face and fainted from the pain. The other attacked me with her fire. Her mind was so muddled that her aim was awry, and I managed to knock her out long enough to locate the sinner at the source of the chaos. Other souls had recovered their former corporeal envelopes by then, or a semblance of them." Flames sizzled over his fingers and chewed into his chopstick.

I clapped my palm over the blaze before anyone could notice. Smoke leaked through my clamped fingers and my skin stung, yet I didn't remove my hand. Asher jerked. He dropped the charred chopstick, which clattered against the bar, then flipped over my hand and ran his thumb over my bubbling flesh, muttering under his breath. New flames licked his thumbs, which he swept over the blisters until the skin pinkened and smoothed.

"I'm sorry," he murmured, stroking the center of my palm with his now extinguished thumb. "I'm so sorry, Celeste."

I closed my hand over his. "I'm the one who forced you to relive this nightmare."

His Adam's apple jostled in his throat.

"Last question, and we'll never speak about it again, but how long were you locked up?"

His gaze set on mine. "Two days. It took me two days to contain the souls. Two days during which I had to knock out the two guards repeatedly, so they wouldn't hurt themselves or try opening the airlock. Two days of burning away flesh and rooting through rib cages to retrieve souls."

The horror of his task made me grip his hand a little tighter.

"If only I'd been a malakim back then." A breath rattled from his lungs. "I could've just coaxed their souls out without mutilating their bodies."

I stroked his knuckles.

"I still smell them sometimes—the burnt flesh, the bitter fumes, the fetid air." His nostrils flared. He shook his head as though to uproot the ugly memory, and then his fist slackened. "Once I contained the souls and unsealed the airlock, I requested a transfer and haven't traveled back to Abaddon since." His fingers spread mine apart before delicately enfolding them. "What a date I make." He raised a diminutive smile. "Regaling you with nightmarish tales of my ascension to power."

"I appreciate you telling me." I swiped the charred chopsticks into my napkin, so their blackened remains didn't raise any eyebrows, and asked for a fresh pair.

Our food arrived then.

One of Asher's hands remained on my body throughout the meal. First, speared through mine underneath the bar, then toying with the ends of my hair, and finally on my bare, pebbled thigh.

He leaned over and, in a voice that sent a thrill down the side of my neck, asked, "Have you eaten enough?"

I frowned. "Were you planning on ordering more?"

"No." Although his hand didn't stroke up my thigh, his fingers encircled my leg. "I was planning on paying and taking you home."

Heart cruising a million knots per second, I whispered, "Take me home."

Although he'd given his cash to the homeless man, he produced a slim billfold from his trouser pocket. I wasn't sure how much dinner had cost, but I doubted it was anywhere near the sum he left.

He stood and pulled my chair back. "Land or air?"

My heart careened to a stop, not from fright—I mean, I still wasn't a fan of dangling over nothing, even though I trusted the archangel with my life—but because he'd given me the choice, and for that very reason, I said, "Let's fly, golden boy."

"I'd rather you not call me a boy, Celeste, even though it is a step above neon swine."

"Neon swine? I would never—oh . . ." The memory of the fluorescent winged pig at his effigy made me dent my lip. "Sorry."

"It could've been worse."

"How?"

"You could've not thought of me at all."

My lips quirked into a smile, but it zapped off my face when, without warning, Asher scooped me into his arms, dumped angel-dust around us, and rocketed skyward.

Chapter Forty-One

" I 'm going to be sick." I squished my face against his white shirt, the small buttons imprinting their shape into my forehead. "I wish there were speed limits up here."

A chuckle reverberated in his chest. "And to think I'm not flying at full capacity."

"You're kidding?" I jerked back to look into his eyes. "You don't consider our cruising speed slow, do you?"

"Not slow per se, but I can go much *much* faster."

"I hope I never find out what full capacity feels like."

He grinned down at me. "At full capacity, we would reach California in . . ." His playfulness withered as his gaze set on something below us.

I turned my head, regretting it instantly. Every piece of sashimi swam up my throat. Clenching my teeth, I forced the raw fish back down as the sparkly-winged woman standing on my balcony came into sharp focus.

"Ish Eliza." Asher's tone was amicable but clipped.

The lavender-feathered ishim's mouth pursed as we drifted lower. "I'm sorry to show up so late and interrupt your evening, Seraph"—she shot me a look as frosty as her wingtips—"but there's a situation in Elysium that requires your presence."

"What sort of situation?" He carefully set me down, and although he removed his hands from my body, he stayed flush against my back.

"The sort that requires a vote," she responded cryptically.

"And it is imperative I vote this very minute?"

Her face tightened in time with her wings. "Seraph Claire asked for this matter to be resolved swiftly. I tried phoning you when I reached the guild, but you weren't answering." She took in my attire with a curl of her lip. "Your daughter suggested you might be helping Fletching Celeste with her latest mission, so I came here."

"No need for titles. Celeste is fine." I added a saccharine smile to show her just how I felt about her regard for my dress and my position on the celestial ladder.

Asher's pecs dug into my shoulder blades and then his hand curled around my hip. "Thank you for coming all this way and waiting, but I need to debrief Celeste on her mission."

Angels, he was a talented liar. Had I not been privy to his plans for our evening, I might've believed we really were about to discuss Jacques at great, tedious lengths.

"Please tell Seraph Claire I'll be in Elysium first thing in the morning and will lend my voice to the vote then."

His dismissal—or was it the hand he'd laid on me—streaked Ish Eliza's cheekbones with two pink slashes. "This vote is extremely delicate and pressing."

The archangel's taut body strummed with annoyance. "What is so pressing about it?"

She jerked her gaze back to his face. "You know as well as anyone, surely better, that Elysium matters don't concern *fletchings*, Seraph."

"And you know as well as anyone that when an archangel asks you a question, it is your job to answer immediately."

Snap.

"The vote concerns Raphael and Sofia."

I expected him to relax since neither Naya nor Adam's name had been mentioned, but his body became quartz.

I tipped my head back to look at him. Between the thinness of his mouth and the somber sheen of his eyes, worry butchered my short-lived relief. "Who are they?"

His jaw formed a perfect ninety-degree angle. "They're—" He swallowed. "Sofia and Raphael *were* . . ." Another pause. Another swallow. "They were Leigh's parents."

I blinked at him. Had they found out about Naya and decided to claim her as their own? Or did they want to annihilate her soul? My blood cooled at the horrific contemplation, then chilled when the archangel pulled away from me. He stepped toward the railing and clutched it, his gaze sinking to the monochromatic park below. I tamped down my desire to erase the distance he'd put between us and ease the tension thundering through his body.

"What is it they want?" His voice sounded cool and collected, but tension bent his tone like the wind bowed the copper edges of his feathers.

Eliza's narrow face scrunched up, as though it physically pained her to share the details of her assignment with a fletching. "They'd like to separate."

Asher glanced over his shoulder at the ishim.

My heart, which had been in the process of derailing, squealed to an abrupt halt. I whipped my gaze off the paving stone beneath my heels and back onto the archangel. Our eyes met and locked, relief simmering in the dark air that separated us. Although he still gripped the railing, there was now a little slack in his arms and spine.

"Ever since they lost their third child, they've been miserable. Everyone understands your reasons for not visiting Abaddon, Seraph, but if you'd paid the erelim there a visit, you would've noticed how Leigh's parents have drifted apart."

Something gave me pause. "Divorces are put to a vote in Elysium?"

"Your education is severely lacking, Fletching. Had you not rejected our world, our guilds—"

"Careful what you say next, Ish Eliza." Asher's growl immobilized her lips. "I made you an ishim; I can just as easily *un*make you. And *without* putting it to a vote."

The anger that sparked in Eliza's dark eyes raised the fine hairs on the back of my neck. I was grateful for the archangel's protection, but he couldn't afford to make an enemy of Eliza. That she didn't like or respect me was one thing. That she stopped lapping the ground beneath his feet was another. I assumed she was smart enough not to directly attack the archangel but vicious enough to use Naya as punishment.

She dipped her pointy chin into her neck. "I apologize, Seraph. I didn't mean to undermine your . . . *protégée*. All I meant by my previous remark is that ophanim are founts of information, who ensure fletchings are equipped for what awaits them after their wings' completion."

Asher shot her a look that would've made anyone else crap their pants, but all it did was make her square her shoulders. The silence that ensued was so loud it reverberated over the howl of the wind, which was growing progressively stronger, carrying the scent of autumn rain.

Eliza pushed the blonde corkscrews carving across her face out of her eyes. "Will you come home, Seraph, or should I inform the Seven they'll have to postpone the vote?"

Asher released the railing just as icy needles began to fall. "I'll go now." He didn't touch me with any other part of his body than his eyes, yet the slow caress sent a shudder right down to my toes. "I'll be right back, Celeste." He pumped his wings and shot into the sky.

Ish Eliza hovered for a moment. "You have no respect for our world." *Dung bug.*

"Do you know what we call women like you up in Elysium? Women who part their legs to lure men? *Zoya.* Temptresses who lead angels astray."

"I'm not a fan of labels or titles, but thanks for being so . . . edifying." I started to turn, done with this conversation.

"I'll have to report you."

"For what?"

"For distracting the archangel, which will hurt his reputation some more. It's presently not at its shiniest up in Elysium."

I gritted my teeth. "Are you threatening him or me?"

"I'm threatening no one. Just explaining our way of life in case you ever make it. Oh, and *verity divorces* are put to a vote; hybrids can divorce without concerning the Seven, their unions not being as sacred." A chilling smile glanced off her lips before she soared, becoming one with the clouds.

Forget dung bug. I thought such harsh and vivid thoughts about her that my wings expelled two feathers.

Thunder growled. Wind howled. Rain drummed. And still, I stood out there, weathering the storm, praying it wasn't a taste for what was to come.

Chapter Forty-Two

I wasn't certain what woke me.

All I was certain about before my lids pulled up was that I was no longer alone in my bedroom.

Someone sat in the armchair by the window. Someone cast in shadows who owned a body composed of hard lines and broad strokes. Someone whose eyes were the color of the ocean at its shallowest.

I rolled onto my side. "How long have you been back?"

"A while." The deadened inflection of Asher's voice made worry spring inside of me.

"What happened?"

His jaw clenched. "I forced a couple, who cannot look at each other without seeing their dead children, to stay together."

I frowned. "You're seven. Surely, the responsibility is shared."

"The votes were three to three. I was the tie-breaker." He squeezed the bridge of his nose. "I couldn't even explain to them why I voted the way I did, because explaining—" A sound came out of him, a keening that made my heart drop like a stone.

I flung the covers off my legs and padded over to him in nothing but my thong. His eyes were closed, his head bowed.

I inserted myself onto his lap and hooked my arms around his neck, tugging his face into the crook of my neck. "I understand the Seven's ruling keeps them legally bound, but can't they lead separate lives?"

"Adultery would cost the adulterer his or her wings."

I pressed my mouth to the windblown waves of golden hair. "I doubt finding new sexual partners was their motive for separating."

"Perhaps not now, but it's their intimacy, Celeste. I should've voted differently. I should've released them from their conjugal contract, but I was so convinced they were leaving each other for the wrong reasons." His arms laced around me. "I'm trying to control everyone's lives, but all I seem to do is derail them."

"That's not true. You set me back on track. Naya and Adam, too. You're derailing no one."

He raised wet eyes to mine. Blinked. I kissed one salty trail all the way down to his mouth, which I kissed in turn. I'd meant it to be a gentle reminder that I was here, but he turned it into something else.

Something so fierce and overwhelming that I found myself gasping for breath.

He jerked away. "I'm sorry. I didn't mean to"—a vein throbbed at his temple—"devour your mouth."

Smiling, I ran the tip of my finger over his wet lips. "I didn't mind. In fact, I'd very much like you to *devour* it again."

Surprise made him straighten, which put a little space between our bodies. His gaze dipped to my exposed flesh before swinging back up to my face. I guessed he was just realizing I was mostly naked.

Which sadly reminded me of what Eliza had said . . . of what she'd threatened.

Letting my hand drift to the back of his neck, I said, "Before leaving, Eliza told me she'd have to report us—well, *me*—for misleading you."

Gone was his grief. In its place, rose an anger as mighty as the storm that had lashed the city mere hours ago. "She. Did. What?"

"She told me it would have repercussions for you. Asher, I don't want to ruin—"

"Are you sure that's what she said?"

I pulled away, a little hurt. "Do you think I somehow misheard her call me a *zoya*?"

"She called you *what*?" he yelled.

Had I just condemned Eliza to a job downgrade? Was it wrong of me to hope so?

"I don't care what she thinks of me, but I do care about repercussions on you and your job. Will being with me hurt you, Seraph?"

"I told you not to call me that," he snapped.

I didn't take his tone personally. I knew it wasn't me he was angry with. "Will it, Asher?"

"No." His hands dug into my back. He could hold on as tightly as he wanted, as long as it was to me. To us.

"Good."

His gaze dipped again to my nipples, but he vibrated with so much ire I wasn't sure he was seeing them. I hoped he wasn't picturing Eliza's head. I didn't want her face anywhere near my body.

"Would you like me to get dressed?"

"No." The word was so sharp the breath that carried it thumped against my chin. He stared and stared, and then he lowered his face and stamped a second, "No," right onto my puckered nipple.

The same fuse that ignited my pulse ignited my skin.

He pulled back, eyes filled with my smolder. Their glow made him seem completely otherworldly. I mean, he was, but in that moment, he was more god than angel. His fingers spread wide, then curved around my waist.

"Are you sure a relationship with a hybrid fletching cannot harm you?" I inquired one final time.

Desire made mortal men feel invulnerable. Was it silly of me to worry immortals could be blinded, too? After all, beneath the feathers and fire, Asher was still a man. A man with wants and needs that all the power in the worlds couldn't slake.

He gripped my hips. "I'm certain no harm will come to you."

"That's not what I asked."

"If I feared this could harm my daughter or anyone else, I wouldn't take the risk. I may be selfish and weak, but I'm not irrational."

I held him away, knowing that the moment my elbows bent, so would my willpower, and there would be no turning back. Not for him. And certainly not for me.

Hadn't we already reached the point of no return, though?

"Okay." My arms unlocked and I stood, and then I reached out a hand to lead him toward my bed.

His breathing stilled, and he stared at me for so long without getting up that I began to wonder whether he liked what he saw.

I'd never been insecure before, but his inaction . . . "Not much to look at, huh?" I started to cross my arms when he rose and pressed them apart.

"There's so much to see that I'm trying to decide where to begin." Before I could roll my eyes, both his palms coasted over my breasts, then lower, over my abdomen.

My breaths hitched, and my heart tipped right over, pinballing into my soul. He leaned in again and swirled his tongue over one nipple and then suckled it, rendering me a thoughtless, shiny, beating organism.

He hovered his mouth over my wet nipple, then with the utmost gentleness, laved the other. I let out a small whimper when his teeth grazed the peaked flesh. A bold smile curved his lips. When he cupped my breasts and caressed their undersides with his thumbs, I actually thought I might orgasm without any other form of contact. He nosed my glittery jaw, then kissed one corner of my parted mouth.

The pulsing at the apex of my thighs intensified with every kiss, every suckle, every explorative stroke of his thumbs. I threaded my hands around his neck to hold myself up.

"Take off your clothes." My labored whisper struck his wet mouth.

"Not yet."

"Asher . . ." I growled a little because I wanted to see him. To taste him.

"Celeste . . ." His amused tone didn't amuse me.

"It's only fair, and you archangels are all about fairness."

Shaking his head, he indulged me and tossed off his black vest, then undid the buttons of his shirt, dropping it in turn. "Satisfied?"

"Not yet." I nodded to his pants. When he made no move to eliminate them, I reached for his trouser button.

As I popped it open, he rasped my name against my forehead. I caught the metal edge of his zipper, but before I could slide it down, he seized my wrists.

"Slow down, *levsheh*. You need to slow down. I want our first time to last." He lifted my hands back to his neck and then lowered his head until his mouth found mine in the smoldering darkness.

His fingertips danced lightly over the pebbled flesh of my arms and then raked down my bare back, making a thrill ripple down my spine. I dragged him closer, crushing my breasts against the golden planes of muscle. He grunted against my mouth as his hard bulge mined my stomach.

I wondered if he was regretting not having allowed me to set him free. And then I wondered about many other things. Not if he would fit, because I knew flesh could stretch, but how deep would he be able to go? And would it feel like my first time all over again? And condoms! I had some—okay, lots—but he wasn't human, and his skin was so warm. What if they melted? What if—

I broke my mouth from his to pant out, "Can you wear condoms?"

"Condoms?"

"Those things made of very thin latex. To prevent . . . um . . ."

He chuckled. "I know what they are."

"Oh." Trying to catch my breath, I asked, "Well, do they work on archangels?"

"I don't know. I've never tried them, nor have I attended a round-table about human contraceptives. The older our bodies get, the harder it becomes to conceive." A veil of somberness drifted over his eyes.

Did he want children? He couldn't want children with a hybrid. A *zoya. Ugh.* Why did that title have to resurface? I wasn't some nefarious temptress.

I shoved Eliza and her stupid insult away. "What did you used to do? When you were younger?"

"I pulled out."

"Every time?"

"Every time." His thumb hooked my lip and dragged it away from my teeth. "But if it makes you feel safer, then we can use a condom."

I nodded.

"Can we go back to *not* discussing logistics, though?"

I nodded again.

"Good. Because I have plans for you that don't require latex sperm-traps." He kissed my mouth with such languor that my soul—and yes, my soul . . . I was sure this time—pressed up against the fence of flesh keeping it corralled from its other half.

Asher must've felt it because his palm slid between our bodies, stroked the palpitating skin, before venturing lower, to some other palpitating flesh.

I inhaled so sharply that I sucked in his lower lip. His mouth curved against mine in a smile as indolent as his kiss.

Twenty years . . . How had he lasted two decades without physical contact?

I stopped contemplating this when Asher dropped to his knees. I also stopped breathing. When I remembered I'd need air to stay conscious, I inhaled so deeply I almost blacked out. And then I almost blacked out again when one of his hands gathered the triangle of lace. Instead of rolling it down, he lifted it until it filled my slit. And then he rocked his hand, loosening the fabric, pulling it taut, until the pressure the lacy rope exerted on my clit dampened the fabric, and I mewled.

I had *never* mewled.

"Does this feel all right, Celeste?"

I snorted. "All right?"

He loosened his grip.

I dropped my chin and glared at him. "Why are you stopping?"

"I thought you . . . I thought you may not have liked it."

"Trust me, I liked it." I didn't yell. At least I didn't think I had but I *had* mewled, so . . .

Even though he was on his knees, the archangel seemed to grow two whole feet. He gripped the lace and gave a hard tug. It scraped across my flesh with such force I gasped. And then he slackened his grip. Again and again, he yanked, released, carefully working my center until the friction created such heat my thighs began to tremble.

He kissed my navel and then the skin around it, pursuing his little game of tug-of-war with my thong. "You are exquisite, *levsheh*." His shoulders rolled as he lowered his head to my thigh and kissed his way up to my sharp hipbone. "Absolutely exquisite."

At his rasped compliment, at the wet scrape of my underwear and his flaring nostrils, the fire he'd kindled between my legs ignited with such violence I threw out a hand and fisted his hair. And then I yelled his name as my body spasmed and quivered.

Eyes on mine, he hooked the lace and slid his knuckle across my still pulsing center, then rolled the string waistband down my legs. Once I'd stepped out of my thong, his hands coasted back up the sides of my calves and thighs, widened my stance. Dragging in my scent on a long inhale, he leaned forward and gave me a slow lick.

My back arched, and my lids closed. "Here I thought angels deemed pleasure a sin . . ."

"If given freely, it isn't a sin." He tasted me again.

And again.

My bundle of nerves hardened, my knees locked, and my fingers, which had been gliding idly through his silken hair, stilled.

I was close.

So . . . feathering . . . close.

He plucked my center with his tongue, and I gasped his name, breaking against his mouth in great, shuddering waves that clapped against my tender flesh. My eyes opened sluggishly, found his locked on mine as he laved and suckled, catching the last dregs of my orgasm.

"Your taste, Celeste." He lifted his head and licked his swollen lips. "Elysian nectar."

I tugged on his hair to get him to rise. "My turn to savor you, Seraph."

He smiled and traced my folds with the tip of his index finger. "Because you called me by my title, it remains my turn."

I shot him a little glower. "What sort of absurd rule is that?"

"I may be on my knees, but I'm still your sovereign."

I wanted to roll my eyes, but he kissed my wet flesh, and it short-circuited my synapses.

"Eventually, the turn will be yours."

The hot brush of his breath and slide of his finger were enough to make me purr in pleasure, but then he added his velvety tongue to the mix and lifted me so high I distantly thought I might reach Elysium before completing my wings.

Chapter Forty-Three

"You're going to end up killing me," I whispered, riding the tail end of yet another orgasm.

"Good thing you have wing bones." There was pride in his tone. Tenderness, too.

"Please come back up here," I breathed, prying his head from between my legs.

Boneless. I was boneless. And even though my feet were planted on the carpet, I felt like he'd carried me into the sky.

"You want me to stop?"

"Yes. No. I mean yes. *Yes.* Come back up here."

Surprisingly, he indulged me and rose, unfurling his giant body muscle by muscle. He smacked his lips, and damn if that didn't set me off again.

This time, when my hands went to his zipper, he didn't stop me. I pushed his trousers down to reveal what, until then, I'd only gotten to feel.

And yep. That part of him was proportionate to his wingspan. He was a beast. *Everywhere.*

I sank onto my knees. "My turn. *Finally.*"

"I don't want to come inside your mouth, Celeste." He grasped the sides of my face, his thumbs digging into my cheekbones to tilt my face up. "I want to come between your legs."

I fisted his hard, impossibly wide and outrageously long dick, and slowly tugged on the silky flesh, letting my fingers glide all the way to the glistening tip. I darted out my tongue and swept the salty bead into my mouth.

"You will, Seraph." I licked the enormous glistening head again. "You'll come in both tonight."

"Celeste." My growled name made me wrap my mouth around his length.

His body tensed, and Angelic words fell from his lips as more of his pleasure coated my throat. I swallowed and gripped his shaft, working him a little faster with my hand but also with my mouth.

He panted my name, growled it, puffed it, snarled it. Never had someone uttered my angels-given name in so many different ways. I ribboned my tongue around him. His hips gave an involuntary buck that drove him so deep I sucked in a breath through my nose. He gasped as a jet of warmth roped down my throat.

Hot and sweet.

So very sweet.

Like honeyed tea which had barely had time to cool.

Like sunshine at the height of summer.

Gripping the hard flesh of his thighs as he thrust into me, I swallowed his celestial seed.

His head tipped back, his throat bobbed, and again, he breathed my name.

I raked my nails lightly over his muscled thighs, then pulled my mouth off him and climbed to my feet.

His head lolled forward. "Fuck . . . me."

"That's my line."

He shook his head but smiled, and then he conjured up his wings and stretched them impossibly wide.

"Are you winging me or reminding me who has the prettier, sparklier feathers?"

"I'm winging you." He gripped my hips, driving his hardening flesh —had it even softened?—into my abdomen.

I wrapped my arms around him to reach the soft vee at the base of his spine which I now had every right to caress. The power this gave me was almost as intoxicating as the feel of him breaking apart inside my mouth.

Pulling in a sharp inhale, he hooked an arm under my ass, and with a pulse of his great wings, sent us both crashing into the middle of my king-size bed.

The ends of his loose hair tickled my cheeks. "Where are those condoms of yours? I want to come inside your body."

I traced the determined set of his brow with my fingertip, the impatient tick of his jaw. "In my nightstand."

As he rose to his knees, muscles and tendons rippled beneath expanses of tanned skin. He reached around to yank open my drawer, retrieved a strip of condoms, and ripped one of the packets.

He frowned at the thin disk, then at me, then tried to unroll it in midair.

"Not like that." I took it from him and rolled it over the tip.

His lips pinched as he tried to tug it down farther. It ripped. He shoved it off. Took a new one. Yanked on it so hard, he plowed right through. Grumbling, he split open a third packet. "You wouldn't happen to have any made for non-human men?"

"Not at the moment, but I'll check the nearest CVS in the morning."

He foiled the next attempt, growing increasingly angrier.

I rose onto my arms. "What are the odds of you putting a baby inside of me?"

"Not very high, but I can pull out."

"Sit." I slid out from underneath him.

He sat back, and I straddled him, then reached out between us to angle him up. His nostrils flared as I lowered myself onto his tip, controlling the speed and depth.

As his girth stretched my pliant skin, I gritted my teeth, breathing through the ache of his body widening mine. When I'd taken as much of him as I physically could, I lifted up, then glided back down, then back up. His lids grew heavy, settling at half-mast.

I pried his fingers off the comforter and set them on my hips. "Come inside of me."

His lids snapped up. "Are you sure?"

"Yes." I leaned over and kissed him, sheathing him inside again.

His mouth was as hard as the rest of him, but slowly, he returned from wherever it was he'd floated off to.

His fingers flexed around me, raising me, lowering me. The shallow ache dissipated as our bodies found a rhythm, and soon, the threads of a new orgasm wrapped themselves around my belly, knotting themselves tighter and tighter. I sped up and moaned his name, and then I gasped and stilled as the threads snapped, splintering me into so many pieces I doubted I could ever be reassembled.

He took charge, manipulating my ragged body, the vein in his neck hammering my slick forehead. I lightly fingered the vee of bronze-tipped down, making his wings spread and snap like windblown sails. He growled and panted, kissed the top of my head, breathed out a few more croaky grunts. And then he stilled, and my name dripped off his tongue like a prayer. It was possibly the most beautiful way he'd ever made it sound.

"You have undone me, *levsheh*." The archangel's deep voice vibrated against my forehead, which was still pressed against his clenching throat.

"And you, me." I languorously stroked the sinewy muscles of his shoulder, my fingertips dipping and curving.

He was still inside of me, still twitching as though he wasn't done pouring himself out. "Thank you." His arms laced around my back and gathered me against him. "Thank you."

"For what?"

"For accepting me with all my flaws."

"Your flaws only add to your appeal." I placed an open-mouthed kiss on the column of his neck that made his entire body jerk. Without disconnecting my mouth, I began to move over him.

"Again?" he rasped. "Are you sure?"

I answered him by sliding him deeper, until he hit every single one of my walls.

Suddenly, I found myself on my back. The momentum tore my lips from his neck and his cock from inside my body. He braced himself over me, forearms bracketing my head.

I frowned. "Did you need a rest, old man?"

His mouth quirked, and then he laughed, serenading me with the glorious sound. "Just thought I'd give your legs a rest, smart mouth." He lined himself up and sank in.

My spine arched off the mattress. "Careful not to break me or I won't be much fun to play with."

He slowed, swallowed. "Never, Celeste."

I could see myself reflected in his eyes—chestnut hair fanned out around my head like a crown of autumn leaves, pale skin sprayed through with freckles, twin dips years of smiles and smirks had dug into my cheeks.

"You may think vows mean nothing to me, but they do." His gaze trekked to my navel, before rising back to my face. "Tonight, I vow to forever protect your body, your heart, and your soul." In slow motion, his hips pulled back, then pressed forward, and a tremor zinged through both our bodies. "*Ni aheeva ta*, Celeste."

"What does that mean?"

"It means: I love you."

Heat pooled behind my lids. Was I really about to cry?

"I don't think you understand how much yet, but I hope that soon, you will."

I batted my lashes, trying to make the tears melt back before they could surface, but they raced right down my temples. I wanted to tell him that I did understand, that I felt it too, but couldn't get my trembling lips to form words.

"I know you still regret Muriel's passing, but I thank every star in the Elysian firmament her soul expired when it did. If she'd held on any longer . . ." He shuddered. Everywhere.

"You'd have had to find me a new body," I croaked. "Preferably one with a few more inches and a few less freckles. I mean, who needs *that* many?"

A scowl made his brows dip. "You're not getting a new body. Didn't you hear me pledge to protect this one?"

"I did, but you can't grow my wings or stop time."

The slant deepened.

"Hey . . ." I raised my thumb to smooth his brow. "This isn't me giving up; this is me contemplating what may happen. We need to be prepared in case—"

"There is no *in case*. You will make it." He pulled out of me, then held still, taunting my pulsing flesh with his throbbing head. "Say it."

I inhaled deeply. Exhaled the words he wanted to hear.

He drove into me slow and deep. "Again."

"Mmm . . ." My hands drifted to his taut ass, settled there. "Why?"

"Because the more you say it, the more you'll believe it."

"Fine. I will make it."

He inched out, then held still. "Again."

"I will make it."

He filled me. "Again, *aheevaleh*."

"*Aheevaleh?*"

"My love," he whispered, his body metamorphosing mine into breath and heat and starlight.

Chapter Forty-Four

I woke up to a body curled behind mine and a sprinkling of little aches in places I wasn't even aware *could* ache. I mean, my waist and toes. How could my waist and toes ache?

The large hand, which had spent the entire night clamped against my abdomen, twitched to life and dragged me into an impossibly warm front.

Warm and hard.

I turned in his arms and slid one hand through his tumbled locks, working out the silken knots. Out of all the men I'd imagined sharing my bed with, Asher had never figured on the list. Not that I'd had a list, but *if* I'd been the type of girl to make one, I would *not* have added an angel's name to it, much less an *arch*angel.

"Show me your wings, *aheevaleh*."

My hand stilled. "Why?"

His lids flipped up. "So I don't have to fly over to the guild and manually research your score on a holo-ranker."

I pursed my lips. There was no way I was displaying my winglets, especially not in the light of day.

"Don't you want me to warm your bed a while longer?"

"Bribery is beneath archangels. Besides, even if I wanted to have sex with you, I don't think I'd be physically capable of it."

Worry replaced his frustration. "Why?"

"Because you're massive, and we did it four times last night. My weak body needs to recoup."

"I apologize."

"You apologize too much." I tapped his nose. "And it was the best sex of my life, so there's really no reason to apologize."

"The best sex, huh?"

"Yes. The best. Want a trophy?"

He pulled the comforter off our bodies, inviting unwelcome cool air.

"Hey! That's a cruel way of getting me out of bed. Especially after the compliment I paid you." I tried to snatch the comforter, but he held it out of my reach as he rose onto his forearm and patted the mattress around my body.

When I realized what he was doing, checking for a fallen feather, I rolled my eyes.

A pleased smile curved the archangel's lips, and he settled back, tucking the comforter around me. "I'm not much into trophies, but I love handwritten notes. In case you wanted to put your feelings on paper."

I smiled. "I'll take your request under consideration."

His hand slid between my thighs. "Please do." When the pads of his fingers began to rub slow, targeted circles, he whispered, "Since you won't spread your wings, at least spread your legs."

"Asher . . . I'm so sore."

"It's just my fingers. Let me have something to think about during my lonely flight back to the guild."

I let out a little moan and rolled onto my back, giving him access. He dipped two fingers inside of me, then returned the wet tips to my throbbing center and slanted his mouth over mine, kissing me so sweetly that I actually considered showing him my wings to keep him at my side. He wouldn't make fun of them. I knew that. Yet, after he wrenched a blissful orgasm from me, I decided I wasn't ready, and he didn't insist. Just vaulted off bed, showered, and got dressed.

As he bound his hair back, I continued debating whether to bring my wings out or not, but the sight of them always spoiled my mood, and I didn't want to stain this perfect morning.

I apologized for my stubbornness.

Sighing, he sat on the edge of the bed, leaned over, and kissed me.

"Soon, I'll get to see them every day. Besides, for all my complaining, I get to have breakfast with Naya. Want to join us?"

I bit my lip. "I don't think I can face her right now." Herein lay the limitations of my friendship with this new version of Leigh. There were things I could no longer confide in her. "Will you tell her about us?"

"I would like her to hear it from me and not someone else." His hand drifted over the duvet and, although it was thick with down, the warmth of his touch penetrated into my legs. "But if you want me to wait—"

"Is waiting an option considering Eliza's threat?"

His lips flattened. "Right." He stood up, shoulders straining his white button-down and black vest.

Sighing, I got out of bed and wrapped my arms around his body, trying to defuse some of his tension. "Make me coffee? I'll come with you."

His mouth finally relaxed enough to ask, "You're certain?"

"That I want coffee? Yes."

The faintest smile softened his expression. I started to spin away from him, when he caught the back of my head and tilted it so our faces were leveled. "Thank you."

I pressed up on my toes, awakening acres of sore muscles. "We're in this together. No reason you get to deal with the unfortunate decision to date a hybrid fletching on your own."

Before I could kiss him, he pulled his mouth out of my reach. "There is nothing *unfortunate* about my choice."

"Unenlightened angels will judge. You're aware of that, right? I will become a blemish on your shiny verity wings."

"Stop it, Celeste."

"Stop what? Reminding you of how your world works?"

"It's yours, too." He trounced out of the room like a bull.

Sighing, I padded to the bathroom and washed my achy body. After towel-drying my hair, I rolled it up into a top-knot and secured it with a coiled plastic hair tie. Wondering if the archangel had waited for me, I picked up the first T-shirt on my dwindling pile. Ironically enough, the shirt read: *I feel a sin coming on*. Seemed quite appropriate for the day ahead. I winced as I wiggled into my leather leggings.

I was so used to Asher dealing with hurt feelings by pulling away that

I hadn't expected he'd still be here. Not only had he waited, but he'd also made me my promised coffee.

He slid his phone into his trouser pocket. "I just received a message that someone will be over between four and six to fix your countertop."

"Thank you."

"I broke it."

I frowned as I finally moved to grab my cup. "So you don't deserve to be thanked? You could've left it broken."

He rubbed the base of his throat. "I'm incapable of it. Leaving broken things alone."

"My fixer."

He stopped rubbing. "I hate fighting with you."

"Really? You do it so well."

He shook his head, but the palest smile fissured his troubled expression. I took a seat next to him and sipped the magic brew I'd become addicted to while I lived in Paris.

He eyed my shirt. "You didn't have one that said: *The archangel is mine.*"

"Surprisingly, no."

"I'll have to remedy that."

I smiled at the idea of him designing a T-shirt for me.

A heavy exhale rattled the air. "I *am* aware many things need to be changed."

"Then why did you flip out?"

"I *flipped out* because I'm tired of hearing you put yourself down. We're all born equal, even though, you're right, we are not given equal opportunities." His fingers rolled into a fist, which he lowered to the island. "Celeste, I swear, I will change that, but—"

"But you have another law to amend first. I know." I covered his fist, then gave it a squeeze.

His fingers slid open, and I threaded mine through. "Drink your coffee, *levsheb*. We have a world to change."

We...

There wasn't much I could do besides be there for him when the going got tough, but maybe that would be enough.

Chapter Forty-Five

The score that showed up on my holo-ranker was a little depressing: 498. I guessed I had to pay Jacques another visit.

Asher frowned at the number. "Why are you down three feathers?"

Three? I thought I'd lost two. *Oh, well* ... I shrugged, spinning on my stool toward him. "You know how well I react to threats."

His jaw clenched as he read between the lines. "Do you want to sign off from Jacques and pick someone else?"

"No. I have one final idea. If it doesn't work, then I'll stop by this afternoon and pick someone else."

He stared at my flickering 3D portrait and stamped score for a few long seconds before rising from his seat. Unable to stomach the pitiful number, I powered off the holo-ranker.

Asher held out his hand; I didn't take it.

"Let me get Naya's approval first."

"You do realize you already have it?"

My heart ticked a little faster. "Has anyone ever told you how tiresomely confident you are?"

Chuckling, he tipped his head toward the curved glass door that slid open when we approached.

Like every time we'd been spotted in the guild together, the sight of us stirred hushed whispers among my peers and drew peaked eyebrows from ophanim. All except Ophan Mira. When we entered the cafeteria, the silence that fell over the breakfasting fletchings was deafening. Even the sparrows seemed to quiet.

Thankfully, a squeal frayed the stifling air as a little body streaked across the pale expanse, two blonde braids snapping in her wake. She raced along the buffet, her pumping elbows knocking over a pyramid of peaches that toppled to the floor. Red spots blooming on her cheeks, she paused on the balls of her soft-soled slippers, eyeing the fruit, then Mira who sat with the faculty a few tables down. When the head of our guild nodded, Naya leaped back into action and slalomed around the remaining tables to reach her father.

He scooped her up. "Good morning, *motasheb*."

She strangled him with her arms and rested her cheek against his shoulder. "It is now, Apa."

I swore I could hear ovaries dissolve around us. And not just mine, although mine were most definitely fusing with the rest of my gooey soul. Which reminded me of what Asher and I had spent our night doing . . . condom-free. He hadn't been worried about it, so I probably needn't be. In truth, I had more pressing matters to worry about, like earning a wing-load of feathers in the next few weeks.

Naya smiled at me, cheeks pink with happiness. "Hi, Celeste."

As I followed them toward a free table at the very back of the cafeteria, I heard him murmur to Naya, "Can you believe she hates flying?"

I side-eyed him. "I hate going fast *and* high."

"In other words, flying."

"Okay, fine. I'm terrified of flying."

Naya released a sweet giggle. "Maybe you'll like it once you have your own wings. I—" Her brow scrunched as though she was remembering a time when she'd flown. She'd told me all about it. All about Elysium the day Asher had returned her to Paris.

"That's what I'm hoping," I sighed, "or I'll be a sorry excuse for a wing-owner."

"Are you almost finished?"

"Getting there." Which was putting it nicely . . . I was very far from the finish line.

Asher set her down into a seat, then took the one next to her while I sat across from the two.

Pushing her long blonde braids over her shoulders, she asked, "Is that why you're here?"

"Um . . ."

When I couldn't get anything besides the dumb sound out, Asher came to the rescue. "Actually, Celeste came along because we have something to tell you."

Naya's eyes began to glitter, and I discreetly checked it wasn't a reflection of my skin. I didn't really feel like smoldering the archangel in a roomful of prying eyes.

"You finally kissed Apa!"

"What?" I squawked, gaze whipping off my wrist.

A low chuckle vibrated from Asher.

"Why, uh . . ." I toyed with the zipper on my bomber. "Why would you jump to *that* conclusion?"

"Because you love him." She rolled her huge, all-seeing eyes.

Not even in her past life had I expressed an interest in the archangel, so it couldn't be a remnant from her soul's time as Leigh.

Wearing a mighty satisfied grin, Asher leaned back in his chair and crossed his arms. "You love me, huh?"

Naya bobbed her head. "When we played *Neither Yes Nor No*, I asked Celeste if she loved you, and she said no, but then she lost a feather."

Asher dipped his chin into his neck. "And when did you ladies play this game?"

I raised an eyebrow. "Why?"

"Just curious as to how long you've loved me."

I was about to say that I didn't love him, that he needed to get over himself, but my wing bones began to itch. Stupid lie detectors.

"Wednesday morning," Naya piped in.

"Huh." Asher rolled his shoulders forward until his forearms landed on the table with a thump that matched the sound of the gulp dropping down my throat.

I was aiming for nonchalance, but the smirk devouring Asher's features told me I was failing miserably.

"So?" Naya bounced in her seat. "Is that what you came to tell me?"

"Yes," Asher said, at the same time I said, "No."

She frowned.

"We came to ask if you'd be okay if we . . .?" My lips jammed. Crap, this was hard. "If we . . .?"

"Kissed?" Naya asked.

"Um. Yeah. That." I tugged the zipper of my jacket so high it pinched the underside of my chin.

"I knew it! And yep. I'm totes okay."

"Totes, huh?" Asher smiled.

"It's a new word Raven taught me."

"Who's Raven?" I asked.

"She's my friend."

I prayed she wasn't another Eve. "When do I get to meet this Raven?"

Naya's gaze cycled around the cafeteria. "I don't see her."

"She's a sweet girl." Asher draped one arm around Naya's shoulders, then flipped his free hand palm-side up, an invitation for me to take it.

I looked at it, looked at him, then relented and placed my hand in his. Intakes of breaths echoed a little everywhere at our PDA.

Naya clutched her chest as though the organ was about to pound right out. "My heart is sooo happy."

I briefly wondered if it was her heart or her soul.

"Mine, too, *motasheh*." Asher kissed the top of Naya's head and gave my hand a squeeze.

Well, damn . . . My skin decided to remedy my lack of verbal sappiness by lighting up.

"You're smoldering!" Naya squealed.

I wanted to crawl under the table or uproot the fig tree in the far corner and hide behind it until my skin could chill the feather down. Instead, I bore my phosphorescence like a big girl.

Suddenly, Naya tilted her little chin toward her father, grin gone. "But you can't marry, Apa."

His mouth set into a grim line.

I hoped that in time he'd stop considering his inability to make an honest woman out of me a shortcoming. "Good thing you don't need to marry someone to be happy."

His thumb stroked my knuckles.

Once my skin stopped being so effusive, I untangled our fingers and stood. "I should go. My mission beckons."

Asher stared at me as I rounded the table.

"I'll come find you when I return from Elysium," he said.

I frowned. "You're going to Elysium?"

"I need to meet with a certain ishim."

I nodded slowly, then came around the table and crouched beside Naya. "Forgot to tell you. I saw this really neat art piece in a gallery yesterday and I wanted to try recreating it with you sometime this weekend. You game?"

"Yes!"

I smiled, kissed her cheek, then straightened and started to turn when Asher caught my wrist and tugged me close. A sparrow swooped over Naya's head, making her giggle and try to stroke its rainbow-tinted feathers.

"What about me?" he asked huskily.

My heart took off, because I knew what he was asking, but I wasn't ready for that. Not with Naya right there. Sure, I'd smoldered him in public but kissing was something else. He must've sensed my reticence because he pressed his lips to my palm and then let go.

Chapter Forty-Six

I t had taken me the whole of Friday, but I'd done it. I'd reformed Jacques. Or at least, I thought I had. Thought I felt the new growths of forty-four feathers but knew that was just my subconscious being optimistic. You couldn't feel feathers grow.

Since it was almost four, I didn't swing by the guild to check my score. I raced home, deciding I would woman-up, stand before my mirror, and pull my wings out of hiding. I could do it. After all, Asher and I had come out as a couple to Naya, and subsequently to the rest of the guild.

When I reached my apartment building, I received a text message that the people tasked with installing my new counter would arrive within a half-hour. I kicked off my boots in the vestibule, then padded toward my bathroom. There, I gripped the edge of the sink, took a massive breath, and popped those purple babies into existence.

I didn't release my breath until I caught sight of the fluff lining the sides of both my scrawny wings. Exhilarated, I whisked my wings back into oblivion and proceeded to do all the human tasks I'd been slacking on. By the time the stonemasons arrived, my sheets had been changed, my clothes were in the dryer, and the dishwasher was running.

As the men removed the broken granite, I texted Asher that I was done with Jacques in case he wanted to sign me up to my next sinner. An hour later, the stonemasons were gone, yet I still hadn't heard back from the archangel. I ironed as I waited, my attention drifting between my balcony and a documentary about mushrooms.

As I put away my neat pile of clothes, a whoosh followed by a gust of cold air made me spring toward my bedroom entrance. Asher filled the doorway, then, gait fluid and impossibly long, he stalked toward me, backing me up against a wall before flicking the switch beside my nightstand to lower my blinds.

I frowned up into his face. "What's going on?"

He kissed me, and the hard press of his lips combined with his simmering silence made me grip his biceps and pull away.

"Asher, what happened?"

My tailbone hit the wall, and then he was leaning over me, and his mouth was on mine again.

Anxiety sank its claws deep. I skated my mouth off his. "Seriously. What happened?"

"Nothing." He chased my mouth, caught it.

I tore it free again. "You're not acting like nothing happened."

He pressed a kiss to my neck, nipping the skin. And then his hands glided beneath my T-shirt. When his fingers caressed the undersides of my breasts, I decided to keep my interrogation for after he blew off some steam. It wasn't as though my mind was at its most cogent when so much raw masculinity was pressed up against me.

With almost violent strokes, he caught the hem of my shirt and yanked it over my head and then did away with my leggings, while I fumbled with the lace ties that ran up the sides of his chocolate suede uniform. He paused his mouth's ravaging to fling his tunic over his head and then shoved down his pants to free his raging erection.

The single-minded beast he was scooped me up and positioned himself at my entrance. I expected him to press himself inside, but he halted. "Are you healed?"

Avoiding answering, because my answer would've been a lie, I reached down between us to rub him against me before sinking him inside. The initial feeling of being dick-punched was rapidly replaced by a bunch of other sensations. All of them mind-numbingly glorious.

Our mouths collided as he pumped his hips and crimped my ass, our breaths tangled, our scents coalesced. He grunted and hissed as I clenched around him, and clenched, and . . .

Oh . . . holy . . . Seven . . .

Oxygen tore out of my lungs as I fell headfirst into a fiery ocean of pleasure, gasping his name, gasping for air. He covered my mouth with his, filling me with his tongue, before filling me with his seed. Panting, he pressed his forehead against mine. Our mouths disconnected, yet we remained joined—our hearts pounding, our souls throbbing, our cores tingling. He rocked slowly . . . slowly. Before our heart rates had even decelerated, he was hard again.

This time, he took me gently, kissing and licking his way across my collarbone, while my stomach muscles gradually contracted and a new orgasm built, twisted, sucked up my organs and sent them spiraling outward. My head fell back and my eyes closed and a string of moans dripped from my parted lips. His fingers squeezed as his thrusts quickened, and then he grunted and reignited my core with his beautiful fire.

Assuming he'd drained his tension and was ready to talk, I cupped his jaw. "Now, please tell me what happened?"

His eyelashes, which had fallen, rose, revealing eyes so dusky they mirrored the night sky beyond my blinds—starless and full of steel smog. He carefully unsheathed himself, then set me on my feet. Warm rivulets dribbled down the inside of my thighs. I grabbed tissues from my nightstand and cleaned myself up as he pulled on his pants and laced them, still silent.

Finally, he said, "I'm on probation."

I waited for him to elaborate, unsure what that meant in Elysium-speak.

"Apparently, I'm not acting like an archangel."

"Because of me?"

His jaw ticked. "No. Because of me. Because I'm allotting too much time to my personal life and not enough to my professional one." He rammed his hand through his hair, yanking strands of it out of the leather tie. The golden waves fell and frolicked around the hard cut of his jaw. "If I don't concentrate on my celestial task, I'm out."

A chill sank into my flesh, dispelling the earlier heat. "Out of the Council or out of Elysium?"

"Out of the Council. My infractions aren't grave enough to compromise my wings." His nostrils flared. "I need to start touring guilds again, offering my time to ophanim and my help to other fletchings."

"Okay . . ." That wasn't *so* bad.

"Which means time away from you. From Naya. I don't want to fucking help other fletchings. I want to help *you*, but they warned me that if I remained at your side in New York, they'd take away my channel key until you were done." A pained rattling erupted from his mouth. "I won't . . . I *can't* stay away from you for two months. Already one afternoon was torture."

"That's just because you have the libido of a thirteen-year-old boy at the moment."

He glowered, but I smiled because there was no bite to his look, just a lot of bark.

"Did you tell them about our bond?"

"Yes. That's why I wasn't kicked off the Council. Soulhalves have a special status." He glared at my carpet. "Not special enough to leave us be unfortunately."

I bit the inside of my cheek so hard I punctured the skin, and the taste of copper coated my tongue. "So let me get this straight. You have to keep away from me for the next two months?"

"I have to concentrate on my archangel duties, and you're a—"

"Distraction." I sighed. "Time goes by quickly. Two months—"

He whipped his gaze to mine, the intensity of his irritation cutting me off.

I placed my hand on his chest. "Or less. Maybe I can make it in less time. I'm already forty-four feathers heavier. Only four hundred and fifty-eight feathers to go." His furious heart shrilled against my palm.

I'd felt victorious when I'd come home and spotted the new growths, but now . . . now I felt a little depressed by the still-high number I lacked. Licking my lips, I walked to my wardrobe and pulled out an oversized sweater and a fresh pair of panties, because this wasn't the sort of conversation I wanted to pursue naked. My hands shook as I got dressed, and then shook some more as I plucked my hair out of the round collar.

Suddenly, Asher's head snapped straight.

"What?"

"I need to travel around the guilds." He prowled languidly toward me like a lion who'd feasted and sunbathed. "You can come with me. While I pay my archangelic dues, you'll reform sinners."

"I thought they said we couldn't spend time together."

"They said I needed to start my rounds again." His palms landed on either side of my face and tipped it up.

"Are you sure that won't get you in trouble?"

"Not if I'm working." His excitement was a tad too manic for my taste, but it did lift my spirits. My soul, too, for that matter. Maybe his loophole was sound. "Pack your bags, *levsheh*. We leave tonight." He dipped down and kissed me. "First stop, Vienna. I got wind earlier that one of Tobias's fletchings got his wing bones today. The ceremony's tomorrow night, and we're going to attend."

Surprise battled with excitement. "Are you certain I can attend? If it's in a male guild . . ."

"Females aren't allowed to sleep in male guilds, but there's no law about spending time there. Besides, I want you to meet Tobias. And his son, for that matter."

A bolt of oxygen suffused my lungs. I was going to meet Adam . . . "You're sure it's not risky?"

"I'm sure." His kiss tasted of so much certainty that it finally shut down my anxiety.

After all, angels were strict, but not inherently cruel. That's what I told myself on a loop as I tossed clothes and toiletries into a small rolling suitcase. I didn't pack more than a week's worth because we'd be back. I wasn't spending my last two months away from Naya.

Besides, we weren't on the run, just on a cultural adventure.

Chapter Forty-Seven

W e landed in the male guild's Viennese channel a little after two in the morning. Even though I was hesitant to keep my hand in Asher's once the pearlescent smoke dissipated, his fingers clamped over mine.

"We have nothing to hide, *levsheb*."

"I'm just not used to handholding."

"And I am? The only hand I've ever held was Naya's. The same way I've only ever hugged the two of you."

I couldn't imagine him not hugging his previous sexual partners, but since I didn't *want* to imagine this, I shut off that train of thought.

The channel's quartz shaft glowed with angel-fire and resonated with the nearby trickle of water and dulcet sparrow song. Like every guild, this one would be fashioned from veined quartz and fake Elysian sky and would contain all of the rooms found in other guilds but laid out differently.

Sure enough, instead of a hallway, the channel opened onto the atrium where glossy emerald vines sprayed through with bell-shaped blue florals climbed the cathedral-tall walls, injecting the sultry scent of sandalwood and silk over the mineral fragrance of the seven fountains.

When I spotted two young men with pale skin and paler hair standing by one of the fountains, instinct had me tugging my hand from Asher's, but again, he tightened his grip, keeping our palms sealed.

"Good evening, Fletchings." Asher's Viennese German was flawless, as mine would be, even though I'd never spoken it.

Once our two-person audience recovered from the surprise of seeing an archangel, they dipped their heads.

"Evening, Seraph Asher," the ganglier of the two said, his voice squeaking a little.

The other peered at me, curiosity so thick it floated atop the sparrows' song and slicked up my skin. His sapphire wings weren't tipped in metal, but they were a lot denser than mine. I suspected he was no more than a hundred feathers away from ascension.

Asher cleared his throat. "Want to meet Tobias tonight?"

I glanced away from the boy and up at the starlit firmament. Although it wasn't real, it indicated the time of day, and presently, Vienna was in its deepest hours of twilight. "Isn't he sleeping?"

Asher smiled. "Trust me, if he is, he won't mind being woken up. Not to meet the fletching whom I've filled his ears with for the past month."

I wet my lips, my stomach folding and folding as though it were a ball of dough being kneaded. "Okay. Introduce me to the man in your life."

Asher snorted at my turn of phrase just as new footsteps echoed against the quartz.

"I thought I heard your cantankerous voice." A man with dark brown hair and sparkling clear eyes stepped out of the office by the guild's front door.

A grin curved Asher's mouth, but he rapidly smoothed his features back into his impassable archangelic mask, probably for the sake of the present fletchings. "I advise you to show your superior some respect, Ophan Tobias."

"Or else you'll set fire to my eyebrows again?"

"You burned his eyebrows?" I whispered.

"By accident." Asher's mouth quirked again. This time, the smile held. "We'd just come into our fire and were learning to wield it."

Tobias stopped right in front of us and grinned, unveiling a swath of white teeth that would make a toothpaste marketing team drool. "I didn't have eyebrows for three entire months."

I couldn't help but chuckle, but my laughter froze when I noticed that Tobias's umber wings were tipped in gold. I had never seen a verity ophanim. Never even heard of one.

"You're a verity," I said, a tad breathily.

Tobias's smile softened. "I'm an angel, Celeste. Like yourself. Like him." He jutted his square chin toward Asher, who surpassed him by several inches . . . who surpassed most people by many inches. "It's a pleasure to finally make your acquaintance. And if you're not in too much of a hurry, I'd love to treat you to some tea and pastries in the cafeteria. We have the best *sachertorte* in all of Austria, baked on premises with jam made from Elysium apricots and Earth-harvested cocoa beans. The best of both worlds."

My stomach, which I'd had yet to feed, released an eager grumble.

"I shall take that as a yes." Tobias's grin grew, and he held out his arm.

Asher released my hand. "Go ahead with Tobias. I'll put your bag in the office and drop by the Ranking Room to find you an interesting sinner."

"We have *many* of those in our city," Tobias said as he led me toward a hallway.

I looked over my shoulder at where Asher stood, watching us retreat, the muscles along his arms and shoulders finally showing some slack.

Tobias patted my hand. "He'll be with us in a moment, Celeste."

I wasn't worried about being without him, simply worried *about* him, but kept this to myself, not wanting to burden Tobias. "So, you two grew up together?"

"Roommates since we were three."

"And best friends for as long?"

"Brothers." When I cocked an eyebrow, he elaborated, "Guild brothers."

In other words, their bond wasn't biological but sentimental. Like Leigh's and mine had been. "Soulmates too?"

Tobias's pupils danced in curiosity, or was it amusement? "I see Asher's been revealing some of Elysium's best guarded secrets." He leaned closer and whispered, "Make sure to keep it a secret, though. The mechanics of soul bonding should be a reward for the ascended."

"How come?"

"So the young concentrate on their wings instead of on their hearts."

The mouthwatering fragrance of fresh bread, tangy dishes, and syrupy confections swelled as we entered the cafeteria, a giant circular room with quartz columns holding up a painted glass dome. I found myself staring open-mouthed because all the guilds I'd visited had favored an unobstructed view of the sky.

"The ceiling," I breathed. "It's magnificent."

"The glass was painted by the very first Viennese ophanim." His voice vibrated with pride.

"I'll be sure to tell Ophan Mira about it. Maybe she'd consider painting ours."

"Oh, she's seen it. She wasn't impressed."

I grinned. That sounded like Mira. Forever sour on the outside. If it hadn't been for our recent interactions, I might never have discovered her gooey center. "So, how come a verity decided to become an ophanim?"

"*Love*. Love for educating young minds and love for a fellow ophanim."

I raised an eyebrow. "How very unangelic of you, Tobias. To let your heart dictate your duty."

He chuckled. "I've learned to embrace my flaws and strive to teach my fletchings to embrace theirs."

"I wish our ophanim were as rebellious."

"It's easier for me to be, Celeste." When I frowned, he gestured to his wings. "I'm a verity, which sadly allows me greater freedom of speech."

I wondered if this had played into Asher's decision to leave Adam here. As a verity, Tobias could probably offer Adam better protection. "I heard you had a son. I'm looking forward to meeting him."

His eyes sparkled as brightly as his wingtips in the glow of the illuminated quartz walls. Although I couldn't see his soul, I bet it, too, shimmered. "Ah, my beautifully temperamental pride and joy."

A half-smile knocked onto my lips, because, even though I wouldn't have used such lovely adjectives to describe the former Parisian mobster, *beautifully temperamental* sounded pretty accurate.

"He'll attend the ceremony tomorrow evening." Tobias gestured to a table, and I released his arm to take a seat. "How is little Naya? I hear she's taken an immediate liking to you."

Since he was still standing, I canted my head. "Sweet. So very sweet."

"Of course, Asher would keep the sweet one. Not that I'm complaining. I wouldn't trade my son for all the riches and honors in the worlds." He winked at me before striding toward the buffet, his tucked wings casting pinpricks of light over his form-fitting navy tunic and matching pants.

I shifted my attention back to the dome adorned with angels— hybrids and verities, young and old—standing at the foot of the Pearly Arch. Behind the vertiginous iridescent arch sprawled a city so pale it seemed carved in bone.

"The celestial capital." Asher slid into the chair beside mine.

I leaned into him, propping the back of my head on his shoulder so I could more comfortably admire the mural. Its beauty reminded me of the long-ago trip to Versailles with Leigh. For days, I'd had a crick in my neck from gazing up at the opulent ceilings of the French palace.

"Does it really look like that?"

"A carbon copy," Asher said.

"Except for the children."

"Except for the children. Did Tobias tell you about the ophanim who painted it? You would've admired the man."

I spun around to face him. "He's dead?"

"Unfortunately." Asher stared upward at the cherublike children playing in what looked like a canyon, probably the Canyon of Reckoning. "He militated for the Seven to reform the law on separating children from their parents at birth. He said it would make for a healthier society if they were raised by their families in Elysium and only moved to guilds once their wing bones came in."

"And the Seven killed him for it?"

"No. They simply refused to consider amending the law, and to show his discontent, he asked for his wings to be burned."

"Our world incurred a great loss that day." The undertone of sadness in Tobias's voice made me turn toward him. He slid two perfect triangles of layered chocolate cake over the translucent white stone. "Let us speak of nicer things while we eat cake." Tobias nodded toward the glazed confection. "I want to hear your thoughts on our national delicacy, but if those thoughts are in any way negative, then I regret to inform you that you and I cannot be friends, Celeste."

I imagined he wasn't serious, but checked Asher's expression just in case. When I saw the corners of his mouth crease into a smile, I decided Tobias was my newest soulmate. *Wait . . .* could we become soulmates or did we have to be born soulmates? Since he'd asked me to keep the Elysium secret under wraps, I saved my question for Asher.

I picked up a fork and took a bite. And, *wow* . . .

Tobias leaned back in his chair, looking mighty satisfied. "Marvelous, isn't it?"

Asher wrapped his arm around my waist and towed me a little closer. "Even if she hated it, Tobias, you have no choice in liking her." Against the crook of my neck, he murmured, "She's my *neshahadza*."

Tobias's smug smile froze. "*Neshahadza*? I thought you weren't sure."

"I'm sure of it now. Not only can this one not stop sparkling in my presence, she can move my soul."

"What does *this one's* smoldering have to do with it?" I asked, my mouth full.

Tobias shifted forward in his chair. "Younger soulhalves can't control their attraction and display it almost every time they find themselves in the presence of their other half. Asher used to make fun of me because I was constantly winging Gabriel when I was still an awkward fletching."

"I never made fun." The ease that clung to his tone made me realize that this solemn man had once been a carefree boy.

"Just laughed your wings off." Tobias scraped a hand through his wavy hair. "By the way, before you get the wrong idea, nothing untoward ever happened while I was still a student. Besides my uncontrollable winging, that is."

I swallowed another bite of *sachertorte*. "Does Gabriel teach here?"

"He does." Quietly, he added, "*Neshahadza* don't function well away from each other."

That made Asher's hands tighten around my abdomen, which in turn made my soul burrow against the ribs he touched. Now that I'd felt my soul, I wondered how I'd spent twenty years *not* feeling it.

I scraped up the last forkful of cake. "How did he take your fatherhood?"

"A tad contentiously. He wasn't too pleased I'd gone and impregnated a woman, but in time, he came around to it. Now, he loves Adam as his own."

I surmised this was the story both Asher and Tobias had agreed upon, that both had fathered these children with mortal women. I did wonder if Tobias had shared the truth of the boy's existence with Gabriel, but filed my question atop the other. Both were better asked outside the angelic dwelling.

I dragged Asher's plate toward me and started on his piece.

"My girl really likes your cake, Tobias." Asher's fingers lazily wore a path up and down my spine.

"And I like your girl. *Because* she likes my cake." Tobias winked at me, which made my heart brim with gratitude.

Gratitude that in this new life, Adam had been blessed with someone as loving as Mimi. After polishing off the second slice, I reclined against Asher and listened raptly as the two men regaled me with tale after tale of their childhood.

It was only when fletchings began to trickle into the cafeteria for breakfast that I straightened, worried that if anyone reported us, Asher would be reprimanded for squandering away his working hours with me.

Asher's hand drifted off my body. "We should get going."

"Wait just one more minute." Tobias's gaze drifted to a space beyond us. When he gestured for someone to come over, I turned, expecting a slightly older-looking ophanim. Instead, I found myself looking at a little boy.

A little boy with a halo of light brown curls and skin to match, which made his deep-set green gaze all the more intense.

Unlike Naya, Adam's gait was measured, careful, and so was his stare. I sensed his young mind evaluating me, determining if I was friend or foe. When he finally reached us, I couldn't decipher the conclusion he'd come to.

Tobias rested his palm on the back of the boy's neck.

"Good morning, Apa. Seraph." He gave Asher a slow nod.

I crouched and extended my hand. "I'm Celeste."

"Celeste." He sounded out my name in a way that made me wonder if he remembered it. He stared at my hand, then up into his father's face.

When Tobias smiled encouragingly, Adam placed his fingers in mine and shook, grip firm but fleeting. Quickly, he glided his hand back to his side and curled it into a tight fist.

When he'd been Jarod, we'd tolerated each other because of our mutual love for Leigh. I hoped that this time around, we might become friends, he and I. For Naya's sake, but also for Mimi's. The thought of her made me swallow. How impatient she must be to see him again.

Asher warmed my back with his front. "Let's go."

He wound his arm around my waist and pulled me away from the little boy, who'd robbed me of my best friend, and yet, for whom I felt no hatred.

Only hope.

Hope that this time around, everything would be different.

Chapter Forty-Eight

As Asher walked me through the dawn-tinted streets of his childhood, I asked him the questions that were plaguing me—did Gabriel know Adam's true lineage, and were soulmates determined at birth?

"You can make soulmates all throughout your life. In regards to Gabriel"—he squinted toward a baroque, limestone church with a curved zinc roof that had greened with age—"Tobias chose not to tell him."

"Because he doesn't trust him?"

"Because he wants to protect him. You can't get in trouble for something you know nothing about."

"He's wonderful. Tobias, I mean. I'm sure Adam will eventually be, too."

Asher side-eyed me. "Adam's a little reserved. And not my greatest fan."

"You were the competition."

"I was the executioner."

I scowled at him. "Don't say that. It's not true."

"Isn't it?"

I pulled him to a stop, and my little suitcase, which the archangel had decided to carry instead of roll, swayed in his white-knuckled fist. "*They* did it to themselves. All *you* did was try to help them."

"If I hadn't intervened—"

"Their souls would've withered in that crypt." An icy chill slinked down my spine as though I was back in the Montparnasse Cemetery. "Leigh and Jarod were doomed from the moment their souls met. Especially if they are what you suspect. I mean, if I lost you—"

He pressed a finger to my lips, silencing me. "You're stuck with me, Celeste, for the rest of your interminably long life."

I swallowed, then swallowed again. My life was still far from interminable. "Tell me about my mission."

As we walked, he fed me background information about my sinner, about her past and about her current situation, and then he gave me her score: 28.

"If only I could take on two Triples. Or four. I'd be done—"

"No Triples." His tone brooked no argument. "Since we'll have to move around every two days for my job, you'll be taking on mostly tens and twenties. Perhaps, a thirty here and there, depending on their sin."

In spite of it being the weekend and still quite early, Vienna was slowly beginning to awaken, and I found my neck swiveling like a tourist's, trying to take it all in. Especially since these were the streets Asher had treaded. The walls he'd marched past. The air he'd breathed.

"It must've looked quite different a century ago," I mused aloud.

He nodded, lost in his own contemplations. "It was a whole other world. When I returned after my sabbatical—"

I raised an eyebrow. "Your sabbatical?"

"Sounds better than century-long confinement, doesn't it?"

I sighed, wishing the Seven would just redact a brand-new constitution. "So what happened when you returned?"

"I flew over Vienna, then returned to the guild and refused to see my city again for years. I couldn't stomach how much it had changed. How my favorite *bäckerei* had been turned into a depressingly, gray government building."

The opulent architecture and wide avenues reminded me of Paris, which in turn reminded me of Mimi. How I wished I could see her, even if just for one day. How I wished channels didn't make ink fade or render cell towers and the guilds' holographic phones useless.

A handful of minutes later, we entered a swanky five-star hotel that resembled a Grecian palace with its white columns, buffed floors, and gold finishings.

"Madame and Monsieur Asher, *willkommen*." The gray-suited concierge came around his desk, extending a hand toward Asher. "May I take this from you?"

Asher set my bag down, and the man clicked his fingers for a bellboy. It was all a little ridiculous, but I let it happen because Asher whispered, "Let them feel useful, *levsheh*."

The concierge smoothed his hand over his lapel. "Your suite is ready."

"Madame Asher?" I murmured as we followed the chirpy concierge to the bank of elevators, my combat boots squeaking on the shiny floor.

"I could've gone with Monsieur Celeste, I suppose. More *with the times*."

I elbowed him lightly in the ribs.

ASHER SAID HE'D BE BACK AT SIX TO PICK ME UP, BUT SIX came and went, and he hadn't shown up, nor had he answered the text messages I'd sent him after I left the plastic surgery clinic where my sinner fixed up humans who weren't broken.

I'd felt enthusiastic when I'd left her office, confident that I'd managed to alter the course of profitability she'd picked—the one that made her urge her customers to change more and more about themselves —by encouraging her to take on less fortunate patients, the ones who *needed* reconstructive surgery but couldn't afford it.

Since actions spoke louder than words, I'd researched people in dire need of her skill and handed her three detailed profiles, complete with pictures and stories that would've thawed even Eliza's icy heart.

I checked the time on my phone, then tried phoning Asher again. My call went straight to voicemail. I tapped the phone against my thigh as I squinted at the horizon where the sun was fading over the Danube river, streaking the foreign city in shadows.

Soul in knots, I turned away from the sunset and strode across the paved balcony—as outsized as the suite Asher had booked—toward the bedroom. If he didn't give a sign of life within the next ten minutes, I would head to the guild. As I tugged on the tie of my bathrobe, I tried to recall landmarks we'd passed. There'd been a small church, although I imagined that wouldn't help considering the number of churches per square mile in European cities.

I was about to toss off the bathrobe when the room door beeped open.

A large, crimson shopping bag flapped from Asher's fingers. "I'm sorry, *aheevaleh*. The salesgirl took forever to prepare my purchase. And then my cell phone went and died. Human technology." His gaze slid up the sliver of exposed skin interrupted only by a black thong.

"I wasn't sure what to wear tonight."

"So, you decided a thong and bathrobe would be appropriate?"

I swatted his bicep, before skating my fingertips across the leather piping accenting the neckline and cuffs of the elegant black tunic he wore over narrow black pants. "You give new meaning to tall, dark, and handsome tonight, Seraph. All that's missing is your golden circlet."

"I left it in Elysium. I worried it would get me too many curious looks from mortals."

"Good call."

Asher smiled.

"Come to think of it . . . I've never actually seen you wear it." The only other archangel I'd met was Seraph Claire, at her daughter's wing bone ceremony. The Seven's crown, a circle of golden feathers, had gleamed in her midnight hair.

"I'm not a fan of how it makes me look."

"You mean, regal?"

"I mean, superior." He handed me the shopping bag. "Here. Get dressed. The ceremony won't start without us, but let's not make the poor boy wait too long. They're always so excited to celebrate."

I peered into the bag, then pulled out a sheath of silk paper. "You *bought* me an outfit?"

"I didn't give you much time to pack last night."

I pulled out a garment bag and set it on the bed. Inside lay a black silk jumpsuit with a deep-cut leather sleeveless top. "Look at that. We'll match."

Asher tugged the bathrobe off my body, then flung it over the foot of the bed. As he stared down at my body, his fingertips drifted over my scanty curves.

When he hooked the sides of my thong and rolled it down my legs, I said, "I thought I was supposed to be getting dressed."

"In a minute." His voice sounded like it had lost a full octave.

He backed me into the bed until my knees bent, and I toppled backward on the cloud-like comforter. Then he knelt between my legs, hooked my knees over his wide shoulders, and kissed me.

Chapter Forty-Nine

We arrived at the guild a half-hour later, which was frankly impressive considering the number of orgasms Asher had wrung from my body. After I'd returned the favor—only *once* because we were in a hurry—he'd zipped me up in the jumpsuit that fit so perfectly I realized he'd learned the shape of my body by heart.

The brand-new leather booties with vertiginous spiky heels he'd bought me to match clipped the glowing stone floor of the atrium and then of the cafeteria from where leaked a level of sound I hadn't heard since The Trap.

My heart discharged a sad little beat. Only one week had gone by since I'd last seen Jase and yet it felt like an eternity. I lifted my hand to my neck and stroked the thin scar. The bruising had resorbed itself quickly, but the mark of the blade, albeit faint, still blemished my skin.

When the inhabitants of the guild spotted us, the noise level quieted so fast that the silence threatened to make me blush. Thankfully, the sparrows kept circling the room, chanting their arias, nonplussed by the arrival of an archangel and his arm-candy.

Hands clasped, we advanced toward Tobias and a man with citrine hybrid wings, a long oval face, and blond hair cropped close to his scalp. I imagined it was Gabriel since Adam linked the two men like a hyphen. The youngest fletchings scrambled out of our path; whereas, the older ones took smaller steps back, seemingly less intimidated by the seraphim.

The rampant testosterone reminded me of the inter-guild dance I'd attended my last year in the guild. It had coincided with the day I'd earned my hundred and eightieth feather. I'd been so pumped I'd proudly displayed my wings. Until some boy with a shadow of a mustache asked if I suffered from feather-alopecia. I'd punched him, and his nose had bled right onto his sparse stubble. I'd lost a hard-earned feather but had walked away with my head held high.

My wings weren't on display tonight, and yet, as I forded through the dense throng of fancily-clad fletchings, I felt their gazes stick to my back, as though if they stared long enough, they'd glimpse them.

"Excuse our tardiness, Tobias," Asher said once we'd reached his friend.

Tobias glanced between us with a conspiratorial curve to his mouth. "I'm certain you have a perfectly valid reason for being late."

How I wished I could fade into Asher's shadow.

"Celeste, Gabriel. Gabriel, Celeste. You two can get better acquainted while I borrow our favorite archangel to officiate the ceremony."

I unwrapped my fingers from Asher's.

Before following Tobias, he kissed my temple and murmured, "I'll be right back. Please avoid smoldering anyone in my absence."

I rolled my eyes.

"Come along, oh Great and Mighty Seraph, we have a boy to put out of his misery."

Asher didn't chuckle, but he shook his head as he trailed his friend toward a young boy sporting a white tunic so large it drowned his smallish frame.

After quick hellos, I parked myself beside Gabriel. "I've heard so much about you."

Without glancing away from the main attraction, he answered, "All exaggerations, I am sure. My husband is quite fond of enhancing my talents and looks." Although Gabriel's lips didn't flinch, his obsidian eyes crinkled at the corners.

I smiled at him. "I'm sure nothing was exaggerated."

The crinkles deepened, accompanied this time by a discreet smile. "Does this remind you of your own ceremony?"

I directed my attention back to Asher and Tobias. They were touching the young fletching's newly formed bones, which protruded from the fabric, wishing him a safe journey through the human world and a successful completion of his wings.

"It was the scariest day of my life—I was only ten—but at least, my best friend was there. She held my hand throughout the whole ordeal and then she helped me pick my very first mission."

"Sounds like a wonderful girl."

I swallowed. "She was."

"Was?" Gabriel cocked an eyebrow so blond it was almost see-through.

"Leigh died a few years ago."

"Oh."

Silence.

Gabriel cleared his throat. "I didn't realize she was the friend you were speaking of."

"You've heard of her?"

"All the guilds have heard of her." His voice was low, probably so that his son didn't overhear us speaking of the poor choices some angels made.

Unless it was low because her fate aggrieved him. I hoped that was the sort of man he was. For Adam's sake.

My gaze strayed to Jarod's reincarnation. Did fragments of his past life haunt Adam like they did Naya? Since his eyes were glued to the masters of ceremony and the blushing object of their blessings, I couldn't tell if he'd even heard me drop Leigh's name.

All at once, I wanted a reaction and didn't want one. I wanted him to remember and hoped he didn't.

"I also heard you gave up because of what happened to your friend." After a beat, he added, "I'm glad you've changed your mind."

"Sadly, a little late in the game."

I tried to brush away the dull ache gripping my heart, but between the solemn crowd, the soulful arias, and the sight of the young boy's symmetrical, curved bones, my throat constricted. I shut my eyes. Peach hair and emerald eyes flared behind my lids so I snapped them open and didn't dare blink. Not once. Not even when my eyeballs began to sting.

She exists. She exists. She exists. Maybe if I repeated it enough, I'd begin to believe it.

"What are your thoughts on nephilim, Gabriel?"

He angled his narrow face my way. "What a loaded question."

Perhaps this wasn't the place or time to ask, but ever since I'd discovered Mira was on our side, I wondered if others might be, too.

He stayed mute for so long I gave up receiving an answer, but suddenly, his mouth moved around a murmur. "We give sinners a chance at redeeming themselves. Why not our own people?"

"Is your belief shared with many ophanim?"

"Would it change anything if it were?"

"Perhaps if enough of you raised your voices."

Regret carved furrows into his strong brow. "Elysium isn't a democracy, child."

I usually bristled when someone called me child, but his inflection held no condescension.

He returned his attention to the fletching of the night. "Not the greatest topic of conversation for such a jolly event."

He was right.

A cheer went up around the room, and the boy's features blazed with excitement. His friends closed in around him, patting him on the back or offering him quick, and slightly awkward, one-armed hugs.

Adam tipped his head up. "Do you remember your ceremony, Papa?"

Gabriel's smile returned as he smoothed his son's unruly curls. "Like it was yesterday."

"Were there dinosaurs?"

"Dinosaurs," Gabriel scoffed. "I'm going to have a word with Ophan Michael about what he's teaching you young minds."

Adam slanted his father a crooked smile that made a dimple appear. A single dimple. Not two like me. "I know you're not *that* ancient. Two-hundred and seventy-nine-years *young*."

"That's right, my boy." Gabriel kept smoothing his son's hair, but the tight curls were like reeds and sprang back the moment they were no longer being flattened. "Now, let's go say goodnight to Apa and off to bed." He crouched and scooped him into his arms. "Say goodnight to Celeste, *aheevaleh*."

Adam laid his cheek against his father's shoulder and looked at me, really looked at me, and for the most fleeting minute, I thought I detected recognition, but then he smooshed his fists into his eyes and yawned.

When he looked at me again, the flicker of recognition was gone. "*Bonsoir*, Celeste."

My shoulder blades jammed together at hearing him speak French. "Goodnight, Adam."

Gabriel readjusted his hold on the four-year-old. "He loves speaking French." He seemed amused by this quirk.

I doubted he'd have been amused had he known the reason for it. I bet Tobias wasn't amused. I bet he shook in his navy tunic every time Adam used French words. I sought out the ophanim, found him standing with Asher on the periphery of the crowd, both of them sipping what looked like Angel Bubbles and chatting quietly. I didn't think they were discussing the children, but whatever busied their tongues had lent them both a grave air.

As Gabriel carried his son toward Tobias, my eyes met Asher's over the sea of bobbing heads and multicolored feathers. All those with wings had let them spill out.

All except me.

Asher's gaze was as soft as the feathers hemming the bottom of his wings, and then suddenly, it was hard. Hard as cooled metal. I frowned at his rapid shift in countenance.

Until I heard a feminine voice say, "Almost six hundred feathers. Color me impressed."

I froze while Asher did the exact opposite. He all but lunged forward, long legs carrying him toward me in six rapid heartbeats.

When he reached me, he wound his arm around my waist and spun me away from the other archangel in the room, and then, with unflappable aplomb, asked, "Seraph Claire, what brings you down from Elysium?"

Two ishim bookended her, one of whom I loathed more than Elysium's obsolete laws and who I'd hoped had been demoted.

Pop went a feather.

Asher must've spotted it because he inhaled sharply, and his lids slammed shut. When his nostrils flared, I realized he hadn't *seen* it; he'd felt it. Was still feeling it. He was reliving the memory inside the shaft. Soon, his eyes reopened, and he was back, in the present, his temper pressing against me, thick and electric like charged clouds about to unleash a lightning storm.

Chapter Fifty

Even though I knew angels didn't age in Elysium, it was eerie to see how much Seraph Claire resembled her daughter. I'd have almost mistaken her for Eve if it hadn't been for her golden circlet and grassy eyes. Besides, Eve was stuck in Elysium for the next ninety-six years.

"I came to congratulate Fletching Celeste on her impressive turn-around." Claire's platinum-tipped fuchsia feathers shifted behind a dress woven entirely with golden seed pearls.

I didn't say thank you. Didn't say a thing. Simply stared between the female archangel and her faithful puppy ranker to figure out their true intent, because commending me was surely not it.

"So wonderful to see how a little motivation goes such a long way." Claire's ruby lips arched into a dazzling smile. "Let's see them."

When Abaddon freezes over.

"Come now, Fletching. Don't be shy."

When I made no move to relent, she clapped her hands and said, "*Lehatsamehot!*"

My wing bones thrummed, and then out poured every feather I owned. My lungs, my heart, all of me held still.

"Never be ashamed of your wings, Fletching. Not everyone gets to have them." Claire's eyes gleamed like the emerald crawlers on her ears. "Or keep them."

Fury shot up my neck and flooded my cheeks. I tried to shove my wings away but they were stuck. Stuck for everyone to see. For everyone to laugh at. I tucked them into my spine as tightly as I could, then wished them away, but they remained.

How?

How had she done this?

"*Habamehot!*" Asher growled, vanquishing the insubstantial weight at my back. "You have no right to force angels to display their wings without their consent."

Even though a hundred or so fletchings surrounded us, none made a single sound.

Claire tittered. *Actually* tittered. "If we had no right, then why possess the power? Was this not explained clearly the day we made you part of the Seven, Seraph Asher? One of our duties is to make fletchings embrace the gift that is their wings."

"Not. Against. Their. Will," Asher gritted out, holding me to him as though worried I might break. Or punch the archangel.

The latter was loads more probable.

"Fatherhood has made you exceedingly lenient, Seraph."

My fingers curled around his forearm because, this time, *I* was worried *he* might punch Claire. Was that her intent? To egg Asher on so he'd commit a transgression. Since he was already on probation—

A sleeve brushed against my rigid shoulder, and then Tobias stepped in front of me, his body obscuring mine and part of Asher's. "Seraph Claire, welcome!" His voice was a warm current in the frigid air.

"Why, hello, Ophan Tobias. How is your darling son?" There was something in her tone that strained the tendons in Asher's forearm and stiffened the ones in Tobias's back.

"Growing like a flower. You must visit when he's awake. I'd love for you to be properly introduced."

A chill that neither Asher's heated skin, nor the surrounding stones' lit veins could temper, crawled over my skin. What was Tobias playing at? Inviting the archangel to meet Adam was risky.

"I would love nothing more," Claire replied pleasantly. "I'm told he is as lovely as Naya."

"They were born on an auspicious day," Tobias said.

"I heard. And the same one. How . . . *improbable.*"

"Asher is fond of copying me. Always has been for that matter, even though I've ceaselessly encouraged him to cultivate *some* originality."

"Copied you down to his choice of companion. No verities for either of you."

Each reply was curated and delivered carefully, like a game of badminton played with a grenade.

"The soul wants what it wants." The agreeable quality in Tobias's tone was fading. "Since you're here, Seraph, may I introduce you to the fletching of the hour? We were celebrating his newly-formed wing bones, and although Seraph Asher has already blessed him, I'm certain Felix would be over the Elysian moon to receive another seraphim's well-wishes. After all, there's no such thing as too many blessings."

"I suppose I can spare a moment."

Tobias gestured for her to go ahead of him.

Her needle-sharp heels clacked twice on the glowing expanse before stopping. Hooking a look over her platinum wing-tips, she said, "Seraph, don't leave before I return. I didn't only come to congratulate your hybrid."

Asher didn't respond, not even with a nod, but the tension wiring his body swelled anew. Not that it had leveled off. It probably wouldn't dwindle until the archangel and her two ishim channeled themselves back up to Elysium.

Eliza was eyeing Asher, no longer in the way of a woman gazing at the object of her desire, but in the way of a verity scrutinizing a hybrid—with a curled lip and a disgusted stare.

"What is the true nature of this visit, Ish Eliza?" Asher's question was barely audible over the sparrows' ongoing arias.

The male ranker standing beside Eliza dropped his gaze to his soft-soled boots and swallowed, his Adam's apple jouncing in his long throat.

Eliza, on the other hand, didn't avert her gaze. "We were informed Seraph Claire required an escort, and Ish Jonah and I volunteered."

Soon, Claire was clip-clopping back toward us, Tobias in tow. I caught his eye over her garishly pink feathers, and the uneasy gleam in it set my teeth on edge.

"I apologize, Fletching Celeste," Claire said. "Although I did make the trip to congratulate you and take a peek at those pretty little wings of yours . . ."

Oh, the curses piling up inside my throat. I forced them down and away from my mind, but one must've broken free, because my wings dumped another feather. This time it didn't hit Asher on the way down. Just drifted past his arm and landed by my pointy black boot.

He shifted his mouth to my temple. "Shh."

Claire glanced at my rocking purple feather. "I also came to borrow your escort for a referendum that necessitates his voice." She lifted her gaze to mine, the corners of her mouth tipping in turn. "No rest for the Seven."

I wasn't sure if she'd intended to be funny, but no one even snickered.

"I'll have him back to you in no time." As though the ishim were hooked to her body, all three turned at the very same time.

A scream built in my lungs. Gained traction. Clawed up my trachea. I clamped my molars shut and forced it back, worried sounding my rage would do more harm than good.

Asher's narrowed gaze trailed his fellow archangel, but his body stayed rooted to mine.

Claire must've sensed he wasn't following because she turned. "Seraph, if Elysium no longer comes first, another referendum, and this time, one that will not require your voice, will have to be called."

The threat throbbed inside my bones. In Asher's, too. He vibrated with barely contained antagonism.

"Tobias," he snapped.

"Won't leave her side, brother."

I choked on the words *don't go*.

Asher gently pried my fingers off his sleeve. "I'll be right back, *levsheh*. I promise."

I scrabbled to cling to him, but he'd already stepped away.

As he pounded after Seraph Claire, he snapped, "Let us be done with this fast."

I slumped against Tobias, whose arm, solid like Asher's but not Asher's, draped around my trembling body.

"He'll be back, Celeste. You know he will."

The only thing I knew was that I hadn't been strong enough to hold on. "Go with him, Tobias. Go with him and make sure . . . make sure he —behaves."

Tobias steered me toward one of the tables that had been pushed to the side to make room for the party. "Asher, misbehave?" He blew air out the corner of his mouth as though it were the most ridiculous thing he'd ever heard.

"He almost strangled her when she made my wings appear." *How did I not know archangels could manipulate wings?*

Tobias pulled out a chair and helped me sit. "Like you said, he *almost* strangled her. He has a temper, but he knows the risks of letting it loose."

"Please, Tobias . . . please go."

The ophanim slid his lips together as though considering my request. "Michael!" he called out, and an angel with shorn hair, ebony skin, and midday-blue wings walked over. "Could you please go up to Elysium and find out what this new referendum is about?"

Michael's gaze flitted to me, then back to Tobias. "Of course. The children are asleep. I'll stay until the vote is cast, if that's all right with you?"

"Thank you." As Michael left, pale blue feathers twitching, Tobias sat and gathered the hands I'd curled like talons. "Everything will be all right, Celeste."

If only I shared an ounce of his confidence.

Chapter Fifty-One

An hour passed. Then two . . .

The cafeteria emptied until the only people left were Tobias, Gabriel—who'd returned Adam-less—and myself. The men spoke in muted tones, but even if I'd strained to hear anything over the rushing in my ears, they used Angelic, the only language I didn't understand. I guessed they were discussing unpleasant scenarios.

Footfalls echoed in the hallway, and then a winged man appeared. My spine snapped straight, vertebrae welding together, until the shape of the body and the color of the wings seeped into my corneas.

Not my angel.

Michael strode toward us, body thin as a blade come to chop off the fraying remains of our hope, and said something in the celestial tongue that had Tobias freezing and Gabriel hissing.

"What?" My voice shook.

Michael's eyes, as pale blue as his wings, set on me. "They seized his channel key."

My body went numb.

"On what basis?" Tobias roared.

"They said he'd been warned and had violated the terms of his probation. But they also said it was temporary."

Tobias shoved his chair back so abruptly the legs screeched across the quartz. "How temporary?"

"Only two months."

"Only two months?" Arms flailing, Tobias shot out of his chair. "Those feathered pricks."

"Tobias!" Gabriel gasped, casting a quick glance around the deserted cafeteria.

"Two months is not a random number! It's how long Celeste has left! They're keeping him away on purpose."

"Perhaps, but insulting them will make them keep *you* away." Gabriel's chest heaved.

My throat burned. My lids, too. And yet the rest of my body felt glazed in ice. A sob jostled my jaw, pushed its way out from my cramping lungs. The desolate sound echoed against the painted dome and glowing stone. I pressed a fist against my mouth, bit down on my knuckles.

Tobias crouched next to me, coaxed my trembling body into his arms. "I'll go up there, Celeste. I'll go talk to them."

I jerked away. "You can't."

"I—"

"Adam," I murmured. "Think of Adam."

He pursed his lips.

"Asher can't help me anyway. On the missions, I mean." My emotions distorted the sound of my voice, distorted the sight of Tobias's face. The room seemed to glow a little brighter and then darken just as quickly. I gripped the curved edge of the table to avoid toppling. "I need to . . . get to the hotel and pack . . . and—"

"Michael will go."

Numb. I was numb. "I need to pick my next mission."

"Not right now, you don't." Tobias flattened my juddering thighs under his large hands. "After a night's rest, you'll sign up."

"I can't stay here. I'm a girl."

"Oh, screw them and their rules."

"To-bi-as," Gabriel gritted out his husband's name.

"What? You want to put her out on the streets?"

"No. Of course not. She can even have our bed. What I want is for you to be quiet."

"Maybe that's the problem. How quiet we all are! Silence is the bane of our existence. I think it's time we all stop tiptoeing around the Seven and turn this autocracy into a democracy, because for all his heart and intent, Asher is only one man. A man who needs *us*. A man who needs *her*." Tobias's hand carved through the air toward me. "Not to mention Naya needs a father. Can you imagine if they took us away from Adam, Gabriel? Can you imagine what it would do to our boy?"

Gabriel paled.

"Michael, can you collect her bag from the hotel?" Tobias asked.

"Right away."

"Michael, please don't . . ." Gabriel gestured to Tobias, worry quarrying his face. "Please keep what you heard here—"

"I have a voice, Gabriel."

Gabriel's head jerked back.

"A slight one but one I intend to join with Tobias's when the time comes."

Gabriel blinked at his fellow guild professor while Tobias whispered, "Thank you."

Once the blue-winged angel was gone, Gabriel asked, "What exactly do you intend to contest, Tobias?"

"Oh, *so* many things."

"Tobias . . ." Gabriel whispered, and it reminded me of all the times Asher had used my name as a full sentence.

A new shiver tormented my body, and however hard I steeled my spine and clenched my fingers, I quaked.

"Don't Tobias-me, Gabriel. It's unfair and you know it."

Gabriel thrust a hand over his cropped blond hair. "Yes! Yes, I know it is, but I don't want to lose you, and I don't want to lose Adam."

"If we don't help Asher, we will lose our boy."

"What are you talking about?"

I shook my head, but Tobias's lips moved. "You really think I cheated on you?"

All of Gabriel's features stiffened. "I . . . I—"

"Asher entrusted me with Adam. Entrusted *us*."

"Tobias, don't . . ." I murmured.

His eyes slid shut. "I can't keep this in anymore. I can't, Celeste. I want to carry Adam up to Elysium and scream at them to look him in his beautiful face and see his beautiful soul."

"Except they won't," I hissed.

"I don't understand," Gabriel said. "Is Adam Asher's son?"

"No."

"Whose son is he?"

Tobias's limpid eyes opened. "Ours. He is *our* son."

Chapter Fifty-Two

After Tobias explained how Adam was born, Gabriel went silent.
Silent and still. Eerily still.

I remembered when Asher had shared his secret with me. How dazed *I'd* been.

Gabriel still hadn't said a word or flinched by the time Michael returned, rolling my suitcase. "If I've forgotten anything, please just send word, and I'll visit the hotel again."

"Thank you, Ophan Michael." I rose from my chair. "Can I ask for another favor from you?"

The man nodded.

"To channel me back to New York?"

"Of course."

I laid a hand on Tobias's shoulder. "Please don't storm up to Elysium without me."

Tobias's red-rimmed eyes lifted.

"Promise me, Tobias. Promise me you'll wait."

The stubborn ophanim didn't utter a word.

"He'll wait." Gabriel's eyes cleared of their haze.

Tobias crossed his arms and shot his husband a glower.

"*We'll* wait because *we* need to prepare." Gabriel scrubbed a hand down his face. "We can't just go up there half-cocked and raise Abaddon."

That dismantled some of the tension.

What dismantled the rest of it was Gabriel scraping his chair closer to Tobias, grabbing either side of his husband's face, and pressing their foreheads together. "No. More. Secrets. We're a team."

My heart ached as I watched them, wishing my teammate hadn't been ripped from my arms. Was this how Leigh had felt the day she'd ascended? Like her heart and soul had been sliced in two?

Throat working, I whispered a quiet goodbye and trailed Ophan Michael out the cafeteria.

"They always make up." He smiled. "In case you were worried. You probably have a hundred other things to worry about."

Not a hundred. Just three. Asher, Naya, and my four hundred-plus missing feathers. "I'm glad to hear it."

Once inside the channel, he held out his palm, and I took it. My hair lifted around me as we rocketed skyward, into the blinding Elysian light.

The trip took mere seconds. When the lavender smoke dissipated, the kind ophanim handed me my suitcase.

"Can you keep an eye on—"

"Tobias?"

"I was going to say Adam."

"I'll keep an eye on all three." Another smile graced the man's lips.

What had possessed me to scorn ophanim? They weren't coldhearted, brainwashing machines returned to Earth to leach the fun and life out of young angels. They were the ones who came back. The ones who stayed. Who devoted themselves to caring for children who weren't even theirs.

My entire life I'd wanted to become a malakim, but as I watched the sparkling cloud blur Michael's dark body, I decided that, if I made it, *when* I made it, I'd train to become an ophanim.

"Celeste?" Mira's voice startled me out of my contemplation, and I pivoted on my heels.

One look at my tearstained face made hers pale. "What happened?"

"They took away his channel key." My voice had no volume.

She frowned, but then she understood. "For how long?"

"Two months. Because of me, Naya's—"

"*You* took away his channel key?"

"No. I meant—"

"I know what you meant." Her red wings bristled. "But I will not have one of my fletchings blaming herself for something she didn't do."

My heart was so squashed it gave a pathetic thump.

"How many feathers are you missing?"

"Four hundred and thirty-two."

"And are you currently signed up to a sinner?"

I swallowed, my throat so raw it hurt. "Yes, but I'm done."

"Well then, let's head to the Ranking Room."

My eyebrows jolted up. "Together?"

"When your mother brought you here, you became my responsibility, and until the day you graduate from my guild, you will stay my responsibility." She clasped my elbow and led me down the hallways of my childhood.

Unlike in Vienna, where night had fallen hours ago, the sky over our heads was only beginning to darken.

"As a baby, you had a set of lungs on you." Her mouth arched into a rare smile. "At night, poor Pippa lost so much sleep trying to keep you from waking the other children that I took pity on her. You won't remember this, but the first year of your life, I stood by your crib every night and told you bits of our history and of human history, until your lids and lips closed."

Not only didn't I remember it, but I could hardly picture it. "Maybe that's why I enjoyed your history classes so much."

She let out a short, *un*Mira-like snort. "You slept through them."

"In my defense, if you used the subject matter to lull me to sleep as a baby, it was a Pavlovian response."

She side-eyed me, which made me smile. It didn't last long. Too soon, the evening reeled through my mind and absconded with my smile.

To avoid turning into a weepy mess again, I redirected my focus back on her. "Did you ever have a child of your own?"

Her gaze fell to the stone floor, which was beginning to glow. "I did."

"Is he or she in Elysium?"

"He. And no. My son chose to follow his heart instead of his calling."

I almost slipped.

"He fell in love with a mortal girl just before his ascension." Her dark eyes traced the fiery veins in the quartz. "I told him I'd take care of her, and that when she died, I'd personally accompany a malakim to harvest her soul. He agreed, but after a year in Elysium, he landed in my guild, his flesh peeling over where his wing bones had once been. He found her again. Married her. They were happy for a while, but then his mind . . ." She inhaled deeply, but the breath barely lifted her narrow chest. "When angels' wings are burned, so is their knowledge of our world. They don't forget instantly, but progressively. This is why they lose their minds."

Here, I'd thought it was another lie. "Did he kill himself?"

"No. He ended up in an asylum, and she . . . she got to go on. Return to a new body. Love again. Live again. I lost track of her after her seventh reincarnation."

I'd always believed Mira's heart impenetrable but it wasn't; it was merely scabbed.

"Enough about me, Fletching." She released my elbow when we reached the Ranking Room. "Turn one of these on and look up Ophelia Simmons."

I frowned.

"I might've heard she was . . . *receptive*."

I slid onto one of the stools and pressed my palm to the cool glass panel. The holo-ranker whirred to life. I traced Ophelia's name. An older lady with a puff of purple hair appeared before me. I scanned her profile. Sin: *marriage counseling*. Number of fletchings previously signed up to her: 23, and 10 of those from our guild. Almost all of them had managed to knock a point off her score.

"My fletchings have been passing around her name, so I looked her up. She's harmless, and I hear, quite entertaining."

"Why is she in the system?"

"Oh. Because most of her customers end up divorcing, even when they don't particularly want to. Unfortunately for her, the ripple effect of her misguidance on their families affects her score." When my swollen lids lifted a fraction, she added, "She's *actively* trying to change her method."

She nodded to the glass panel, and I pressed my palm into it. Once my name appeared over Ophelia's face, I switched off the holo-ranker and followed Mira out.

Keeping my voice low, I asked, "What will you tell Naya?"

"A version of the truth. That her father has much work in Elysium."

"How long will she buy it?"

Her gaze perched on one of the atrium's angel statues. "We'll keep her distracted."

"What's the longest he's stayed away?"

"A week."

Guilt layered itself over my grief. Because of me, Naya wouldn't get to see her father for several weeks. Even if Mira pointed me toward a bunch more thirty-point sinners, it would still take time to get through to them. Sure, some could be steered toward a better path in a day, but most would require two or three days. Not to mention I'd need to take breaks or I wouldn't have the energy and mental wherewithal to help anyone.

"I'll talk to my fletchings about their easier missions over dinner tonight. I should have a new sinner ready for you tomorrow."

"Thank you, Ophan. I really appreciate your help." My voice caught, and I swallowed. I wouldn't break down. Not here.

Mira grazed my knuckles with her papery skin. Although she was immortal, she'd been born in Italy in the fifteenth-century. Six hundred years had taken its toll on her body. "Celeste, this is still your home. I can find you a single bedroom if you don't want to share."

Laughter drifted from two girls entering the guild. One of them blinked when she saw me, then discreetly elbowed her friend, who was still bent double. She instantly sobered up. As they speed-walked past us, both glanced over their shoulders, and then, although muted, I heard my name whispered.

No. I couldn't live here anymore. Be gossiped about or stared at like the under-feathered heathen everyone considered me. Instead of explaining this to Mira, I used another excuse, one that was just as true.

"If I stay here, I'll run into Naya. Even if I skirt the truth, she'll eventually guess something's wrong."

Mira pinched her lips.

I turned and started toward the front door, my suitcase's wheels whispering over the buffed stone. Before leaving, I called out, "The Viennese guild's cafeteria has a lovely ceiling."

She scoffed, which brought a smile to my lips. It lingered a moment but faded like the last. When I arrived home a half hour later and took in my unmade bed, I wondered how my lips had managed to bend at all.

Chapter Fifty-Three

I spent the night in Mimi's old room, curled up between sheets that didn't smell of Asher, and woke up so exhausted that I wondered if I'd slept at all. Mind fuzzy, I got up and went through the motions, picking out clothes from my suitcase, so I wouldn't have to go back into my bedroom. I'd have to face the space I'd shared with Asher eventually, but I didn't feel brave enough this morning, the same way I hadn't felt brave enough to press the buttons on my coffee maker.

Silly . . . so silly.

I dug out a thick scarf from the foyer closet and wound it around my neck, my fingers trembling on the burgundy yarn, then traded my bomber jacket for a thick wintry one. Still, I shivered because no amount of fabric or insulation could warm up hearts and bones.

I ordered an Uber and input Ophelia's Brooklyn address. The moment she ushered me into her brownstone, I understood what Mira had meant about the woman being receptive. I'd had some easy missions but this one felt like cheating. Like one of those college courses students took for easy credits.

After posing as a specialist peddling a novel type of therapy, I excused myself to use her restroom, and although I still detested the sight of my wings, I magicked them into appearance.

I thought I'd be able to tell whether I'd succeeded, but yesterday's feathers were still so fluffy I couldn't tell new growths from day-old ones. Just in case, I spent another hour with Ophelia, who seemed only too delighted for my company. How odd our ranking system was . . . that they'd attribute such a high score to this woman.

Some claimed the celestial scales were infallible, but Ophelia and Jarod . . . they proved our system had flaws.

After leaving Ophelia's house, I headed for the guild. Even though I wanted to seek Naya out and take her in my arms, her touch would make me disintegrate like a collapsed feather and fill her with all the hateful memories of my evening in Vienna.

Keeping my distance wasn't a choice; it was a necessity. For her sake and for mine.

I stopped by the front office and asked my former etiquette professor, Ophan Greer, to inform Mira I'd arrived. She didn't ask what I needed from her older colleague, just offered me a cordial smile and set off across the atrium in search of the woman who'd taken me under her wing.

As I waited, I followed the sparrows' lazy swoops, watched them spread their rainbow wings. *Ah* . . . to be born with all our feathers. Granted ten years was generous, and each feather we earned was a true prize, but still, I found myself envying the guilds' avian pets like I'd envied the city pigeons.

Red feathers appeared in my peripheral vision. I turned away from the sparrows and met Mira's weathered stare.

Sighing, I made my way toward her. "I think I'm done with Ophelia."

"Let's go check."

We walked side by side toward the Ranking Room. The verity fletching I'd bumped into back at The Trap was propped up in front of a holo-ranker. She watched Mira and me approach a holo-ranker without saying a word, coiling one of her long brown curls around her finger.

I pressed my palm into the panel and checked my score first. My heart lifted at the sight of it: 601.

"Good. Now look up Harold Newman," Ophan Mira whispered.

I traced his name on the panel. A balding man appeared along with a score that wasn't frankly that enticing: 8. "Do you have any higher scorers?"

"He will be quick."

I sighed and was about to press down on the panel when the brunette with the gold-tipped blue feathers blurted out, "Milo Jenkins."

When both Ophan Mira and I twisted around to look at her, she blushed and cleared her voice. "I heard you were trying to find high scorers. Milo Jenkins is worth thirty-one feathers." Her hand dropped from the lock of hair she was toying with. "I started on him earlier in the week. He's . . . ripe. Just trace his name."

So I did. The face of a young man with a mohawk and more piercings than skin appeared in place of the older one Mira had suggested. She peered at his rap sheet. "You're still signed on to him, Fletching Liv."

"I know. But if Celeste would like to take over, I'll sign off from him."

Perhaps because my mind was scrambled and aching, I didn't instantly comprehend what she was offering, but then it penetrated, and my lips parted around a shallow gasp. "You did all the legwork, Liv. *You* deserve the reward."

She wrung her fingers together against her denim-clad thighs. "I have four years ahead of me."

"That's very generous of you, Fletching." Ophan Mira's sharp bob cut through the warm air as she pivoted toward me.

"It doesn't feel right to usurp her mission," I murmured.

"Many things aren't right about this situation, Celeste, so accept Liv's offer." As though she'd bitten down on a lemon, wrinkles creased the skin around her mouth.

Liv's voice breezed through the room, "Tell me when."

Mira set her hand on my shoulder, and even through the thick puffy material of my jacket, I felt the crush of her slender fingers. "You don't have any time to waste."

I sighed and poised my palm over the glass panel. "I'm ready."

The second Liv's holo-ranker dinged, I pressed my palm against the glass and the words: ASSIGNED TO CELESTE FROM GUILD 24 appeared like a stamp over Milo's face.

As I stared at my name and guild number, I said, "I don't even know what his sin is."

"Sins." Liv had twirled around on her stool, blue-gold wings haloing her body.

Mira got up. "I'll leave you two to it. As soon as you feel like you're done, come back and sign on to Harold. I know he's not worth much, but I was guaranteed he wouldn't take much time."

I touched her arm. "Thank you, Ophan."

In the softest voice I'd ever heard her use, she murmured, "I know you want to protect Naya, but last night . . . letting you go off on your own . . ." Her gaze drifted to Liv, who busied herself scrolling through sinners on her holo-ranker. "In case you change your mind, I've had a room prepared for you. Number thirty. It's a single and it'll stay vacant until your wings are complete," she murmured before heading out the sliding doors, leaving me alone with Liv.

Liv, who'd gifted me her sinner without prompting.

The light from the 3D projection caught on the golden tips of her pretty wings.

Huh. When did I start considering verity wings pretty?

Since Asher. The answer was a punch to the heart.

I powered my holo-ranker off and crossed the room. Climbing atop the seat beside hers, I asked, "Have you reformed Ophelia Simmons yet?"

Her pupils widened, and after almost a full minute of silence, she shook her head. I nodded to her holo-ranker, and she traced my ex-sinner's name. The woman I'd spent the better part of my day with appeared in all her puffy lavender glory, her score one point lower.

"Take her on."

Liv pressed her palm to the glass panel without even glancing at Ophelia's card, and my heart twanged because I remembered all the times Leigh had recommended some pleasant sinners to me.

After explaining what Ophelia was guilty of and what I'd done, I asked her to tell me about Milo. We parted ways wearing tentative smiles. I wasn't on the market for a friend, especially one I wouldn't see for years to come, but it was nice to know that, perhaps, I wasn't completely despised. Then again, people disliked what they didn't understand, and they hadn't understood my decision to renounce my wings. Now that I'd clambered back atop the celestial wagon, I was no longer a conundrum.

As the green door clanged shut behind me, I wondered if the next time I returned, it would be to stay because, besides an untidy bed that smelled of Asher, what did I have left out in the human world?

Chapter Fifty-Four

After an entire afternoon spent inside the brick loft Milo shared with six other struggling artists, all of whom contributed to the counterfeit art business Milo had created, I headed back uptown. Stanley told me I'd gotten a delivery, which he hadn't even had the slightest inclination to do away with. After he'd wheeled it out of the back room, I told him how proud I was of him.

The crate was long and wide but slender enough that both he and I fit inside the elevator alongside it. As we rose toward the penthouse, he asked which football team I was rooting for this season. The mention of the Superbowl spread goosebumps across my skin. I'd watched last year's game at The Trap with Leon and Jase.

The realization that I truly had no one left in the human world made me wonder what I thought I'd built outside the guild. The disheartening answer was: *nothing*. I'd learned and experienced plenty of things, sure, but these were all things I would take with me. I'd leave nothing behind . . . besides a trail of purple feathers stuck in the Parisian sewer system or floating atop the murky waters of the Hudson.

After Stanley settled the crate against my kitchen baseboard, he rubbed his palms. "Want help opening it, Miss Moreau?"

The brilliant sheen in his eyes, the one that belied his unboxing excitement, made me nod. Using one of my kitchen knives, he popped the wood open.

I froze at the sight of what lay inside—the skyline of our city, the one made up of verses.

Stanley stared between the painting and my face. "Are you . . . all right?"

I tried to speak but couldn't, so I raised a watery smile, which made the poor man shift around as though he wanted to offer me a hug or a tissue but wasn't sure if either would be welcomed. Before the awkwardness could suffuse all the air in the apartment, I pulled a twenty out of my wallet and handed it to him. My hand trembled so hard the green bill bobbed.

He shook his head. "Just doing my job."

"Please," I croaked.

He stuffed the twenty in his pants pocket, then offered to remove the crate.

Once alone, I kneeled in front of the art piece. Although there was no note, I knew it was a gift from Asher. Probably the reason why he'd gone to talk to the gallery owner. How cruel was our universe? Sending me a reminder of the man I'd lost when I was at my feeblest.

I ran my fingertip along the lines of text, the words blurring and wobbling like the city during the pinnacle of summer when the temperatures hit the triple-digits and the concrete steamed. If I was lucky, I'd never get another summer in New York.

At least, not in this century.

My heart felt too shredded to press a smile into my cheeks. As I palmed the tears away, I finally made up my mind about my living arrangements.

I picked myself up and packed.

An hour later, I arrived in front of the guild with only one suitcase and my new painting. I couldn't take it to Elysium, but I could keep it inside the guild. Sure, it would win me raised eyebrows and a puckered brow from Ophan Mira—fletchings weren't supposed to decorate their bedrooms with material things, especially ones foraged in the human world—but I dared anyone to pry it from my warm, lively fingers.

As expected, I received my share of wide-eyed stares as I slid it through the atrium and then down the hallway toward the door carved with a thirty. I pushed it open, and although I knew exactly what to expect—quartz walls and floor, a domed glass ceiling overlooking the fake Elysian sky, a queen-size bed wedged beside a nightstand also whittled from quartz and an adjoining bathroom, made of . . . *drumroll* . . . the celestial white stone—my heart gave a small kick of relief. Everything had changed, including myself, yet this hadn't.

Doors clacked open and shut, followed by animated conversations and leisurely footfalls. After the glaring silence and emptiness of my apartment, I was glad for the noise. The chatter lost volume when my peers passed my open doorway and then died off completely when I smiled at them. Who would've thought a vertically-challenged angel with stunted hybrid wings could inspire such fear?

I tilted my painting against the wall beside the bed, then unzipped my suitcase and unpacked, first Naya's purple feather painting and parrot drawing, then the clothes and shoes beneath. I'd just dumped my underwear in a drawer when a flurry of arms and wavy blonde hair erupted inside my room.

"Celeste!" Naya launched herself at me, almost tipping me over. "I heard two girls say you were here, and—"

"Fletching Naya!" Pippa panted, sidling against my doorframe. "You can't just run off like that."

I readjusted my hold on Naya, who bit her lip, a deep blush tinting her face. "I'm sorry, Ophan, but I wanted to see Celeste."

Smoothing a tangle from Naya's hair, my gaze met Pippa's worried one. "I'll have her back before bedtime."

"No!" Naya whipped her dark eyes toward me. "I want to stay with you. Please." She cupped my jaw with her tiny hands. "Unless Apa's coming . . ."

The lump, which swelled and shrank but never vanished, grew so large I could barely manage a swallow. "Maybe you could stay with me tonight. If that's all right with Ophan Pippa, that is."

Pippa gulped in breath after breath as though she'd just run an Olympic sprint instead of given chase to a four-year-old. "I, uh . . . would need to ask Mira, but"—another gulp—"but maybe—"

"I'd really like Naya's company tonight."

"Okay." Pippa dragged her hands through her long brown hair. "Okay. I'll go inform Mira that you're here and that Naya will stay with you tonight."

"Yes!" Naya pumped her fist the second the door shut.

I laughed and then pressed a kiss to her warm, milky cheek. She wasn't Asher's and yet, somehow, she felt like a piece of him. When my lids began to prickle, I pressed my cheek against the side of her head and hugged her tight, so she wouldn't catch the sheen of tears. And then I slid my lids closed and breathed until the grief subsided.

When I felt strong enough to speak, I said, "Remember that painting I told you about? The one I wanted us to do together?"

She pulled away, and her large eyes roamed over my face. "Yes."

"I brought it." I tipped my head toward the wall against which it was slumped, then set her down on her slippered feet.

She padded over and studied it with such focus her face sprouted tiny creases. "What does it say?"

I crouched next to her. *That's right, she can't read yet.* So I read her the long poem, stumbling a few times, not because the scrawl was unclear, but because of the memories it dredged up.

When I was done, Naya draped an arm around my neck. "Why does it make you sad?"

Not rending my eyes off the word *love*, which shaped the antenna atop the Chrysler building, I said, "Because your daddy gave it to me."

"But you love Apa, so it should make you happy."

I swallowed.

"So why are you crying?"

"Because soon, I'll have to leave it behind . . . I can't bring it up to Elysium."

"Channels are *soo* stupid."

"They really are."

"Welcome home, Fletching." Mira had opened my door and was standing in the doorway, the glowing quartz highlighting the edges of her crimson wings. "I heard Naya will be staying with you tonight. Are you pleased with this arrangement?"

I smiled, understanding she was giving me an out. "I know it goes against the guild's guidelines, but I'd love for Naya to stay with me."

After a beat, Mira notched her chin a little higher. "Ah . . . the guild's guidelines. They require some updating."

The implications flew over Naya's head, but not over mine. Change was happening. It had begun at the top, with an archangel going against his ingrained values, and spread to the bottom. Would the rumble at the base be strong enough to fissure the pyramid of power, or was our system as indestructible as Elysian quartz?

Mira's gaze strayed to the painting. If she disapproved, she didn't let on. "Don't go to bed too late. You both have much work to do in the morning."

Naya groaned.

"Starting with my history lesson, Fletching Naya."

Another groan.

My dimples dug into my cheeks. "History was my favorite." In a stage-whisper, I added, "But don't let Ophan Mira know or her wings will get all puffy."

In an extremely low voice, Naya asked, "Why will they get puffy?"

Mira released a snort so breathy I wondered if I'd imagined it, but her eyes were aglow, so perhaps the austere professor had produced such a sound. "I'll leave you two to your whisperings, but if Naya comes to me with the seditious idea of painting over the skylight in the cafeteria, I will know where it came from."

I grinned.

Mira drummed her sensible fingernails—unpainted and short—against the stone doorframe, then turned on her sensible heels—short and square—and walked away, leaving me with Naya and the feeling that tomorrow would be a little brighter.

Here, I'd thought I was still sinking but perhaps I'd hit rock-bottom and was slowly drifting back up. I raised my gaze to the dark sky beyond the glass dome, a projection of the same one Asher was looking upon.

I'm coming, neshahadzaleh.

Chapter Fifty-Five

The sun revolved thirty times around the Earth and Elysium, and although it saw the loss of six feathers, it also saw the birth of two hundred and eighty-seven new ones.

I was a hundred and eighteen feathers away from joining my soulhalf.

A soulhalf who'd sent news through Tobias. Even though the Viennese verity had promised not to get involved, two days after they'd locked Asher in Elysium, Tobias had traveled to the celestial capital almost daily and phoned Mira through the inter-guild system just as often. Asher was behaving himself and tracking my progress in the celestial Ranking Room. He was still an incumbent member of the Seven but no longer an active one. The referendums and daily decisions were carried out without his input or vote. According to Tobias, Claire was seeking to have him removed from the Council, but the archangels had said his infraction wasn't grave enough a motive to unseat him. Selfishly, I wished he was no longer a seraphim, but then I'd look over at Naya and remember all the reasons he needed to keep his position.

Her father's absence was beginning to take a toll on the child. Her eyes were less bright, her smiles less frequent, her energy less giddy. Even her blonde mane seemed somehow tamer. It was as though, in the space of a month, she'd caught up to her soul's true age. She'd still smile or kiss my cheek when I'd come find her between my missions, but sadness clung to her like the chill in the autumnal air.

"She's *my* student. *My* responsibility." Mira's voice snapped my attention off my boots, which I was trying to rid of mud and dead leaves. "You do *not* get to go around my guild and corner my fletchings!"

A detestable face peeked from beyond Mira's juddering red wings. Only wind or strong emotions had the power to make wings tremble. Since not even a breeze slinked through the atrium's forever tepid air, I was guessing my history professor was well and truly incensed.

The exhaustion of having undertaken three missions in one day evaporated, and energy roared through me. "Who did Eliza corner, Ophan?"

"*Ish* Eliza." The ranker bit out her title.

I didn't even gratify her with an acerbic smile. "Who did the ranker corner?" I sensed I knew but wanted confirmation before I did or said anything that would ruin today's hard work.

"Naya," Mira said.

This time, I looked at the ishim. "And why did you corner a child?"

Eliza lifted her pointy chin. "That is none of your business, Fletching."

"Naya is very much my business now that you've removed her father from her life." Fingers curling at my sides, I took a step toward her.

Although she was several inches taller and her feathers sparkled, she backed up.

A hand landed on my forearm, eased me back. "Go to your room, Fletching." I popped my mouth open to object when Mira added an inflexible, "*Now.*"

Glowering at Eliza, I did as I was told, but not without visualizing myself yanking out fistfuls of the ishim's feathers. And yeah, the fantasy cost me one of mine and made Mira's already sour expression curdle some more, but damn if it wasn't worth the stabbing pain.

Instead of my bedroom, I went in search of Naya, whom I found huddled next to Ophan Pippa in a corner of the children's playroom, behind the quartz shelving stacked with colorful board books. When I reached them, the children's supervisor shot me a worried stare but rose from her crouch and went to stand guard by the door.

I dropped down in front of Naya. "Hey, little angel."

Naya picked her head off her kneecaps, eyes so red her irises looked golden instead of dark brown.

"Tell me what happened. What did that ranker do?"

Her lips wobbled, and new tears pitchforked down her blotchy cheeks. "She t-told me Apa was in trouble. She said I c-could get him out of trouble if I answered s-some of her questions."

My heartbeats teemed, turning into one long, uninterrupted clang. "*What* questions?"

"She asked if I . . . if I kn-knew Lee."

Heat and cold slammed into me in alternating waves. Lee? Did she mean Leigh? Rare were the people who'd pronounced my friend's name the way she'd preferred it: Ley.

"And what did you say, sweetheart?"

She wiped her nose on her sleeve. "I said I d-don't know a Lee."

I didn't ask her if she remembered the name pronounced differently, afraid she might, and even more afraid it would stir up a memory.

"And then sh-she asked if I l-liked Paris." Naya sniffled, and I pulled her onto my lap. "I d-don't know if I like P-Paris."

"How could you know? You've never been."

She pressed the side of her head to my chest. I hoped that, in spite of the layers of fabric, she couldn't hear my now-furious pulse.

"And then she asked"—she took a slow breath—"if I still loved Jarod Adler."

I kept my calm, even though on the inside I was a geyser about to feathering blow. "That's a silly question. You don't know any boys named Jarod." Did my voice sound as strangled as it felt?

A tremor racked her small body.

"Naya?" I stopped running my hand up and down her hunched spine. "What did you tell the ishim?"

"I told her the only man I loved was Apa."

Good girl.

"Who's Jarod, Celeste?"

"No one, honey."

"Why does his name make my heart hurt if he's no one?" She swiped her cheek, and it was so slick with tears, the friction made it squeak.

"Maybe you read a sad story about him?"

She looked up at me. "I don't know how to read."

"What I meant was, maybe Ophan Pippa read you a story about a boy named Jarod?" I smiled, even though my insides felt like they were being pulped. "You didn't tell the ranker that it made your heart hurt, did you?"

Naya pushed a strand of hair off her forehead.

"Did you?"

"Ophan Pippa says lying is very bad."

Oh . . . no . . .

Naya sniffed. "Did I do something wrong? I just wanted to help Apa." Her lips wobbled. "Is he in trouble because of me?"

"No, Naya." I swept up some of her tears with my thumb. "He's in trouble because of me."

"*You?*"

A bitter smile contorted my mouth. "Seraph Claire wants him to concentrate on his work instead of on my wings."

"Fletching Celeste!" Mira's strident voice boomed through the playroom. "A word."

"Geez . . . I'm not deaf," I muttered, which made a smile pop onto Naya's face. I kissed her forehead, then set her down and got up. "I'll be right back. Don't go anywhere."

Mira tipped her head to the hallway, and I trailed her out. "You need to earn feathers, not *lose* them."

Her reproach was coming from a good place, but really? "Eliza's a giant rumphole."

She inhaled a sharp breath and gaped at the air around my thighs.

"Relax, Ophan. That descriptor doesn't cost me any feathers. Tried and tested."

Her shoulders stayed at ninety-degree angles. She was *not* amused. "Do you know where Seraph Claire spent her afternoon?" She paused. "In Vienna."

I was no longer amused either.

Mira sighed. "Tobias says we shouldn't worry. That Adam gave the archangel nothing."

Dropping the volume on my own voice, I whispered, "Perhaps he didn't but Naya told Eliza the name Jarod made her heart hurt."

"She's four and extremely sensitive. A lot of things make her heart hurt."

"Claire knows, Ophan! She wouldn't be rooting around if she—"

"She *suspects*, but she doesn't know," she hissed. "No one knows."

"*You* know."

"I *suspect*. But rest assured, suspicions aren't admissible in the Seven's court."

I bit my lip. Perhaps suspicions weren't admissible, but they would spur Claire's digging, and at some point, she was bound to find hard evidence. *Admissible* evidence.

"Eve!" I gasped. For all her flaws, she'd loved Leigh, and love was a powerful weapon.

"What about the archangel's daughter?" Mira asked.

"You need to talk to her. She was Leigh's best friend. She—"

"No!" Her complexion turned as scarlet as her wings. "Absolutely not! Have you lost your mind, Fletching?" Suddenly, her mouth clapped shut as her gaze dropped to something behind me.

Someone.

Naya.

"Pippa!" Mira screeched. "Please do your job."

"Sorry, Mira." Pippa coaxed Naya from the doorway.

Once the door shut, she said, "The only thing you need to worry about are your wings. The quicker you get to Elysium, the quicker she'll get her father back."

I stared at the closed door of the playroom, my pulse finally quieting. Not because I was relieved, but because Mira was right; the quicker I ascended, the quicker Asher would be able to travel again. High on adrenaline, I spun around and strode to the Ranking Room. I scanned profile after profile, single-digits blurring into double-digits. Too low. All of them too low.

Sucking in a breath, I stopped scrolling and traced a name I'd memorized and then I flattened my palm against the glass of the holo-ranker.

Leigh had reformed a Triple and so had Seraph Claire's husband. Since it wasn't the motivation I lacked, I couldn't see a single reason why I'd fail.

Barbara Hudson. Attorney at Hudson & Mintz. 100.

Here I come.

Chapter Fifty-Six

After a night animated by more nightmares than dreams, I arrived in front of a narrow, brick townhouse painted a pretty greenish-blue and sandwiched between a dusty music store and an apartment building with saggy air-conditioning units. I tossed my empty cup of coffee into a bin, wiped donut crumbs off my fingers, and rang the doorbell beneath the gold plaque that read *Hudson & Mintz, Family Law.*

No fancy high-rise for this Triple and her associate, a young lawyer with a single-digit score. I'd decided upon visualizing his low number, that *she* couldn't be all that bad if her associate was *that* good.

A woman sporting a sleek navy dress, kitten heels, and a gray bob opened the door. Her bifocals slid to the tip of her nose as she eyed me. "Welcome to Hudson and Mintz. Do you have an appointment?"

"I don't, but I'm in a real bind. One which Mrs. Hudson can apparently help me out of."

"Mrs. Hudson won't be in for another hour and her schedule's packed, but you're welcome to take a seat in the waiting area."

"Thank you."

She led me into a small, comfortable cream-colored waiting area with a large glass table covered in pamphlets ranging from safe sex to adoption to allergy nasal sprays.

The secretary left the room, then returned a moment later with a plastic clipboard. "Could you please fill out this form?"

I took the proffered clipboard and read over the two-page questionnaire.

The older lady watched me for a second, then instructed me to bring the completed form to her office across the hall. The questions were a little odd but nothing that set off alarm bells, no *Can you build a dirty bomb?* or *On a scale of 1 to 10, how do you feel about being tortured?*

They were more along the lines of: *Do you still have any living relatives? Are you presently in a relationship? When was the last time you were in contact with a loved one? Do you use drugs? Are you currently pregnant? Why should we take you on pro bono?*

I'd read articles about Hudson and Mintz's benevolence—most of their customers were either teen runaways or women in bad marriages. Hudson had to have a dark side, though. My guess was that she pretended her cases were pro bono but actually made her clients pay for her services some other way . . . some illegal way . . . a way her partner was oblivious to since his soul was so pure.

As I dropped the clipboard off with the secretary, a man in tan corduroy slacks and a blue shirt with a toothpaste stain on the collar walked into the building. Thrusting his fingers through uncombed hair, he shot me a quick, slightly frazzled smile, as though he'd literally rolled out of bed and smacked into his floorboards.

"Good morning, Griff," the secretary said. "Your nine o'clock just phoned to say she'd be ten minutes late."

"Great." His hair flopped back into his eyes. "Great. Just send her in when she gets here." Another quick smile my way, and then he climbed up a set of stairs to what I imagined must be where his and Barbara's offices were since the lobby area was on the cramped side of small.

I'd read every pamphlet front to center to back by the time a blonde woman dressed in dark denim, a white linen shirt, and cowboy boots appeared in the doorway, peering down at the form I'd filled out. "Hi, Celeste. I'm Barbara." A grandmotherly smile pressed in a plethora of deep wrinkles. "Maisie said you didn't have an appointment."

I stood up. "Sorry. I don't. Could you still see me?"

"I just had a cancellation so I guess it's your lucky day. Come with me. We'll talk in my office." She gestured to a door at the far end of the foyer, which I'd assumed led to a bathroom or a storage cupboard.

I trailed her to it. Sure enough, it led to a basement, but it wasn't creepy. Quite the contrary. It was sort of homey, done up in beiges and creams with bright lighting and a wall shelving unit filled with law books. She gestured to one of the chairs, then propped herself against her desk, her hands loosely gripping the edge.

"So, what is it I can help you with?" Her face was clear of makeup, and her nails clear of blood.

Yes, I checked. After all, she'd been in the celestial system for 400 months. She might not have spent all thirty-three years as a Triple, but still . . .

I folded my coat over the back of the chair and sat. "I hear you take on pro bono work, and I was wondering if there was some sort of catch."

"A catch?"

"Gifting your time seems so generous, and I guess I'm worried I'll end up with a bad surprise."

Her eyebrows pulled together. "You mean, hidden fees?"

"Yes." I looked around the room for bricks of white powder or stacks of money but found none. Why couldn't the ishim be more descriptive?

"Why don't you start by telling me what you'd need my help with?"

"Um. Well, I've been living on my own for a while, but then I got tangled up with this guy, but he got in trouble and had to go home, and his family, they're very strict, so they've basically locked him up, and I'm trying to set him free, but pleading with them didn't work, so I thought, maybe legal action could get him emancipated."

"Is your boyfriend a minor?"

"No."

She linked her hands together, almost blinding me with her huge bulbous ring. "Then I'm not sure I'm the right person for the job."

"I have no one else to turn to, Mrs. Hudson."

She glanced at the questionnaire plopped on her desk. "You have no one? Not even a close friend who'd . . . *help*?"

I shook my head, hoping the ishim wouldn't consider my charade a lie and pluck my wings. Technically, there was truth in all I'd said.

She sighed. "Okay. Well, let me have a think about your case. If I believe it's right for me, I'll give you a call later on in the day." She extended her hand, and I shook it.

I kept expecting something to happen. Something terrible. Something that would explain why this lady was a Triple.

She led me back up the stairs, opened the door, and sent me away with a warm smile and a little wave.

As I stood on the street in front of *Hudson & Mintz*, the adrenaline rush of signing on to a Triple waned, and my mood inched toward despair. What if she didn't call me back? Or what if she did, but it was to say she wouldn't take me on? Sinners weren't always easy to read, but never had one baffled me as much as Barbara Hudson.

I began to walk away, resolving to try again even if she turned me down. Maybe the key to seeing the evil side of her nature was to annoy her until it leaped out of her.

So I waited, killing the hours wandering the neighborhood, buying things for Naya—colorful clothes, cute headbands and glittery barrettes, a squishy turquoise unicorn with a golden horn, and books with pretty drawings and stories to match. I was at the cash register of the bookstore when my phone finally chirped with an unknown number.

I shifted all my purchases to one hand and picked up. "Hello?"

"Celeste? It's Barbara." A beat. "So, I've thought about it and I don't think I'll be the right person for the job. However . . ."

I held my breath.

"Griff, my associate, is an extremely smart and dedicated man. If you're interested, I'll gladly refer you to him. Would you like me to do that?"

No. No. And no. It's you I want, not him. "Um, that's very kind of you, but I don't feel comfortable working with a man on this."

"I can assure you that you'd have nothing to worry about." Papers rustled on her desk. "Anyway, I'll be at my office until six tonight. If you change your mind, just call back our firm's number and ask Maisie to connect you to me."

Frustration made my fingers curl around the phone. "Okay. Thank you for calling me back."

Once the line went dead, I tossed a large packet of roasted nuts atop my purchases, paid, then returned to the blue building and took a seat on the stoop across the street. Snow began to fall, not quite accumulating, simply dusting the sidewalk like icing sugar. I read through all the picture books I'd bought Naya, glancing up from time to time. At five-thirty, the secretary left, followed a couple minutes later by Griff. The lights were still on, so I imagined Barbara was still there.

I dusted the snow off my thighs and crossed the street. I was just about to ring when the door opened, revealing a man with greasy black hair gathered in a ponytail.

He looked at me as he zipped up a leather jacket. "Can I help you?"

"I was hoping to have a word with Mrs. Hudson before she left."

"She's busy."

"It'll just take a minute."

His pin-sized eyes strayed to the fluffy unicorn peeking out from my shopping bag, then back up to me. "Wait here."

"Can I wait inside? It's really cold."

He stepped to the side to let me through, slanting me a look that made me glad I'd had the foresight to pack pepper spray.

Not that it had saved me last time . . . but it had helped. *A little.*

After he headed back to the basement door, I set my shopping bags down and transferred the canister from my bag to my coat pocket. A moment later, he was back with my sinner.

"Celeste." Barbara pinched out my name, clearly displeased I'd returned. "You're back."

"I don't want your associate's counsel. I want yours, Mrs. Hudson."

Her gaze dropped to my shopping bags, and I could see the wheels spinning. I'd said I had no one in my life, and yet here I was with fluffy toys and children's clothing.

"I think working together could be mutually beneficial." *Open your closet to me. Show me those skeletons. Come on . . .*

Her hazel eyes returned to my face. "What do you think, Fred?"

"Why does it matter what he thinks?" I asked.

"Because Fred's my ex-husband."

Ex-husband? I tried to remember if I'd read about him in one of the many articles I'd found on Barbara, but his name didn't ring *any* bells.

Fred cocked his head to the side. "She doesn't seem like a runaway."

"That's because she's not," Barbara said. "But she did recently lose her only living relative—Muriel Moreau."

"You looked me up?" I licked my lips as I slid my index finger over the Mace's trigger.

"You don't think I'd take on someone I haven't checked out?" She tipped her head to the shopping bags. "I also know you're attending Columbia and don't have any kids. So, who's the lucky recipient of all those toys?"

My mind scrambled to find an explanation that wouldn't cost me feathers *or* this mission. "A little girl who's growing up in the same orphanage where I spent my childhood." I braced myself for the uprooting of a feather. It never came.

"How magnanimous of you."

"Look, you don't have to take me on pro bono."

"I don't have to take you on at all." She turned and started toward her basement office. "Fred, please show the girl out."

"I know about your shady side business, and I want to help," I blurted out, desperate.

She halted, then looked over her shoulder. "My shady side business?" She laughed, but I knew I'd hit a nerve because it was slightly shrill. Not to mention her ex's boxy forehead furrowed. "I don't have the faintest idea what you're talking about."

Was he not aware of what his former wife was up to? Or maybe he did know, and that was why they'd divorced.

My heart sped up, punching the side of my throat. "I think you do."

She was no longer laughing. "Fred, search her."

The man was on me faster than a fly on dung.

"I'm not the enemy! I just came to help." I swatted his hands away, but he locked both my wrists in one giant, hairy fist, then shoved my coat open and ran his meaty palm down my front, probably looking for a wire or a weapon.

When his intrusive hand sank into my coat pockets, a smile creased his square face. He removed my pepper spray and tossed it to Barbara, then dug through my bag, pinched out my phone, and dropped it on the floor.

The crunch of glass beneath his boot had me growling. Oh, if I'd had angel-fire . . . the things I'd do to him.

"Better not bite me." He grinned, then hooked his arm around my shoulders and spun me around, pressing my back to his front. "'Cause I bite back." When his teeth grazed the shell of my ear, a full-body shudder shook me.

As Barbara approached me, I kept my head held high, the weight of my invisible wing bones reminding me I would be safe no matter what these two psychopaths had in store for me.

She traced the shape of my face with her fingertip. "Humans are incredible. You give them an out, and they don't take it."

"I didn't take your out because, like you said, humans *are* incredible. Even if they do terrible things, they're capable of changing."

She tipped her head to the side. "Capable perhaps but willing . . .? Now, that's the question."

"Are you willing to change, Mrs. Hudson?"

"Depends. What are you offering?"

"Redemption."

Her lips quirked, making her skin ripple with wrinkles. "Redemption? Aren't you the sweetest, Celeste Moreau. Sweet and so very naïve."

I bristled. "Just because I'm young doesn't mean I'm naïve."

"Being naïve isn't a flaw. God, I wish I could be naïve, but you take one wrong turn, and suddenly, no matter how many right ones you make, you just can't get out of the ditch. So then you make the most of being in the ditch."

"I can help you out of your ditch."

She was uncomfortably close. So close I could smell she'd eaten garlic at lunch. "But you see, Celeste. I like my ditch." She flipped open the dome of her golden ring and a needle glinted.

Fred shoved my head sideways, exposing my neck.

"Don't," I cried out. "Don't hurt me. I'll come willingly."

Barbara stroked my skin once. Twice. "Can't take the risk of you seeing where we're going."

"I'll keep my eyes shut."

"You certainly will." She tittered and pressed the needle into my neck.

I hissed from the sharp jab.

She wobbled. Or maybe I wobbled.

The ground bucked, liquefied, and I melted right into it.

Chapter Fifty-Seven

lank. Clank. Clank.
  The rhythmic sound made me groan awake. My forehead throbbed like the night I'd inhaled vodka. The night Asher had carried me out of a bar.

Oh, Asher...

"Hey, you."

I held still.

"Hello?" The soft voice made my lids spring open.

I was assaulted with light so bright I thought I was back at the guild, but soon my eyes adjusted and made out a popcorn ceiling striped with halogen tubing.

Clank. Clank. The sound of metal striking metal had my head turning. Medical equipment littered the room. Oh, angels ... was I in a hospital? I tried to roll myself up, but my ankles and wrists were immobilized.

"Are you awake?"

The hushed voice snapped my attention to another bed where a lone figure lay beneath a white sheet. The person's hair was chopped short and a band of gauze was wrapped around their eyes, obscuring part of their sallow face.

"Yes." My throat felt like it was filled with the same scratchy wool as my head. "Where are we?"

"Are you chained too?"

Again, I tried to lift my hands. "Yeah."

333

The sound of approaching footsteps set my attention on a glass-paneled door. The only door in the room.

"Where are we?"

"They call it *The Farm*," my neighbor whispered, just as two familiar faces appeared in the glass pane.

When the door clicked, the kid with the gauze sucked in a breath.

Barbara Hudson walked in, cowboy boots squeaking against the linoleum floor. "That wore off fast. I thought you'd be out for another hour at least."

"What is this place?" I stared at the man in the lab coat who'd walked in behind her. Fred. Her ex.

She sat at the foot of my bed. "This is the place where miracles happen."

"Miracles?"

She gazed at the kid with the bandaged eyes. "Yes, miracles."

"What sort of miracles?"

"I thought you knew *all* about my little side business." The lilt in her voice made my skin break out in goosebumps.

"I know it's an amoral business."

She frowned. "Amoral? Why, that's incredibly harsh. We save lives here, Celeste."

"Is that what you're doing to that kid? Saving his life?"

"That kid's corneas just helped a man recover his sight."

The Farm . . . "You took his corneas?"

"He'll be fine."

"Fine? You took his corneas!" I repeated. "What is wrong with you?"

Her eyes narrowed on mine. "Maybe I'll take yours too. Or maybe I'll take one of your kidneys. We just got an order for a kidney."

I jerked, my chains rattling, my brain, too. What in Abaddon had she injected me with?

"Fred here's going to check your blood type and prep you for surgery if you're a match. And don't worry. My ex has his medical license. You'll have anesthetics and discreet scars."

"You're not taking my kidney!"

"Would you rather I take your heart, Celeste? Those are in high demand. Just last week we harvested one for the Venezuelan president's niece. The child would've died without us."

Revulsion warred with absolute abhorrence. "You cut out someone's heart?"

"To save a child."

"And the person you took it from survived, too, I suppose?" I spat.

"The donor had no one and the President's niece . . . well, she had a lot of people."

"You're insane."

She toyed with her large gold ring, popping the bulbous top open, then pressing it closed. *Click. Click.* "That's not very nice. And highly untrue. I save people."

"By killing others!" I gritted out.

She loomed over me, eyes frighteningly wide. "Who would've died eventually. Most of these kids are vagrants with no prospects."

"That doesn't give you any right to steal their organs!" And I'd wondered why she was a Triple.

She stood and walked toward the door. "Everyone here sought *me* out. Not the other way around. I don't abduct unsuspecting people."

"You don't abduct people? I didn't walk into your little farm!"

"No, but you walked into my office. *Twice.* And then you offered to come. *Willingly.*" She fished a keycard from her jeans pocket and swiped it over the electronic lock. "Should've taken my out."

"You're a monster!"

Before letting herself out, she shot me a chilling smile that made Seraph Claire seem like a powderpuff. I yelled, my throat already so hoarse, my shouting had little volume, but maybe . . . maybe someone would hear me. Maybe a malakim was wandering around the place, collecting squandered souls.

I yelled harder when Fred wheeled a metal tray table toward my bed, greasy ponytail swishing. He strapped a rubber band around my bicep and then thumbed the inside of my arm until my vein bulged.

"Don't do this," I said.

He didn't even look up at me, just grabbed a catheter and slipped it inside my vein, and then he hooked me onto a drip.

"You don't have to do this," I croaked.

His gaze flicked to the transparent bag he'd hooked me up to. As the cold liquid flowed into me, the contours of his face grew hazier and hazier, his features becoming mere smudges before dissolving completely.

Chapter Fifty-Eight

I gasped as pain sawed into me.

"She's awake, doctor." A pair of eyes covered in surgical glasses swam before mine.

"Impossible. The dose I gave her was fit for a horse."

Cold.

I was so cold.

Another head popped into my line of sight. Even though he was wearing scrubs and glasses too, I recognized Fred. "Give her another pump."

I opened my mouth to speak, but my shallow breath simply bounced back into my face, powerless.

Tears curved down the sides of my nose.

I shaped Asher's name.

Why didn't I listen to you?

FIRE SINGED MY VEINS AND LIT UP MY WAIST.

"I've fucking never seen anything like this. I can't get past the subcutaneous tissue. Call Barbara."

"Stop," I whispered.

Something rattled.

Perhaps my heart?

"How many pumps did you give her?" Fred's voice was so loud it echoed inside my skull.

"Asher," I croaked. *Find me.*

But he wouldn't, because he was locked up in Elysium and I was locked up in the human version of purgatory.

I AWAKENED TO THE RHYTHMIC RESONANCE OF BEEPS. I shifted, and the violence of the pain that streaked across my waist felt like acid chewing through my skin.

Was this the pain I would experience when I lost my wings? *Had* I lost my wings? Oh, angels, what day was it? No more than a day could've gone by, right? Two at the most. I searched for a window or a clock, but all I saw were machines and the boy with the gauze-covered eyes.

"Hey," I croaked.

The kid stirred, turning his face in the direction of my voice.

"What's your name?"

"Will."

"I'm Celeste." I tugged on my restraints, but it only made the chains rattle. "How long have you been here?"

"I don't know." His voice was so faint I had to concentrate on his mouth to make out what he was saying. "My face hurts so much."

"I wish I could take your pain away, Will." My eyes heated with anger. Anger at myself for being so damn stupid, and anger at that soulless doctor and his evil boss.

"My parents said I was dead to them. They're not coming. No one —" His voice broke. "No one's coming for me." His chains rattled. "We're going to die in here, aren't we?"

"No. Someone will come for us." Mira or Naya would notice my absence and then check my profile and see my name beside Barbara Hudson's.

What if that took days? And where the hell were we? Underneath the townhouse? I asked Will.

"I don't know. She gave me something, and I blacked out, and then I woke up here."

I thought of the human whose heart Barbara had harvested. If they'd killed him or her here, then a malakim had come. Another realization hit me. If a malakim had come, then the angels knew about this place, this *farm*. How could my people let this go on? Even if Barbara or that doctor only got a single lifetime, how was this right? How was this fair?

I knew we weren't gods and that we were supposed to teach humans to fight their own battles, but how could we turn a blind eye?

The door buzzed.

Barbara pushed her limp blonde hair behind her ears. "I hear you're giving us grief, Miss Moreau."

Will shrieked, "Help!"

"Silence him!"

A woman in scrubs walked over to his side of the room and pressed a button.

"No!" Will wailed, chains clanking. "HELP! Help," he sobbed. And then his sobs turned into sniffles that turned into hiccups, and then . . . into nothing.

Barbara walked up to me. "What are you?"

I tried to slide my hands through the restraints but the metal bracelets were too tight. "I *was* your ticket out of Hell."

"Don't speak in riddles. Your skin breaks and you bleed, but Fred cannot cut through your flesh. He tried a drill and it broke. How?"

"I'm an angel." My shoulder blades spasmed as my confession cost me a feather.

She pursed her mouth, making each wrinkle dig deep. "Do you work for the government? Are you some underground project of theirs?"

"No."

"We're going to study you."

"What day is it?"

"Why?"

"I want to know how long I've been in here."

"No one's coming for you. At least, not here."

"The least you can do is tell me what day it is."

"Friday."

I'd been gone two days. Unless . . . "Friday what?"

She backed up to let her ex through.

I thrashed. I must've hit my feather because I collapsed into an old memory. When I came to, a saw glinted between Fred's gloved hands.

"What are you going to do with that?" I croaked.

"We're going to study you." Barbara returned to the door, which she beeped open.

"No!" I wrung my body from side to side, trying to break the chains, but I possessed no magic, only meek fletching muscles. "No!"

The door suctioned shut just as Fred positioned the saw over my wrist. I tried to pull my hand back, but all that did was make the cuff dig into my skin. And then the serrated blade was tearing through my skin.

I screamed, my ears roaring with heartbeats. "STOP!"

The doctor didn't.

"Asher," I sobbed. "Asher, help . . ."

Suddenly he was there. Right there.

He lifted me into his arms and pushed off the floor, shooting through the ceiling, which wasn't a ceiling but open sky. With stars. So many stars.

I reached out to catch one, but pain tore through me. I screamed until it ebbed, and the stars flicked off, one after the other.

Pop. Pop. Pop.

"Asher," I whispered.

"She keeps repeating that name," I heard someone say, and then I heard nothing at all.

SCREAMS. INHUMAN SCREAMS WRENCHED ME FROM A DREAM. A dream where I was chasing Naya through the guild, and she kept morphing into Leigh, and I kept hissing at her to stop, worried someone would see.

I cracked my lids open, and the hateful popcorn ceiling with its bright halogens flooded my eyes. I tried to raise my arm to shield them, but pain like I'd never felt radiated through my bones, and I whimpered.

Wet heat rushed into my eyes, blurred the room. I squeezed my lids shut, and tears tracked down my temples.

Someone screamed again. *Will.*

Fred growled something at the nurse about anesthetics. There was a rustle of plasticky paper, and then Will grew quiet.

I was so useless.

So pitiful.

How could I save humans if I couldn't even save myself?

"So?" Barbara's voice resonated through the now quiet room.

I kept my lids shut, hoping she wouldn't spy the wet tracks along my temples.

She poked my wrist, and I winced. "Her hand's still there. How is her hand still attached? Give me that saw, you useless fool."

My lids flipped open. "No."

"How is your hand still attached?"

"Take away the cuffs, and I'll tell you everything."

"Nice try, Miss Moreau, but no. What." She poked my wrist, and I gritted my teeth. "Are." Another prod. "You?"

I wouldn't sob. I wouldn't scream.

"I'm a patient woman. We can wait. Weeks. Months. Whatever it takes . . ."

I didn't have months. I wasn't even sure how many weeks I had.

Grunts and gunshots sounded outside the hospital room. My lids snapped open.

"What the hell was that?" Barbara jolted toward the door.

Hope that someone had come, human or angel, sprang through me, numbing my atrocious pain. When a spray of bullets pinged against the wall of the hospital room, she swung the blood-soaked saw in front of her. Groans echoed outside and then the glass panel in the door filled with a sight that made the rest of the world fade.

Asher.

Asher had come.

I blinked, because it was an illusion. He was locked in Elysium. He couldn't have come.

After the third flutter of my lashes, he was still there.

The door flew open, and not on its hinges, but downward. Just banged into the floor. And there he stood, beautiful wings vibrating with unbridled fury. The nurse screeched, but Fred, he pulled a gun from his lab coat and fired it. The bullet pinged off Asher's bicep.

He looked at the man, and then held out his palm and shot a bolt of fire at the doctor who threw himself on the nurse, begging for help. They went down, a mess of limbs and flame.

"What the hell are you people?" Barbara shouted from where she stood with her saw.

Dipping his chin into his neck, Asher advanced toward her, flames zipping along his fingers. She swung her saw. He caught the blade and melted it. Shock made her fingers loosen, and the handle clanged against the floor. She scrambled backward, but he cuffed her around the neck and lifted her. She squirmed, legs kicking out.

I'd witnessed feral animals, feral humans too, but never a feral angel, and yet the clustered darkness in Asher's eyes . . . it was the most terrifying and mesmerizing thing I'd ever seen. It was a darkness that promised retribution.

Justice.

"Look away, Celeste," he growled.

I didn't.

"Look. Away."

"No."

He glowered at me, but I still didn't avert my gaze as he pressed his palm against the Triple's abdomen and extracted the soul from her still-writhing body. She looked down at the glowing orb seeping from her body and then she gasped as though he'd punched her, and her eyes rolled back.

He tossed her body, then closed his fingers around the shining soul. Dark, glittery smoke began to curl through his clenched fingers. Something popped, not like a gum bubble, but like a bone displaced from its socket.

Was that . . .? Had he . . .?

His lids slid shut, and his chest . . . his chest, it went still. He dragged his fist to his side and slowly pried his fingers apart, releasing a thin trail of ash.

When his eyes opened again, they set on me. He stalked toward my bed, gripped my chains, and liquefied them. And then he started on the cuffs. When he saw the butchered mess that was my wrist, his eyes narrowed. The violence I saw inside of them . . . it made me shrink away. Not from fear but from shame.

Shame of what I'd brought upon myself.

I bit down hard on my lip, so he wouldn't see it wobble.

Asher ran his fiery palm over the gash, mending the skin, and burning away some of the dried blood, then directed his fire on the cuff, warmed it, and pulled it apart as though it were playdough. He repeated the process on my three other restraints, and then, still in complete silence, he scooped me into his arms.

"Will," I whispered. "We need to help Will." I tipped my head toward the boy with the band of gauze.

"Erel Brutus!" he yelled.

A white-robed angel soared into the room. An erelim had come down from Elysium? The celestial sentinels rarely visited the human realm.

"Break the kid free," Asher roared. His heartbeats punched into my body as he spun and pounded out of the torture chamber.

I gazed at the underside of his rigid jaw, and then at the world surrounding us. A darkened warehouse milling with winged bodies and non-winged ones—humans in uniforms. Cops. EMTs.

"Forgive me," I whispered.

He looked down at me, and although he didn't utter a single word, his pain, his fury, his relief . . . it seeped out of him and sank into me. We were suddenly outside, and it was snowing, and although all I had on was a hospital gown, I didn't feel cold.

Snowflakes caught on his lashes.

Melted.

I wrapped my hand around the arm cradling my legs, unable to reach any higher. I squeezed once, but then my trembling fingers skidded, falling limply. He readjusted me in his arms, seized my limp wrist, and tucked it between our chests, and then he spread his beautiful wings, curled himself around me, and sprang into the raging blizzard.

Chapter Fifty-Nine

I didn't look around as we flew over the city. Not that I would've seen much. Snow was pouring hard and fast, smacking into our bodies, pushing us sideways. The rocking motion reminded me of a long-ago boat trip with Mimi where the ocean had swelled and churned, tossing us around so violently that I'd spent the dreadful trip sprawled on the floor of our cabin.

My stomach heaved as a gust of wind dug against my skin and sent Asher swinging upward. Had there been anything in my stomach besides whatever drugs they'd pumped me with, it would've found its way out.

I wondered where he was taking me—my apartment or the guild? The wind blew so hard that even if I'd tried to ask, my words would've been lost in the frosty torrent. As long as Asher remained with me, it didn't matter where we went.

Oh, angels . . . What if he dropped me off in the land of fletchings and then returned to the land of angels? What if those were the terms of his release from Elysium? *Save your incompetent soulhalf and get your ass back through the channel.* Swallowing, I tried to look up at him, but flakes stung my eyes, so I burrowed my face against his chest and stockpiled my questions for when we were no longer exposed to the harsh elements.

A sharp jostle sent a jab of pain through the side of my spine where the monsters had tried to retrieve one of my kidneys. Was I still bleeding or merely bruised? Gritting my teeth, I peeled my face away from the seraphim's suedes. My fear that we'd bumped into a skyscraper subsided at the glare of white quartz, the melody of sparrows, and the scent of honeysuckle. Voices rushed all around us. Feathers swung. Bright, lustrous.

"Fletching Celeste!" *Ah* . . . that shrill, nasal voice. Mira's complexion made her face smudge into her scarlet wings. "A Triple! What in the worlds possessed you to sign on to a Triple?" Her eyes, bright with . . . tears? No, those couldn't be tears. This woman never cried. "What did she do to you?" She peeled my wrist away from Asher's torso.

"It"—I wrinkled my nose as she prodded my swollen purplish flesh— "feels better than it looks."

She glowered, and then the strangest thing happened. A tear rolled down her cheek.

"Ophan, it's okay."

She tucked my battered wrist back between my body and Asher's.

Asher who still hadn't said a word, but whose torso was vibrating with adrenaline.

He swung around, striding down the dormitory hallway. "Tell Naya Celeste is home but keep her away until morning!"

"Immediately, Seraph." It was Pippa who answered, her pitch high with nerves.

Had she also been worried about me? I knew Naya and Mira would care, but the others? Sure, fletching abductions were unusual, but this was me we were talking about . . . Me, who'd walked out on all of them four and a half years ago. Me, who always had an opinion about everything. Me, who'd ornamented the guild's floor with purple feathers.

"What day is it?" I croaked as Asher flung my door open.

His loose, wet hair flogged his shoulders. "Sunday."

"And it's still November?"

"Yes."

I expelled a relieved sigh.

He kicked my bedroom door shut. I thought he might toss me on the bed and scold me, but instead, he walked straight into the shower and turned it on.

"Your clothes!"

As the warm spray steamed around us, Asher's bright eyes raked over my face. "Can you stand?"

"I've got feet, so I don't see why not." My recycled joke did *not* make him smile. "Set me down, and I'll try."

He pried his arm off my legs first, sliding me onto the shower's slick floor. When the soles of my feet hit the quartz, the sensation of twin blades hacking into my flesh made me release a soft whimper. Asher's gaze flashed to my ankles, which were ringed in bruises. I didn't tell him that the pain hadn't emanated from them. He was worried enough as it was. He didn't need to hear that they'd tried to remove one of my kidneys.

Keeping his other arm around my back, he undid the ties of my hospital gown, then gently peeled the damp fabric off my body. The gown sloshed to the floor like a dead snake, reddening the water around the archangel's boots.

The nightmarish memories played out in my mind as I watched the blood sluice down the drain. I shuddered and leaned my forehead into his shoulder, the drenched suede sticking to my clammy skin. His hand slipped delicately over my shoulders and spine, the flowery fragrance of soap assuaging the sickly-sweet reek of blood and wet hide.

When his fingers collided into my belt of injuries, I stiffened and sucked in a breath. He froze, and then he gathered my long hair and lifted it. He must've peered over my shoulder because his already rigid stance solidified until I felt like I was showering in an atrium fountain with a stone angel.

He didn't ask what they'd done. I supposed the wound was self-explanatory. As crackling heat kissed my ruined flesh, I fisted my fingers. Gradually, the sting ebbed, became a dull ache. How I wished he could use his fire on my mind, rid me of the last five days. No . . . the entire last month. I didn't want to remember a single day without him.

"I missed you so feathering much." I curled my arms around his waist and held him so no one—neither angel nor mortal—could take him away from me again.

Wordlessly, he went back to his slow ministrations, soaping my skin and hair and then he pressed me away so he could work his way down my front. His touch was gentle but not like a man's, like a nurse caring for his patient. It wasn't that I was in the mood for sex, but I wanted him to see *me* . . . the woman he'd loved, the curves he'd cherished, the skin he'd kissed.

"Asher, say something . . ."

His gaze flicked off the foam sliding down my stomach.

When he went back to being a silent sponge, I added, "Yell at me. Tell me I'm an idiot but say *something*."

His throat bobbed as he worked the soap over my hips and then down my legs, lightening his touch when he reached my ankles.

"How did you find me?"

"After Mira alerted me you hadn't returned . . . after *five* days," he growled, "I went to check your profile in the celestial Ranking Room and saw who you picked!"

"She probably assumed I'd gone back to my apartment."

"She did, but she shouldn't have waited five days to tell me, and I should've visited the celestial Ranking Room sooner!" He rose from his crouch, his long hair plastered to his razor-edged features. "I told you not to pick that woman."

"I know but I was trying to get to you faster. I didn't think she'd—" I chewed on my lip. "I didn't think," I admitted.

Water drummed against our bodies, against the sinuous rope of damp fabric that lay between us like a fault line.

After a long, long while, he said, "I've never used my fire to kill."

My heart held still. "I'm sorry."

"I'm not. I'd kill them again if I could. You called me a monster once, and it took me until tonight to realize that I truly am one. And the most dangerous type. The type who thirsts to rid the worlds of every ugly soul and who possesses the power to do so."

I cupped his face. "You're not a monster. Those people you killed . . . they were the monsters. Not you."

"I believe my nickname will change after word spreads of my unchecked vengeance. I'll no longer be the Golden Boy of Elysium, but the Angel of Death, or maybe they'll just change my name to Satan."

"Shut up, Seraph."

"I hate when you call me Seraph."

"I know."

"Of course you know. That's why you do it. To irritate me."

"Most of the time, but I'm using it now to remind you of who you are. An archangel. One who delivered death tonight but who brought life back four years ago. One who saved me tonight. Asher, if you hadn't come—"

"Don't. Don't say it."

"Don't say what? That I owe you my life? I do. I owe you my life. My eternal life."

"A hundred and twenty feathers and twenty-five days."

"I can do it," I whispered, because I *could* do it.

His fingers threaded through my wet strands and curled around the nape of my neck. "Oh, you can and you will. And whether you like it or not, I'll be holding your hand throughout each one of your missions."

My pulse hitched. "You're staying?"

"I'm staying."

"What about Claire?"

"I told her she could put me on trial for my un-Sevenly behavior once you've ascended."

I wanted to smile but dread tautened my lips. "Trial?"

"Yes . . . trial."

"So she knows?"

"That I love you? All of Elysium knows. And surely, most of Abaddon. There are no bigger gossips than erelim."

Interesting, and I'd definitely revisit that later, but first . . .

I licked my lips. "I meant—"

"I know what you meant." He bumped my nose with his, then slanted his mouth over mine. Before he kissed me, he said, "She's going to bring it up, bring *them* up, but she has no proof."

Chapter Sixty

I woke up curled onto my side with a heavy arm draped over my
chest, a hand splayed over my stomach, and something thick and
warm hardening along the backs of my thighs. If I was going to live
forever, *this* was how I wanted to wake up each morning—cocooned
body and soul against this giant, sometimes grouchy, but always glorious,
winged man.

As the illusory sky beyond the domed glass lightened to the dusty
lavender of early dawn, I thought of what Asher had told me while the
shower sluiced the night off my battered body. That he'd have to stand
trial. After which he'd kissed me. And although there'd been need and
hunger in that kiss, I sensed he'd used his mouth to silence mine.

He shifted, which made his heavy length drag up the inside of my
thigh. However eagerly he'd kissed me last night, however close he'd held
me, he'd kept out of my body, claiming it needed to rest. And it did. It
really did, but my body also needed him. Sleep had unfortunately won
me over before I could win over my stubborn archangel.

But this morning . . .

I wasn't leaving this bed until we'd made up for lost time. I scooted
myself at an angle to accommodate his swollen tip. When I began to
grind against him, his hand clamped down on my stomach, stilling my
wriggling.

"Celeste." Was there *anything* sexier than Asher's sleep-roughened
voice? "You're bruised."

"Not between my legs." I tried to slide more of him in, but his grip tightened, halting my progress.

For an achingly long moment, he kept my body still, stretching my entrance but not the rest of me. Angels, how I wanted him to stretch the rest of me. If he pulled out, I'd—

He pressed himself in, and *holy baby demons*, our month apart must've revirginized me because my walls stuck to his cock like luster on verity wingtips.

Fully sheathed, he stilled. "Are you all right? You're tense."

"I can guarantee you'd be tense, too, if our positions were reversed." I turned my neck to look at him.

His lids were at half-mast, yet the cyan depth beneath was so much brighter than last night. "If you're too uncomfortable, I can pull out."

I inched my face closer until our mouths almost touched. "It's wholly tolerable." My hips gave a little buck, for friction's sake.

He snared my mouth, then took over my clumsy grinding, slowly thrusting our bodies toward the slippery edge of bliss and down its velvety precipice.

SHOWERED AND CHANGED, WE WALKED TOWARD THE cafeteria. Heads turned; gazes darted to our clasped hands. Bringing boys back to the guild was against every celestial rule, but the rulebook didn't mention archangels, which was probably why I wasn't molting. I bet Seraph Claire was drawing up some new guidelines to make it illegal, so she could pin yet another crime on her fellow seraphim.

"Are you feeling up for a mission?" Asher asked as we passed by the Ranking Room.

I'd rather have spent my day in bed with him, but time was of the essence.

I answered by drawing him inside the circular room and powering on a holo-ranker. "You already have someone in mind?"

He leaned over me, caging my body between his bare arms that smelled of soap and male and fire. The urge to stroke the dips and swells of his biceps, the stretched tendons in his tanned forearms, the—

"Do you need me to write it for you?"

"Huh?" I tipped my head up and slanted him a rueful smile. "Sorry. I was distracted. What did you say?"

He shook his head, but his eyes shimmered as he lowered his mouth to my ear. "The name is Timothy Granger, and you are smoldering me."

Ah. That explained his glittery irises. "Technically, I'm smoldering your arms. You have really nice arms."

"Timothy Granger. Reform him, and I'll let you admire my arms for however long you please. Maybe I'll even let you pet them."

Ha. "Again with the bribes."

"After what I did last night, I'm no longer above bribery."

My smile warped off my lips, and my smolder off my skin. "Please stop saying that."

He pressed away from the countertop. "Timothy—"

"Granger. I got it." I let out a little huff as I traced the sinner's name.

His score: 12. His sin: relabeling expired products in his supermarket. I supposed the worst that could happen to me on this mission was getting E. coli.

I scanned my palm, applying my name over the man's narrow face, then hopped off my stool and jammed my index finger into Asher's torso. "What you did last night, that's called justice. True justice. You saved me and so many helpless kids. Their lives might never be perfect, but at least they get a chance at having one."

He curled his hand over my fingers and dragged it down, but instead of letting go, he held on. And not just to my finger but to my entire hand.

"That woman whose soul you burned, she had someone's heart cut out to gift to the Venezuelan President's niece."

"It is not my job to mete out justice in the human world."

"It should be! It should be *every* archangel's job." My head jerked as a feather was cleaved from my wings and drifted like a purple snowflake, settling beside the extra pair of boots I'd thankfully carted over from my home when I'd moved back into the guild. The leather was stiff and they had more buckles than my last pair—my favorite pair, the ones which had perished along with my favorite leather pants and my cell phone. "I need a phone," I grumbled, annoyed my zeal had cost me something that was becoming a priceless commodity.

Asher crooked a finger underneath my chin and tipped my face up. "Save your subversive opinions for Elysium, *aheevaleh*. I'll make sure to amplify your voice there, but until then . . . *shh.*" He pressed his finger against my mouth to silence me, then replaced his finger with his lips.

The kiss was fleeting but defused some of my anger. What defused the rest of it was the sound of Naya's voice calling for her father, and then the sight of her flushed face as she swung to a stop in front of the Ranking Room. She squeezed herself between the curved glass doors that were sliding open too slowly for her taste, then came to a brutal stop in front of us, tears shining on her cheeks. She looked between me and Asher, as though unable to decide whom to hug first. In the end, she curled one arm around one of his legs and her other around one of mine, and hugged us both.

Chapter Sixty-One

The days passed.

November melted into December, and December inched toward my wing bone's expiry date. And although I was no longer worried about making it, having gained ninety-one feathers since Asher's return, I was also not sabering open champagne.

I may have been twenty-nine feathers away from eternal life and from Mimi, but I was also twenty-nine feathers away from leaving Naya behind. The pain of my impending departure rivaled the one that had sawed through my chest the night I'd believed her dead forever.

"Why are you looking at me like that?" Naya put down the fork with which she was battling her mound of peas.

Asher, who was sitting across from us in the cafeteria, raised a single eyebrow.

I swallowed back the lump clogging my throat. "Like what?"

Raven, Naya's newest friend, a little seven-year-old with pale blue eyes and ghost-white hair looked up from the story she was reading out to Naya, a chapter book about sister dragon slayers I'd spotted in a bookstore on my way back from a mission.

"Like you're about to cry," she said.

"Me? Cry?" I puffed air out.

Asher shifted forward and slipped his hand under the table, curled it around my knee, squeezed it.

I bit down hard on my lip before blurting out, "I don't want to leave you."

Naya blinked her big eyes at me. Had she not realized that once my wings were whole, I'd be gone? "Apa's a seraphim."

I frowned.

"Ophan Pippa says seraphim are almighty."

Did she think his position would win me a special pass? I looked over at him for help in explaining that I wasn't above the law.

"Unfortunately, *motasheh*." His hand slipped off my knee. "Celeste won't be able to return."

Her mouth burst open. "What?"

All around us, dinner conversations ceased, and eyes turned in our direction, reminding me of the first meals Asher and I had shared with Naya. And then with Raven. Sometimes, other young fletchings joined us. Especially when Asher would get into storyteller mode.

"I . . . I—" Naya's lower lip overtook her plumper upper one. "How could you not tell me this!" She jerked out of her chair.

She stabbed my already agonizing heart with a look of anguish before dashing down the hallway toward the children's section of the guild. I gaped at Asher, then back at the corridor of white stone.

Shocked, I stammered, "I, uh . . . I—"

Raven shut her book and got up. "I'll go see her, Celeste. When she's calm, I'll come get you."

"Okay." Once Raven was gone, I plopped my elbows on the table and grasped my throbbing forehead. "I can't believe she thought I was coming back."

"It explains her enthusiasm for your missions."

I closed my eyes. "This was already hard, but *ugh* . . ." Yeah, that was the best I could come up with: *ugh*. I thrust my fingers through my hair, sighed long and deep, and pulled my lids up. "I understand why we can't come back to Earth but being unable to visit guilds makes *no* sense." My wing bones prickled as though warning me to stop there.

"The reason for it is technical," he said softly.

I lifted an eyebrow.

"We have channel keys but not guild keys."

I blinked. "You mean, we're imprisoned in Elysium because the Seven fear we'll wander out into the human world if we're allowed to return to guilds?"

He nodded.

"You realize how crazy that is, right?" The ishim pilfered a feather in their eternal hope to tame me. "Have they never heard of the honor system? If you're dishonest, you're out. The Seven could implement the same rule for angels. Their first infraction could cost them a year of traveling through the channel. A second one could cost them ten years. And—"

Asher reached over and gathered my hands in his. "*Levsheh*, it's not me you have to convince."

I lifted my eyes to the clear dome and the night sky beyond. "Just the rest of your gang," I sighed.

He nodded. "After my trial, however it goes, you should bring it up."

I pressed my lips together. Although I was actively trying not to dwell on his damn trial, it was never far from my mind. I was spared from thinking about it by Raven returning hand-in-hand with a mottled-faced Naya. I stood up and walked toward both little girls.

And then I kneeled in front of Naya and took her hands in mine. "Even though I refuse to make you a promise I can't keep, I swear I'm going to fight tooth, nail, and feather for the right to visit you."

"No," she croaked, "No fighting."

Frowning, I pulled away.

"I don't want them to hurt you."

"Hurt me?"

"Take away your wings," she murmured.

I pushed a blonde lock off her wet cheeks. "Oh, honey . . . no one's going to take away my wings."

The sound of knees clicking had me glancing sideways. "I'll make sure they stay attached to her back, *motasheh*." Our kind didn't have guardian angels, and yet never had a man so fervently guarded others.

Naya's lower lip hooked her upper one again. "Pinky-promise, Apa?" She stuck out her small pinky, and it threw me years back, to the guild in Paris where I'd made Leigh pinky-swear she'd stay signed up to Jarod to earn her wings and get her ass up to Elysium to marry Asher.

Suddenly lightheaded, I sat back on my heels and watched Asher wrap his pinky around Naya's and shake. If she'd kept her promise to ascend and marry the archangel . . . my soulhalf . . .

"Celeste?" Naya was waving her hand in front of my face.

I blinked. "What?"

"You want to play a game?"

"I, uh . . ." Leigh's face overlaid itself upon Naya's, as though I were staring at a beamed image from my holo-ranker.

"I actually need to borrow Celeste for a little while." Asher grazed my shoulder. "But I promise that tomorrow morning, I'll leave the two of you to play while I go visit a few guilds."

Although he hadn't returned to Elysium since he'd freed me from Barbara Hudson's warehouse, every time I was off-duty, he'd get back on duty, touring fletching houses across the planet.

"Fine." Naya shrugged a shoulder. "I wanted to know if the dragon stepmother set Penny's house on fire anyway." She turned to Raven, and the two of them ambled back to the table.

I rose in slow motion and walked out of the cafeteria beside Asher. I thought he was taking me to the Ranking Room, but we ended up back in my bedroom. Although most nights, we used my apartment, for privacy's sake, the bedroom in the guild had remained mine, just as Mira had promised.

He shut the door. "You look like you've seen a ghost."

I bit my lip. He freed it.

"Pinky-promises. That was a thing I did with Leigh all the time."

He caressed the side of my face.

"Want to hear what our last one was?"

"Only if you want to talk about it."

"I made her swear not to sign off from Jarod."

"Don't blame yourself."

I shook my head. "That's not . . ." I inhaled. Started over. "I made her swear not to sign off from him, so she could earn her wings and marry you. I was just imagining an alternate reality where she hadn't fallen for Jarod. Where she'd fallen for you. And it . . . it really hurt." I studied his brilliant irises. "Asher, for a second back there, I was glad she was gone. I was glad—" My voice broke. "I'm a horrible person."

He wrapped his arms around me and pulled me into his chest. "You're not a horrible person."

"Didn't you hear what I just said?" I dug my palms into his chest to pull away.

His hands floated to the base of my spine, giving me space but keeping me close. "I thought you finally enjoyed my hugs."

I stared at him, stunned that after such a sordid confession, he even wanted to take me in his arms. Let alone joke about his hugs, which, for the record, I adored.

"If Jarod was her soulhalf, the moment they touched, nothing and no one could've separated them. The same way nothing and no one could separate us now."

"What if they hadn't touched when I'd made her pinky-swear? What if she'd signed on to someone else, and—"

"And what if Muriel hadn't died when she did?" His tone was so brusque I sucked in a breath. "Sorry. I didn't mean for it to come out so harshly." His throat bobbed. "The moment your soul and mine would've collided, we would've become inseparable. Whether it happened here or in Elysium, whether I was married or not. You can rewrite this story a million different ways, Celeste, but it will always end the same. It will end with you and me."

Chapter Sixty-Two

F our days.

    I had four days left to earn nine feathers.

    In the past, I might've found it daunting, but I'd learned to believe in myself and had no doubt I could get it done.

Although Asher's faith in me had never wavered, there was a nervous energy about him. One shared by all the ophanim in the guild. Only Naya wasn't nervous, too grief-stricken to worry. She'd made me promise —pinky-promise—that the moment my wings were complete, I'd spend every second of my last twenty-four hours on Earth with her.

Each beat of my heart felt like the tick of a bomb, one that would leave a mess of tears once it detonated. Especially since the detonation would also mark the start of Asher's trial.

I looked at him, at the strong cut of his jaw that had only grown stronger in the passing week and that probably wouldn't soften until my wings bonded with my bones and the Seven issued their verdict. He must've felt my eyes on him because he looked at me as we crossed the street toward my penultimate sinner, a young boy worth four feathers.

He'd wanted me to sign on to a ten-pointer, but I'd begged him for one more day.

Just one more.

He squeezed my gloved hand; I squeezed his ungloved one. Yes, ungloved, because what need did a man made of fire have for gloves? Soon, I'd have fire, too. Not the moment I ascended, but a year or so later. My fire wouldn't be hot enough to burn souls, but it would be warm enough to seal wounds, clean up messes, and keep my body forever toasty.

My phone vibrated in my pocket. After my old phone had gotten smashed, I'd bought myself a new one with a new sim card but with my old phone number. Not that I received or made many calls.

A week ago, after I'd stumbled upon Fernanda's profile and found her score had improved by eight points, I'd sent her a message apologizing for how I'd acted the last time we'd spoken. She'd changed her ways, and although my wings hadn't benefited from it, my soul and heart had. She'd never texted me back, but as long as she kept bettering herself, it didn't matter.

I frowned when I saw MAYBE: MOUNT SINAÏ light up my screen. Why would a hospital be calling me? I stopped walking and removed my glove with my teeth to take the call.

"Hi, is this Celeste Moreau?" a woman asked.

"Yes."

Asher's eyebrows dipped.

"You're listed as Jason Marros's emergency contact, and . . ." Everything else she said came at me disjointedly. "Overdose. Heroin. Stable."

My gloved hand climbed to my gaping mouth. "Can I see him?"

She said yes, but I would've come even if she'd said no.

Once the call ended, I filled Asher in. "I need to see him."

Asher looked at the glass façade of the bank where my sinner worked. I could feel his desire for me to go inside and get another mission under my belt, but even if I'd wanted to, I wasn't fit to help anyone.

He sighed. I didn't fight him when he scooped me up and tossed a handful of angel-dust to cloak our bodies, before soaring off the slush-covered sidewalk into the pearly sky. I still wasn't a fan of being airlifted, but at least my stomach no longer bottomed out. Progress.

Minutes later, we were landing. And then I was tearing through the hospital lobby toward the front desk to find out which room was Jase's. Although Asher didn't run, he kept up with me. He shadowed me all the way to my friend's door.

I curled my palm around the handle. "I think it's better you wait out here."

Even though it seemed to take everything in him to accept, he nodded. He was anxious, not about my affection shifting to anyone else —our souls plaiting had made sure that was impossible—but that this would delay my ascension.

I pressed up on my toes to kiss him. "Don't worry."

He grunted in response.

I entered the room without knocking, then closed the door, separating me from my antsy soulhalf, who'd undoubtedly start pacing the hallway and make nurses faint from his prettiness.

My wet soles squeaked as I approached the hospital bed, trying not to think of the one I'd been cuffed to not so long ago.

Jase turned his head, and time . . . it just stopped.

"Celeste?" His cheekbones tented his sallow flesh, and his dark hair, which he'd always taken great pride in keeping neat—cropped on the sides and gelled on top—hung limply and haphazardly around his face.

I tried to rid my expression of shock, but he saw it, because his throat bobbed, and he averted his pained gaze.

I fiddled with a button on my coat. "The hospital called. You didn't take me off your emergency contact list."

His lashes swept down, shielding off his brown eyes. "Sorry."

"That's not . . . You don't have to apologize." I neared the top of his bed.

His lids flipped up, and the hatred that flared from him was so intense I took a step back. "I wanted to remove your name but the only other person on my *list* is in jail, so"—he gave a bitter laugh—"that wouldn't have worked out too well. I doubt they let convicts take field trips to the hospital."

Jase's accusation wrung my heart the same way my fingers were twisting my coat button. I wondered which would snap first.

I eyed the door. I could walk out and wish him a good life, or— "Your brother landed himself in jail, the same way you landed yourself in this hospital. He made poor life choices, and so did you." I released my button, done with feeling guilty. For what I'd done. For what he'd done. For what we'd said.

Jase needed a wake-up call, and maybe the shock of an overdose would be enough to jolt him out of his funk, but what if it wasn't? And what if the next one killed him? What was his score now anyway? I doubted it had gone down but had it gone up?

"Now you listen to me, Jason Marros. I don't care if you hate my guts for the rest of your life. What I do care about is you taking responsibility for what went wrong. You *stole* from people. You stole from *me*! Me, Jase. Me, your best friend. Your feathering emergency contact." I tossed my hand in the air, exasperated. "And then you dumped my stuff. You dumped our friendship."

"You dumped us first."

"How? When?" I shrilled. "When I tried to talk some sense into your brother?"

"When you lied!"

"What did I lie about?" I shouted back.

"That guy! Abercrombie. You said he meant nothing to you."

I jerked back in surprise.

"I thought—" His pale lips pinched shut, a white line in a sea of dark scruff. "I thought we had a chance. The day they booked Leon, I was coming to tell him I wanted out, but then you were in Abercrombie's arms, and you . . . you left. With him. You left with him." He covered his face with his hand, jostling the tubes attached to his arm, and let out a howl of pain that made me sink onto his mattress.

"I never meant to lead you on." Tears rolled down my cheeks. "But I swear, back then, I wasn't with him."

"You weren't with me either."

My throat squeezed and squeezed.

"And now?" He lowered his hand, peeking at me through clumped lashes. "Are you with him now?"

I weighed the consequence of telling him the truth against telling him a lie. In four days, I'd be gone. If I said no, I'd lose a feather but I'd gain a friend. But then what? What happened once I vanished into thin air and Jase was alone again? Who would be his emergency contact? Although I'd reformed high scorers in a day, he needed long-term support.

"Scoot over, will you?"

He did, and I curled up next to him.

"I'm going to tell you a story. A story I'm not allowed to tell. And you won't believe a word of it, I'm sure. You'll think I'm crazy. Probably even call me crazy. And that's okay. But you have to promise to listen. To every word. And maybe one day, maybe you'll see something happen, you'll *feel* something happen, something unexplainable, and you'll realize that your friend might not have been as zany as you imagined."

I took a breath. A long one. And then, word by word, I drew him a picture about where I came from and where I was heading. And for each secret I spilled, a feather dropped. My wing bones ached, but my heart ached more.

For Jase.

But also for Asher.

Not only had I deseeded my wings but also our people's secrets.

I didn't count how many feathers I lost. Didn't dare.

I simply closed my eyes and prayed I'd have enough time to make up for their loss before it was too late.

Chapter Sixty-Three

J ase didn't speak for such a long time after I'd finished that I opened
my eyes to make sure he wasn't asleep.

His eyes were wide open. "So that's why you use so many
strange expressions . . ."

I bit the inside of my cheek. "Old habits."

"And in four days, you're going to go up to Heaven?"

"Elysium." Another feather. I gritted my teeth.

"For a hundred years?" His tone was still so brittle.

"That's the plan."

A beat. Then, "I'm still high, right? This . . . *you* . . . it's all in my
head?"

"No." I refused to regret my confession. Refused to truly worry.
"You're not high, I'm really here, and all of what I said is the truth."

Silence. So much silence.

"Please say something, Jase."

"Why?"

"Why what?"

"Why tell me all this?"

"Because I want you to get your shit together." I gritted my teeth as
another feather fell.

He stared and stared at me. "Do you know how many fucking déjà-
vus I had when we lived together?"

My heart tripped. Was he beginning to believe me? "I molted a lot

362

back then."

His features were preternaturally still even though there was nothing otherworldly about him.

"I still do. There's a whole bunch of feathers on your floor."

"There is?"

"I'm not allowed to share forbidden secrets."

"You're really not shitting me, Cee?"

"I'm really not."

"Fuck."

"Yeah."

"I feel delirious."

"Deliriously happy?"

A smile crept over his lips. "More like, *in shock*. You're a fucking angel." He tentatively grazed my cheekbone as though to check I was real. "How come sharing what you are is forbidden?"

"I'm not actually sure but I imagine it's like that hive-mind chicken thing."

He cocked a thick eyebrow. "Hive-mind chicken thing?"

"That's probably not the right term."

His lips quirked again, bringing a little rosiness back into his cheeks. "Enlighten me about your poultry theory."

I smiled, too, because his eyes were no longer hateful or bereft. "Apparently, there were these railroad tracks that bisected a field, and the owner of that field had chickens that he would let roam free during the day. And some of the chickens got squashed—"

"Poor chickens." His eyes twinkled.

"Don't make fun of the chickens."

"I wasn't."

I flicked him, but that simply intensified the twinkle. "Anyway, fast forward a few years, and there's no more train, but there are still chickens."

"The ones that didn't go splat."

I made a face, and he laughed. And the sound . . . it was a balm to my tender wing bones.

I must've stared at him a long time without speaking because he shifted to his side and said, "The suspense is killing me, Cee. What happened to those chickens?"

"They didn't cross the tracks."

He frowned.

"They didn't cross the tracks because they somehow remembered what happened to their ancestors."

"The squished ones?"

"Generations later, and the tracks are overgrown with grass, or gone, I forget, and the chickens still don't approach the area."

"For real, Cee?"

"Yes. For real." But was it? I glanced over my shoulder to check if the pile had gotten denser. If it had been a lie my wing bones would've ejected another feather. Maybe they had.

"What are you looking at?"

"The purple mound under your bed."

He pushed himself onto his elbow to glance over my body. "I don't see it."

"You can't see it if you don't have angel-blood, remember?"

He swung his legs off the side of his bed.

I sat up. "What are you doing?"

He grabbed onto the IV pole and took a step, then another, but then he faltered, stumbling against the mattress before flopping onto the floor, which set off a bunch of alarms. I rushed around the bed as nurses raced in, demanding why he'd gotten out of bed and tossing me sour looks as though it were my fault.

As they helped him back onto the mattress and quieted the machines, I turned toward the doorway. Surprisingly, Asher hadn't barged in along with the nurses. Was he on his way? I braced myself for the agony that would streak across his face when he'd spot the decimated feathers.

The two nurses asked me to leave. Jase barked a *no* that made both women's expressions pinch.

Once they were gone, I sighed. "Thanks to you, I'm now on Mount Sinai's watchlist."

His earlier exhilaration was replaced by annoyance, probably at his body's weakness.

"What exactly were you trying to achieve? Besides making me look like an unfit emergency contact?"

"I was trying to get to your feathers."

"Oh. Why didn't you ask?"

"Because you said they disappeared once they were touched."

"Only if touched by bare skin." I pulled a glove out of my pocket and wiggled my fingers into it, and then I crouched, grabbed a handful of feathers and dumped it on the mattress beside him. "Palm up, Mr. Marros."

He opened his hand, and I laid a feather inside. His eyes closed, and his nostrils flared. A couple seconds later, the purple down burst into glittery dust.

A little vertical groove formed between his eyebrows. "Again."

I gave him another. He wouldn't see the full memories, but he'd feel *something*.

"Another one."

I was about to make a quip about him being an addict and me an enabler when I remembered why he was here. I held the feather out of his reach. "Only if you promise that you'll never *ever* take drugs again."

"Done. Hit me."

"I'm not kidding, Jase. I want you to live a long, full life so that when you join me up in Elysium, you'll have plenty of stories to tell. I can't stand dull people."

The corners of his mouth scooted up. "Deal."

"You mean it?"

"I mean it. I'm meeting a drug counselor this afternoon. To assess my need for rehab."

"And?"

"I only snorted heroin once. Doc thinks it was cut with something because my reaction to it . . ." He shuddered.

"Okay." Here, I'd imagined he'd spent the last two months stabbing himself with needles under city bridges. "By the way, no tell-all, or they might ship me to Abaddon."

"What if I call it fantasy fiction?"

"I guess . . . I guess that'd be okay."

He smiled again. "Chill, Cee. I was kidding. I still want to be a lawyer."

"You're still enrolled at Columbia?"

"I haven't attended classes or answered emails in a while, but I didn't drop out." He ran his hand across his scratchy jaw. "I just need to apply for a dorm room and hope they have a free one. The apartment was in Leon's name, so it was foreclosed."

Shock parted my lips. "Where have you been living?"

"Alicia's couch, but then she told me to get my shit together, like someone else . . ." He leveled an almost playful glare my way. "And instead . . . well, I did the opposite of that."

"Do you have any money?"

Shame stained his eyes. "Hard work doesn't scare me."

"That's not what I asked."

"I don't, okay?" he growled.

I touched his forearm, a swirl of ink shaped like a rose, and he flinched. "I'm not judging you."

"Aren't you?"

I sat down again. "Remember how I told you I'll be gone for a little while?"

"A little while?" He let out a snort. "You mean a century?"

"And remember my apartment?"

He side-eyed me.

"It's going to be empty. You think you can take care of it?"

His pupils flared. "Cee, that's—"

"I'll leave money in an account to cover any and all expenses."

"I can't move into your apartment."

"Why not?"

"Because."

"If you're going to be a lawyer, you're going to need to improve your appeal verbiage. *Because* is weak."

He gaped at me.

"Look, this wouldn't be a pity loan. I really do need someone to take care of it for the next hundred years."

His fingers shook as he scratched his chin.

I lifted a palm as though I was weighing something. "Squandering away your life and destroying your soul." I lifted my other palm. "*Or* being responsible and elevating your soul. What'll it be?"

"Cee . . ."

"Fine. I'll send Asher to check up on you once a week. Hope you're looking forward to your celestial nanny." Oddly enough, my wing bones didn't even vibrate.

Jase made a face.

"I take it you choose the apartment. Am I correct?"

A smile poked back out.

"Good. I have one rule, though." I took out my keyring and placed it on his side table since I could get in through my balcony. "No smelly-ass leather couch is allowed to pass the threshold. Deal?"

He gifted me a weak smile. "Deal."

I leaned over to hug him. "I need to go now, Jase. Make me proud, all right?"

"I'm going to miss you a hell of a lot," he rasped, as I pulled away. "An Abaddon of a lot."

The contours of his face blurred. "I'm going to send my family lawyer an email with your contact information. He'll take care of everything." I got up and walked toward the door, licking salty tears off my lips. "One last thing. When my people come to help you, because my people will come . . ." I'd make sure someone signed up to him right away. Maybe Liv. "You be nice to them, all right? And whatever you do, do *not* mention you know anything about us or our world. They'll have to deny it, and lies—"

"Cost feathers. Got it. I'll be the perfect sinner." He pressed two fingers to his forehead in a little salute.

Again, no feather fell. Was it because I was just reiterating things I'd already said?

"Hey, Cee?"

"Yeah?"

"From the moment I first saw you, I knew you were an angel."

I rolled my heated eyes. "I wasn't very angelic back then."

"Don't sell yourself short. You might not have a halo, but you always had the aura."

"My eyes are never going to level out if you keep spouting crap like that."

He chuckled.

"Love you, you moron. Be good."

"Be better."

I looked at him one last time before walking out. Whatever tenuous hold I'd had on my emotions snapped, and tears streamed down, washing out the hallway. After I'd bumped into a nurse and then into a stretcher, I sagged against the wall. Someone approached me to ask if I was feeling okay.

Without thinking, I said *yes*.

A giant lie, and yet the ishim didn't pocket a feather. What a strange bunch. Maybe they were on a lunch break.

My shoulder blades tightened and a tickle began at the tops of my wing bones and curved to the very tips.

I'd spoken too soon. No rest for the wicked.

"Celeste!" The lines of Asher's strong body and glittery wings swam in and out of focus.

Keeping one palm on the wall, I reached out to him.

"I'm so sorry," I whispered at the same time as he said, "Please don't be angry with me."

"You're the one who's going to be furious."

A frown touched his brow.

"Asher, I told Jase things. Things about us. Our kind. I thought that if he knew there was something more after this life, he'd get back on his feet. It cost me"—my voice splintered—"it cost me so many feathers, but I was desperate to save his soul."

His lips pressed together, not so much in anger but in wariness.

I opened my mouth to apologize again but a sob lurched out instead. I wrapped my arms around his waist and rested my cheek against his thumping torso. "I'm so sorry, Asher. I won't sleep. Won't eat. Won't do anything but reform people to make up for—"

He enfolded me in his arms, threaded his fingers through my hair, and although he didn't say I was forgiven, his embrace made me feel absolved.

Suddenly, I frowned and tilted my head up. "Wait. Why did you ask me not to be angry with you?"

He dipped his chin, and his eyes cut to something beyond my shoulder. I followed his line of sight, wrinkling my nose at the sight of my wings. I'd been so lost in my anguish, I hadn't heard him mutter the incantation to make them appear.

"Are there great big holes in them?"

His neck straightened, and it jostled his topknot. "Holes?"

"I lost a lot of feathers."

Furrows carved up his brow.

"I'm not mad, Asher. I understand why you made them appear without my consent. You were trying to assess the damage."

His grip on my hair tightened. "Celeste, I didn't make your wings appear."

"You didn't?" *I'd* made them appear? "Since they're out, can you tell how many feathers I'm missing or do we have to go back to the guild to find out?"

"*Aheevaleh.*" He untangled his fingers from my hair to caress the top of one wing, tracing its shape all the way to my spine.

I shivered at the delicious, foreign sensation. No one had ever touched my wings. *I'd* barely touched them. His other hand swept down the outer edge of my second wing. And another deep shudder raced up my spine, making the shafts vibrate.

One caress, and I already didn't want him to stop. How dangerous. Thank Elysium I hadn't found out about this sooner, or I would've spent a lot of time with my winglets hanging out.

"They're exquisite, Celeste." He pressed his forehead to mine, his nose to mine. "*You* are exquisite."

I wanted to brush off his compliment, but it swaddled my ego and . . . well, it didn't give me wings since I already had a pair, but it damn near caused me to flap them.

His fingers danced over the inverted vee, and the pleasure that shot through me was so alarmingly potent I took a step back. "We're in public. In a hallway. The ishim are going to shred what's left of my feathers."

His brows pulled together as though I were the oddest celestial specimen he'd encountered, and then they jolted apart.

I jerked my gaze to the linoleum, expecting to find at least one feather loitering there. "Do the rules not apply to archangelic groping?"

He blinked at me, and then a laugh burst from his mouth. It wasn't loud, and it wasn't at my expense. In truth, I wasn't sure *why* he was laughing.

My fist perched on my hip. "What's so funny, Seraph?"

He captured the sides of my face, crooked it farther up. "You're done, *levsheh*. They're sealed."

The blood drumming inside my ears must've distorted his voice because I'd just heard him say I was done. Which was impossible.

"While you were in there with Jase, I went back to the guild." His thumbs swept over my cheeks as though playing connect-the-dots with my freckles. "I signed you off from the banker and signed you up to Jase."

"You did *what*?"

He slid his jaw from side to side. "I'm sorry. I didn't want to take the decision out of your hands, but I was . . . I was worried."

My mouth began to gape a little, then a lot.

"I knew you'd want to spend time with the guy before you left, and I was coming back to tell you to take your time. That he'd be your last sinner. But you, *extraordinary* you"—his thumbs stilled—"you managed to reform him in a single hour. I had no doubt you'd get his score down, but I thought it would take you at least a day or two. I thought I'd get a chance to warn you. To prepare you."

I lifted my hands to his.

"You're shaking."

"I'm . . . my . . . they're . . ." My lips began to tremble as hard as the rest of me. "I'm done?"

"You're done."

My eyelashes flapped wildly, batting away tear after tear.

Asher frowned. "I can't tell if you're happy or angry right now."

"Happy," I croaked. "I'm happy. I'm so happy." A breath ratcheted down my crumpled airway. "I thought—I lost so many feathers. I thought—" I cupped the nape of his neck with my gloved hand. "I made it!"

I extended my wings and curled them around us. Their reach wasn't half that of Asher's but their density, it was the same, so thick they shielded us from the bustling, surrounding world.

A slow smile glided onto his mouth, carrying so much pride and love that emotion threatened to choke my very soul. Of course, the adoring blaze in his eyes lit me right up, on the inside and on the outside. I really needed to learn to control this whole smoldering business. The good thing was that I now had an eternity to do so.

An eternity . . .

Face steeped in sparkles, Asher stretched out his gorgeous appendages, and unhurriedly, so . . . very . . . unhurriedly, the bronze edges bent, brushed over my purple ones, and overtook them. "Are you ready for the rest of our lives, *neshahadzaleh*?"

"I'm ready," I murmured, pressing up onto my toes to seal my lips to his, the same way my feathers had finally fastened to my bones.

Chapter Sixty-Four

A knock made my paintbrush skid across the canvas I was working on with Naya. "Celeste, we have to go."

"I'm not ready."

Asher walked toward where Naya and I were crouched in a corner of the art room, paint smeared across our clothes and probably our faces. He stroked the top of my right wing, and I shivered.

"I'm sorry, *levsheh*. If I could give you more time, I would, but your wings need exposure to the Elysian atmosphere to properly fasten to your body."

"Are you sure that's not another unsubstantiated rule?"

"I've sadly witnessed the effects of delayed ascensions—feathers that tarnish, wings that seize up, or sometimes . . . rarely though, cannot be flapped at all."

Naya, who'd been trying to be brave since I'd gotten back to the guild yesterday, wings bared for all to see, let out a little squeak, that turned into a whimper, that punched me right in the heart. As I released a similar sound, more of a honk-sob combo, her arms locked around my neck so snugly she cut off my air supply.

"I'm going to come back. I'll find a way, okay, little angel?" I whispered.

She nodded, or maybe her bobbing head was just an extension of her convulsive shaking.

"Don't grow up too fast."

"I c-c-can't control that."

I grinned into her blonde hair and inhaled her sweet scent, and then I got up, scooping her right along with me, and carried her all the way to the channel, murmuring a million times over how much I loved her.

"Can I get a hug too, *motasheh*?" Asher gently untangled her arms from my neck.

As though she were more monkey than child, she swung herself into his arms and dampened his suedes with her tears. He spoke softly into her ear, then set her down and kissed her cheek.

Mira snuck her arm around the little girl. Never had the red-winged ophanim draped her arm around any of our shoulders. Instead of jealousy, relief teemed within me that Naya had our crotchety old professor in her life, that she'd be taken care of. Her father would return as soon as his trial was over, but until then, she'd get to lean on Mira. On Raven, too.

Naya's friend must've gotten word we were off because she appeared with Pippa in the hallway, along with a whole gaggle of fletchings.

Raven's white hair settled like fresh milk over her shoulder as she stepped close to Naya and took her hand. "Bye, Celeste."

Another sob cramped my chest. I clapped my palm over my mouth to muffle it in case it managed to wriggle out. Why couldn't I be stoic like Leigh had been?

Asher slid his fingers through mine and murmured, "Completing your wings has made you alarmingly soft, *aheevaleh*." His warm breath fluttered my long hair.

"Soft," I grumbled, slapping his large bicep.

The collective intake of breath made me peer around. Except for Naya, who was finally smiling, everyone else looked as though I'd smashed up one of the quartz angels in the atrium.

The atrium I wouldn't see again.

These hallways I wouldn't tread through.

The cafeteria I would no longer eat in.

The stupid fake sky I would no longer look upon.

My lips trembled, and the waterworks started anew. Could something start anew if it had never stopped, though?

"Wait." I broke away from Asher and strode toward Mira whom I hugged fiercely. "Thank you," I whispered.

Her arms were slow to encircle me but eventually they did. "This isn't goodbye, Celeste."

"I know." But it felt like it.

She squeezed me, then let go. "I'll come visit." She smiled. Mira. Smiled. What an unexpected sight. "I promise."

Stealing a lungful of honeysuckle, I returned to Asher, who tucked me into his side.

Blue wings tipped in gold nudged my mind off my rising nostalgia. Liv smiled at me and gave the slightest nod. A nod that promised she had everything under control. This girl I'd met at The Trap months ago had not only accepted to take Jase on but to check on him until it was her time to ascend. I didn't think she realized the depth of my gratitude, but one day soon, she would.

Asher turned me away and guided me into the channel. As lavender smoke curled around us, he took my hands in his and slanted his face down to mine, transporting me out of one world and into another on a gentle, lingering kiss.

Chapter Sixty-Five

"I'm not lost, Erel." The raspy feminine voice made my mouth slip off Asher's and my hands claw at the glittery smoke that hadn't yet cleared.

"Mimi!"

She spun away from a flying, white-clad sentinel, her eyes lambent with joy. "Celeste!"

She opened her arms, and I fell into them, new tears tumbling over the ones that hadn't yet dried.

"Oh, Mimi," I sobbed.

"How I've missed you, my beautiful girl. How I've missed you." Her arms crushed me to her, carefully avoiding my wings, and it struck me that she had arms, that she had a body, but then everything I'd learned about the celestial world over the years slotted into place, and I remembered that once souls made it to Elysium, they could pick the form of their choosing.

I pressed her away to see which form she'd chosen. "You look like . . . like you, but—"

"But younger?" She tipped a finely arched eyebrow. "I made sure to keep some wrinkles, so that you'd recognize me."

She had kept some, it was true, but instead of sixty, she looked two decades younger. She'd gathered her hair into a sleek twist that shone a richer auburn than any dye she'd ever used on Earth.

"Can you change your appearance at will?"

"No. Not at will. I'll be permanently locked at thirty-eight, which I thought a sensible age, unless I decide to return to Earth." Alarm must've registered on my face because she said, "Which I have no intention of doing."

Her ocean-colored eyes took me in from wing to boot, and the smile that blossomed over her face made me reach out for another hug. Although I'd left a chunk of my heart behind, I'd recovered a lost piece.

"*Ma chérie*," she murmured. "The family is almost reunited."

My pulse stuttered. "Almost." For all of Asher's assurances that everything would be fine, fear coated me like an oily film.

"Muriel, it's nice to see you again." Asher's voice was so light it sounded like sunshine and burned away some of the viscous residue encasing me. Unfortunately, not all of it.

"It's nice to see you, too, Seraph. You had me worried when you didn't return with news. Thankfully, though, Tobias spared a thought for my old soul."

Tobias. Of course, she knew Tobias.

"My deepest apologies."

"You brought my Celeste, so you are forgiven."

They smiled at each other, and that smile made my heart seesaw with joy. I tipped my head up, and while they exchanged a few pleasantries, I absorbed my world, from its salt and citrus fragrance to its gleaming white stone to its unfathomable cerulean sky and iridescent Pearly Arch.

A light weight settled on my waist and a warm breath at my ear. "So, what do you think, *levsheh*?"

"It's . . . heavenly."

Two candy-colored furred creatures clambered up the canyon walls, chasing after one another.

"*Haccouls.* The heavenly version of wildcats," Asher said. "They inhabit those crevices dappling the rock walls and rarely wander out of the Canyon."

"*Haccouls*," I repeated the word, adding it to the tiny pile of Angelic Asher had already taught me. To think that soon, I'd be fluent.

"I tried to domesticate one," Mimi said, coming up beside me. "I assumed that after domesticating Jarod and then you, it would be a breeze."

Snorting, I found her hand in the folds of her sleek navy trousers and gripped it tight even though I could no longer lose her to death . . . only to life, if she one day changed her mind about taking another spin on the earthly carousel.

"Asher!" Claire's voice boomed through the canyon. "You have returned." Bracketed by a dozen erelim, she flew toward us, a gray smear with lavender wings and curly blonde hair at her side.

Oh, Eliza . . . how I'd missed her. The daydream of strapping her down to a slab of quartz and plucking each one of her feathers drifted through my mind, raising a smile surely as white as the vertiginous walls entrenching our merry group. Especially when *not a single* feather fell.

"I said I would. I do not break my promises, Claire."

"Only your vows," she replied pleasantly.

Where Mimi's fingers tightened, Asher's surprisingly didn't. They merely remained perched on my hipbone, protective and gentle.

"Welcome, Celeste. You made it in the nick of time."

"Hope you didn't bet against me?"

"Angels don't bet or gamble." As Claire landed in front of us, her pink chiffon dress embellished with ribbons and platinum grommets twisted around her legs.

"Whatever do they do for fun?"

"They?" She tilted her head to the side, her golden circlet gleaming against her black locks. "You are one of us now."

I hummed. "That's right."

"You have a hundred years to acclimate to celestial life. I have no doubt you will uncover plenty of entertaining pastimes." She reeled in her fuchsia wings, their tips glittering as brightly as the grommets on her dress. "Ah. Daniel has arrived. We may proceed to the removal of your channel key. Your hands please, Asher."

As he uncurled his arm from around my waist, a black-skinned man wearing a golden circlet and a matching tunic bound by overlapping straps of black leather over black leather pants landed beside Seraph Claire. Like Leigh, the man possessed the rarest type of wings, entirely metallic—a pure verity. Unlike Leigh's, his were golden.

"Congratulations on your ascension, Celeste." Even though his face bore fewer wrinkles than Mimi's, Daniel was one of the oldest archangels. I remembered that much from Mira's history lessons. Over six-hundred years old, or was it seven?

Asher held out his hands, palms facing up.

"Is it truly necessary to remove his channel key, Claire?" Daniel asked. "Our brother returned as he promised he would."

The ends of her glossy black hair lifted in the sea-scented breeze. "He wasn't on trial before. Only on probation."

The male archangel sighed. "Very well."

Claire hovered her hand over one of Asher's and Daniel over the other.

I clutched Mimi's fingers so hard I was probably strangling the blood out of them. Or whatever coursed through her veins. Did she even have veins? Maybe I should've listened more closely in celestial biology.

Twin beams appeared between Asher's palms and his fellow archangels', and then two golden keys—actual old-fashioned sculpted door keys—slid out of Asher's skin and flickered upward into Daniel's and Claire's. I blinked, not so much at the extraction process, but at the fact that channel keys were actual keys. Once they vanished, all three lowered their hands.

"Your trial begins at sundown. This'll give you time to show Celeste around Elysium, teach her to use her wings, and get her settled in the Hadashya as I'm sure you're eager to do." Claire backed away, extending her wings for takeoff.

Asher's brows lowered, darkening his eyes. "How generous of you, Claire." He smiled, but it was tighter than Daniel's belt. "Purely for practical purposes, I'm informing you that Celeste will not be moving into the Hadashya. She will be cohabitating with me in the Shevaya."

Claire's circlet glinted in the Elysian sun. "The Shevaya? She isn't your consort."

"No. She is my *neshahadza*, and soulhalves are lawfully allowed to cohabitate, unless that law was amended in my absence."

Claire seemed to grow straighter, stiffer.

"Would you like me to prove it, or will my word suffice?"

Claire stared up at Daniel, who'd already taken flight.

His great wings shimmered as though they'd been plated in actual gold. "I require no proof."

Claire's emerald eyes narrowed on me. Sure, my wings didn't glitter like hers, but did I deserve a look of such condescension? I narrowed my eyes right back.

"How fortunate you have found your soulhalf. So few do." She tilted her head up and then she snapped her wings and shot into the sky.

The erelim, who'd remained airborne throughout, ribboned behind the two archangels like the contrails of a jet. Only Eliza remained, features pinched with disgust but eyes shiny with something else . . . disappointment. Was she disappointed that I'd made it or that I was Asher's soulhalf?

Asher stepped in front of me, obscuring my sight of Eliza and plunging me into his inky shadow. "Time to fly."

Mimi released my hand and stepped out of the way, and then she was hovering over me. My stomach twisted even though my boots were still firmly planted on the ground.

A slow smile lifted the corners of his lips. "Muriel, can you tell Celeste how wondrous it is to fly?"

"It's possibly the best thing about the after-life. Second only to being able to conjure up whatever food you desire. Although nothing will ever beat the art of cooking." When I didn't spread my wings, she frowned. First at me, then at Asher. "Celeste? What is it, *ma chérie*?"

"Celeste has vertigo." Asher spoke with such smugness that I rolled my eyes.

How they stung . . . The stinging made me glance over my shoulder at the channel, at the glittery filaments still billowing out. To think Naya was a heartbeat away, and yet completely out of my reach.

Fingers clutched my chin, drove my face off the only exit out of this world of quartz and feathered beings. "Spread your wings, *aheevaleh*."

As though he'd commanded my very wings, they snapped out.

He took both my hands in his and brought them between our bodies. "I won't let go."

"Okay," I murmured.

"Ready?"

"No."

He leaned over and, although Mimi was waiting much higher out of earshot, whispered, "I'd really like to show you my bedroom, Celeste. Especially my bed. It's round. Did I ever mention this?"

I swallowed. "You did not."

"Huh." He straightened, rolling his shoulders, his wings rippling in their wake. "Would you like to see it?"

I licked my lips, then, stomach in a vise, flapped once and shot into the air so fast my fingers were ripped from Asher's.

I gasped and retracted my wings just as Asher shouted, "Keep them out."

Too late. I plummeted like an inanimate object but squealed like a very animate one. As the ground rushed at me, I closed my eyes. Silver lining, I couldn't die.

Oompf.

Two solid arms plucked me from the air, and suddenly, I was swooping upward again. "I'm proud of your enthusiasm."

I snorted.

He chuckled softly. "Now I'm going to let go—"

"No!" I strangled his neck.

He fell back until his back was parallel to the ground and I was resting atop him. "Give me your hands."

I made the mistake of glancing at the arch, which looked like a toy bridge.

"Soon, I'll have to stand before a Council and defend my choice of having saved two souls. Before then, please fill my heart with peace and my eyes with beauty. Let me see you soar, *aheevaleh.*"

How exactly could I resist such a request? Especially requested in such a way. My fear of heights may have been real, but it paled in comparison to my fear of the trial to come and of its outcome.

Stealing a lungful of briny courage, I let him wrangle my hands and tow them in between our bodies. His fingers slid through mine, sealed our palms together.

"Now spread your wings and do not close them until you're ready to land."

Easy enough. I snapped them open, muscles cramping from the strange flexion.

"Now pump once. Nice and slow."

"That sounds dirty."

A grin seized his lips.

"Hope you don't give too many flying lessons, Seraph."

The grin eased into a melancholic smile. "The only other person I taught to fly was Leigh."

"I bet she picked it up fast." Leigh had been so easygoing, so willing to learn new things.

"As fast as you have."

"Have?"

Asher had sunk a little lower, but I hadn't, and a slender divide of air separated our bodies. My fingers clamped around his, and again he laughed.

"How many times must I tell you until you believe it? I will never let go." Tendrils of gold twisted around his chiseled jaw, snaked into his jeweled eyes before blowing sideways. And his wings, his magnificent wings, so vivid and bright, sparkling like the soul locked inside this man's body. A soul that belonged to me. "You're smoldering, Celeste."

I eased my wings up an inch and then down another, repeating the motions, each shallow pump deepening my confidence. "Just want to make sure I have my flying instructor's attention all to myself."

His face smoothed, and his smile returned with a vengeance. "I thought the sight of your naked body unraveling was spectacular but watching you fly . . . now that is a true thing of beauty."

My pounding heart threatened to trip right out of my chest. "It's the smoldering."

"It's the *woman* doing the smoldering." Barely beating his wings, he tugged on my hands, easing my body lower, and leaned in to kiss me.

It took everything in me, and I do mean everything, to remember not to fold in my wings and sink into him, body, heart, and soul.

Chapter Sixty-Six

"Ah, young love," someone cooed somewhere to my right. Mimi.
I freed my smiling mouth from Asher's. "The tour guides here are pretty handsy."

Mimi laughed; Asher just smiled, not even the slightest bit rueful.

He drifted low again. "I'll need to turn over if you want a tour."

When he glanced down at our hands, I understood he needed me to let go.

"I'll stay right underneath you, Celeste."

I eyed his wingspan, guessing flying hand-in-hand wasn't an option. "Okay." I relaxed my grip and steeled my spine.

Once our fingers disengaged, he didn't flip over immediately. Just kept gliding, inspecting the line of my body, the breadth of my wings. "If you want to go faster—"

"That'll *never* happen."

His eyes sparkled with amusement. "Just in case, simply propel your wings up and down faster. It's a lot like swimming actually. If you keep your wings out and immobile, you'll float. If you angle your body downward, you'll dive. Upward, you'll rise."

I bit my lip as I unpacked his instructions and stored them. Suddenly, he tucked in his wings, and his body plunged. I gasped. Like a rotary blade, he spun, then snapped his feathered appendages out and the force of the movement raised him right back up.

I wasn't the one who'd just freefallen and yet my blood was swooshing as though I had. "What in Abaddon was that?"

He craned his neck until I could see his profile. "I didn't want to bump you."

"Hope you don't mind being bumped because I am *never* doing that."

"You also said you'd never do a verity."

Had the archangel really just made a sexual quip? In front of Mimi no less? I glanced toward where she floated, wingless and mirthful.

"No need to blush, *ma chérie*. I wasn't born yesterday. Besides, I approve of your verity. Definitely the best of the flock." She winked, then floated nearer and carved her fingers through my fluttering hair. "Purple suits you."

I peered over my shoulder, then back at her. "Did you always know what I was?"

"My soul knew."

"Ladies, the tour is about to begin," Asher announced, as two angels soared past us and then another swooped low to get out of our path.

All of them stared. I supposed the archangel strolling with a hybrid and a human soul was an odd sight.

"We need to fly a little lower. You think you can do that?"

I pulled in a breath, my gaze going to a pond dotted with iridescent water lilies and seven winged colossuses shooting water from their open palms. I guessed if there was a place to test my skydiving skills, above a body of water was an ideal one. Swallowing back my nerves, I performed a sort of breaststroke.

"You need to pull in your wings, Celeste. Just a little."

"How much is a little?" I called back.

"You'll feel it. And when your body begins to tilt, whatever you do, don't stretch your wings back out or you'll swoop upward."

Okay. No stretching. Check. I reeled in an inch and then another inch. When my body began to tip, instinct to push my wings back out drove me hard, but I fought it, and then I was diving, and Asher was saying, "That's it!" and Mimi was keeping pace with me, and I had the briefest realization that I was suspended in midair on my own, and although there was definitely some freaking-out happening in a part of my brain, in another part, there was some fist-pumping because. I. Was. Flying.

I laughed. "Asher, I'm flying."

"I see that, *levsheh*." He'd drifted sideways and was staring at me with that heady mixture of love and pride. "Now press your wings back out as slowly as you gathered them into you."

I followed his instructions, and my body leveled off. Amazing. This was amazing.

"How's the stomach?"

"Fine. Why? Oh." I blinked at the silvery expanse below, at the angel statues so tall I must've resembled a sparrow beside them. Slowly, my lips stretched into a smile. "It's gone!"

"I assumed as much."

When Mimi asked what was gone, I filled her in on my motion sickness. And then I remained quiet as Asher pointed out various landmarks, starting with the fountain below us—the Lev—the heart of the capital. Of course they'd have a fountain here. And of course it would be outsized. What glistened inside wasn't liquid, but it was water, the celestial kind—*ayim*—gaseous instead of liquid.

Around the fountain stretched a horseshoe-shaped quartz wall down which coursed seven waterfalls. Openings resembling bay windows were carved into the rock.

"I live down at the bottom. Next to the restaurant with the solid gold tables." Mimi gestured to the lowest tier of the rock. "The Neshamaya. It's the soul quarter, also called Kefimya, which means fun quarter in Angelic. It lives up to its name. That's where all the newer angels spend their evenings. Especially since they live right above the Kefimya, in the Hadashya."

Where I was supposed to live.

Asher was no longer flying underneath me, but beside me. Too far to touch with my hands but every so often, the edge of his wing grazed the edge of mine. "The third level is the Yashanya where older angels reside until they decide to retire to the Nirvana Mountains belting the Nirvana Sea."

"And where is your residence, Seraph?"

"*Ours.*" Another brush of his wings.

I tipped him a smile. "And where is *our* residence?"

"Above the Emtsaya."

"The Emtsaya?"

"Where angels are sorted by calling and trained."

"Have you decided what you'll become, Celeste?" Mimi asked.

"I was thinking . . ." I licked my lips. "An ophanim."

Asher swerved a little as though my revelation had thrown him. "Ophanim?"

Mimi patted my wrist. "You'll make a wonderful teacher. Don't you agree, Asher?"

"I believe Celeste would be wonderful at whatever she set her mind, heart, and soul to."

"Biased much?"

"Absolutely not."

"Well, I'm going to retire for a little while and let you two rest. I'll see you in the canyon." Mimi stared past me at Asher. "I'll be there before sundown."

"Thank you, Mimi."

"No. Thank *you*." She cupped my cheek, her skin soft instead of roughened by time and dishwater. "See you later, *mon amour*." Eyes shining like polished lapis, she lowered her hand and then her body, drifting like a dandelion floret toward the bustling fountain banks before slipping through a trench between two waterfalls.

Without even realizing it, my body had become vertical and was bobbing, treading air.

Asher glided in front of me, the bronze tips of his feathers and golden hair refracting every particle of Elysian light, making him look as though he'd been dipped in sunshine. "Ready to see that bed I was telling you about?"

"You mean the round one?"

He smiled slowly and then completely. How could he exude such joy when so much was still at stake? Confidence was part of his character, but wasn't he even slightly anxious? His thumb swept across my forehead, probably to smooth out a groove.

"If I'd known the shape of my bed would cause you such anxiety, I'd have asked to have a square one made."

"It's not your bed."

"I know." He threaded his fingers through mine and tugged until my body bumped into his. "Do you trust me?"

"With my soul."

"Then trust that I have everything handled." He kissed my knuckles, before letting go and sinking underneath me. Like synchronized swimmers, we soared up toward the top of the horseshoe cliff from which rose a seven-pointed quartz edifice.

The structure bobbed atop the smoky *ayim* like an unanchored star, the tallest point in the capital, but not in Elysium. The mountains beyond the Nirvana Sea reached so high their peaks pierced the thready clouds.

Thanks to Mimi, I'd gotten to travel to many exotic places on Earth, but never had I seen anything like this land. This realm of silver smoke, glistening quartz, and cobalt sky stippled by flamboyant feathers.

Asher glided underneath me, upside-down again, and took my hands. "Come. I'll teach you to land. The key is getting as low as possible horizontally, then pulling up your body, so your feet touchdown first."

"Sounds like I'm going to be busting many a kneecap."

He chuckled. "Your knees will be fine." I mustn't have looked convinced, because he added, "It's intuitive. You'll see."

And I did see. It was less daunting than what my mind had conjured up during his explanation. Admittedly, though, he held my hands throughout the entire process.

"Each of these elongated triangles is a seraphim dwelling."

"How do you know whose is whose? They all look the same."

After we'd folded our wings, he tugged me toward the center of the star—an amphitheater. At the heart of it blazed a firepit surrounded by seven thrones. Although they were all carved from the same milky stone, each seat bore a different golden letter. An A gleamed on the throne nearest our perch.

"Nifty. So how do we get into your oddly-shaped home with its oddly-shaped bed?"

Asher smirked. "We have to get down to the wrap-around deck."

"And how do we—"

My sentence died on a whooshed exhale as Asher hopped off the flat, mirrored roof, towing my body down with his. We landed on the quartz deck below—far below—in a crouch.

"Alternatively, you could fly down."

My pulse was striking my neck too fast for me to shout at him that I would've greatly preferred the alternative method. As I straightened, testing for broken bones—surprisingly all seemed in place, besides my heart which was presently lodged in my throat—I found myself staring at a massive gold door framed by grapes of heavy blooms shaped like wisteria, but iridescent like the fountain lilies.

Just like on the throne below, an A was engraved at the heart of a seven-pointed star that stretched across the breadth of the door. As Asher pulled it open, I ran my fingertips along the carvings, marveling at the finesse of the work but then became sidetracked by the bright space sprawling before me. As Asher had warned, a round bed was recessed into the quartz floor and covered in taupe silk and satiny pillows, ranging from emerald to amethyst.

I craned my neck, realizing that the roof we'd stood upon was actually a half-silvered mirror. Asher pressed his hand against the base of my spine, guiding me down one of the tapered walls and into the star's point —a bathroom with a tub as large as the bed.

"Fancy bachelor pad, Seraph. Hope you didn't show it to too many girls."

He swiped his finger up the wall, and the same silvery water that filled the fountain in the Lev began to rise from the bottom of the tub.

"Twenty years, I've been waiting for you, Celeste."

"Since my birth," I mused.

"My soul must've felt its other half's existence."

Fallacious but so very romantic.

He tucked a lock of hair behind my ear. "Magick away your wings, Celeste."

"Already bored of seeing them?"

"Bored? Never." Asher raised a smile so sensual it slowed my pulse. "I merely want you naked, and then I want you winged." He'd already banished his, along with his suede tunic and boots. His pants were off before I'd even discarded my favorite jacket and unzipped my boots.

Muscles rippling like polished armor, he stripped me until I stood naked as the day I was cast out of my mother's womb, save for the sixteen rings forever twinkling around my fingers.

"Wings back out, *levsheh*."

They jolted from their bones. As his arms laced around my waist, his mouth dipped along the slope of my throat, depositing open-mouthed kisses that made my neck fall back. My eyes began to close but then I spotted a skein of angels flying over where we stood. My body must've locked up because Asher stopped.

"They can't see inside, Celeste. Not even at night when the sky darkens and the quartz glows."

I hummed with relief and then hummed again when his hands stroked up the inverted vee at the base of my wings. Although his hands were nowhere near my core, it heated as though he'd set it on fire.

Keeping one hand on that delightful feathered vee, he glided his other hand underneath my ass and lifted me. I wrapped my legs around his waist and sheathed him inside of me. As his gorged tip struck my walls, his caresses sped up. Out of nowhere, an orgasm detonated with such power that I clawed his shoulders and screamed his name for all of Elysium to hear.

Holy. Feather. What in the world was wrong with me? I'd had this V-spot for a decade and never explored it? That was my last lucid thought before another orgasm banged into me and I do mean banged. I wasn't sure whether it had emanated from between my thighs or between my wings, but damn if it didn't fill my vision with fireworks.

I cupped the hard edges of Asher's face and pulled it against mine, pressing our lips as bruisingly close as our bodies. Groans slipped from his mouth as his hips pistoned faster and his fingers turned almost clumsy before falling from my wings to grip my ass, lifting it before slamming home.

My body throbbed around his steel length, vibrated from his harshening grunts, and then slickened from the jet of warmth that gushed out of him and into me with such violence that its strength alone sent me careening right back into a new precipice of ecstasy.

Asher and I had spent the afternoon christening every square inch of his dwelling, from floor to wall to ceiling. Yes. Ceiling. Although I offered no objections, I assumed he was using sex to get our minds off the trial.

When the sun began to fade behind the Nirvana peaks, I pared my sore body off his cloud-like mattress to hunt down my clothes.

"Here." Asher pulled open one of the closets along his tapered wall, revealing a neat row of finery that ranged from hides to silks, dresses to pants, simple to complicated, tight to flowy.

"I didn't know you were into cross-dressing, Seraph," I teased, fingering a burgundy beaded top.

He shook his head and smiled, but his smile was edged with friction, probably because the blue over our heads was now streaked with peach and gold. "That rack's all yours." He came up behind me, already dressed in his archangelic suedes, and reached for a white dress. "I think you should wear this one." He held it up in front of me.

"To make me look purer?"

"No." He kissed my clavicle. "You wore white the first time we kissed and you looked . . . there are no words that would do the way you looked justice."

A thrill thickened my blood, made it ooze slower. "Your wish is my command, oh great ruler."

As I plucked the dress from his fingers, he playfully tapped my ass.

389

I pulled on the dress, the bodysuit sliding into place over my tender flesh. "Where's your circlet?"

"In a drawer."

"Shouldn't it be on your head?"

"I'd rather my actions define me than my status."

Angels, this man. This wonderful, extraordinary man. Tugging my hair free from the halter tie and sliding my wings back out, I walked up to him and pulled him down for a kiss.

An aria rose around us, sweet and soulful. At first, I thought it was playing in my head, but when it grew louder, I craned my neck. Spearheaded by a dozen rainbow-winged sparrows, a swarm of erelim soared over our glass ceiling with Claire's unmistakable fuchsia wings and Daniel's gold ones in their midst. I gathered the four other angels not dressed in white were the remaining members of the Council.

"Time to go." Asher's deep voice seemed to have grown raspier. For all his confidence, his nerves had to be getting the better of him. "Ready?"

No.

Was he?

THE CANYON OF RECKONING WAS PACKED WITH ANGELS. Some airborne, some standing, all of them dressed in such finery one would think they were attending a gala.

When we approached the white gorge, necks craned, heads tipped, feathers fluttered, voices hushed. All six archangels were aligned beneath the Pearly Arch, the golden circlet Asher refused to wear gleaming atop their tilted heads. Their wings were pulled in tight, their hands clasped in front of them, their expressions solemn as though they were part of a funeral procession.

Even though Asher seemed nonplussed by their somberness, goosebumps skittered over my skin. In fact, I was so perplexed I royally screwed up my landing, crashing right into my beloved's retracting wings. Thankfully, I didn't knock him over, only myself. Ears ringing, I barely registered the snickers at first. But then I heard them, and instead of blushing, I smiled deprecatingly, glad to have livened up the depressing crowd.

Asher helped me onto my feet, concern flitting over his brow. "Are you all right?"

"My immortal ass is fine, Seraph."

Grunting, he brushed a lock of hair out of my eyes. "Go stand with Muriel." He tipped his head to the right, toward where Mimi was fording through the multitude of wingless bodies instead of attempting to fly through the denser horde of hovering ones.

Her expression rippled with alarm. "Hand her over, Seraph."

He relinquished my forearm into Mimi's care, then kissed me chastely, eliciting a whole bunch of gasps—was PDA not a thing up here?—before making his way toward his comrades.

"Nice entrance, winglet." The familiar voice had both my shoulders and wings constricting.

Without glancing over, I flipped Eve off. I thought she got the message, but suddenly, she was standing right next to me, grinning.

Actually. Feathering. Grinning.

"Did you think I was crooking my finger so you'd come over?" I asked.

"What's it been? Four years? Five?"

"Not long enough."

Her grin broadened, pushing up her already high cheekbones.

"It's about to begin," Mimi said, putting an end to the inimical reunion.

Eve's gaze slid over to Muriel, to her hand wrapped around my arm in support and affection. Even though the air was as balmy as the one in the guild, I shivered.

"Silence. Silence." Claire's voice ricocheted against the blazing quartz, amplified by the shape of the canyon. "As you all must have heard by now, Seraph Asher was put on probation two months ago for neglecting his duties as archangel in order to aid a fletching. Last month, we showed him leniency and allowed him to return to Earth because the fletching in question"—she gestured to me, and all eyes turned in my direction—"found herself in dire need of rescue."

Wow . . . Could she make me sound any more the damsel in distress? I mean, I *had* been distressed, but shame on her for making a spectacle of my predicament.

"Heard you took on Barbara Hudson." Eve kept her voice low.

"Can't decide if you're fearless or reckless. Everyone knows signing up to that butcher is a massive no-no."

"The ishim should've labeled her sin better." I no longer shuddered at the memory, but my bones still went cold. "Lawyer was misleading."

Claire continued, "Although Seraph Asher promised to return once she was safe, he remained on Earth for the extra month his protégée took to ascend, leaving the six of us to oversee his celestial duties."

Eve puffed out some air. "Dramatic much?"

I side-eyed the archangel's daughter. In typical celestial fashion, Claire hadn't been very present in Eve's life, but I'd imagined that once she'd ascended, the two would've reconnected over their complementary viperous, vapid personalities.

"In the end, our brother made good on his word to return, thus we, the Council, have voted to forgive his negligence. However . . ." Claire let her voice trail off.

Asher had his back to me, so I couldn't read his expression, but there was a looseness to his shoulders, a suppleness to his stance. How was he this relaxed? I mean, yeah, we'd had *a lot* of sex, and plenty of endorphins were still loping around my system, but my stomach was a snake pit.

I examined the line of sparkly winged archangels, trying to discern their expressions in the refracted glow of the arch, to distinguish friend from foe. Except for Daniel, who wore a placid smile, and Claire who was clearly out for blood, the others' expressions were ominously enigmatic.

"However," Claire repeated, her thunderous voice frightening a pair of chanting sparrows off their mother-of-pearl perch. "We have two subjects of contention. The first, I am sure, will be dealt with expeditiously; the second, well the second is the true reason for this public hearing."

Eve crossed her arms over her neon-blue frock.

"The first matter concerns Asher's decision to extinguish a soul when we allowed him to travel back to Earth. As you all know, archangels aren't in the business of burning souls. Especially Triples' souls, which, *usually*" —she put great emphasis on the word, as though to prepare the crowd for the second part of the trial—"remove themselves. Now, this Triple tortured Asher's protégée, so his reaction wasn't incongruous per se—"

"Barbara Hudson's soul was putrid, Claire. How many times have we debated to remove it from the guild's ranking system? If memory serves,

Gideon brought it up again last year." Seraph Daniel flicked his wrist toward the pale-haired archangel with sparkly-cranberry wings and an Elvis jumpsuit.

"I didn't know they could manually remove sinners from the system," I murmured to no one in particular.

Eve snorted. "Of course you didn't. Ophanim enjoy keeping it all nice and vague. The privilege of ascension."

"Claire, had it been your daughter in this Triple's clutches"—if spun-sugar had a sound, it would've been Gideon's voice—"you would surely have done the same."

Claire's gaze settled on Eve. "You're right. I would've terminated the woman's life."

"Yeah right," Eve grunted under her breath.

Her voice couldn't have carried to Claire, but her expression must have because Claire's slender throat straightened.

"I thought you two loved each other," I whispered.

"Leigh sacrificed her wings because my mother wouldn't hear of giving Jarod a chance at redemption. I will *never* forgive her for that."

"This truly is a non-issue, Claire," Daniel continued. "But if the Council must put our brother's action to a vote, then let us do it now and close the subject once and for all. All those in favor of pursuing action against Asher's decision to eliminate a soul, that would've eliminated itself, please speak now."

No archangel—not even Claire—spoke.

I frowned. Why had she made such a spectacle of the matter if she was on Asher's side? Had she felt cowed into absolving my soulhalf of his crime? Her expression was smooth, her carriage relaxed. Nothing about her spoke of intimidation. If anything, she seemed pleased by the outcome.

Oh, angels . . . This was all part of her plan, the perfect segue to the main event. Her display of leniency painted her as levelheaded, whereas the crime painted Asher as hotheaded, an angel who delivered death on a whim.

"Now, onto the crux of this trial." Claire stepped toward Asher, like a prosecutor approaching the witness stand. "An ishim recently brought to my attention something truly troublesome, something which the Council has deliberated on for several weeks now." She paused dramatically. "Our brother has saved not *one* but *two* recently deceased nephilim by transferring their noxious souls into infant bodies, infants who were then abducted and dropped off in. Our. Guilds."

That got her lots of gasps.

"With. Our. Children," she continued.

The air grew rife with tension.

Daniel clapped his hands. "Quiet, please!"

The crowd settled, silencing so completely I could hear the Nirvana Sea foaming against the distant shore of the canyon. Unless that was the sound of my pulse dashing itself against my eardrums.

"Seraph Asher's gross misconduct is enough to repudiate him from the Council, and we will, of course, address this, but first and foremost, we need to address the fate of these fallen. I have seen and interviewed both children, one whom Asher is raising as his daughter, and the other whom he has entrusted to Ophan Tobias of our Viennese guild, and whom Ophan Tobias and his consort are raising as their son. Both four-year-olds carry an alarming amount of memories from their past lives, memories that concern me by the violent emotions they provoke in both nephilim. Yes, they're young and relatively harmless, but what will happen once they grow into teenagers and take this violence out on their peers? On *your* children?"

"Who?" Eve's voice was lighter than the warm breeze twisting the long strands of her black hair.

She hadn't been told . . .

"Who?" she repeated, this time spearing me with her intent hazel eyes.

"Who did we lose four years ago, Eve?"

She frowned, but then her eyebrows jolted up. "Leigh? He saved Leigh?"

"He saved Leigh."

"Fuck," she breathed. "Fuck." A long beat passed. "Who's the other one?"

"Jarod."

Eve's glossy lips fell open as her mother resumed her soliloquy.

"I have put the children's fate to a vote amongst the Council, but since the Seven are currently six, and the Council is divided, we have not been able to draw a conclusion."

Daniel's smile intensified. Okay, I liked him. *Really* liked him. Clearly, he was on Naya's side.

"Naturally, Seraph Asher cannot vote on the matter."

"Naturally," I heard Asher repeat, which earned him the mother of all glares from Claire.

The five archangels next to Claire shifted. Two stepped nearer Daniel —pale-haired Gideon and a raven-haired male with gilt-tipped lime wings and a black suede uniform. The other two assholes lined up beside Claire.

Whoa. I'd just called them assholes and my wing bones hadn't even strummed. Even though now wasn't the time to rejoice, I couldn't help but feel a twinge of delight.

"For this reason, we are requesting *your* help. However, only angelic voices will be taken under consideration. We mean no offence to our wonderful neshamim, but their verdict would surely be biased since we are dealing with human souls. And—"

"Pardon me for interrupting, Seraph Claire, but we aren't dealing with human souls. We're dealing with celestial ones." Asher slowly turned around to face the sea of people abounding the gorge. "Since my sin has been unmasked, let it be unmasked fully. The souls I've saved belonged to Leigh, daughter of Sofia and Raphael."

A pained whimper arose at the edge of the crowd from a blonde with powder-pink feathers tipped in silver. Sofia, I guessed.

"And Jarod," Asher continued, "son of Mikaela, a nephilim who gave up her wings to remain with her mortal lover. Now, Seraph Claire touched upon their violent temperaments. I can assure you that neither reincarnated nephilim possess a violent streak, but you may think me biased, and perhaps I am. Therefore, to ease your minds, I've invited the ophanim of both children's guild to come tonight as character witnesses. Before casting your votes, I beseech you to hear them out. And lastly, none of the ones who've agreed to testify are aware of the children's origin."

Claire let out a snort. "You actually expect us to believe this?"

Asher hooked a look over his shoulder. From the subtle broadening of Claire's nostrils, I assumed it contained plenty of barb.

"I don't expect *you* to believe anything, Claire, but I am hoping our constituents will. Ophan Gabriel, could you let the ophanim from both guilds know we are ready for them to ascend."

I leaned over Mimi to find one of Adam's fathers stepping into the channel. Was Tobias here too? I looked for him, but if he was in attendance, I couldn't spot him. Deep down, I hoped he'd stayed with Adam.

For a moment, the lavender smoke that had puffed out of the channel in Gabriel's wake cleared, and then it thickened and the angels I'd met only briefly during my trip to the Viennese guild appeared from the cavity carved into the rock wall. A moment later, the female ophanim from Guild 24 walked out with a jittery Gabriel.

I looked for Mira, but like Tobias, she was notably absent, and her absence eased my thundering pulse. I didn't believe Claire capable of going into the guild and flinging Naya into the street, but still, I preferred knowing Naya had an adult with her. A full-fledged one.

Asher walked calmly over to them, greeting each one with words, except for Gabriel whose shoulder he squeezed. "Ophan Gabriel, like I, will not be speaking as he's recently been made aware of his son's origin."

The poor ophanim was white as chalk.

"Claire, would you like to interrogate the ophanim or should I?" Asher asked.

"By all means, continue." She swept an arm toward the twenty professors, whose expressions ranged from confusion to discomfiture.

"Ophan, as you may have heard, I've been accused of negligence these last few months, but the seraphim have graciously voted to forgive me for it. However, Seraph Claire, Seraph Hillel, and Seraph Louis have raised a new motive for prosecution, one that affects two fletchings. Tobias and I have entreated you to attend because these two fletchings are our children, Naya and Adam."

"Naya," Eve murmured, rolling Leigh's new name on her tongue. "Dawn."

"What?"

"Naya means dawn in Angelic."

"Oh." I glanced at her expression, found surprise but no repugnance.

"Before I explain the reason our children are being judged tonight, I would like you to speak about them, about their personalities and their sociability. And please be aware that your opinions will neither affect your job nor your social standing in Elysium." This assurance seemed to allay their wariness. "If any one of you would like to begin, please rise, in body and in voice, so that the assembly may hear."

Pippa was the first to flap her wings. "I'm the children's keeper, which means I've had Naya under my tutelage since she was born. I'm not sure what's going on tonight"—her gaze zipped over the crowd, lashes beating in time with her wings—"but I can vouch that she's one of the sweetest fletchings I've had the pleasure of teaching in my century-long career and beloved by all of her peers. And I really do mean all of them. You will not find a single girl in Guild 24 who doesn't have a soft spot for our little Naya. Even my colleague Mira, who tries not to get attached to her fletchings, is fond of the child. So fond, in fact, that when our colleague came to collect us, she refused to leave Naya on her own."

"Well, that's . . . unexpected," Eve murmured. "I didn't think that old bat cared an iota for Leigh."

"She's not an old bat."

Eve's forehead grooved but then smoothed as Ophan Greer took to the sky to share her opinion—also glowing. And then blue-winged Michael took a turn. Mimi seemed to straighten as the angel, who'd transported me from the Viennese guild back to New York, spoke of Adam with the same fondness as Pippa. Pride wafted off Mimi, even though Michael didn't use the words sweet or beloved, choosing instead, inquisitive and bright. It was clear the ophanim was fond of his ward. Two others from his guild followed, and then the rest of my professors presented their opinions of Naya. All of them, complimentary.

I didn't expect any bad words to be spoken about the little girl, but the fact that none were spoken about either child relieved me to no end.

"Thank you. For your endorsement but also for your kindness toward Naya and Adam. I can only hope that what I'm about to reveal will not alter your view of either." Asher rubbed the edge of his jaw. "Ophanim of Guild 24, four and a half years ago, you lost one of your fletchings. She decided, after ascending, to return to the human world, and I"—his voice wavered—"burned off her wings."

Eyes rounded; mouths parted.

"In case you haven't guessed, I'm speaking of Leigh."

Greer slapped her mouth where Pippa gasped. "Naya is . . . she's . . .?"

"Yes. Naya carries Leigh's soul inside of her." Asher spun to face the Elysian crowd again, his feet still firmly grounded on the lit quartz. "And before I can be accused of body snatching, Naya's form belonged to a stillborn, as did Adam's. I revived both, once I guided their souls inside—

souls I did my best to cleanse of memories. As any malakim can attest, some memories are impossible to extract without causing irreparable damage. Perhaps those are the memories Claire was referring to."

"And Adam? Who was he?" one of the Viennese ophanim asked.

"His soul belonged to a man named Jarod Adler. He and Leigh were —I believe they were soulhalves. He's the reason she forsook our world."

From the corner of my eye, I caught Eliza traipsing up to Claire and murmuring something in her ear. Something that made Claire's gaze drift over the assembly. Were they revising their strategy, or looking for character witnesses of their own?

"Claire, the stage is yours for further questioning," Asher announced. "Unless you'd prefer Ish Eliza to do your bidding. She seems quite fond of being your lackey."

The collective sucking of air was epic, and if I weren't worried about how it might harm the vote tonight, I would've smirked. Eve certainly did.

"Not fond of your mother's pet?" I asked.

"I've harbored a few fantasies of charring off her eyebrows and hair since my fire unfortunately doesn't take to feathers."

"You tried?"

"Maybe." She slanted me a smile.

I'd never understood Leigh and Eve's friendship, but perhaps Eve wasn't *so* terrible. After all, she seemed an assiduous judge of character. I'd give my final verdict once she cast her vote.

Claire wound an arm around Eliza's hunched shoulders. "How dare you demean one of our people this way. Ish Eliza is a diligent and faithful ranker who, unlike certain angels, has never shown disregard for our laws."

"Ish Eliza recently cornered my child, interrogated her, and made her cry!" Asher roared, pinning everyone's wings nearer their spines. Even the still hovering angels seemed to pitch down. "Not to mention she blatantly disrespected my soulhalf on more than one occasion, so forgive me for not feeling more compassionate at the moment."

"Soulhalf?" Eve gasped, along with a bunch of people.

Of course, that made everyone turn toward me again. It also made Mimi's fingers dig a little harder into my forearm. Could no one focus on the more significant part of what he'd said? The part about Eliza being a royal bitch to Naya?

"Well that explains it," Eve said.

"What? You didn't think he could be attracted to a hybrid?"

"Oh, no. I don't doubt our resident softy's attraction to you, but had you not been his soulhalf, being with you would've gotten him kicked off the Council."

Claire asked for everyone to land, so the voting could begin.

"And what exactly are we voting for?" someone yelled.

"Why, the children's dismissal from their respective guilds," Claire answered. "All those in favor of repudiating the nephilim from our midst, rise. All those in favor of letting them exist alongside *our children*, stand."

Even though I'd felt it coming, the blow of her words stilled my heart and iced my blood. I looked toward Asher whose eyes were already on mine.

Mimi unwrapped her hand from around my arm. "Go stand by your man, *ma chérie*."

I stepped gingerly over the glowing quartz until I reached his side. He held out his hand, and I took it, and then we craned our necks to see how many would rise to make two innocents fall.

Chapter Sixty-Eight

Claire, Eliza, and the two other archangels had been the first to rise, but *many* followed.

So many that my eyes began to sting. This couldn't be happening. Hadn't they heard a single word of what the ophanim had said? The neshamim stayed standing, but their votes didn't count, so even if they stood out of solidarity, it wouldn't alter the children's fate.

Eve's feet were on the ground. I'd be eternally grateful to her for this. *Eternally . . .*

If they kicked Naya and Adam out, there would be no eternity for Asher *or* for me. I wouldn't stay in a world where they judged children for faults committed in past lives.

Even though I was trying to remain stoic, a sob began to vibrate in my chest.

Asher let go of my hand to curl his arm around my waist and gather me into his side. "It's going to be okay."

"How will it be okay?" I croaked. "*How?*"

He didn't answer, and his silence made my dread balloon because he was my rock, and for all of Mimi's talk of sand becoming glass, I didn't want my rock pulverized to sand or transformed into anything he was not.

Suddenly, I heard Tobias cursing the hovering voters, his voice so scratchy with emotion it made more tears overflow. I wasn't sure when he'd arrived, but I hated that he was here, witnessing gratuitous cruelty, because who were these people to judge children they hadn't even met?

That's it! I pulled away from Asher, palming my wet cheeks. "We need to postpone this vote. All of the people who are voting against Naya and Adam need to travel to the guild and meet them. If they met them, then they wouldn't be voting to . . . to . . ."

His thumb stroked the crease of my waist. "*Shh.*" Even though his eyebrows hung low over his eyes, Asher was still trying to reassure me.

"I agree with Celeste." Tobias's eyes were crimson.

"Are those of you standing still undecided?" Claire's voice rang from right above our heads.

I'd thought Barbara Hudson evil, but Claire was cut from the same pitiless cloth. Instead of scalpels and drills, though, she tortured with words and condemnations.

"Daughter?"

Eve cranked her neck back. "Leigh was my best friend, and she's dead because of you. I know you find me lazy, but rest assured that tonight, my body isn't beached because I don't care to exert myself."

Claire's lips pinched and then pinched some more when a man, who had Eve's hazel eyes and tall frame, approached Eve and draped an arm around her shoulders. Even though he looked barely older than her, the resemblance was so striking I assumed he was her father since Eve had no siblings.

He shot us a sad smile I didn't have the force to return. Although he had my gratitude too, there were still too many angels swarming the sky and not enough amassed in the canyon.

"Well, Seraph Asher, Elysium has spoken." Although Claire didn't gloat, I still abhorred her for what she and Eliza had accomplished tonight.

I hoped they'd rot in Abaddon for this. No, I hoped they'd rot in the human world, with twin crescent scars on their backs.

Asher's arms tightened around my waist, eyes rimmed so red his irises glowed like The Trap's neon signs, and although he didn't cry, his face was as washed-out as the abounding quartz. It was the look of a heart breaking, of a man shattering.

"Wait!" Seraph Daniel's voice boomed through the Canyon of Reckoning, and the force of his command had me jumping. "Wait! All of Elysium has not voted yet."

"All of Elysium is here, Daniel."

"No. But all of Elysium is coming."

The channel began to toil and haze, blustering an endless stream of glitter and smoke through which materialized angel after angel.

"You've forgotten the ophanim," Daniel said, "but the ophanim, for all your talk of negligence, have not forgotten our brother."

Thousands of angels poured out of the channel, and then thousands more.

"Do they at least know what they've joined us for?" Claire asked, as the guild professors joined the hundreds of thousands assembled.

"They know!" Gabriel was rushing back toward Tobias. "Mira and I called all the guilds to explain what was happening."

"Where's Adam?" were the first words out of Tobias's mouth.

"Michael went back down. I needed to be here."

Tobias clutched his husband's hand the same way Asher gripped my waist, as though it was the only thing keeping them from drifting and drowning.

"And we stand by Seraph Asher!" a handful of ophanim called out.

A few didn't stand. A few floated upward, but too few for it to matter.

I wasn't sure how long it took for the channel to stop heaving glittery smoke and fletching professors, but when only pale threads licked up the canyon's glowing walls, Daniel spoke, "I believe all of Elysium is now present, Claire." He gestured to the ocean of colorful feathers filling the gorge. "Would you like us to take a wing-count, or do you deem this as unnecessary as David, Gideon, and I do?"

Claire bobbed over our heads. "In the past, verity votes counted double. I don't see why today's vote should be treated any differently. So yes, let's proceed to a wing-count."

"You are so hateful," I hissed. "They are children."

"They are nephilim," she growled.

"This isn't right, Claire," her consort said.

"It's the law! As for verity votes counting double, that's the law, too."

I raked my gaze over the crowd. I didn't need to count to see there were as many hybrids as there were verities, which meant that if the latter's votes counted double—

I balled my hand into a fist. "It isn't fair."

One of the seraphim who'd risen with her said, "Claire, we've lost. Concede."

"Look around, Hillel. We won."

"Because you keep changing the rules," Tobias shot out.

"Watch your tongue, Ophan," she snapped.

"In this case, you've lost my support." Seraph Hillel landed next to us. "Which means the Council is no longer divided, and this referendum is null and void."

Claire's lashes rose, making her eyes appear crazed. "You cannot change your vote."

"I can. And I have. Concede."

Time held still.

I didn't dare hope she'd set aside her vindictiveness and pride, and yet hope wiggled its way into me.

Above the hushed conversations which had sparked like little fires throughout the canyon, Claire barked for all to hear, "Although I still believe it's a mistake that will cost our people dearly, I leave Naya and Adam to the ophanim and to their fathers, who, I can only hope, will raise them properly."

I threw my arms around Asher's neck. Even though tears still rained down my face, they were now tears of joy instead of sorrow.

Naya and Adam would live.

They'd get a chance to prove the worth of their souls and the righteousness of what Asher had done.

Chatter erupted. Loud, happy chatter.

Claire sank back onto the canyon floor. "You're setting a dangerous precedent, brothers."

"Not a precedent. An experiment," pale-haired Gideon said. "One that will not be repeated until Naya and Adam have both earned their wings. Those were the terms of our backing Asher. We will review the law tomorrow, all *Seven* of us. I bid you all a good night."

Before I could thank him, his great cranberry-gold wings carried him into the starlit sky.

"His key, Claire," Daniel said.

Asher let go of me, so the two archangels could return his channel key.

His face was rife with so many emotions that I wasn't even sure he registered his access to the channel being returned to him. He just went through the motions, extended his palms, absorbed the beams.

"May I have your attention for one last minute!" Tobias's voice rose in time with his body. "Even though Naya and Adam's origins are no longer a secret in Elysium, we'd like to preserve the children's innocence a while longer, keep the story of how they came to exist from swarming the guilds. We hope we can count on your discretion on the matter."

Asher kissed my temple, then bent his legs to join Tobias in the sky. "Ophanim! People of Elysium who stood alongside me tonight! You've earned my eternal gratitude." His timbre was deep but clear. "Thank you for lending your voices to ours to save our children." The air churned around his wings, blew locks of my hair onto my damp cheeks. "Those of you who voted against us, we understand your reservations. And although we'd prefer for no one to interrogate our children, we are happy to organize for you to meet them." Another beat of silence echoed throughout the canyon. "Thank you." His voice broke, and he pressed his palm against his heart. "Thank you."

And then he was drifting down, along with Tobias. Once they'd landed, the two men embraced.

Mimi touched Gabriel's arm to garner his attention. "We haven't had the pleasure of meeting yet. I'm Muriel."

He raised an eyebrow, which jostled his tired face.

"I was Mimi to Jarod."

His eyebrows leveled out. "The woman who raised our son in his past life," he whispered reverentially.

"Take excellent care of him for me. And the day he finds out, please tell him how much I love him." Mimi smiled. "And tell him I'm waiting."

He nodded.

Two verities approached Tobias and Asher. When I caught sight of the sparkle of pink wings and the luster of fully metallic wings, I moved toward my soulhalf.

"Seraph." Sofia's feathers trembled like her voice.

Asher tipped his head toward Leigh's mother. "Sofia. Raphael."

I wrapped my hands around Asher's arm, fearing she and her husband had come to claim Naya.

"You saved our daughter," Raphael said.

She's no longer yours. I bit down on my lip to keep the words from shooting out. *You didn't even care for her all that much when she was yours.*

The tendons beneath Asher's skin strained as though his thoughts aligned with mine. "It was the least I could do after I damned her."

I squeezed his arm, hating that he still blamed himself.

"She damned herself, Seraph," Raphael said.

Sofia glanced up at her husband. "Existing without him would've damned her soul, whether she'd kept her wings or not."

I stared at Asher, at the sharp lines of his face, the lambent shine of his eyes, his aquiline nose, and strong brow. I loved his corporeal form because it was what I could see, but I loved it for all I couldn't.

"I apologize for having impeded your desire to divorce." Asher inhaled deeply. "Now that you're aware she's alive, if you still want to—"

"We don't. We tried living separate lives, but we were more miserable apart than together." Raphael clasped his consort's fingers, a sheen entering his eyes. "Thank you for saving our daughter's soul." He raised Sofia's knuckles to his mouth and kissed them. "For saving us."

Sofia batted her lashes over eyes as green as Leigh's had been. "Sofia and I would also like—"

"Please don't ask me not to be her father." The pain in Asher's voice carved the balmy air.

Raphael's lips tightened.

Don't you dare. Don't you dare. My nails and rings dug into Asher's forearm.

"We would never ask this of you," he finally said.

Relief filled my chest, my wings, my head, my very soul.

"We would like to meet her, though. This time, before she ascends."

"You don't have to tell her who we are," Sofia added.

Asher gave a sharp nod. "Just tell me when, and I will arrange it."

"Whenever suits you, Seraph." Raphael's silver wings spread and retracted, spread and retracted, like a fist clenching, like a heart pumping. "You know where to find us."

Unlike most of the angels in the ravine, they walked, and I understood why once they reached the rock wall opposite the one housing the guild channel and stepped into a similar cavity. This one, though, puffed with dark smoke that licked up their black leathers and shimmering wings before swallowing them whole. I remembered Leigh telling me her parents were underworld sentinels, so I assumed the channel led to Abaddon.

"Well, I best be going." Tobias gripped Asher's shoulder and Asher clutched his friend's. "Don't be a stranger."

Asher smiled, the first real smile since the trial began.

"Celeste, you take good care of this man for me, all right? See that he doesn't break too many more laws. We'll always have his back, but I wouldn't mind a little respite first."

I laughed. Oh, how nice it felt to laugh. "No more law breaking for him, only law *amending*."

A smile brightened Tobias's haggard face. "What a fearsome political duo you two will make."

"Elysium will quake," Gabriel added, Mimi at his side. "Home? I promised Adam an extra-long bedtime story."

"Let's go give him that story." Tobias took his husband's hand. Before turning, he added, "Dinner next week?"

My grin faded at all the things I'd miss out on because I was cooped up here.

"In Elysium, Celeste," Tobias said. "Dinner in Elysium."

Oh.

"Muriel, say you'll join us?" Gabriel smiled. "I want to hear your memories of Jarod. All of them."

"It would be my pleasure."

I unwound one of my hands from Asher's arm to grip her hand, this extraordinary soul who'd mothered two children, neither of which had biologically been hers. But biology didn't matter when it came to affection. Look at my real mother.

My gaze strayed to the guild channel. Had she even come tonight?

After Tobias and Gabriel walked away, and Mimi wished us a good night, Asher rounded on me and tucked a lock of hair behind my ear, his fingers lingering, curving around my neck and dipping beneath the fabric of my white bodice. "I will find a way for you to see Naya again."

I gave him a paltry smile. "I know you will. But that wasn't where my mind had gone."

"Where did your mind go?"

"To my mother. I was wondering if she'd made the trip to support us tonight."

His chin dipped and then his brow. "I didn't see her, but the ophanim were numerous. She might've been among them."

Wouldn't she have sought me out, though? Did I really mean absolutely nothing to her? Naya wasn't my daughter, and yet I would move Elysium and Earth for that little girl. I decided it didn't matter. I already had a family.

I smiled up at Asher, and although his worry took a while to clear, eventually his eyes regained their dazzling radiance.

"I hear most human love stories end with the phrase *happily ever after*." His wings began to curl around us.

"Aren't we lucky to be angels, then?"

His fingers wound through my hair, tipped my head back. "And why is that, *neshahadzaleh*?"

"Because our love story"—I touched my lips to his—"gets to begin this way."

Naya's wing bone ceremony was two days ago, and already our brilliant thirteen-year-old was off to earn her first feathers.

Yes, *ours*.

Mine and Asher's.

There were no formal adoption papers because there was no need for those in our world, but everyone knew Naya as Asher and Celeste's daughter. It had felt strange at the beginning, but then the strangeness had faded and I could not imagine being anything else to Naya.

Especially after she called me by the Angelic name for Mom: *Ama*. The first time she'd said it, on my second trip back down to the guild, I'd cried so hard that she'd worried her lip and apologized. I'd hugged her, tucking her little blonde head beneath my chin, and told her I wanted her to call me Ama for all of eternity.

After the trial, Asher had waited a few months to bring up the Guild Honor System Law with the Seven, and although it wasn't a unanimous vote, the majority was favorable to it. Surprisingly, Claire was the tiebreaker, but her vote came at a cost: one strike and you were out. And not out of the channel, but out of Elysium and its earthly guilds.

I was convinced Claire had agreed in the hopes I'd break the law. By punishing me, she'd get to punish the man who'd made her lose face in Elysium, because she knew Asher could no longer exist without me. My soulhalf didn't believe Claire that perverse, but he was magnanimous to a fault and believed every angelic soul redeemable. I, on the other hand, believed some souls—essentially Claire's and Eliza's—were beyond saving.

I burned the blue paint coating my fingers before pressing them into the glass plate beneath the holo-ranker. As soon as it whirred to life, I traced Naya's name.

I'd been maniacally checking up on her score to see if she was done, which earned me headshakes from Mira. For all her pretending my behavior was absurd and all her repeating, "Let the fletching be," every time I returned to the cafeteria where I was painting over the glass dome, she'd drop by and linger until I said, "Not yet."

And then she'd stick around and scowl at the ceiling I was desecrating, but the glint in her eyes and lengthy inspection of my burgeoning mural betrayed her true feelings: she didn't hate it. She simply refused to acknowledge this for fear it would incite others to defile her guild.

Naya's cherubic face leaped out of my holo-ranker, along with her score.

4.

My heart missed a beat and then recouped it, pounding so frantically I expected I'd go into cardiac arrest any moment. I ran out of the room and screeched Mira's name.

She burst out of the front door office. "What?"

"She did it! Naya's done!"

Mira notched her chin higher as though excitement was beneath her, but her subsequent silence told me she was proud. We stared and stared at each other, and then I swung out of the atrium and dashed to the channel. A couple seconds later, I landed in the Viennese guild where I'd sent my soulhalf after I'd caught him trying to sneak out of the guild after Naya this morning.

However much Asher longed to bubble-wrap our daughter, she needed to learn to navigate Earth and reform humans on her own. So I'd put Tobias in charge of distracting him until she came home.

I found them both in the cafeteria—Tobias sitting, Asher pacing. "She's finished!"

"Thank all that is angelic." Tobias yawned. "Our favorite archangel was wearing the quartz thin."

Asher stopped dead in his tracks. "She's—Naya—finished?"

"Yes, brother. Your beautiful, extraordinary daughter has accomplished her four-point mission in less than thirty-six hours." Tobias squeezed my shoulder. "Her very first feathers are growing as you stand here, gaping at the air like a beached pike."

I laughed; Asher didn't. My poor soulhalf was in too much shock to react to the humorous taunt.

"Apa?" the voice made me step to the side. "Can I play one more game of pool?"

I took in the boy standing beside me, the boy Asher had made the same night he'd made Naya, from his curly toffee-colored hair, deep olive complexion, and incisive green eyes. "Any signs of wing bones?"

"I'm surprised you're asking, Celeste." His voice was still breaking, but I could already tell it would be deep. "Don't you know my fathers? You think my bones would appear without them making a public announcement to all the guilds?"

I grinned.

He didn't, but his green eyes sparked. "I heard Naya got hers a few days ago."

"She did! And she just accomplished her first mission."

Where Naya already possessed the curves of a young woman, Adam was still gangly and soft-jawed, but a shadow darkened his upper lip. "Tell her I say bravo."

"I will."

Sometimes I couldn't believe they'd never met, but fletchings weren't allowed to travel through the channel until their wing bones formed, and even then, they were only allowed to travel to guilds housing angels of the same gender.

Asher, fiercely protective as he was, hoped the children wouldn't meet until they both completed their wings and rose to Elysium. He didn't want either distracted, especially since he feared they truly were soulhalves, and there was nothing in our worlds more distracting than that sort of bond.

Tobias released Asher's shoulder. "One game and off to bed with you, Adamleh."

"Thank you, Apa." Adam retreated out of the cafeteria.

"What are you two still doing here? Go and give your girl my warmest congratulations." Tobias shoved Asher. "Oh, and, Celeste, I will gladly babysit Asher's jittery ass again, but on one condition: if it's a boy, he grows up in *my* guild."

I cupped my enormous belly as Asher finally walked over to me, turquoise eyes aglow with exhilaration.

"I don't know, brother . . . The New York male guild has an air hockey table *and* a pool table."

Tobias scowled eloquently whereas I laughed as Asher fit his fingers through mine, then caressed my abdomen where my soul had made space for a new one. One which we'd created together and which was due any day.

"If it's a boy, he's coming to you, Tobias," I promised.

He winked at me as I towed the love of my eternal life through the hallways of his youth toward the hallways of my youth.

When we landed back in Guild 24, Mira was emerging from the cafeteria.

In her haughtiest voice, she said, "Celeste's mural is coming along messily, in case you were wondering, Seraph."

Asher grinned.

I rolled my eyes. "Oh, Mira, you adore my mural." Clutching Asher's hand with both of mine, I drew him into the atrium just as the front door opened. "Naya!"

She jumped, apparently not expecting her welcome committee—how she hadn't expected us to await her was a mystery.

Asher studied the sliver of face visible behind the golden swells of her hair, hunted the velvet depths of her obsidian eyes. "So, *motasheh*? How was it?"

"Incredible." Her lips curved. "I think I may even have accomplished my mission."

"And what makes you assume this?" he asked, pretending he wasn't aware she'd succeeded.

I wanted to shake my head but let him go on with his farce.

"Well, first off, Mirabelle called her stepbrother and stepmother before I left and asked for their forgiveness in front of me. Secondly"— Naya curled her arm to reach her back—"unless I picked up lint from the couch I sat on most of the day, there's something soft growing right . . . *here.*"

I rocked on the balls of my feet like a child, the word victory balancing on the tip of my tongue.

"And lastly, Ama looks about to burst, and I don't mean because of the baby."

Asher side-eyed me. "She does, doesn't she?" He splayed his fingers on my swollen waist, receiving a little flutter in return.

I covered his hand with mine. "If you don't tell her already, then I will."

Naya's grin widened. "I completed my mission, didn't I?"

"You did, Nayaleh," I gushed.

Our unborn child nudged Asher's hand with such force he could no longer mistake the tiny knock for my soul.

"Eek!" Naya twirled on herself, hair fanning out like the gold blades the erelim wore strapped to their thighs. "I completed my mission, Ophan!"

"It's about time, Fletching," Mira said, in a tetchy tone that no longer fooled anyone. "Well, let's see them."

Naya spun around, wing bones poking out from her black tank top. My gaze ran along the curved bones, hunting for colorful down. It took me two lengthy sweeps to catch the small tufts growing at the top of each bone.

Naya peered over her shoulder. "So? What color are they?"

My eyes met Asher's and then Mira's before finally settling back on Naya's.

Her smile wavered. "What is it?" She gathered her wild hair and pushed it off her shoulder. When her eyes finally alighted on the new downy growths, she sucked in an audible breath, and her gaze jerked to her father.

In shock.

In question.

In distress.

We'd never told Naya about her origin, and mind-bogglingly enough, the ophanim had all kept silent, but how much longer could we keep it a secret now that it had stained her feathers?

I supposed that until Adam's appendages appeared, my theory was pure speculation, but if his feathers too were black . . .

Asher's throat bobbed. "They're magnificent, *motasheh*. Absolutely magnificent."

I released Asher's hand to thread my fingers through Naya's. "I, for one, am *incredibly* jealous. You get my favorite color while I'm stuck with a shade that clashes with everything in my wardrobe."

Mira squinted at Naya's feathers, lashes fluttering ever so slightly. "They sparkle."

Naya grimaced. "But they're black. Which, by the way, isn't even a color."

"Yeah, yeah," I said. "It's the absence of light. I remember you schooling me about this when you were four, smartywings."

"Have I mentioned how proud I am?" Asher's timbre was roughened with emotion. Was my soulhalf about to cry? Possibly. His eyes were *very* shiny, and I wasn't smoldering him—for once.

"For getting black feathers?" Naya untangled her fingers from mine to give her father a hug.

"For earning *four* feathers on your very first venture out into the world."

She laid her cheek on his chest. "Why are they black, Apa?"

Until Adam's feathers came in, our answer would be pure speculation.

"They're not black, *motasheh*. They're the color of starlight."

"That's just a nicer way to say black," she mumbled. "I really wanted rainbow wings."

"And I really wanted your mother to take it easy during her pregnancy. Some things are out of our control." He pressed her away and cupped her cheeks. "But remember this always, *motasheh*, feathers define who you are, *not* their color *or* their luster."

She bit her lip. "What do I say when people ask me why they're black?"

"You send them my way."

"I'm serious, Apa."

"You tell them, Starlight, that your wings are black because your father made you this way."

She squeezed a smile onto her lips. "Is this going to be a thing, now? You calling me starlight instead of sweet doll?"

"Yes. It's going to be *a thing*. I hope you like it."

"How do you say it in Angelic?"

"*Kalkohav*."

She wrinkled her nose. "I like it better in English."

"English it will be then, my darling girl. My starlight."

Epilogue
5 YEARS LATER - ADAM

As I sipped my pale ale, I twirled my girlfriend's ponytail around my fingers, her hair so fine and sleek it slipped through my fingers like silk. Emmy and I had met when I'd signed up to reform her two months ago. After I'd completed my mission, I'd stayed signed on to her because she'd been fun. Her mind wasn't particularly riveting, but her body and skill in the bedroom more than made up for this.

After I'd selected her, my best friend Noah had railed me about using my holo-ranker as a dating app, but I'd caught him more than once lingering on the profiles of pretty sinners. Where he always made himself scroll toward particularly unattractive ones with heftier scores, I selected mine based on superficial criteria—usually their looks or their uncomplicated, sometimes amusing, sins.

My fathers weren't particularly fond of my system, but as long as I earned my feathers and didn't waste too much time between my missions, they didn't interfere. Once I exceeded the one month's mark, they interfered, though. Usually, they threatened Seraph Asher would pick all of my next sinners, since seraphim were almighty like that. I never took this menace seriously.

The archangel was so busy grooming his daughter to become the youngest ascended I doubted he'd waste any time on my ass. I had yet to meet the girl and yet knew everything about her: from the color of her wings—black, like mine, because we were both byproducts of extra-conjugal affairs, but sparkly, unlike mine—to how precocious she was—she'd already earned over nine-hundred feathers. I'd even heard her mother prattle on about how Naya's voice rivaled the guild's sparrows. Whoop-de-effing-doo.

I was so sick of hearing about her accomplishments that recently, when my fathers compared me to her, apparently to motivate me to improve my feather-netting ways, I lost my cool and transferred to another guild where I didn't have to hear about the archangel's precious princess.

Eventually, though, I found my way back to them. For all my irritation, I loved both too much to drag out their unhappiness, and Elysium, how miserable those two were when I snubbed them.

At the moment, I was approaching the one-month anniversary of my mission's completion, which meant, it was time to wish Emmy goodbye. The problem was, I didn't want to leave. I was really enjoying life in her London mews. Her neighborhood was just the right amount of colorful, the pub on the corner made the best fish and chips, and the sex was bountiful.

Speaking of . . .

"Let's go home," I murmured into her ear.

She turned her blue eyes toward me and laughed, a choppy, shrill sound that reminded me of the bleating sheep that littered the English countryside. I kissed her mouth to make it stop, then left enough pounds to cover our drinks and meal, and towed her out of *King's Whistle*.

As I held the door open for her, a blonde exited a black cab. My gaze stuck to her ass, then swept up her body to the face peeking from behind long, ropy curls. She glided toward the entrance of the pub, the door of which I was still holding open.

"Thank you," she said softly, probably imagining I was being a gentleman and holding it for her.

My fathers had hammered good manners into me, but that wasn't the reason I was acting like an inanimate doorstop.

I wasn't actually certain why I was acting like one.

"Adam, come on," Emmy whined.

The blonde glanced over her shoulder as she shrugged out of a jacket with silver angel wings, but not at me.

At Emmy.

I frowned.

After almost a minute, her gaze slid back to me, and a small groove formed between her brows.

What in Abaddon was wrong with me? Why was I staring? She wasn't particularly pretty or anything. I mean, her hair . . . Did she not own a brush?

Color crawled up her throat and spread into her cheeks from my enduring scrutiny. Then suddenly, she said, "Emmy Rogers?"

Damn, that voice . . . pure, effing velvet.

Emmy tapped one of her white sneakers impatiently. "Yeah?"

"I thought I recognized you. We chatted about a flat you were renting out." The blonde slid past me and extended her hand to shake Emmy's. "I'm Naya."

My fingers froze around the door handle. Naya? As in Asher and Celeste's Naya?

I gave my head a firm shake. What was I raging on about? There wasn't only one Naya in the damn worlds.

Emmy gave Naya a long once-over, a smirk creeping onto her lips. "My boyfriend and I were just heading back, actually."

I unbolted my fingers and finally stepped onto the sidewalk, wishing the door would slam instead of settle noiselessly. I glared at Emmy until the smirk disappeared from her face and then I glared at Naya, who took a step back. The irrationality of my aggressiveness toward this stranger spurred my strange behavior.

My eyes narrowed. "What's your last name, Naya?"

Her hands slid to her hips. Perched there. "Moreau. What's yours, Adam?"

My heart calmed. Angels didn't have last names, so this couldn't be Elysium's faultless princess. I checked the pavement for a fallen feather in case she'd lied.

Only smooshed dog poop and trampled gum.

Relieved, angels only knew why, I glided my gaze back up the length of her.

When I reached her chest, my head jerked back.

My breathing stilled.

Fuck.

Me.

I grimaced as the expression fleeced me of a feather.

Her gaze followed its collapse, while mine traced the wings curled around her, wings that looked like someone had sheared off a piece of starry night sky and fit it to her spine.

When her eyes settled back on mine, glittery black as her feathers, I murmured, "And so, we finally meet."

You can rewrite this story a million different ways Celeste. But it will always end the same. It will end with You & Me.

Acknowledgments

When I set out to write *Feather*, I meant for it to be a standalone, not the first book in a series. But Jarod and Leigh's ending slayed so many of my beta-readers that I squeezed in that epilogue, which led to a second book.

I adored returning to Elysium with Celeste and Asher, even though their story was a difficult one to write. The pressure to deliver a love story worthy of my first couple made me want to give up many times. Not to mention the complexities of the plot, which had to showcase not only Celeste's innumerable missions but Asher's agonizing battle.

I know many of you were hoping to find Jarod and Leigh in their original forms, but that was never my intention. Not even when I was still debating whether to write *Celestial*. Know that Naya and Adam will grow into all you loved about my angel and her sinner in their book, *Starlight*.

Yes, I'm writing a third book.

So much for *Feather* being a standalone . . .

Thank you to my all-star beta-readers: Theresea, Katie, Astrid, Maria. You girls transformed *Celestial* into its very best version.

Becky Barney, this was our first editing collaboration but not our last.

Kate, as always, nothing slips past your keen eyes.

To my precious family—I love you to Elysium and back, or as my angels would say: *Ni aheeva ta.*

And last but never least, thank you, dear reader, for getting lost in my crazy, fantastical world. I truly hope this story has lived up to its predecessor, and that you were both entertained and moved.

ETERNALLY YOURS,
OLIVIA

Also by Olivia Wildenstein

PARANORMAL ROMANCE

The Lost Clan series
ROSE PETAL GRAVES

ROWAN WOOD LEGENDS

RISING SILVER MIST

RAGING RIVAL HEARTS

RECKLESS CRUEL HEIRS

The Boulder Wolves series
A PACK OF BLOOD AND LIES

A PACK OF VOWS AND TEARS

A PACK OF LOVE AND HATE

A PACK OF STORMS AND STARS

Angels of Elysium series
FEATHER

CELESTIAL

STARLIGHT

The Kingdom of Crows series
HOUSE OF BEATING WINGS

HOUSE OF POUNDING HEARTS

HOUSE OF STRIKING OATHS

The Quatrefoil Chronicles series
OF WICKED BLOOD

OF TAINTED HEART

CONTEMPORARY ROMANCE

GHOSTBOY, CHAMELEON & THE DUKE OF GRAFFITI

NOT ANOTHER LOVE SONG

ROMANTIC SUSPENSE

Cold Little Games series

COLD LITTLE LIES

COLD LITTLE GAMES

COLD LITTLE HEARTS

About the Author

Olivia is the byproduct of a meet-rude in a Parisian discotheque that turned into an epic love story spanning several decades. Naturally, this shaped the way she viewed romance.

After meeting her own Prince Charming—in a Parisian discotheque of all places—she decided to put fingers to keyboard and craft love stories for a living.

None of her characters have ever met in a Parisian nightclub... as of yet.

WEBSITE
HTTP://OLIVIAWILDENSTEIN.COM

FACEBOOK READER GROUP
OLIVIA'S DARLING READERS

9 781948 463874